"Thoughts are the most
powerful force in the universe."
—Metamorphosis, Sage of the Ages

"Begin at the beginning and go on till you come to the end; then stop."

—Metamorphosis

Hunter Wainright
The Way

By

Mel Wayne

Cataloging In Publication Information

Wayne, Mel.
   Hunter Wainright : The Way / by Mel Wayne.

ISBN - Soft Cover - 13: 978-0-9862942-4-2
ISBN - Deluxe Color Edition - 13: 978-0-9862942-7-3
ISBN - E-Book - 13: 978-0-978-0-9862942-0-4

1. Philosophy. 2. Fantasy. 3. Science Fiction. 4. Esteem.
5. Self-Actualization. 6. Mythology.   I. Title.

Artwork, Maps & Illustrations by: Peka, Ignacio Abad Donado,
   and Mel Wayne, Creator of Imaginary Places.

• Editor and Voice of Reason: Pamela Wayne.
• Thanks to Clifford Robbins for his inspiration, his gift of story telling and imagination.
• In gratitude to my friend, Dennis Fletcher, for his belief in Millennium.

Songs: Open Road ... Free Me ... Bridge of Words
   Lyrics by Jamie Browning, from the album, Open Road: Rock Odyssey.
      © 1974 Rock Solid Songs, BMI, and Universal Music Publishing Group, BMI.

Songs: Love Teaches All ... The Purpose
   Lyrics by Jamie Browning, from the album, Open Road: Rock Odyssey.
      © 1996 Rock Solid Songs, BMI.

Printed in the United States of America

www.Octilogy.com

www.Planet-Millennium.com

www.MillenniumAdventures.com

www.FreedomWithinFoundation.com

Deluxe Color Edition available!

Visit Mel Wayne on:

YouTube   Facebook   Twitter

www.Facebook.com/Octilogy

www.Twitter.com/MelWayneAuthor

Mel Wayne
Author
Creator of Imaginary Places

With the vision of inspiring you to discover
personal insights into who you truly are,
how to change your life by
changing your thoughts,
Mel Wayne's inspirational novel,
Hunter Wainright
The Way
unites philosophy with adventure,
epic fantasy and science fiction,
as his timeless odyssey takes you into the
magical and mystical world of Millennium,
a journey of empowerment and self-discovery.

More novels, books, videos, maps, and music by
Mel Wayne featured in the Appendix.

Table of Contents

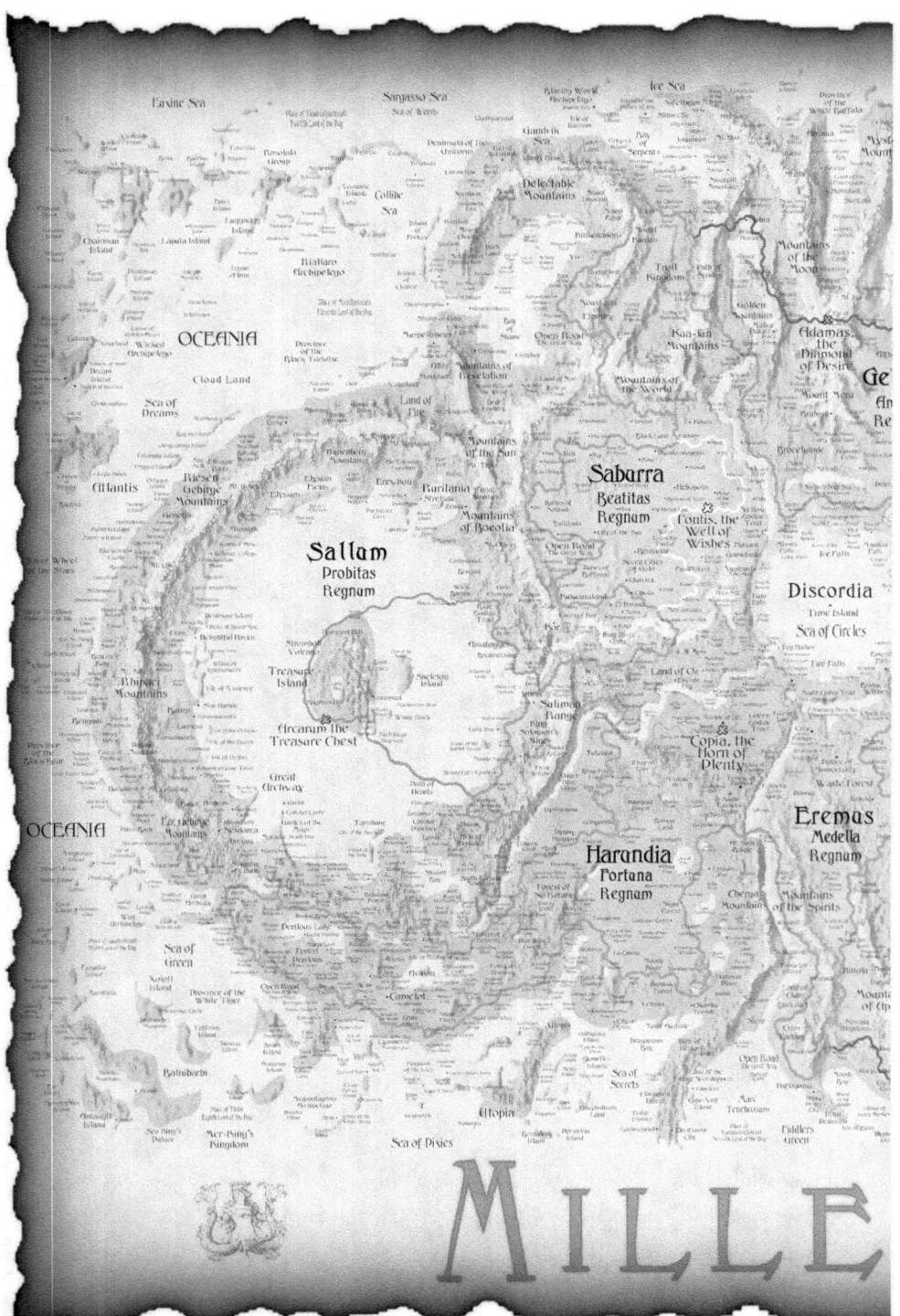

MILLE

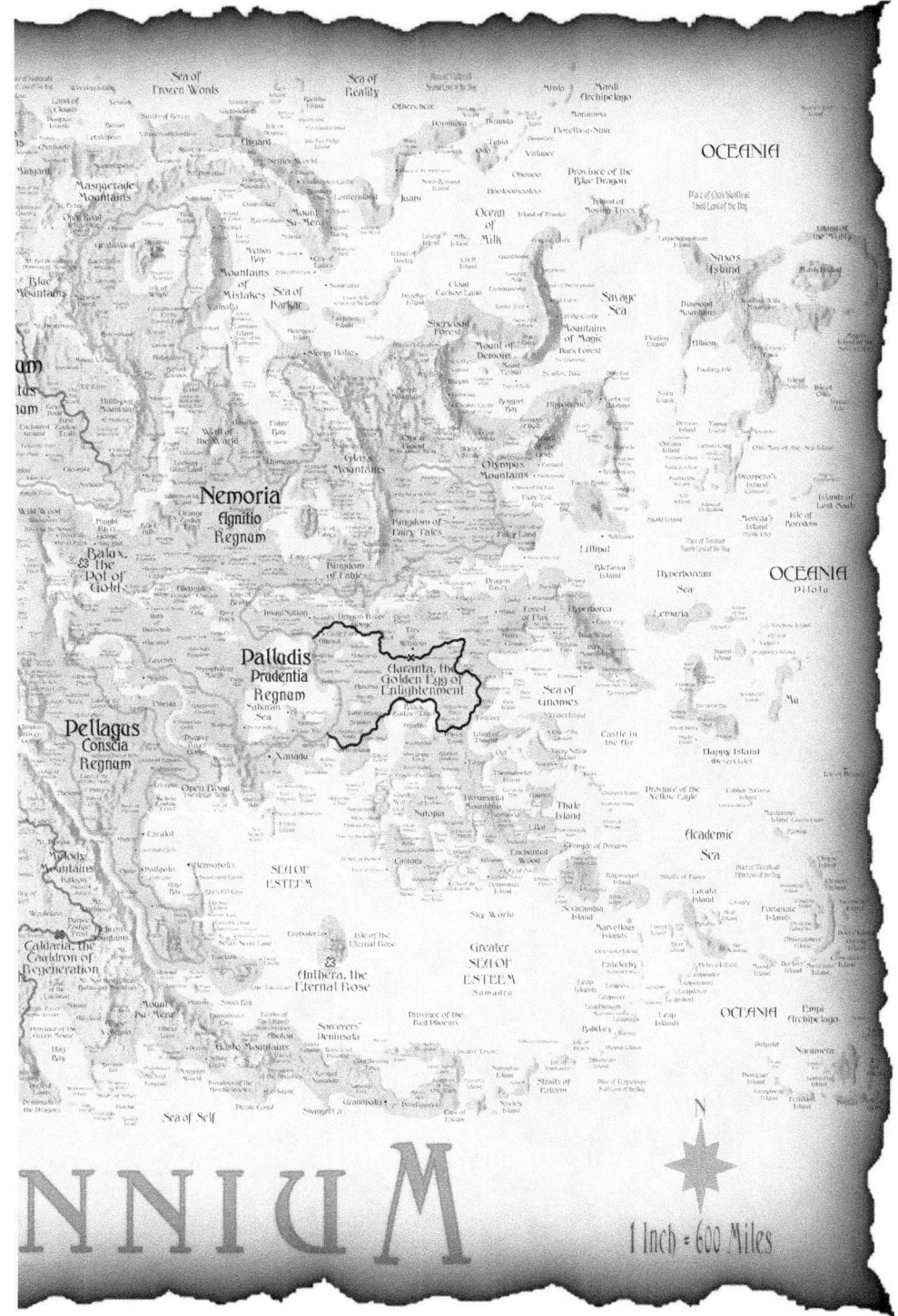

Daynight of the Boar

Aries the 17th
Year of the Dragon

"If you seek to understand the whole universe,
you shall understand nothing.
If you seek only to understand your Self,
you shall understand the whole universe."
—Metamorphosis

Chapter 1
Triamulet

The aftermath of my father's decision to wear the gold Triamulet has changed our lives forever. What I mean is, for better or for worse, my family has survived a chain of unworldly events that only happen in dreams. We are the Wainrights. All thirteen of us. My parents decided to have eleven children. As my twin sister Julia says, "I don't know what they were thinking!" And I say, "The more the merrier!"

Of course, that's easy for me to say since I'm the oldest and can do whatever I please, as long as Father's not around. Julia tells everyone I'm a spoiled brat because my mother never says "no" to me.

But that's another story.

My sister forgets that, in our family, there is a heavy price to pay for being the oldest son.

My father, the renowned Dr. Wayland Wainright, named me Hunter. I'm happy with my name. I'm just not happy with my father. He and I never seem to get along. I know he's a good man, that he means well, but he's relentless in his weekly, sometimes nightly, lectures about how I'll be attending Stanford University and following in *his* footsteps. How he wants me to become someone that I have no interest in becoming. You know, a doctor or lawyer or politician, or as he puts it, "Someone who is well known and respected."

I just want to be an artist. Create great things.

Before I go on and on about my father and my complicated family, you need to know that right now I'm alive and well on Millennium, a planet located in the Andromeda Galaxy.

Standing here alone, I'm looking out a second-floor window of the Crossed Harpoon's Inn, in a seaside fortress called Escalot, perched above the Sea of Esteem.

I've just opened the shutters to breathe the fresh Millennium air and to gaze at the surreal landscape. If only I had my camera to capture the spectacular scenery. The atmosphere is like nothing you've ever seen. Overhead, the sky is red. Fiery red. To the east, a black sky creeps across the horizon. To the west, a blue sky looms overhead, filled with white thunderheads.

All of this, because Millennium is a gyro planet. Two cosmic belts, gigantic red and black rings, spin around her body every twenty-four hours. This is why the sky changes color, from blue to red, and blue to black, every daynight.

Here's the weird part. For each daynight I'm here, fifty days pass me by on Earth. It's hard for me to accept that for every week on this planet, one year goes by at home.

It's been nine daynights since my arrival. That means I've been gone one year and three months. Away from home. Away from friends and family.

12

The sage I've been traveling with, Metamorphosis, has gone downstairs to make arrangements for tomorrow's journey. At sunrise, we will continue our pursuit of the *Walrus*.

We're going to go find—I mean, we're going to rescue—sorry, I need to slow down and not get ahead of myself.

Before I tell you about the past nine daynights on this Andromeda planet, I need to explain my story from the beginning, so you understand *how* I got here and how it's possible for me to exist in two separate bodies—one body lying in a coma on Earth, and *this* one, my active body here on Millennium. So, I'll begin with the day my father made his decision to leave us.

When you were a little kid, did you ever experience a day in your life when everything changed radically? When things were never the same?

If so, you'll know exactly what I'm talking about. If you haven't, you're really lucky.

Our lives were turned upside down the day my father did not wake up. Mom found him unconscious and made a 911 emergency call. The ambulance came and rushed him to the hospital in Monterey. That's in northern California.

"That bad day in July", as my mother called it, happened right after my seventh birthday in 2004. The trauma of the ambulance leaving our home burned permanent images into my memory, like freeze frames in my mind.

Ugly photographs. Sad pictures.

After the ambulance sped away, sirens blaring, I had to take care of my crying, hysterical brothers and sisters until my grandparents arrived. Julia always took care of my siblings. But that day, Mom took seven-year-old Julia with her in the ambulance. My sister didn't return home until later that evening.

While my grandma and grandpa stayed with us at our house, my mom, pregnant at the time, kept a twenty-four-hour vigil beside my father's hospital bed. We didn't see her that entire week. She never came home. That week without my parents was really stressful for Julia and me.

Can you imagine not knowing if your comatose father is going to live or die? Ever wake up? When I was a little, I had positive memories of my father. I remember he always read to Julia and me from the books in his library. Our favorite stories came from *Brothers Grimm Fairy Tales*.

Finally, on the eighth day in a row without seeing our parents, Grandma answered the telephone. She dropped the receiver and shouted, "He's okay! He's not in a coma any more! He's coming home!"

Father had awakened.

According to the doctors, his sudden consciousness was a miracle. No one could explain his bizarre coma.

Julia and I hugged each other, thinking of Mom. How happy she'd be when my father came home. How she'd behave *normal* again and not act so hysterical.

That overcast morning when my father returned home, the last week of July, 2004, will always be remembered as one of the ugliest times of my life. Our father acted differently. Our mother acted differently. Everything felt different—empty. Like a ghost or evil spirit had stolen the happiness from our home.

Have I told you that our home is on the coast of the Pacific Ocean, in Carmel? Carmel-By-The-Sea is in Northern California. It's really beautiful there, peaceful. But no amount of tranquil scenery could cure the tension in our home.

To my mother's chagrin, all my father talked about was the magical world he had visited. She kept telling him to hush and relax, not to worry about his vision, that he had been in a coma, that he had been dreaming.

He kept telling everyone he wasn't dreaming, that he had visited another world. Grandma and Grandpa smirked at each other. Momma's face turned red with embarrassment.

The day after he arrived home, my father locked himself in his library. His obsession with his world—Millennium—had created a rift between him and Mom.

Father held on to his story of the distant planet like a stubborn child.

Night after night, my mother knocked on the library doors, begging my father to stop working, to come to bed, to get some sleep, to be with her. I'll never forget all those lonely nights my mother cried herself to sleep. Over time, she became depressed.

Lonely nights. Depressed mother.

Like a cancer, her depression slowly ate away some of the love she had for my father. Mom searched for her true self for years to come. Meanwhile, my father began spending the family fortune on his quest to prove that Millennium truly existed. He talked about a sage, Metamorphosis, all the time.

I asked him what the sage looked like. He told me that Morph, his nickname, looked like a comic book hero or a role play character.

I'd laugh and say "I want to meet Morph."

"You will never meet the sage, he lives too far away," my father said with a distant look in his eyes.

Based on his descriptions, I drew pencil sketches of Metamorphosis. The illustrations depicted the sage character as having a long white beard and butterfly-like wings with four arms and a tail and wearing a medieval outfit with knee-high boots.

Drawing the sage inspired my passion for fantasy and science fiction artwork at an early age.

When my mother saw my fantasy illustrations, she grew irritated with, as she put it, "Your father filling your heads with nonsense." One time I made the mistake of pinning my illustrations of Morph on my bedroom wall. Momma scolded me as she tore down the pictures and threw them in the waste paper basket. As I grew older, the stories about the great sage and the fantasy planet became a heated topic in our home.

Mom always reminded my father, "Don't talk about such foolishness around the children."

He'd grin and reply, "Honey, please relax. You're about a nine on the tension scale."

She'd give him a dirty look. He'd wipe the grin off his face and remain silent. As he would say, "To keep the peace."

Then, he'd wink at me and Julia.

My parents argued for hours and days and months and years about my father's dream planet. He continually talked about the amazing journey he had experienced during his coma. Over and over and over again. Divorce was a word I became familiar with. All I knew was, it meant that my mother and father wouldn't be together. I learned to live with uncertainty. That led to locking myself in my room and drawing illustrations. Always drawing. Sometimes by hand with a pencil, or ink, or oil and acrylics. As I grew older, I'd create digital artwork on my computer. All I know is, my parents acted a lot happier before my father's coma.

Mom happened to be pregnant with her fourth daughter when father was rushed to the hospital. To me, my mother always looked pregnant. By my sixteenth birthday, I had four brothers and six sisters. Let's see, after Julia and me, Ruby was born. Then, Zachary and Alexander came along. Next, my mother had five girls in a row—Emily, Grace, Astrid, Pearl, and Crystal. Momma gave birth to baby Sebastian in January, 2014.

That year, just a couple of years ago, became the turning point of my life, the year I decided to leave home.

Some of my fondest childhood memories took place in my father's library. Julia and I would beg Mom to let us visit Father's office and study. She'd knock on the library doors, requesting that "the twins", as she called us, could visit for a moment and see their father.

"Sure, let the twins come in," he'd announce to my mother.

When the two of us bolted through the library doors, Julia always ran faster than me and jumped in Father's arms first. He'd pick both of us up and twirl us around. He felt so strong, so invincible. My sister and I loved the salt water aquarium built into the library wall.

Our mother hated the library. "My absentee husband's hideaway", as she named it, because he spent every day consumed with, what she called, his "La La Land Project". Even if he did spend a lot of time in his favorite room, at least he lived with us and spent most of his time at home, with his family. It made us kids feel secure to have our father in the house.

Whenever we asked, my father grabbed a book from the shelf and he'd read to us. We loved the leather-bound, illustrated edition of *Brothers Grimm Fairy Tales*.

For years I thought he read us all those children's stories for our enjoyment. I had no idea the fairy tale characters and fantasy lands really existed, that Jacob Grimm and his brother, Wilhelm, had visited Millennium and returned to Earth to write down what they had witnessed on their journey.

I recall school had just started. Julia and I had entered the third grade together. A year had passed since my father's hospitalization and his eight-day coma. Father finished reading us a fairy tale and Julia pointed to the aquarium.

"Daddy?" my sister asked, "Where do the fish come from?"

"The ocean, Julia," he replied.

"That one?" She pointed through the doors, past the hallway lined with glass, through the windows that revealed the endless Pacific Ocean.

My father nodded, *yes*, while I asked, "How did they get from that big sea to this fish tank?"

He explained how the fish had been caught in a net at their underwater ocean home and transported to a pet store and then to our house. He described how the fish now lived in a different place, a *new* world. They needed to adapt—survive—make the best of their new home.

"Don't they miss their families?" Julia asked.

"Yes, but we don't always have a choice to live where we want. Life takes us on unexpected journeys."

My father always talked to us kids like we were adults. Maybe that's why I've always acted older than my age.

"Sometimes we wish we could live somewhere else," he said, gazing out the library doors at the restless ocean.

"Mommy says you want to be somewhere else," I said, not shy to repeat what I heard adults say, mostly my relatives.

Ignoring me, Father patted Julia on the head, took a deep breath, and pointed at the clown fish. "There's Nemo, sweetheart. Our little friend."

Giggling, Julia watched her favorite red and white clown fish swim in and out of the wiggling sea anemone with the pink tentacles. I loved the spotted octopus that changed colors.

I remember thinking about the helpless creatures being captured and taken from their homes.

Julia must have read my thoughts because she asked, "Is he sad?" pointing to her clown fish.

"What do you mean?" Father asked.

"Nemo's all alone," she replied. "Where are his mommy and daddy?"

"Far, far away," my father replied.

Gazing at the ocean, she asked, "How far?"

"So far away they might as well be on another planet."

Frowning, she replied, "That's sad. Families should always be together."

I tapped my father's chest and said, "Like us. We're together."

My sister nodded and said, "Nemo's mommy must be really unhappy that he's gone. Not home."

"Don't worry, Julia. His mother must learn to be happy without him around."

When I was eight years old, I couldn't image being away from home, away from my family.

Silently, the three of us sat together and stared at the miniature world where the creatures wanted to be somewhere else—back where they came from—back home.

Julia and I often talked about catching the clown fish and the octopus, going down to the cliffs, and returning them to their ocean home.

So they could swim free. So they could find their families. Reunite with them.

Speaking of the library, Julia and I loved to sneak into my father's sacred space when he wasn't there. We told Mom we were playing *Hide-And-Go-Seek.*

She'd tell us, "Stay out of that room." But we'd always forget what she said on purpose, tiptoeing into the sacred space and hiding behind the leather sofa.

When my father discovered our hiding place, he'd tickle us until we begged him to stop. Then, he'd tell us he had a lot of work to do and he'd yell to Mom, "Come and get the twins."

It didn't take long for us to figure out a *new* way to sneak into the forbidden library. We were smarter than my parents gave us credit for when we turned eleven years old.

We abandoned *Hide-And-Go-Seek* for a new game—*I Spy.*

Julia and I discovered that we could hide inside the cabinets under the aquarium. We had plenty of room below the ten-foot-long tank that held five-hundred gallons of salt water.

The cabinet doors had louvers, so we could see and hear everything in the room through the openings between the slats. The aquarium had been built into the wall adjacent to the garage, so, an extra set of doors had been installed on the garage-wall side for servicing the tank equipment.

The cabinet became our perfect hiding place. We learned to sneak out our bedroom windows onto the tile roof, climb down the metal garden trellis covered with star jasmine, squeeze through Pooh's pet door into the garage, scamper past the twelve cars in our father's auto court, and enter the library cabinets from the back side—our secret hiding place under the aquarium.

Quiet as church mice, I learned that phrase from Grandpa, we learned to move silently. Sometimes I took Pooh, my golden retriever, inside the cabinet with us. So he wouldn't whine and bark. He never made a sound; he just wanted to be with me.

All those times we played *I Spy* in the library, the clandestine games became our childhood bond—our special secret. Having secrets made us feel like detectives. Julia would tell me about her Nancy Drew mystery books. I would tell her about Sherlock Holmes. Little did I know that Julia and I would uncover clues leading to amazing adventures in faraway places.

I mean, *far* away!

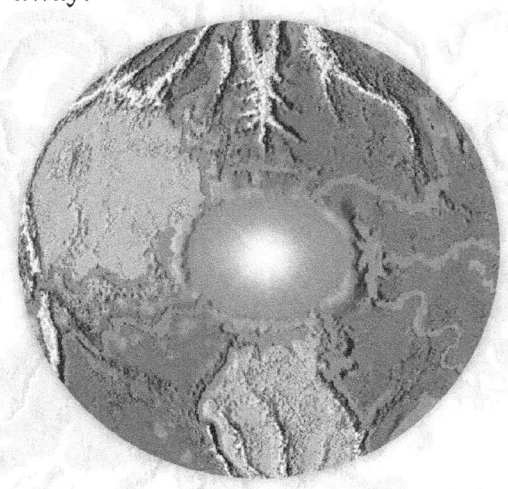

Chapter 2
Wainright Foundation

My father created the Wainright Foundation in November, 2004, four months after his coma. Against his friend's and family's advice, he quit his tenured professor position at Stanford University and proudly announced that he planned to prove Millennium existed.

Are you familiar with the saying, "Put your money where your mouth is?" Well, that's exactly what he did! As it turned out, my father would spend his inheritance money to finance his research foundation. That really stressed Mom out. His father and grandfather had been really smart with real estate investments and the stock market, so Father ended up with a lot of money. As I grew older, I learned that he spent his entire fortune on his obsession with Millennium, mostly on his research project: Coma-X.

The Wainright Foundation staff consisted of dedicated research scientists, mythologists, clairvoyants, and philosophers who shared a common belief—that extraterrestrial life existed.

"A bunch of strange people," as my mother often called them.

During my childhood, Father entertained many people at our home, but mostly his best friend and mentor, Professor Johan Van Campbell. Hunter and I called him Professor Johan.

If it wasn't the professor dropping by unannounced, we'd welcomed a parade of Wainright Foundation doctors who insisted on visiting my father.

Many of my father's meetings took place on the weekends. Often, Julia and I would wait until after dinner, pretend we were asleep in our beds, and then we'd sneak downstairs into the library so we could hide in the cabinet under the aquarium.

When I think of all the times Julia and I hid in our secret

hiding place, we were really lucky that Mom never checked our fake bodies made of blankets and pillows stuffed under our bedspreads.

It wasn't until I turned twelve that I understood the significance of what my father and his colleagues discussed during their closed-door meetings in our library. In fact, by our twelfth birthdays, Julia and I knew all about Millennium and the Triamulet and Coma-X.

It was a Friday night. I remember I had just turned fourteen years old and had started junior high. Mom said I could go to renaissance faire with my friends. Instead of a typical medieval costume, I dressed like a swashbuckling pirate.

No sooner had I climbed into my friend's parent's car to leave, when my father came running out and told everyone, "Hunter is no longer allowed to attend renaissance faires."

Embarrassed, I walked back into the house while Father lectured me on how my grades needed to improve and how I needed to straighten out. He told me how I had to stop playing those stupid role playing games and get my head out of the clouds. All this coming from the man who claimed to have visited another planet!

That night he put me on restriction. Sent me to my room.

The doorbell rang. Special guests had arrived. Father's colleagues.

Still dressed in my pirate costume, I climbed out the window and made my way to Julia's window. She wasn't in her bedroom. I knew where she had gone. I climbed down the trellis, made my way through the garage, opened the aquarium cabinet doors, and crawled into the confined space.

Julia laid on her stomach, peeking through the louvers.

Startled, she asked, "What happened?" in her low, whispering voice.

I looked through the louvers at the stacks of mythology books, *Brothers Grimm Fairy Tales*, medical journals, and hand-drawn maps laid on the library tables and the marble floor.

Still upset, I complained to Julia how Father had mistreated me in front of my friends.

"What did you say to Daddy?" she asked.

"Nothing. Nobody talked. "

"Sorry, Hunter. I know how much you love going to the faire."

"Father's going to be sorry for embarrassing me in front of Kirk and the guys."

Hearing voices and footsteps approach the library, Julia put her index finger to her lips.

"Shhh."

I nodded, staring through the louvers. In the dim light, the library doors open.

Professor Van Campbell and a man we had never seen before walked into the room with my father. He was a newly hired Wainright Foundation doctor who had come to our house for his orientation. Or, as our mother called it, his "indoctrination and brain washing" initiation.

My father poured his guest a glass of scotch and offered

Wayland

him a cigar. Professor Johan lit their "havanas", as they called them, and they puffed away while my father grabbed paperwork from the top drawer of his cherrywood desk.

Clearing his throat, he began his presentation. Father always spoke with passion, like he was behind a podium in a grand lecture hall at Stanford University.

"The Wainright Foundation's research team has initiated

Project: Coma-X, consisting of two study groups. The first group is comprised of five people who remain in a comatose state. The second group, two men and one woman, have awakened from their comas."

The young doctor with coal-black hair scribbled notes on his yellow pad.

"As for the group still in a coma, the people who have yet to awaken, our scientific data indicates that the five Coma-X patients possess different heart rates, abnormal brain-wave patterns, and astonishing metabolic life signs when compared to typical coma patients."

My father handed the doctor a chart. "Here are the vital statistics of our five Coma-X patients that we have researched since 2004. All five are men. One lives here, in the United States, the others are in Europe, Latin America, Asia and Africa."

"Their numbers are right here," Professor Johan said, puffing on his Cuban cigar while he pointed to the charts. "Look at their vital signs. Notice that the data listed under all five names have the same numbers. Each patient's heart rate indicates sixty-four beats per minute. Their body temperatures all read ninety-six degrees Fahrenheit."

The doctor glanced up at my father. "Are these identical numbers correct?"

Father smiled, combing his fingers through his goatee. "Yes, Dr. Shankar, they are accurate."

"Please, call me Hari," the doctor said, half-grinning.

My father nodded and continued. "I need to share some details not on these charts. Just like the three awakened survivors, all five of our Coma-X study patients share one trait that defies scientific explanation. They are living miracles."

He stood and held up his glass of scotch like he had been invited to toast a grand event.

"They haven't aged," Father yelled. "Like modern-day Rip Van Winkles, they have not grown older."

The bewildered doctor remained silent, sipping on his scotch.

While my father continued to explain Coma-X, I grinned, imagining Rip Van Winkle's long white beard that hung to his knees. I recalled Father reading that story to me and Julia, telling us, "Rip slept for more than twenty years".

"Three people have awakened from their coma. My investigations determined that these individuals, two men and one woman, have never met or communicated among themselves. I interviewed the children and grandchildren of these Coma-X survivors. They told me the coma lasted years, sometimes decades. In one documented case, she had been unconscious for more than ninety-four years. Almost a century!"

Dr. Shankar raised his hand to ask a question. Father ignored him and continued to talk. When my father focused on a subject, it was impossible to get his attention. We kids learned that at an early age. Don't interrupt him when he's talking. Do *your* parents ever do that to you? You know, ignore you?

"I also spoke to the relatives and neighbors who confirmed the awakened ones had maintained their youth during their extended coma episodes," Father said. "I believe these witnesses because the three Coma-X survivors have outlived their brothers and sisters by several decades. I have three birth certificates to substantiate their birthdays. They do not look anywhere near their chronological age, especially the one woman."

"She is Elizabeth Dow," Professor Johan said. "She has given us the best descriptions and the most valuable information so far. Elizabeth will be the focus of our Coma-X research, as it pertains to the awakened group."

Gloria Wainright

25

"When I interviewed Elizabeth in London," Father said, "her experience matched mine perfectly. She had awakened on Millennium, met Metamorphosis, and she was given the choice between staying there to see the Eight Great Treasures and learn the Secrets of Time & Space, or return to Earth. When you know you can never go back to Millennium, it's a difficult decision. The Triamulet's only good for one trip. Like a round-trip ticket to paradise and back."

"Don't get sidetracked, Wayland," Professor Johan said. "Stick with the coma information."

Father took a gulp of scotch and continued. "I have more astounding information. Unlike typical coma patients, our Coma-X group does not suffer from muscle atrophy. Their muscle tissue does not waste away, no matter how long their coma lasts. Our group can breathe without a respirator. Their skin does not break down. No ulcers or wounds develop from inactivity. Just like in the *Professor Josef* movies, after years of coma, they wake up and can walk, talk, and function normally. The final miracle is, they never enter into a permanent vegetative state...no PVS!"

Lying on our stomachs, Julia and I listened to our father explain that the Wainright Foundation doctors and scientists were convinced that the Coma-X patients could survive without requiring special coma apparatus or monitoring, that Elizabeth Dow fell into her coma during the late 1800's, when modern medical equipment was unavailable. She survived without a feeding tube.

Hari asked, "What is the scientific evidence that confirms the Coma-X patients' decelerated aging?"

"They are not with us right now," Father yelled, stepping over to a color map mounted on the wall.

He loved to sit in front of that map with Julia and me on his lap and point to the Eight Great Kingdoms and fairy tale lands and mythological places.

My mother accused him of loving the map more than her. I never thought that was true, but he sure spent a lot of time looking at that map on the wall.

Pointing, he said, "They're all alive *here*, on Millennium. This is the world where one daynight equals fifty days here at home. Try to comprehend that six months on Millennium equals twenty-five years on Earth. That's why they don't age."

"How did you get that geographical information?" Hari asked.

"Hand drawn by my associate," Father said, pointing to Professor Johan.

Hari leaned forward, staring at the map. "Based on what?" he asked.

"Show him," my father said, gesturing to his best friend.

"I'm not in the mood to take my shirt off," Professor Johan responded.

"You owe me one," my father said, smirking.

Professor Johan sighed, putting his cigar and drink on the end table.

He unbuttoned his shirt.

I wondered what was going on as I watched the professor take his white dress shirt off and turn around.

"There's our evidence," my father said, pointing at the inked artwork.

A breathtaking, inked map of the planet Millennium had been tattooed on Professor Johan's back! It matched the one on the wall perfectly.

Whispering in Julia's ear, I said, "Look at that tattoo."

She poked me with her elbow, placing her index finger to her lips, reminding me to be quiet.

"I never thought I'd wear a tattoo," the professor said, "but this one was worth it."

While Hari stood and examined the beautiful body art, the professor explained how Andvari, a gnome aboard the *Skipbladnir*, had inked the Millennium map on Johan's back during their voyage on the Sea of Circles.

"So I could remember all the geography upon my return to Earth," Professor Johan said, putting his shirt back on. "I hope you're satisfied, Wayland. Now, please, tell Dr. Shankar about our Coma-X research project."

My father's face glowed with passion; the library's amber lights twinkled in his eyes.

"During my Coma-X episode, I wasn't just on Earth. My other body was alive and breathing on another planet."

Tapping his index finger on the center of the map, he said, "When I awakened on Time Island and talked to Metamorphosis, I became confused and disoriented. I decided to return to Earth instead of beginning my journey on the Open Road for the Eight Great Treasures. I wanted to see, Anthera, the red Eternal Rose."

"Since you insist on talking about that," Van Campbell said, "it *would* have been beneficial if you had stayed a little longer."

"I should have stayed a lot longer," my father replied.

Running his fingers through his black wavy hair, Father looked so sad and dejected, like a child who never got to open all his birthday presents.

"Because I loved Gloria and the children so much, I made the decision to return to Earth, to come home."

"It's okay, Wayland," Professor Johan said. "Don't beat yourself up all the time. You made the right decision. Like Metamorphosis told us, 'All things happen in perfect order.' We can send someone else to Millennium. We have two Triamulets."

"Go ahead, Wayland," the professor said, "show Hari the Triamulet."

Dr. Shankar set his drink on the end table. He must have felt intimidated because he never said a word. Just took notes.

Father nodded and retrieved a safe deposit box from the bottom file drawer. Setting the box on the cherrywood desk, he reached into his pants pocket and pulled out a shiny chrome key.

He opened the grey metal box and showed his guest a radiant gold necklace with a triangular medallion attached to the chain.

"Here she is," he said, smiling. "The Triamulet."

My heart skipped a beat. When I moved my face to the louvers, Julia grabbed my arm, fearful I would make noise and give us away.

The gold medallion shined brightly in the lamp light, swaying back and forth between my father's fingers.

It sound's strange, but I felt the golden charm's energy twenty feet away.

Hari jumped out of his seat.

My father let the doctor hold the sacred medallion.

"After we finish our research and prove that Coma-X is real," Father said, "we will find the perfect person to visit Millennium. Once our volunteer returns, we will have the evidence that dimensional shifting exists, that teleportation is real, that extraterrestrial life exists in the universe, that mythology and folklore and fables and fairy tales are accurate and that—"

"Slow down," Professor Johan said, interrupting my father. "Let's not get

PLANET MILLENNIUM REPORT

SCIENTIFIC THESIS PROPOSING THE EXISTENCE OF DIMENSIONAL SHIFTING INVOLVING ASTRAL TRAVEL, DECELERATED AGING, INTERGALACTIC TELEPORTATION, AND TERRESTRIAL LIFE FORMS INHABITING A PLANET IN THE ANDROMEDA GALAXY.

Carmel, California
8 December 2014

Dr. Wayland Wainright, CEO, Wainright Foundation

Wainright Foundation

ahead of ourselves. Your team has several more years of research before the *Planet Millennium Report* is finished."

My father returned the Triamulet to the safe deposit box, locked the lid and pointed at the doctor. "That's why I've hired you, Dr. Shankar. With all your experience with brain computer interfaces, those magic caps you make, you'll help us complete our report in the next thirty-six months. Welcome to our team."

Hari grinned and nodded his head in agreement as he crushed out his cigar in an abalone shell ashtray.

My father escorted his guest out of the library, into the corridor. He turned to close the doors and looked straight at the aquarium. When he switched off the light, I swear he stared right at us!

Making our way out the back of the cabinet and through the garage it occurred to me that in three years Julia and I would be seventeen. We'd be seniors in high school.

As it turned out, we *would* be seventeen when my father released the controversial *Planet Millennium Report* to the world.

Wanderlust.

My sister Julia told me that was her favorite word.

I had to admit, living in our sea-cliff home in northern California always gave me a sense of wanderlust too. When the Pacific Ocean is your backyard, you learn that the world is bigger than you, larger than life. Whenever I had the chance to sit on the cliffs behind our house and watch the relentless waves crash onto the jagged rocks below, my thoughts drifted to other lands. I don't mean Africa and Australia and Europe and the Orient; I mean Millennium.

By the time Julia and I turned fourteen years old, we knew more about Millennium than our mother. Much more.

Whether I believed my father's stories of a distant world or not, we learned to not upset my mother. The decision to never discuss our father's coma or his dream world became an easy one. I learned the hard way when I brought up the taboo subject as a teenager.

My mother really freaked out and screamed at me, "Never talk about that damn planet again!"

I learned that the cliché, "Some things are better left unsaid", made perfect sense.

Because of our secret library visits, Julia and I talked about Millennium all the time. We loved to look at the color map of the planet on the wall. We memorized the names of the Eight Great Kingdoms.

I knew in my heart the planet existed. Julia wanted the distant world to go away. She was always afraid that "Daddy", as she always called him, might someday leave us and go back to Millennium. She had nightmares that he would never come home, or that he'd be gone so long that she'd be an old woman when he returned to Earth. What that means is, Father would be our age, or younger than us! How weird would that be? Have you seen that movie where the teenage boy travels to the past and meets his father who is the same age?

Can you imagine your parents being the same age as you?

Our relatives gossiped that my father had gone mad, that he had lost his mind during his coma. My aunts and uncles and grandparents always upset my mother with their nasty rumors. They couldn't help themselves. Talking about someone behind a person's back had become their nature. Gossiping was in their blood, their DNA.

Actually, I would discover later that they all suffered from an emotional virus. A contagious disease.

Their gossip and rumors kept my mother and father in a constant state of quiet anxiety.

No matter how stressful things became for my parents, nothing could prepare them for my seventeenth birthday.

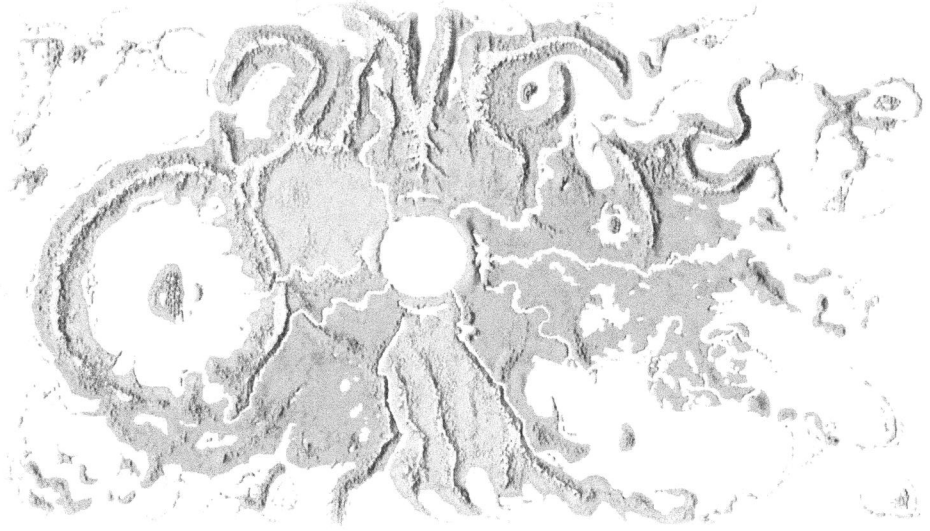

Chapter 3
Astral Journey

July 7th, 2014. The day before my birthday. Actually, the day before *our* birthdays. Julia and I were scheduled to celebrate our seventeenth b-days in Monterey with the family. All Julia talked about was some boy she had just met in our backyard. All I could think about was secretly borrowing my father's Triamulet. Doing something he had failed to do ten years earlier; that is, go to Millennium and stay there long enough to see the Eight Great Treasures.

That evening, certain that everyone had fallen asleep, I slipped out my bedroom window, down the trellis, through the garage, and crawled into our secret passage under the aquarium. I pushed open the louver doors and entered the sacred library.

For several weeks in a row, I had become a late-night visitor to the library, obsessed with seeing the gold Triamulet, holding it in my hands.

Breathing heavily, I turned my flashlight on, pointing the white beam at my father's desk. Holding my breath, I stepped behind my father's desk chair, unlocked the bottom drawer, and placed the metal box quietly on his desk. If you're wondering where I got the keys, I managed to borrow my mother's keys to open the desk and metal box.

Unlocking the lid, I opened the box and shined my flashlight on the gold necklace and medallion. Then and there, I realized how much I loved the darkness, the suspense, the thrill of doing something I knew would change my life.

Setting the flashlight down, I picked up the gleaming gold Triamulet between my trembling fingers. Grinning, I put the necklace over my head.

Knowing the talismans hidden promise of unimaginable

adventure, the Triamulet gave me a sense of power I had never experienced. Something changed inside me, a feeling of freedom. The amulet felt magical around my neck.

Returned the metal box to the bottom drawer and made my way to the louver doors. Switched off the flashlight just as the library clock struck twelve. Crawled through the passage, through the garage, and into the back yard.

It's my birthday, I told myself, gazing at the yellow waxing moon rising steadily above the black ocean. The gold Triamulet looked mystical under the starlight. I lifted the chain and dropped the medallion inside my black sweatshirt. With each beat of my pounding heart, I felt the warm Triamulet pulsate up and down, up and down, up and down against my chest.

Out of my mind with excitement, I climbed the trellis and jumped through my bedroom window. Undressed and crawled into bed, staring at the sacred Triamulet, sensing my destiny. My heart pounded in my chest.

Have you ever felt light-headed when your mind becomes filled with too many ideas?

What if I go to Millennium and I can't get back? I thought. *Wonder what it feels like to be in two separate bodies? Will I feel my Earth body when I'm on Millennium? Mom's going to freak out when she sees me in a coma.*

Breathing deeply, I gazed out the window at the river of stars drifting across the northern night sky.

With my mind spinning with thoughts of the unknown, I stared at the Triamulet. Holding the triangular-shaped medallion and feeling its incredible power, I had already made my decision.

The choice of a lifetime.

Tuesday.

My decision to leave home came on a Tuesday.

At 2:22 a.m., on the 8th day of July, 2014, I made the decision to do what my father had failed to do. Stay on Millennium for as long as I needed to, as long as I wanted. I had the Triamulet on, all I had to do was go to sleep.

Lying in bed, clutching the gold medallion, one of Julia and my favorite poems came to mind. I would learn later that it had been written by one of the Millennium visitors.

The verse went like this:

> Thus grew the tale of Wonderland,
>
> Thus slowly, one by one,
>
> Its quaint events were hammered out,
>
> And now the tale is done,
>
> And home we steer, a merry crew,
>
> Beneath the setting sun.

Yes, Wonderland. Somewhere magical like my father always talked about.

Closing my eyes, I murmured, "Go to sleep, Hunter. You'll be hero when you return."

Pretending I breathed air into my lungs from the other side of the universe, I stopped worrying and slowed my mind down, imagining myself floating above my bed, looking down at my body.

Floating.

Detached.

Free.

"Relax, Hunter. Go to sleep. Let go."

The exact moment I fell into a dream state I felt warm all over. Completely weightless. A fantastic white light flashed and then pulsated within my mind. Not in my eyes, but within every cell of my body. The light never blinded me, it had become me. The warm illumination overtook my body, radiating and absorbing itself within my spirit, my soul. The glowing light lifted my spirit up and pulled me toward somewhere mysterious.

Upward.

I sensed the light carried my body to another dimension, to somewhere else, a place far, far away. Like I had been lifted up and shot out of a cannon, from slow motion to an incredibly-fast warp speed.

What a wild, exhilarating feeling I had. A true, out-of-body experience. Everything seemed to be happening at once; yet, all things remained static—the same. Time stood still while I sped through endless space. A timeless void overwhelmed me. A magical place with no sky and no physical boundaries.

The experience felt real, nothing like a dream.

DAYNIGHT
OF THE
CRAB

Aries the 8th
Year of the Dragon

*"There is no calamity greater than lavish desires.
There is no greater curse than discontentment.
There is no greater disaster than greed."*
—Metamorphosis

Chapter 4
Millennium

ithout warning, the uplifting, inner white light within me dimmed. The warm illumination disappeared and my body became heavy again. My astral journey lasted but a moment in time, but to me, it lasted an entire lifetime. My bright world had gone dark. Immediately, I knew what had happened. I had awakened. Or, at least I thought I had.

Remember those times when you woke up out of a dead sleep and you couldn't decide if you were still dreaming?

Opening my eyes, everything looked blurry. Blinded, I held my hand in front of my face to shield my eyes from the glare of a red sky. The atmosphere appeared to be on fire, the same crimson skies that were described in vivid detail by my father and Professor Van Campbell whenever I spied on them in the library.

At that moment in time, I knew I had arrived on the planet Millennium. My awakening, as predicted, had begun at the center of Time Island.

Sat up to gain my bearings.

Everything I heard about and studied in the *Planet Millennium Report* had been correct. Time Island, an obelisk rising 300 feet above the surface of the Sea of Circles, did indeed have a pyramidal platform of ancient rock at the top, 100 feet wide by 100 feet long. The center of the rock platform—my exact location—displayed a gold Triangulum, inlaid on the rock, encircled by a band of white opaque stone. This sacred circle, spewing beams of radiant light into the red sky, was the entry point for all galactic visitors who inhabited the eight planets known as the Amalgamation.

Eight stone benches, five feet long, formed a circle around the center entry platform. Directly behind each bench sat an ornate wooden chest. Between each of the stone benches, a path, made of opaque white stone, led to a stone pedestal.

Climbing to my feet, I turned in a circle to confirm that the eight paths led to eight pedestals surrounding the center circle. A spinning, illuminated globe floated in midair above each of the stone pedestals. As I turned in a circle observing each of the three-foot-diameter globes, they all spun at different rates.

Eight opaque paths radiated like spokes on a cosmic wheel, stretching from the center circle and connecting to the pedestal, what Father called a Time Oracle in his *Planet Millennium Report*. Each of the pedestals had a podium-like shelf just below the globe that held a parchment scroll.

The moment I stood, an illuminated path began to glow and pulsate, like a heartbeat. The path led to a globe, some thirty feet away. The spinning sphere, a replica of Earth, beckoned to me. Following the three-foot-wide opaque path, I took five steps,

Time Island

stopping at the stone bench and the wooden chest that my father described during his meetings with Professor Johan.

Looking down at myself, I couldn't tell if the goose bumps covering my body came from the cool air or my adrenaline rush. My Triamulet, hanging from the gold chain around my neck, along with my black briefs, were the only Earthly possessions that had made the galactic journey with me.

The air felt cool and damp. Patches of crimson-grey fog, as far as I could see, encircled the rock platform.

In the far distance, above the eerie mist, a flat plateau of land surrounded the tiny island, a complete 360° circle of towering vertical cliffs—the rim of the Discordia Crater. Directly above me, ghostly stars pulsated in the scarlet haze. On the horizon, the blazing red sky melted into a blue sky with billowy white clouds. On the opposite horizon, an ominous black sky hugged the crater's rim. Three moons, white and orange and purple, move across the Millennium horizon. The two suns cast a strange, double shadow, one I was not accustomed to.

The chest displayed EARTH etched in the leather lid.

I opened the rustic chest. The ornate hinges creaked and popped, as the escaping odor of musty air reminded me of my home attic—antique trunks stuffed with moth-eaten clothes. Several reddish-brown furs lay crumpled inside the chest.

Rubbing my hand over the soft pelt, I picked up the bizarre coat with four arm holes, two on each side, and put it on. Lined with satin, the fur smelled musky, like my dog, Pooh, after a bath. I didn't care; it was something to wear.

If I would have dug deeper into the chest, below the furs, I would have discovered clothing, swords, knives, and other magical paraphernalia that many visitors find helpful. But, I was in a hurry to get the Time Oracle, so I closed the creaking lid.

The brown and black rock felt warm under my bare feet as I walked toward the pedestal revealing the globe and parchment scroll. I overheard the professor tell Father that touching the globe and reading the parchment instructions are important for survival, and that I would learn my time dilation. That means the exact ratio between the 3rd and 11th dimensions, the time difference between Earth and Millennium.

When I arrived at the Time Oracle, I reached for the parchment scroll and noticed rows of engravings that had been chiseled into the front of the pedestal. Hundreds of names had been etched into the stone that surrounded the scroll.

"The names," I mumbled, "these must be the famous people."

Father and Professor Johan described the engravings on Time Island and how they wished they'd written down all the Earth visitors, the people that had visited Millennium and returned to Earth to share the wisdom of Metamorphosis, Sage of the Ages.

Kneeling down to get a closer look, the rows of names had been chiseled in vertical rows. I immediately recognized many of the famous people—historical figures.

LAO TZE · SOCRATES · PLATO · PYTHAGORUS · CONFUCIUS · ARISTOTLE · SIDDHARTHA GAUTAMA BUDDHA · ZOROASTER · HOMER · AESOP · ZENO OF ELEA · NOSTRADAMUS · CLEOPATRA · GALILEO · DANTE · MICHELANGELO · LEONARDO DA VINCI CERTEUX · · NICCCOLO MACHIAVELLI · CHARLES DARWIN · HANS C. ANDERSON · CERVANTES · LEWIS CARROLL · VOLTAIRE · FRANCIS BACON · WILLIAM SHAKESPEARE · SIR ISSAC NEWTON · JACOB GRIMM · WILHELM GRIMM · VINCENT VAN GOGH · DANIEL DEFOE · RALPH WALDO EMERSON · ROBERT L. STEVENSON · WALT WHITMAN · AMADEUS MOZART · OSCAR WILDE · BENJAMIN FRANKLIN · SAMUEL CLEMENS · KENNETH GRAHAME · HERMAN MELVILLE · HENRY DAVID THOREAU · CHARLES DICKENS · SIR JAMES BARRIE · H.G. WELLS · HENRY W. LONGFELLOW · JULES VERNE · BOOKER T. WASHINGTON · EMILY DICKINSON · JOHAN VAN CAMPBELL · WAYLAND WAINRIGHT ·

The list of names was longer than I had imagined.

GLOGG	LAO TZE	SOCRATES	XENOPHANES
ZULU	PLATO	COPERNICUS	ZENO OF ELEA
PYTHAGORUS	PLOTINUS	APOLLONIUS OF RHODES	PTOLEMY
ARISTOTLE	AVICENNA	ARISTOPHANES	DIODORUS SICULUS
CONFUCIUS	GAUTAMA BUDDHA	EPICTETUS	LIU CHING-SHU
THALES	ZOROASTER	SANKARA	CAROLUS LINNAEUS
PLINY THE ELDER	MO TZU	TUNG-FANG SHUO	NOSTRADAMUS
HOMER	CLAUDIUS AELIANUS	AVERRHOES	SENECA
ALEXANDER THE GREAT	LUCIAN OF SAMOSATA	MARCUS AURELIUS	CLEOPATRA
NICCOLO MACHIAVELLI	DIOGENES	HYPATHIA OF ALEXANDRIA	PATANJALI
MEISTER ECHART	JACOPO SANNAZARO	MICHELANGELO	AESOP
LEONARDO DA VINCI	GALILEO	THOMAS FULLER M.D.	JOHN MILTON
DANTE	SIR ISSAC NEWTON	KABIR	CHARLES DARWIN
SIR FRANCIS BACON	HAFIZ	FRANÇOIS RABELAIS	RUMI
WILLIAM SHAKESPEARE	BRAM STOKER	WILLIAM DEAN HOWELLS	LUDOVICO ARIOSTO
CERVANTES	ROBERT-MARTIN LESUIRE	CHARLES F. DE MOUHY	JEAN J. D' ABLANCOURT
DANIEL DEFOE	CERTEUX	SIR WALTER RALEIGH	SAMUEL BUTLER
SIR THOMAS MALORY	MARIE ANNE ROBERT	TOM HOOD	VOLTAIRE
ROBERT PATLOCK	GRANT ALLEN	MARGARET CAVENDISH	GUSTAVO BECQUER
GEORGE MACDONALD	NICOLAS DE LA BRETONNE	JEAN PAUL	PHILLIPPE AUGUSTE
SIR JOHN MANDEVILLE	WILLIAM MORRIS	SIMON DE PATOT	EMILIO SALGARI
SAMUEL BRUNT	EDWARD LEAR	GODFREY SWEVEN	CHARLES SOREL
JOHN BUNYAN	CHARLES KINGSLEY	WILLIAM BRADSHAW	SAMUEL T. COLERIDGE
GUYOT DESFONTAINES	MATTEO MARIA BOIARDO	DENIS DIDEROT	SIR THOMAS BULLFINCH
GIOVANNI BOCACCIO	LEPRINCE DE BEAUMONT	MARQUIS DE SADE	ELEAZER DE MAUVILLON
EDWIN A. ABBOTT	FRANK CARELESS	ABBE BALTHAZARD	PIERRE DUPLESSIS
ANNE MARIE HENRIETTE	WILLIAM BECKFORD	THEODOR STORM	ETIENNE CABET
RENE DESCARTES	CARLO COLLODI	LORD LYTTON	PERCY BYSSHE SHELLEY
HANS C. ANDERSON	SIR RICHARD BURTON	UNCA ELIZA WINKFIELD	EDGAR ALLAN POE
LEWIS CARROLL	JONATHAN SWIFT	ALEXANDER POPE	EMMANUEL KANT
JACOB GRIMM	ELIZABETH BARRET BROWNING	DISRAELI	RALPH WALDO EMERSON
WILHELM GRIMM	AMADEUS MOZART	NIETZSCHE	SIR THOMAS MORE
WALT WHITMAN	WILLIAM WORDSWORTH	LOUISA MAY ALCOTT	JOHN LOCKE
OSCAR WILDE	ROBERT L. STEVENSON	MONTAIGNE	VICTOR HUGO
BENJAMIN FRANKLIN	NATHANIEL HAWTHORNE	A. LORD TENNYSON	HERMAN MELVILLE
HENRY DAVID THOREAU	HOWARD PYLE	ANDREW LANG	SIR JAMES BARRIE
CHIEF SEATTLE	TATANKA YOTANKA	J. WOLFGANG VON GOETHE	JOEL C. HARRIS
H.G. WELLS	HENRY W. LONGFELLOW	KENNETH GRAHAME	WASHINGTON IRVING
WILLIAM M. THACKERAY	BOOKER T. WASHINGTON	JOHANNES KEPLER	HENRY RIDER HAGGARD
CHARLES DICKENS	JULES VERNE	HARRIET BEECHER STOWE	EMILY DICKINSON
SAMUEL CLEMENS	KAHLIL GIBRAN	L. FRANK BAUM	MANLY HALL
ALEISTER CROWLEY	D.T. SUZUKI	JAMES LEGGE	A. EINSTEIN
J.O. LENNON	JAMES EARL BROWNING	PROFESSOR VAN CAMPBELL	WAYLAND WAINRIGHT

At the bottom of the engravings, my father's name popped out like they had been written in neon lights.

All the names confirmed the controversial story my father told about humans visiting Millennium. These famous people returned home with knowledge and wisdom beyond their years. They changed the course of human history. They changed human thought.

I stood up and took one last look at the famous peoples' names before I looked up at the illuminated sphere, a replica of our planet, Earth. The globe spun slowly, twenty-four inches above the rock pedestal. I moved my hand back and forth under the floating globe and felt a strong magnetic force.

Reaching down, I grabbed the rolled parchment scroll and, before I read it, looked over both my shoulders, like someone was watching me.

You'd be nervous too.

Unrolling the twelve-inch-wide parchment, my heart pounded in my chest as I read:

Welcome to Millennium,

As our esteemed visitor from Planet Earth, please be aware that I, or one of my eight fellow Utopians, is racing to greet you and inform you of your circumstances, which, as you shall soon discover, has happened at the right and perfect time in your life. Enjoy your journey, wherever it may lead you, however it may unfold, for all things happen in perfect order.

Please place your hand on the spinning Earth globe to discover your Time Dilation.

Namaste,

Metamorphosis, Utopian Master

Following the instructions on the scroll, I placed my hand on the illuminated replica of Earth. Immediately, a deep, resonating voice from inside the globe startled me, saying,

Greetings. You have arrived on the Daynight of the Crab, the 8th of Aires, in the Autumn of Sol, Year of the Dragon, 9001 A.E.. Therefore, your time dilation from the 3rd dimension to the 11th dimension has been calculated at a fifty to one ratio, Earth to Millennium.

Because of my library spying sessions, I had a good idea of what the instructions meant, so I rolled up the scroll. Clutching the parchment, I walked to the edge of the obelisk, between two giant slabs of stone, three feet taller than the platform.

Looking down, I recognized a symbol made of three stone blocks. It was one of the eight Trigram emblems that encircled Time Island. Professor Johan would lecture Father on Trigrams being the core symbols of Feng Shui and the I Ching.

I stood at the top of a steep stairway that led down to a stone ledge below, peering down at the foamy-white waves breaking on the treacherous rocks below. Looking back across the platform at the eight pedestals in between the eight Trigrams, I scanned the entire perimeter, thinking about my fate.

Questioned myself if I'd made the right decision. I knew I'd caused my family a lot of stress. *Mom must be really freaking out by now*, I told myself. *What if the Utopians don't show up? What about food and water?*

Calmed myself down while I gazed at the fabulous scenery with two suns and three moons. Walking the four hundred feet perimeter edge of the platform, I confirmed that Time Island was a 300-foot-tall tower of ancient stone blocks encased by volcanic rocks with jagged outcroppings.

I wondered if I should follow the Time Oracle's instructions and wait, or take the stone steps and see what lay below.

What would *you* do? Go exploring?

I considered climbing down the steps, but my intuition told me to wait for a Utopians. So I did.

Kept reminding myself I had read the *Planet Millennium Report,* so I knew what to expect, recalling how my father and the professor both got to meet Metamorphosis on Time Island.

I'd be next to meet the great sage, I told myself.

Carrying the scroll, I walked to the stone bench and sat down. From my galactic seat, I gawked at the crimson sky and the towering granite cliffs on the distant horizon.

The feeling of total freedom overcame me. Independence. At that moment, a peaceful calmness overcame me, an inner feeling I had never experienced before. I no longer felt afraid of anything. Surrounded by the surreal landscape, I waited patiently for the unknown.

Chapter 5
Time Island

rom my stone bench, 200 million light years from my planet, Earth, I stared in amazement at the tri-colored sky. The red, blue, and black atmosphere reminded me of my unworldly location. Three moons and twinkling stars sat on the horizon, visible through the red sky. White thunderheads emerged from the blue sky. I looked down at my double shadow cast by the bizarre heavens holding a pair of shining daystars—two suns. Having read the *Planet Millennium Report*, I knew that Helios shone at one end of the binary solar system, and its twin star, Sol, burned brightly at the opposite end.

Relentless waves broke on the granite rocks that surrounded the obelisk. Becoming frustrated, I couldn't help but think, *What if no one shows up? I have no food or water. Did I made a mistake coming here? What if—*

The faint sound of voices broke the silence, interrupting my negative thoughts. I ran to pyramid's stone steps and held my breath. The splashing of oars and the cadence call of a ship's crew cut through the crimson-grey blanket of fog.

"Rrrrrooooow! "Rrrrrooooow! "Rrrrrooooow!"

Moving straight toward me, cutting the primordial fog like a gigantic knife, a ship's mast emerged from the crawling mist.

Was it the Skipbladnir, I thought, *the grand ship that Father and Professor Johan described during their meetings?*

The cadence call stopped. In the silence, a mysterious form appeared through the fog. Swaying up and down, the carved figurehead of a dragon adorned the front of the mystery ship.

A row boat appeared through the mist.

I knelt on one knee and peeked over the edge of the rock obelisk. My heartbeat throbbed in my head. Approaching the granite rocks at the base of the island, a solitary figure in the wooden skiff rowed toward me.

"It's Metamorphosis," I murmured under my breath. "He has a long white beard and four arms, just like father described."

"Hello up there!" the man in the skiff shouted.

Signaling acknowledgment of the stranger's presence, I stood, raised my right hand and yelled, "Are you Metamorphosis?"

Metamorphosis

"Very perceptive, young man," he yelled. "I need to talk to you. Explain your fate."

I motioned with my hand, *come up*. The sage secured the swaying boat to a wood mooring. He jumped from rock to rock, climbed the wall of rock, and ran up the stone steps in no time.

Before I knew it, the Sage of the Ages stood in front of me, face to face.

"Hello, I am Metamorphosis," he said, smiling.

Stepping forward to shake hands, I said, "My name's Hunter."

Metamorphosis shook my outstretched hand and said, "You may call me Morph."

My hand, then arm, then body, tingled with energy, like a mild electric current.

The Skipbladnir

I saw white spots before my eyes. I could not comprehend what had happened, but I felt exhilarated as the sage smiled and let go of my hand.

"How do I know I am not dreaming right now?"

Morph grinned. "Your question reminds me of the man who dreamt he was a beautiful butterfly, and when he awoke, he wondered if he was a butterfly dreaming he was a man."

The sage's facial expression had a calming effect on me. His blue-green eyes looked hypnotically tranquil. His olive skin glowed. He wore a leather headband that displayed a gold triangular medallion on his forehead. The same medallion I wore around my neck.

Morph wore a four-armed purple tunic, a brown leather vest with shoulder pads, black breeches, and knee-high, brown leather boots with buckles. His belt buckle was also a replica of the sacred gold medallion.

He carried a scepter, or wand, in a sheath on his leather belt with a blue, glowing crystal ball on the end.

While Morph looked down to find a pair of spectacles in his vest pocket, I stared at his long, green tail. Then I gawked at the pair of wings that protruded from his shoulder blades. The wings moved slowly back and forth in unison. The wing patterns looked like an exotic moth or butterfly. Translucent black with fluorescent red, orange, purple, green, and turquoise patterns, the pair of wings displayed perfect symmetry.

"Go ahead, you can touch my wings if you wish," Morph said, now wearing the glass spectacles on the bridge of his nose.

Reaching out, the wing felt warm and soft, like skin. The arteries and veins formed a red and purple network that separated the mosaic of colors. Instead of insect scales or feathers, a colorful, translucent membrane stretched across the wing's surface.

Morph pointed at the stone bench. "Perhaps we can sit and discuss your destiny."

I nodded, *yes,* and we sat together.

"I have brought you some nourishment," the sage said. "A cosmic traveler cannot think on an empty stomach, especially after a journey across two galaxies."

He unhooked a leather pouch from his belt and placed it between us. Opening the flap, he gestured to me, *reach in.*

"Go ahead, son, help yourself," Morph said. "It shall make you feel better, energize you."

He pulled out the oval piece of bread, bit off a piece, chewed, and swallowed.

"So delicious," he said, smiling with bread wedged between his teeth. "And here is water to wash it down with."

He took a small leather water bag out of the pouch and set it on the bench.

I picked up the bread and smelled it. The loaf had a sweet, familiar aroma, like honey and corn bread.

"Ambrosia, my son," the sage said, "Food of the gods and goddesses."

Recalling that my father had mentioned ambrosia, I took a small bite off the end of the loaf and grinned. "Mmm, great tasting bread."

Morph nodded, saying, "Ambrosia."

I bit off a larger mouthful. Swallowing the honey-laced ambrosia, I felt a burst of energy I had never experienced in my life.

Morph offered me the water bag. "Try some amrita, our Millennium well water. It is especially tasty."

Accepting the leather bag from Morph, I sipped from the spout.

"This water tastes great."

After drinking the amrita, I felt a second rush of exhilaration. Euphoria.

"My father told me you teach visitors the Universal Truths, the Secrets of Time & Space."

"Before I share such wisdom, I must ask your father's name."

"Dr. Wainright," I replied.

"Wayland Wainright?"

"That's right."

"Wayland and I met a short time ago," Morph said. "He was, indeed, a fine human being. In fact, we sat on this very bench, ate ambrosia and drank amrita together. After I explained the time conversion factor between Earth and Millennium, your father looked devastated, telling me that he could not justify being gone so long, that he would miss his children growing up. He made the decision to return home. So, he left us."

"I know all about that," Hunter said. "My family heard the story of the bad decision Father made. Heard it for years. Ever since I was seven years old."

"I told your father that whatever decision he made would be the correct one. I am sorry to hear he is living in the past. Regretting his choices."

"Yeah, all he talks about is Millennium."

"We shall discuss your father later. While you enjoy your ambrosia, I need to share some important issues with you. They involve your future. I request your full attention."

I motioned, *go ahead*, chewing on a piece of ambrosia.

The sage said, "Do you understand where you are and how you arrived here?"

"I read my father's *Planet Millennium Report*. I know about the Triamulet and dimensional shifting between the 3rd and 11th dimension. My twin sister and I heard Father and his staff talk about the Millennium treasures. Professor Van Campbell has a tattoo on his back, a map of Millennium."

"Ah, yes. I truly enjoyed Johan's company."

"Just like my father, the professor wishes he had stayed longer. That's why I won't make that mistake."

"Since all things happen in perfect order, mistakes are a misconception."

Not sure how to respond to his philosophical statement, I said, "I need to show my father that I can make my own decisions. I'm tired of him telling me what to do."

"We shall discuss your relationship with your father another time. Did he give you that gold Triamulet?"

I looked down and blushed, saying, "I kind of borrowed it without his permission."

Knowing the truth, Morph said, "Well, young man, your curiosity has helped decide your destiny. Listen carefully while I explain your options."

"Okay, But first, can you explain why you're speaking English?"

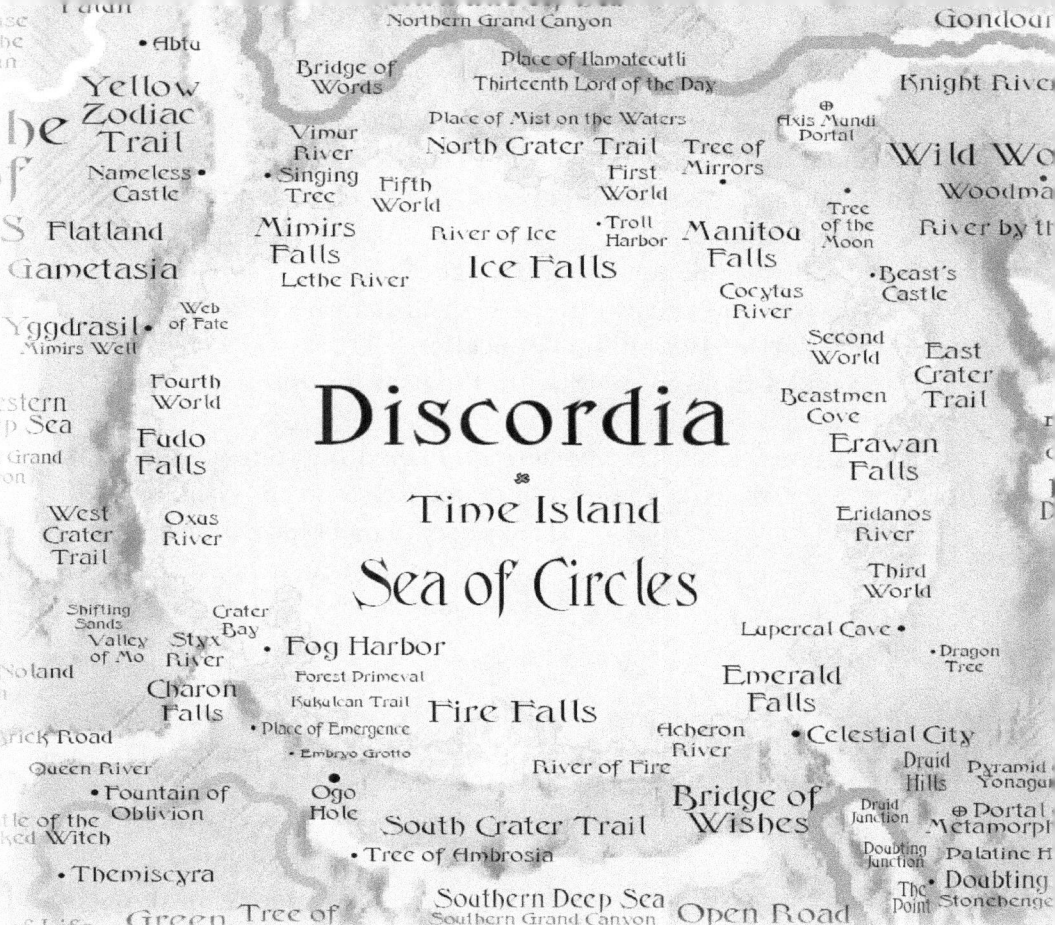

"We are both speaking Millennish. Some of the early Earth visitors did not speak at all, so we taught them Millennish. The first human who returned to Earth spread the language and now it is called English."

"You mean, those people who have their names carved in the rock?" I asked, pointing to the pedestal—the Earth Time Oracle.

"Correct. Those are the visitors who decided to return home, to Earth."

Morph grinned and asked, "My son, how do you know so much about our planet, Millennium?"

Told the sage how my twin sister, Julia, and I would sneak into father's library when we were children. How we had discovered a secret hiding place inside a cabinet. How we would spy through the openings in the louvers. How we listened to dozens of meetings between our father and his research staff.

How, by the time we turned twelve years old, we knew all about Millennium and the Triamulet and Coma-X.

The sage said, "You shall have to tell me some of your spying stories some other time."

"I can tell you one now, if you'd like."

"Thank you, but this is not the right time. I need to enlighten you on the Earth-Millennium connection."

The Sage of the Ages pointed to the heavens and began his explanation.

"Ever since the Extractor Asteroid crashed into our planet, forming the Discordia Crater, the crater we stand in, visitors from other planets have arrived here on a regular basis. The aliens who have visited here, like you, have all been friendly. They have always materialized right here, on Time Island. Our records prove that eight other planets exist in the surrounding galaxies that share the exact climatic conditions and similar humanoid life forms as Millennium. We know this, of course, because we communicate with the intelligent life forms upon their arrival here. Then, we document all information. We have enjoyed numerous visitors from the Milky Way galaxy, including *your* planet, Earth."

Hearing that intelligent life existed throughout the universe excited me. The sage continued by explaining that there was a direct correlation between the asteroid disaster on Millennium and the subsequent arrival of alien visitors, intelligent life forms, like me. Before the asteroid crash, Millennium never had interplanetary or intergalactic visitors.

His white eyebrows drew closer together.

"And with the Extractor Asteroid came the *Extractor Virus*, the *Dark Essence*, and with it, the dreaded—"

"Virus?" I asked, interrupting.

"The emotional virus, known as the *Extractor Virus*."

Seeing the confusion in my eyes, the sage said, "Allow me to clarify. Prior to the cataclysmic asteroid collision with our planet, all intelligent Millennium creatures, humanoid or otherwise, lived together in perfect harmony. Paradise. Eden. When the infected asteroid crashed and spread the emotional thought virus, everything changed.

The sage ran his fingers through his white beard. "The *Extractor Virus* infected paradise. Many Utopians, members of our noblest race, caught the contagious disease and became Extractors. Brother turned against brother, sister against sister. Even the gods and goddesses began quarreling amongst themselves.

"Prior to the *Extractor Virus*, we enjoyed a utopian society, a social paradise. No creature on Millennium, large or small, suffered from bad behavior. Good behavior prevailed. No evil. In fact, soon after the asteroid crashed, we observed the first symptoms of the crippling disease."

"Symptoms? Like what?"

"The hideous viral diseases, once they infect a person's thoughts, develop into recognizable symptoms. The most common is *emotionalsclerosis*. On your planet, Earth, the symptoms are commonly referred to as personal and social disorders with names such as anger, violence, jealousy, lying, cheating, stealing, gossiping, making fun of others, and revenge, just to name a few. Unfortunately, the viral infections always result in terrible family disorders such as emotional abuse, physical violence, alcoholism, drug addiction, and broken homes. The result has been world-wide social disorder: poverty, starvation, corrupt governments, riots, war, and genocide."

"An emotional *virus* causes all those bad behaviors, all that misery and death?" I asked.

"Yes, a *thought* virus that infects human thinking and critical decision making."

"It causes all that evil?"

"Evil is simply another name to describe out-of-control egos. In other words, low self-esteem in its lowest of lowest forms."

I frowned. "I know you asked me not to talk, but I'm still confused."

"Go ahead, speak."

"What does the Extractor Asteroid crashing into your planet and spreading this *Dark Essence,* this *Extractor Virus,* have to do with my planet and with me being here? I don't remember reading that in the *Planet Millennium Report.*"

"I understand your anxiety. I shall clarify all issues. Keep in mind, the privilege of wisdom is to listen. Those who talk do not know. Those who know, do not talk."

I nodded and took another gulp of amrita.

"We are certain the Extractor Asteroid that struck this planet 9000 years ago was merely a small fragment of the Dark Star, the Star of Evil. The diseased supernova exploded, sending infectious asteroid fragments into stellar space. We know this because our alien visitors, intelligent beings like you, have reported evidence of a cataclysmic event on their *own* planet."

Morph raised his index finger. "Each of our Millennium visitors from eight other planets tell the same story, 'A gigantic asteroid, Extractoroid, collided with their planet in the distant past. The asteroid collision caused total chaos. The catastrophic explosion created severe climatic changes and mass destruction, resulting in the eventual extermination of numerous plant and animal species, culminating in the evolution of a dominating life form, an intelligent race of creatures with all the symptoms of the low self-esteem *Extractor Virus,* the *Dark Essence.*'"

"Infected asteroids brought the emotional virus to all eight planets?" I asked. "To Earth?"

The sage nodded, *yes,* and placed his hand on my shoulder. "A fragment of the Dark Star struck your planet, Earth, some 50,000 Earth-years ago. Your species, humans, have evolved into the viral life form, carriers of the disease, which leads me to the very reason that you have journeyed here."

Morph grinned. His eyes sparkled in the crimson light.

"Millennium, our noble planet, remains Eden. A social

56

Planet Millennium Elliptical Solar Path

∞

Iridium   Osmium   Helios   Planet Millennium   Sol   Radium   Xenon
Krypton   Argon

Path of Helios
180 Daynights
6 Months

Binary Star System
Total Distance = 372,000,000 Miles
Helios System = 186,000,000 Miles
Sol System = 186,000,000 Miles
Planet Millennium Annual Elliptical Solar Path Cycle = 360 Daynights = 1 Year
Planet Millennium Speed = 134,000 Miles per Hour = 37 Miles per Second
1 Millennium Daynight= 50 Earth Days

Path of Sol
180 Daynights
6 Months

Planet Millennium
12 Months

∞

8 Month of SCORPIO
9 Month of SAGITTARIUS
7 Month of LIBRA
1 Month of ARIES
2 Month of TAURUS
3 Month of GEMINI
Helios
Sol
10 Month of CAPRICORN
12 Month of PISCES
6 Month of VIRGO
4 Month of CANCER
11 Month of AQUARIUS
5 Month of LEO

Path of Helios
180 Daynights

30 Daynights = 1 Month

Path of Sol
180 Daynights

paradise. This is because, unlike Earth and the other seven planets infected with the *Extractor Virus*, our planet has only a small percentage of contagious, viral populations; that is, dysfunctional creatures suffering with the emotional virus. Earth and the other seven planets are experiencing epidemics, pandemics, of major proportions. Our planet is not. Millennium still enjoys paradise compared to our sister planets infected with the contagious thought diseases."

The sage raised his white eyebrows.

"Please keep in mind, like the other planets, we have Octilogy, the Eight Great Treasures, but unlike the other planets, we have not lost our treasures to the Extractors. We have successfully guarded our sacred treasures, preventing the Extractors from destroying Octilogy, and with it, The Great Way. The eight treasures, if protected, help prevent the spread of the emotional virus and can cure all infected creatures."

Morph paused to look skyward, and then said, "I shall explain Octilogy in a short while. Right now, I shall focus on the Cosmic Force."

Clenching my jaw, I wondered how humans had become, as Morph had explained, a viral life form. He continued by saying, "The Dark Star possessed a phenomenon known as the Cosmic Force, a wave length of unparalleled magnitude. The nuclear explosion that fragmented the Dark Star intensified the waves of the Cosmic Force. The fragments, thousands of asteroids, maintained a magnetic connection to one another even though they traveled in different directions millions of light years through space. This, of course, is the Law of Attraction, in action. Each asteroid's path created the Astral Highway, a universal matrix of vibrating energy."

The sage stopped to study my eyes. He sensed that I understood the concepts as he continued.

"The Astral Highways, like the spokes of an infinite wheel, connect the eight planets to our planet, Millennium. This is because our world is located in the exact center of the Cosmic Force Zone. We are the nucleus of the vibrating energy wave field. The resulting phenomenon is that we receive visitors to Millennium. Visitors worthy of the journey, worthy of astral body travel."

"Worthy?"

"Worthiness is a virtue. You see, there are two requirements a creature must possess in order to make the intergalactic journey to Millennium."

Morph held up his index finger. "First, the intelligent life form must have the potential for greatness." He held up his second finger. "The second requirement is rare indeed. The creature must wear a gold talisman, known as a Triamulet, prior to entering a dream state."

I held my Triamulet between my fingers. "Can you explain astral body travel?"

"Astral body travel is quite simple," Morph said. "The Cosmic Force between Earth and Millennium, the Astral Highway, allows dimensional shifting to occur. This shifting between the 3rd and 11th dimensions allows astral body travel, at the speed of thought."

The sage grinned. "As I said, only intelligent life forms with the potential for greatness are capable of dimensional shifting.

No other creatures have this capability. This is because the Cosmic Force became completely reversed during the formation of the universal matrix. I would compare it to the reversal of a major magnetic field from negative to positive. In other words, instead of creatures with emotional viral infections being able to travel the Astral Highway, life forms *without* severe symptoms of the emotional virus, life forms with a potential for greatness, became the exclusive travelers on the Astral Highway to Millennium."

Seeing the curiosity in my eyes, Morph said, "Allow me to clarify. It is time to expand your mind. First, I shall explain dimensional shifting. I am going to ask you to imagine you are in two different places at this moment. After visualizing it, believe it, because it is reality. After all, believing is seeing. At this very moment in time you sleep on Earth, a deep sleep. And, you sit here with me. Your astral journey from Earth to Millennium involved dimensional shifting. Your body's atoms and DNA, every cell in your body, traveled the Astral Highway and went through reconstruction, perfect re-assembly, here on Millennium. The dimensional shifting included your sacred gold Triamulet. The dimensional shift created the exact you, not a replica, but you."

Remaining silent, I absorbed the sage's knowledge.

"But there is something more important than your physical self that traveled the Astral Highway."

The sage paused. "Can you guess what that would be?"

I thought for a moment. Then, shook my head, *no.*

"Your thoughts," Morph said. "Your spirit. Your soul. The divine spark that makes you who you are. Although your body on Earth is alive and breathing, it no longer houses the personal energy of your thoughts. Your sleeping body no longer contains your soul, that which sits in the center and knows."

Morph raised his eyebrows. "Am I making sense?"

"Sort of. I read about some of this in my father's report."

"Allow me to clarify. We are what we think. Our thoughts are pure energy, more powerful than electricity. In fact, thoughts are the most powerful force in the Universe. That very statement happens to be our third Secret of Time & Space."

"I remember Father discussing those secrets with Professor Johan."

"More on those later. Our thought waves are alive with energy, a rhythmic energy flow, similar to a radio transmitter. Here on Millennium, it is known as a being's personal energy. When we talk to ourselves, self-talk, that voice inside our head determines exactly who we are and how we behave. Each of us, every creature in the universe, possesses personal energy, wave patterns that radiate in all directions from the center of our being. Our personal energy transmits signals, vibrating energy waves that transmit out and into the universe. We call this energy the music of the universe. We all hear it, if we listen."

Morph looked up and pointed to the sky.

Looking up at the stars, I swear I heard the music of the universe at that moment!

If you're wondering it sounds like, the next time you sit in a quiet room, or visit a wilderness area under a river of stars, just listen. You will hear the music. I promise.

The sage said, "Think of this energy as the invisible intelligence flowing through everything and between everything, every creature. For instance, right now, your thought energy and mine meet exactly midway between us. Do you feel the energy filling the air between us?"

Closing my eyes, I replied, "I think so. Now that you describe it that way, I think I do."

Morph nodded in approval.

"Imagine all the air, the space in the universe as a matrix, a vibrating grid filled with this personal energy. It affects everything. The energy field of the universal grid constantly shifts and changes, just as your personal thoughts, feelings, moods, and behavior continually change. I believe you humans refer to this phenomenon of the thought matrix as collective consciousness. It affects every event on your planet. Everyone, everything in the universe, emits energy in every direction."

Morph smiled and held up one index finger. "The first Secret of Time & Space is, 'Like attracts like.' Like thoughts attract like thoughts throughout the vibrating grid of the universal matrix. Good attracts good, bad attracts bad. This is the universal Law of

Attraction. Let me remind you again, all personal energy waves meet midway between creatures. The closer you are to someone emotionally, the more intense the energy. When two creatures come together, it often results in the dance of life and—"

"The dance of life?" I asked, interrupting.

"Ah, yes. More on that later," the sage said with a twinkle in his eyes. "Do you understand that your body on Earth has no spirit? Your essence, your soul, what I like to call your divine spark, has traveled the Astral Highway along with your new body."

"I'm trying to understand. All I know is, I feel exactly the same."

Morph raised his two right hands to prevent me from interrupting.

"All you need to know for now is that your sleeping body on Earth is perfectly healthy, physically, but has no spirit. No soul. Your bodies are chemically connected through space and time, but not spiritually."

"I think I get it, but I have another question."

The sage placed his hand on my shoulder. "No more questions. We have run out of, what you humans call, precious time. Right now, I must inform you of your fate."

I remained silent, looking north. The horizon had become darker, 'the coming of the black sky', as Morph called it.

"The astral journey is a trip that may be taken one time with the Triamulet you are wearing. Once." Morph said. "If you decide to return to Earth, you may never return to Millennium wearing that Triamulet. Before I offer you the adventure of a lifetime, I need you to know you are not a prisoner here. You may leave anytime you choose."

Morph smiled, pointing to the center of the island. "The way you return to your home is simple. With your Triamulet on, you lie down at the center of this sacred obelisk, the galactic portal of Time Island, and go back to sleep. You, your spirit and your thoughts, shall awaken within your physical body on Earth, wearing the gold Triamulet."

"That's it? Just go back to sleep?"

"Anytime you wish, you may return to Earth. Keep in mind,

the return journey must begin right here on Time Island, wearing your gold Triamulet."

"I'm staying for sure, I just don't know how long I'll be here."

The sage arched his eyebrows. "Does your father's *Planet Millennium Report* explain the time difference between Earth and Millennium?"

"I should have read more. I know that people in a coma never grow older."

"Allow me to enlighten you. After our visitors experience dimensional shifting and arrive here, there is a dramatic difference between their planet's time and Millennium time, between the 3rd dimension and the 11th dimension. This is why your father decided to return home. Known as time dilation, each visitor, depending on the date and time of arrival from his or her planet, experiences either a dramatic increase, or decrease, in time."

"So, what does that mean for me?"

"What did the Time Oracle tell you?"

"The voice in the globe told me that my time dilation from the 3rd dimension to the 11th dimension has been calculated at a fifty to one ratio, Earth to Millennium."

"If your conversion factor is based on a fifty to one ratio, this means for every fifty days on Earth, you are on Millennium for one daynight. For every fifty years on *your* planet, only one year passes here, on our planet. That is 360 daynights on Millennium. Six months on Millennium equals 25 years on Earth. For every 100 years on Earth, what you call a century, only two years pass here on Millennium. For every 1000 years on Earth, what you call a millennium, only twenty years pass here. Divide your Earth years by 50 to figure the Millennium years."

"How long is a day, I mean, a daynight? Wait a minute, forget all the mathematical equations, how long have I been here and what time is it in California?"

"Excellent point. Let us calculate the exact answer."

Morph thought for a moment. Then, he held up eight fingers, two on each of his four hands.

"Eight? Eight hours?"

The sage shook his head, no. "Eight Earth *days.*"

"Eight days! That seems impossible, I just woke up."

"As I told you, the time conversion factor is fifty to one. You have been awake on Time Island for approximately four hours, so we multiply four times fifty. This equals 200 Earth hours. Then, by dividing one Earth day, twenty-four hours by 200 hours, we get the answer of eight Earth days, give or take a few of your Earth hours."

EARTH

Morph pushed his spectacles up the bridge of his nose. "See how simple the formula is? Take the Millennium hours, multiply times fifty. Then, divide by twenty-four for your answer."

I frowned. "If it is now eight days later on Earth, what happened to all that time?"

"Ahhh, time. Now there is a concept you humans have difficulty with. I do not have time," Morph said, chuckling, "to explain time properly to you, right now. You shall learn that all events occur at once, that all the things in the universe exist simultaneously, that there is *no* time. In other words, you move, not time. You humans count movements and call them time. My point is, all things that have ever happened, all events that are ever going to happen, are actually happening now."

"Can you explain that again?"

"Be patient, my son. If you stay long enough, I shall gladly explain the space-time continuum to you. Right now, we do not have time. Understand?"

Without warning, a low-pitched, reverberating horn interrupted Morph.

The monotone note bellowed from the ship.

"That is our signal. We must set sail as soon as possible. Earlier, the captain spotted another ship on the horizon."

Before I could ask about the ship, Morph placed his upper right hand on my shoulder and said, "You must now make the decision of a lifetime. I have a ship ready to take you ashore. From there we shall escort you to Pellagus, home of Octilogy's first great treasure, the Eternal Rose. During your journey on the Open Road, The Great Way, you shall see amazing things you have never dreamed possible. When you arrive at the first treasure and embrace Anthera, the red rose, you shall discover self-awareness, that is, who you *really* are."

I stared into Morph's calm blue eyes. "And I can return anytime I choose?"

"My promise is, if you are not satisfied with the gift offered by the first treasure, the awareness of Self, we shall bring you back here to Time Island so you may return home."

The sage grinned and asked, "Would you mind if another new arrival joins us on our voyage?"

"Who would that be?" I asked.

"Three daynights ago, we had another visitor materialize here, on Time Island. She is from another planet in the Amalgamation, Epiphany, and—"

"Wait," I said, interrupting. "What do you mean, Amalgamation?"

"I will explain it more in depth later," Morph replied, "but the Amalgamation is comprised of Millennium and the eight other plants within the Cosmic Force Zone I spoke of earlier. Earth is one of them. Another is Epiphany."

Morph held up his right upper hand so I would not interrupt him again, and said, "As I was saying, our female guest is aboard the *Skipbladnir* right now. The young lady, about your age, decided to stay on Millennium and journey with us in quest of the Eternal Rose."

"A young lady?"

Nodding, *yes*, the Utopian Master knew he had my undivided attention.

"Yes. The young lady from Epiphany, who had arrived prior to you, was on the *Skipbladnir*, ready to go ashore, when our ship's captain received orders to turn around and sail back to Time Island."

"To get me?"

Morph grinned, removed his spectacles and placed them in his left vest pocket. "Correct, to get you. The young lady became quite upset having to make the return two-daynight voyage back to Time Island. I told her that we had to return to the galactic portal to greet a young man, a human from Earth, so he may join us on our voyage. Suddenly, she became calm and began asking questions."

"What questions?"

"Oh, questions such as, 'What do young male humans look like?' 'How tall is he?' Simple questions any young lady might ask."

"What did you tell her?"

"The truth. That you, like many of our Earth visitors, were probably tall, physically fit, high spirited, and full of curiosity. Possibly rebellious. She also asked if you looked handsome. I told the young lady I did not know the quality of your facial features, that I had not met you yet. And, of course, I reminded her that beauty is merely in the eyes of the beholder."

"What does this girl my age look like?" I asked, gazing through the fog at the ship.

Morph's eye's twinkled.

"As I have said, beauty is merely in the eye of the beholder. In my opinion, she is the most beautiful young lady I have laid my eyes on in many a Millennium moon. She is tall, slender, with ebony hair falling down over her shoulders, and eyes so green that I mistook them for sparkling emeralds."

I looked back toward the ship, masked by the primordial fog. The dragon's head bobbed up and down in the choppy water.

"In fact," Morph continued, "the young maiden told me that—"

The ship's horn bellowed again.

"There is our final signal to board ship," the sage said.

"I don't need to think about my decision. I'm going with you. Do you promise I can return to Time Island anytime I choose?"

"Anytime you desire. That is my promise."

"Let's go," I said.

The sage smiled and held out his upper right hand.

"Congratulations, young man. You shall cherish your decision to remain as our guest."

Returning the smile, I shook Morph's out-stretched hand, thinking, *I still can't believe this is happening to me.*

Except for the crashing waves below, an eerie quietness surrounded Time Island. The black sky, visible on the northern horizon, crept closer. The red sky moved steadily toward the western horizon, blotting out the blue sky. I couldn't take my eyes off the three Millennium moons.

Morph told me, "Before you descend the rocks, please do me a favor. Jump. A small jump, if you do not mind."

"Why?"

"You are in for a surprise. Please, jump."

I bent slightly at the knees and sprung upward.

"Whoa!" I shouted.

Effortlessly, I had thrust myself above Morph's head, jumping a body's length higher.

"Easy does it," Morph said, grabbing my arms as I fell back down, off balance. "You are not yet accustomed to our atmosphere. Millennium's about three-quarters the size of Earth. This means our gravity is lighter, has less gravitational pull than where you come from."

"This will take some time to get used to," I said.

"Exactly," Morph replied. "Please remember, you are also much stronger here than you were on Earth. Use your new-found strength wisely."

I shook my head, *okay,* not knowing the extent of my strength.

Morph and I walked down the ancient stone steps, taking us from the top of the pyramidal platform to the bottom third tier of the obelisk.

"Please be careful on the rocks below," Morph said, pointing down the face of the obelisk to the skiff below. "You are too heavy for me to carry while flying, but I shall hover next to you in case you slip during your descent."

I peered down the edge of the obelisk. Straight down, a *long* way down. My breathing quickened. My fear of heights, a phobia I had experienced since childhood, embarrassed me. I closed my eyes and murmured, "It's higher than I thought."

"You are lighter here than your Earth weight," Morph said. "You can jump twice as far. You must jump from rock to rock below, so judge your distance carefully, compensate for the longer distance."

Metamorphosis flapped his vibrant wings. The turbulent wind created by his wings caused my wavy black hair to blow in my face. The sage's wings flapped faster and faster. His leather boots lifted off the rock platform, followed by his curled green tail. I squinted from the force of the air turbulence. The bearded man with wings flew directly over my head, hovering like a human butterfly.

Just like father told me, Morph *could* fly!

"Hold on tight. Do not look down."

I began my descent.

Morph hovered next to me, making sure I maintained secure footing. The heavy fur coat made climbing awkward. The granite rock felt slippery on my hands and bare feet.

"Steady as she goes," Morph yelled.

Near the base of Time Island, my fur coat became wetter, and wetter from the crashing waves. Because I spent many weekends surfing the northern California coastline, I had experienced dangerous shoreline conditions before—rocks and treacherous waves.

The pounding surf splashed warm mist and foam in my face. My fur coat became saturated, twice as heavy as before. My arm and leg muscles began to ache.

The waves looked bigger than I remembered, but I knew I could jump twice as far. My eyes darted from the jagged rocks to the crashing surf.

"You are almost there," Morph yelled.

A wave crashed at my feet. White, foamy water exploded in my face. I bent down to steady myself, drenched.

"The water feels warm," I murmured, licking my lips. The water tasted like mineral water, not salty.

Morph flew to the skiff and signaled to me, *hurry*.

The sage untied the rope, releasing the small boat from the iron mooring.

Shouting, "Here I come!" I judged the distance to the first rock, two body lengths away. Wishing I had my wet suit on instead of the heavy fur coat, I stopped, questioning whether I should swim to the rock, or jump.

Morph coaxed me toward the skiff with his hand signals. I had to trust that I could jump farther than I had ever had without a running start.

Bending at the knees, I sprung up and forward, gliding effortlessly through the air. It felt like a slow motion movie as I landed on the opposite rock with a heavy thud.

Feeling super human after each long leap, I focused on Morph and the skiff. The pounding surf drenched me as I clung to the rocks to avoid being grabbed by the massive waves. From my surfing experience, I knew that surviving crashing waves and jagged rocks was unlikely, no matter how well I could swim.

"Two more rocks to go!" Morph shouted, waving from the swaying skiff.

I had timed my leaps between waves perfectly, but the final jump to the skiff proved too difficult. A monster wave snatched me during my final leap toward Morph's four outstretched arms.

Entering the water upside down, I frantically gulped air before I submerged. Sinking immediately, my fur coat became dead weight underwater. My years of surfing had taught me to remain calm when pulled under water by a big wave, so, I rolled over to a feet-first position.

The clear, fluorescent water surprised me, glowing with vibrant pink, violet, and yellow swirls. It looked as if the water had been illuminated with a giant aquarium bulb, like my father's tank in our home library.

Sinking fast, I attempted to untie the sash around my waist, to calm myself and not swallow water while I struggled with the knotted sash. The more I struggled, the tighter the sash felt. Pain shot through my hands as my fingernails tore at the fur.

The weight of the waterlogged fur dragged me deeper.

Suddenly, my feet landed on a rock outcropping, preventing me from sinking into the black abyss.

Through the clear water I spotted the rotting hulls of three sunken ships, the reality of death.

I panicked and tugged desperately at the sash's double knot. My lungs burst with pain, craving oxygen. I knew I was about to swallow water, maybe for the final time.

My hair swayed back and forth in the current while I stared at the sunken ships. My thoughts slowed down as I watched a black whale swim by, singing in a high-pitched voice.

The final breath of air bubbles escaped from my lips as I stopped tugging at the sash around my waist.

I watched the bubbles float upward toward the surface of the Sea of Circles, toward the shadowy silhouette of the skiff's hull.

I realized I was going to drown.

Die there, all alone.

God, did I come all this way to die?

Losing consciousness, I prepared to swallow my last gulp of water when an object drifted in front of my face.

A sea snake?

No, a rope! A brown rope swayed in the underwater current.

I grabbed the knotted end, wrapped the rope around my arm, pulling myself upward.

Swallowed another gulp of the warm liquid, filling my lungs with water.

Unexpectedly, the rope tightened and I lunged upward, toward the surface at a rapid speed.

Closing my eyes from the force of the water, my face burst through the surface of the Sea of Circles.

Morph grabbed the back of my fur coat and pulled me into the boat. Gasping for air, I choked violently, puking up water.

"Outstanding. Great recovery, young man," Morph yelled.

Lying flat in the skiff, I choked and gasped for oxygen while Morph rowed away from the treacherous rocks of Time Island, holding four wooden oars in the water, two on each side of the boat.

"I apologize. It is my fault you had to tolerate such treacherous waves," Morph said. "We should have left much earlier, before the big surf arrived."

Breathing hard and spitting up water, I said, "I've dealt with bigger waves at home, but never wet suits made of heavy fur like this one."

"Excellent attitude. Your life was in danger and you faced the challenge head on. You are a brave young man."

I nodded in appreciation. My teeth chattered uncontrollably from the cool air hitting my face, arms and legs.

Stared at Time Island through the fog.

Half the sky had turned black, the other half, red. The three moons reminded me of my unearthly location.

"We shall get you out of that wet coat soon," the sage said. "We have comfortable clothing for you, outfits that are quite fashionable."

Calming myself, my attention turned toward the *Skipbladnir.*
Still no movement on board.

The skiff pulled up to the ship's port side and I grabbed the rope ladder that dangled from the deck's railing.

"Look at all the hand carvings," I muttered. The intricate carvings that covered the ship's hull fascinated me. Many of the figures and hieroglyphs I recognized were famous Earth deities—gods and goddesses—that I had seen illustrated in my father's mythology books.

Morph told me that the *Skipbladnir,* pride of the great inland sea, had been constructed of the finest oak from the forests of Nemoria, the richest teak from the jungles of Harundia, and the sturdiest redwood from the northern regions of Gellum.

I told Morph how I remembered the names of the kingdoms from the maps in Father's library.

He went on to say that the royal vessel had been meticulously hand carved and crafted from prow to stern. A "floating work of art", as he put it. At 150 feet in length, the *Skipbladnir* ranked as the largest vessel on the vast Sea of Circles.

The sage dropped the four oars and tied the skiff to a cleat on the ship's hull.

The red sky cast an eerie light on the Sea of Circles.

"Before we go on board," Morph said, "I must warn you about the physical appearance of my friends. Please keep in mind, they all are friendly and would never harm you. Once you open your mind and heart, get to know them, their physical features shall look natural to you."

The sage paused and placed his left hand on my shoulder. "There is nothing to fear."

I grinned. "If they are your friends, I won't be afraid."

"Good attitude my son. Let us board the *Skipbladnir* so we may get you some clothes to wear."

The sage clutched the rope ladder, saying, "Tonight we shall celebrate your arrival."

"At dinner?"

"Of course, my son, at dinner," Morph said, chuckling.

Using all four arms, the sage climbed the ladder, saying, "Come aboard; the black sky approaches."

"Here I come," I said.

The skiff bucked up and down in the splashing waves.

Looking down at my coat, I gasped, feeling my chest. Thinking I had lost my Triamulet, I grabbed my neck and fumbled to feel the gold chain. Found the necklace, realizing the gold talisman had slipped around my neck to my back side, between my shoulder blades.

Thank God I didn't lose it, I thought.

Letting go of the Triamulet, I clutched the rope ladder and followed Morph up toward the ship's deck, watching the underside of his segmented green tail disappear over the ship's brass rail. Taking a deep breath, I reached for the top rung of the ladder.

The *Skipbladnir* creaked and groaned. She seemed to say, "Welcome aboard, Hunter.

The Skipbladnir

Chapter 6
The Skipbladnir

olding on to the top rung of the ladder, I clutched the brass rail, pulled myself up, and peered over the railing to catch a glimpse of the crew. Only Metamorphosis stood on deck. I looked up to see a billion stars twinkling in the vast Andromeda blackness. Silhouetted against the Millennium sky, one the ship's three ivory-white sails displayed a triangle—the *Skipbladnir's* insignia.

Above her sails, three full moons reminded again me of my unearthly location. Looked over my shoulder at Time Island. Shrouded in primordial fog, the ghostly obelisk stood alone in the turbulent Sea of Circles.

"Come aboard," Morph said.

The ship swayed on the waves while I climbed over the slippery rail and stumbled down onto the wooden deck. The polished planks felt warm under my cold, bare feet.

"Welcome aboard the *Skipbladnir*," Morph announced. "I want you to meet Captain Gog before I escort you to your cabin."

"Okay. This fur smells really awful."

Morph chuckled, turned, and walked to the main mast. He rang the ship's brass bell. The *Skipbladnir* surged forward. The long oars moved in unison to the rhythmic cadence.

"Rrrooowww! "Rrrrooowww! "Rrrrooowww!" bellowed from the bowels of the mighty vessel.

Morph rang the ship's bell two more times.

The *Skipbladnir* looked magnificent by all seafaring standards. Every plank of polished wood displayed carved figures and mythological deities of ancient symbols and legendary creatures. I recognized many of the figures and symbols carved on the ship's woodwork.

The carvings looked like Egyptian, Greek, and Roman gods and goddesses. Some were Aztec, Mayan and Inca symbols. Others were Indian, Japanese, and Chinese in ancestry. I liked the knight on horseback slaying the fire-breathing dragon.

Standing near the capstan, I balanced myself at the midway point of the surging, swaying ship. Although the hull of the *Skipbladnir* had the appearance of an ancient Viking galley with the dragon figurehead at the prow of the ship, the upper decks looked more like a Spanish galleon.

Morph told me that since there were no steady trade winds in the Discordia Crater, the ship required oars.

The rear decks resembled a fifteenth-century galleon, a caravel, the ships Columbus and Magellan sailed to explore the seven seas. The stern's aftercastle, bordered with bulky balustrade, rose two levels up and around a deckhouse. The massive ship's wheel stood on the first-story level, in front of the deckhouse with a door that looked unusually tall, out of scale with the structure.

I wondered why no one stood at the ship's wheel.

Morph rang the ship's brass bell three more times.

The rowing cadence quickened.

"Rrrooowww! "Rrrooowww! "Rrrooowww!"

The ship picked up speed, surging through the choppy waves.

Morph and I turned toward the prow. The front deck's forecastle had two raised decks, split level platforms surrounded by ornate balustrades. At the main deck level, a carved door stood underneath the first platform's staircase.

I heard a flapping sound and looked up to see the front sail wave helplessly in the steady breeze of the ship's forward surge. An embroidered triangle, the same symbol as my Triamulet medallion, adorned the sail.

75

"What does that emblem mean?" I asked, pointing up at the flapping white sail.

"That is our Triangulum. Most Millennians will tell you the three L's mean: Live Life as a Leader. The three L's also mean: Long—Live—Love, and Love—Life—Laughter. All mantras are correct, but the emblem has a much deeper meaning."

I stared at the Triangulum on the main sail. Then, I looked down at the Triamulet on the chain around my neck.

Morph pointed at the sail. "The eternal Triangulum represents the three levels of enlightenment. The relationship of body—mind—spirit. Physical—non-physical—meta-physical. Energy—matter—anti-matter."

The Sage of the Ages held up his upper left hand, raising three fingers.

"Simply, the inter-relationships of past—present—future. Before—now—after. Thought—word—action."

Morph grinned. "Does that make sense?"

"I think so," I replied.

"My apologies, I am sharing a bit too much information regarding our Triangulum. Until we have more time to talk, think of our triangular symbol as a sign of love, peace, and ultimate wisdom."

"That makes sense."

Morph waved and shouted, "Hello, Captain Gog!"

I spun around to see the captain. A massive man with a braided red beard stood in the deckhouse door. A helmet with two curved horns adorned his rugged, rust-colored face.

He looked like a Viking.

The captain took two giant steps down the staircase.

"Do not be alarmed," Morph said, "Captain Gog is a Vanir giant. He is our friend."

The wooden deck vibrated from each footstep of the approaching giant.

I stood my ground, forcing a grin.

The captain stopped and chuckled. "Ya, Morph, der youngin' is one goot lookin' lad."

"Captain Gog, it is my pleasure to introduce our esteemed guest, Hunter Wainright."

Gog stuck out his hairy hand in a gesture of friendship.

Reaching out to shake the captain's giant hand, I said, "Glad to meet you, Captain Gog."

My hand disappeared in Gog's grasp. He released my hand and pointed toward the ship's stern. His expression changed from a cordial grin to one of concern.

"Time to get der first mate on der ship's vheel und bring der crew up on deck to lower der flappin' sails. They be slowin' us down."

"Secure the ship, Captain; I shall take our guest below."

Captain Gog

Strutting across the deck, Captain Gog towered eight feet tall. The giant wore a brown fur tunic, brown breeches, and leather boots. Atop his shoulder-length red hair sat a fur-lined helmet with ox horns protruding from both sides. His braided red beard hung to his thick leather belt.

The captain shouted orders. "All hands on deck!"

"Remember what I requested of you regarding my fellow companions?" Morph asked.

I paused. "I must not let their looks frighten me, they are my frien—"

Speechless, I did not complete my sentence. At the ship's wheel stood a monstrous creature, shouting orders.

"That guy doesn't look very friendly," I said.

"Although some claim that half-orcs can be unpredictable," Morph said, "the crew is loyal to Captain Gog. Do not be alarmed, they shall not harm you."

Morph told me that 208 half-orcs comprised the ship's crew. Endowed with enormous strength and endurance, forty-eight of the faithful beasts volunteered to man the forty-eight oars, twenty-four on each side of the ship. The remaining half-orcs worked as the ship's crew, handling the main deck rigging and providing protection against hostile attacks.

Before I could ask what *hostile attacks* meant, I became overwhelmed by the crew of half-orcs emerging from the deckhouse door.

Wearing fur-lined breeches and boots, they stood seven feet tall, with muscular bodies and greenish-grey skin. They wore their long black hair like barbarians, tied with a metal band on the top of their bald heads. Tusk-like teeth protruded from their lower jaws. Their heavy brows and pointed ears gave them a beast-like appearance.

A high-pitched sound drew my attention skyward. Rusted turnbuckles creaked and moaned while a crew of half-orcs lowered the three flapping sails from the top yards to the main yards. Like giant curtains piercing the fog, down came the billowy sails.

"Due to wind," Morph said, "the crew must lower and secure the ship's sails."

"So they don't slow us down?" I asked.

"Correct, so the sails do not impede our progress."

Then, I spotted him.

A bizarre creature had emerged from the stern's pavilion

door. Gigantic, he bent over to get through the door, the same door Captain Gog had just walked through *without* bending over. The winged creature stood proudly on the upper deck, his dragon-like face smiled as he raised a tall staff with his left arm, acknowledging me.

The two-legged beast balanced himself with his scaly-blue tail. A green dorsal crest ran from the back of his neck to the end of his serpentine tail. The horns of a ram adorned the creature's head. Blue-grey wings emerged from his back, like dragon's wings. The behemoth's muscular body shone with silver fur, except for the bare, human-like flesh that covered his neck, arms, and chest.

"I am proud of you, young man. I see you have accepted all my fellow Millennians as your trustworthy companions."

"And who is *that* companion?" I asked, pointing at the creature with the dragon face and wings.

"That is Pendragon, my fellow Utopian. You shall meet him at dinner."

As I watched Pendragon, he shouted to Gog, "*Paralus!*" and pointed his staff toward the stern of the ship.

Captain Gog took a spy glass from his belt and aimed the telescope northeast.

"Extractor ship comin'!" Gog shouted. "Dat be Kraken und Barbus und der beastmen pirates!"

Looking behind me, I spotted a ship emerging from the hazy fog. The main sail displayed an x-shaped emblem. The ship's figurehead, breaking the waves, looked like a gigantic red demon with horns.

Captain Gog ran to the main mast and rang the ship's bell three times.

The cadence call quickened, reverberating from the voices of fifty half-orcs rowing below deck.

"Rrrooowww! "Rrrooowww! "Rrrooowww!"

Morph placed his upper right hand on my shoulder. "Do not worry about the *Paralus*. We can easily outdistance her with our superior ship. Let us get you to your cabin. Please, follow me."

"Who is on that ship that everyone's so concerned about?", I asked.

The sage pointed toward the *Paralus* and said, "Unfortunately, your arrival here has not gone unnoticed. A group of malevolent beings, known as the Extractors, will do everything in their power to stop you and drain your life essence for their own evil purposes. The Extractors invaded this world long ago. They carry with them the *Dark Essence*, a virus that twists each mind it infects into acts of evil and despair. They feed off this negative energy and are spreading it not only here, but along the dimensional bridges to the populace of every world tied to Millennium, what we call the Amalgamation. This group of nine planets includes your planet, Earth."

Pendragon

I stared into the sage's eyes. With a grin, Metamorphosis continued. "But fear not, these Extractors are not unopposed. Here on Millennium their force is countered by we Utopians and our loyal followers. You shall learn, my son, that we ageless avatars of hope and knowledge protect the Eight Great Treasures by combating the evil Extractors at every turn."

I raised my right hand to speak, but Metamorphosis spoke first. "Please, hold your thoughts and questions for later, we will discuss more on our voyage to Fog Harbor. Now, we must get you to your cabin."

I nodded, *okay*, and followed the sage toward the prow of the *Skipbladnir.*

Stopping at the entrance beneath the forecastle deck's staircase, Morph swung the door open and shouted, "Master Hunter aboard!"

The sage stepped three paces forward and descended a narrow stairwell lined with oil lanterns. Morph's tail slid across the top step as he disappeared down the stairs. I ran my fingers along the ornate carvings on the walls. Bizarre creatures and symbols, ones I had never seen before, fascinated me.

"There shall be plenty of time to admire the ship's artwork," Morph said. "Please, close the door behind you."

Shutting the door, my eyes adjusted to the flame-lit stairway. I held the brass railing at the top of the stairs. Dancing flames cast shadows on the carved walls and ceiling.

Morph waited at the bottom of the steps, signaling to me, *come down.*

I descended the stairwell, enjoying the warm temperature below the deck of the *Skipbladnir.* Smelling the aroma of food cooking, my mouth watered. Other fragrances permeated the air. Recognizing the scent of vanilla and cinnamon, the aromas reminded me of home. The food smelled really good, like Mom's cooking.

Holding the copper rails, I descended the steep stairs. The sage pulled his scepter, *Joyease*, from his belt and walked down a narrow corridor. The crystal ball on the end of the scepter glowed with a blue, ultraviolet hue.

He stood next to an open door, saying, "Your room is ready."

I walked down the corridor and entered the cabin. The room looked awesome. The brass oil lamps mounted on the walls made the reddish teak walls and beamed ceiling glow with a warm, yellowish hue.

A parchment map hung on the cabin wall. It looked like the map of Millennium I saw on Professor Johan's back.

"You may clean up in there," Morph said, pointing to the latrine door. "Andvari has laid out your new clothes."

"Andvari?" I asked. "Is he the same guy who drew the tattoo on Professor Van Campbell's back?"

Mom will kill me if I came home with a tattoo, I thought.

"Yes. Andvari is a gnome from Nemoria. He shall personally assist you on our voyage."

Before I could respond, Morph said, "Please get ready. Dinner in one hour. Everyone is excited to meet you."

The sage smiled and closed the door. The sound of his tapping boot heels faded down the corridor and up the stairs.

I used the latrine to shed my fur coat, clean myself up, and try on my new clothes. Reentering the main cabin, I walked toward the full-length mirror to see what I looked like.

The heels of my black leather boots with silver buckles clicked on the hardwood floor.

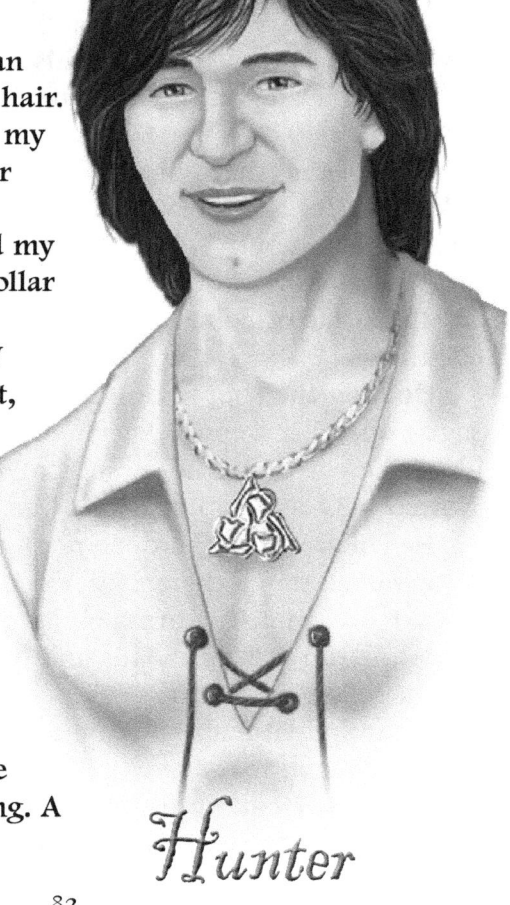

Smiling in the mirror, I ran my fingers through my wavy hair. Turning in circles, I admired my black breeches and my leather belt with the gold buckle, a Triangulum. I especially liked my white silk tunic, the v-neck collar with leather-laces.

All I need is a sword and I can battle a dragon, I thought, grinning with self-approval at my reflection, swishing the air with my make~ believe saber.

Full of restless energy, I strutted back and forth in front of the mirror. Happy with the way I looked, I walked to one of the open portholes on either side of the bed and gazed out the opening. A cool breeze brushed my face.

Hunter

Through the patches of swirling fog, the sparkling stars lit up the black sky. The ship surged ahead in perfect rhythm with the forty-eight oars.

Looking back toward the stern of our ship, I saw no sign of the *Paralus*.

I felt empowered. Ever since my childhood, I had dreamed of exploring uncharted territories. Now, I could live out my fantasies, my dreams.

My thoughts were interrupted by the unmistakable sound of a harmonica outside my cabin. The playing got louder, accompanied by a clacking sound.

A knock on the cabin door was followed by, "Hallo, Marster Hoonter. 'Tis me, Andvari."

The cabin door swung open and there stood the gnome, smiling from ear to ear. Andvari waddled in with his hand outstretched. His wooden clogs clacked against the cabin's wooden floor.

The gnome stood three feet tall, half my height. Andvari's squatty body and jolly pumpkin face put me at ease. The gnome sported a slate grey beard that stopped at his pot belly. The curly hair under his cap stuck straight out.

I greeted the smiling gnome, who wore a scarlet-red tunic and matching cap that hung to his shoulders, like a miniature Santa Claus. Tucked in his belt, a copper spyglass hung to his knees.

"Hello, nice to meet you," I said, reaching down to shake the gnome's outstretched hand.

"Aye, me pleasur', Marster Hoonter."

After a vigorous handshake, he let go of my hand. The gnome looked me up and down, nodding in approval.

"Hoot mon! You're lookin' gude 'n black an' white, laudy."

"Thank you for the clothes. They fit perfect."

"An' w'at aboout your boots?"

"The boots fit great."

I asked. "Was that you playing harmonica?"

"Aye, laudy, twas me," the gnome said, showing me his gold plated harmonica he keep in a leather pouch on his belt.

"I can play harmonica."

"Aye, you cun play fer me later. Are ye ready fer dinner?"

"I'm starving."

"Tis gude Marster Hoonter, follow me. Oooh, wait a blooody mument! You might be needin' a vest. The fog 'as lifted a bit, 'tis gettin' cooold on deck."

Andvari opened a wooden cedar chest and showed me a red fur vest.

"Aye, try this 'ere on."

Accepting the vest, I felt the soft fur.

"Is this mink?"

"Hoot mon, no. 'Tis pygmy weaselsnatcher."

Hesitant to ask what a weaselsnatcher looked like, I put the vest on and glanced in the mirror. The red vest complemented my white shirt and black pants.

Grinned at my reflection, pleased at the way I looked.

"Kenn we gooh?"

"I'm ready," I replied, still looking at myself in the mirror.

"Aye, folla' me."

Andvari waddled out the cabin door. I followed the gnome down the corridor to the stairwell. Andvari struggled to climb the steep steps. At the top landing, the gnome bent over, winded.

"Aye...excoose, me, Marster...Hoonter," he said, panting. "I be...ar' little slooow...goin' up...these 'ere stairs."

"Don't worry, when I was a little boy, I used to struggle going up my stairs at home."

"Hee~hee~hee...haw~haw~haw...uck-uck."

Andvari high-pitched laughter echoed in the stairwell.

"Sorry," I said, "I didn't mean that like it sounded."

"'Twas' nooo mistyke. You're merely sharin' a fond child'ood mem'ry. Aye, me'd like to 'ear mooore aboout your planet Earth 'hen you got time."

"Sure. I'd like to hear all about *your* planet, Millennium."

"Aye, you shall, laudy," Andvari said, turning the crystal knob and opening the forecastle door to the top deck.

A cool breeze hit my face. Taking a deep breath of Millennium air, I knew I'd made the right decision.

White fog danced in swirling patches on the Sea of Circles, encircling the mighty *Skipbladnir*. A veil of sparkling white stars lit up the pitch-black sky while a shower of blazing comets crisscrossed the cosmos.

A voice from the top of the main mast shouted, "Captain, the *Paralus* sail be out of sight!"

"Das is goot!" Gog shouted.

Looking up, I recognized the silhouette of a half-orc in the topcastle's crow's nest, perched sixty feet above the deck.

As we walked across the wooden planks of the top deck, the half-orc in the crow's nest shouted, "Earthlin' n' gnome walkin'!"

When Andvari and I reached the bottom of the deckhouse, Captain Gog stood in the lantern light at the top of the stairs.

"Hurry up, dinner is ready to serve," the captain yelled.

With me right behind him, the gnome climbed the steep stairs, one at a time. Wanting to be polite, I patiently followed the gnome.

Without warning, Captain Gog took two giant steps down the stairs, grabbed Andvari by the back of his collar and lifted the gnome up in the air.

"Come up here, little fella'," the captain said. "Vee do not havin' all daynight to be vaitin' on ya."

I froze on the deck steps as the Vanir giant swooped up Andvari and plopped him down on the second deck.

Andvari's angry face matched the color of his red tunic. Tucking the ruffled shirt tails back inside his breeches, he shouted, "Captain Goog, pleeease. 'Tis nay your job to 'elp me climb the blooody stairs!"

85

Gog grunted and turned his attention to me.

"What might you be waitin' on, young man?"

"Coming up now, Captain!" I shouted, running up the steps.

"Goot," Gog yelled. He turned and rang a triangular chime mounted on the deckhouse wall. While he clanged the triangle, Gog shouted, "Ya, I be so hungry I can eaten' der sail on yonder mast. Ho-ho-ho…ho-ho-ho…ho-ho-ho."

The upper deck shook with the roar of forty half-orcs laughing with their captain.

Andvari tugged on my breeches and said, "Ya' must pardon the cap'in. He gets blooody awn'ry when 'e is 'ungry."

"I understand. He's got a huge mouth to feed."

"Hee-hee-hee. 'Tis gude Marster Hoonter. Vary fuuny."

The deckhouse door swung open. There stood Metamorphosis, bathed in a flood of yellow light escaping through the doorway.

The captain stopped clanging the triangle and said, "Here is der boy. Supper must be burnin' up by now."

The sage patted the giant on the back. "Thank you, Gog. You may take your seat at the dinner table. I shall escort our guest from here."

The captain lumbered past the sage through the doorway.

"Did I cause dinner to be late?" I asked Andvari.

"Nae, o' curse not. Folla' me," he replied, entering the main entrance to the deckhouse.

Morph gestured with his hand, *follow Andvari.*

I entered the elegant foyer covered with wood-framed mirrors soldiered with crystal oil lamps. The mirrors gave me an opportunity to admire my new set of Millennian clothes. The more I saw, the more I liked the outfit.

Morph walked past me and stood in front of the ornate double doors. The plush rug displayed embroidered scenes of gods, goddesses, and mythological creatures. The sage's wings, semi-folded, radiated in vibrant colors under the lamp lights.

"Hunter," he said, "tonight is the beginning of your enlightenment, a new way of seeing yourself, and others. Embrace it."

I grinned, unsure of how to respond.

Andvari stood by the sage and winked at me.

Morph spun around, turned the crystal doorknobs and swung the double doors open. A roar of applause and cheers erupted from the group seated at a long banquet table.

Adjusting to the brightly-lit dining room, I stood dumbfounded. The room looked breathtaking, as did the many creatures seated at the table. Above the banquet table, a crystal chandelier with dozens of burning blue candles hung from the copper tile ceiling. The teak-wood walls displayed oil paintings and tapestries displaying grand castles and surrealistic landscapes of Millennium.

Pendragon sat at the far end of the banquet table, smiling and gesturing, *come in*. To the dragon's right sat Captain Gog, tying a white napkin around his neck and red beard. Next to the captain sat a huge woman, every bit as big as Gog. She had one eye, like a cyclops. She smiled at me, blinking nervously.

Across from the captain and the one-eyed woman sat two half-orcs. They both continued to smile and clap their hands in honor of my arrival. Four gnomes, who looked like Andvari, sat on both sides of the table. The gnomes giggled in high-pitched voices, chiming their crystal goblets with their silver spoons.

The three winged-back chairs nearest to me sat empty.

"Folla' me," Andvari said, waddling into the banquet room.

"Go ahead," Morph said. "Remember, they are your friends."

Forcing a smile, I followed Andvari to a winged-back chair, catty corner from the half-orcs. The gnome pulled my chair out.

"Thanks," I said, taking my seat, fidgeting in my chair while the group quieted down. I made eye contact with the gnomes sitting across from me, but I found myself looking back at Morph for reassurance. I avoided looking to my left. The one-eyed lady and Pendragon still bothered me. Made me feel uneasy.

Andvari closed the double doors and took his seat to the left of me. Metamorphosis seated himself at the head of the table.

In the middle of the table, between two crystal candelabras, a silver platter held a humongous fish with a green apple stuffed in its mouth. The weird fish reminded me of a prehistoric coelacanth. Whatever it was, it smelled delicious.

The oversized silver plates and dinnerware featured

embossed Triangulums. Ornate crystal bowls, overflowing with fruits and vegetables, adorned the table. I recognized apples, oranges and bananas, but could not identify the other strange, oddly shaped fruit. Baskets of ambrosia, the 'bread of life', as Morph called it, sat at both ends of the table.

Piano music played from the corner of the room. Looking behind me to find the source of the music, I had never seen anything like the musical quartet in the corner. On a miniature stage stood three frog faeries dressed in minstrel attire. The faeries, twenty-four inches in height, bobbed their amphibious heads to the rhythm of the piano. One faerie held a miniature cello, the other two held tiny violins. A chubby toad faerie sat at center stage, his grey head covered with bulbous pink warts. Wearing a black and white Mozart-like outfit, he played a miniature white grand piano.

The music sounded great. I grinned at the faeries. All four nodded. Their bulging eyes sparkled in the candlelight.

When I turned back around, everyone stared at me. I felt my face turn red. I felt like a bug under glass, as Mom would say whenever she felt someone was staring at her.

The instant I placed my white napkin on my lap, the eclectic group burst into spontaneous conversation.

Andvari

Feeling more at ease, I did my best to comprehend the bizarre scene before me. It reminded me of a Thanksgiving dinner at home, except that I was surrounded by a creature with wings, a giant, a cyclops, gnomes, half-orc sailors, faeries playing classical instruments, and a sage with wings, four arms, and a tail.

I loved fantasy novels, science fiction movies and role-playing games, but in my wildest dreams I could never have imagined anything like the dinner party being held in my honor. I felt positive energy in the room, something special, extraordinary.

88

Winking at me, Morph picked up his silver spoon and tapped on his crystal goblet. Knowing he had the group's attention, he announced, "Before our other guest of honor arrives, allow me to introduce Hunter to our crew."

He pointed at a gnome and said, "Sitting next to Andvari is Vestri. And next to him is Norori. These two gnomes handle the ship's maintenance chores."

Vestri and Norori nodded with childish grins, their gnomish faces red with excitement.

Morph continued. "And next to Norori, we have our ship's cook. Oh, excuse me. Our resident chef, the charming, Menja."

"Ya, dat is my yab, to cookin' ze meals fer my husband's crew, ya," Menja said, blinking the red eyelashes of her single, green eye.

Morph said, "Menja happens to be Gog's lovely wife."

Menja blushed and stuck her giant head in the captain's chest. She continued giggling. Her red hair, braided in pigtails, framed her humanoid face. Gog wrapped his tree-trunk arm around his wife, patting her on the back.

Morph continued. "Next, we have my trusted friend and fellow Utopian, Pendragon."

Smiling from horn to horn, Pendragon said, "My pleasure, Hunter. I admire your courage in joining us on our journey."

The table vibrated from his deep voice. Pendragon, the largest guest at the table, sat with his furry knees above the table. His claw-tipped wings almost touched the ceiling.

"Thank you, Pendragon," I replied, thinking to myself, *a talking dragon. Wait until the guys at school hear about this. Kirk is going to freak out.*

The sage continued with his introductions.

"Next to Pendragon, our ship's first mate, Balder."

"Ahh, Master Hunter," the half-orc said in a low, slow voice. "Balder at your faithful call." He bowed his bald, green head.

"And next to Balder is the *Skipbladnir's* second mate, Lycus," Morph announced.

"At your service, Master Hunter," Lycus said.

"Then, there is Fundin, our ship's recreation director, our faerie game master," Morph said. "He conducts our gaming activities during our voyages."

Fundin looked smaller than Andvari, with finer features. The game faerie wore a checkered jester's hat, complete with bells dangling from the hat's three peaks.

"Games?" I asked. "What kind of games?"

Morph chuckled. "We Millennians must have our beloved tabletop games for entertainment. They are part of our heritage."

"Do you play tabletop games, Master Hunter?" Fundin asked.

I thought about the term, tabletop games, fixating on Fundin's orange and green checkerboard shirt with the black, white, red and blue chess pieces dotting the silk fabric.

"Games play'd on a table. You know, *board* games!" Fundin shouted in a high-pitched voice.

"Board games, of course," I replied. "My father taught me chess when I was a little boy."

"Exc'llent," Fundin said. "Tomorrow you must visit o'r game room. We'll play a rousin' game o' Gametasia Chess, ur I'll show you 'ow to play Open Road, ur me fav'rite game o'—"

"Excuse me, my gaming friend," Pendragon interjected. "We have another daynight to play your tabletop games. Our other guest is about to arrive."

Fundin blushed, saying, "Excuse me enthusiasm."

Morph nodded. "And last but not least, we have the lovely Miss Alfrigga. All the way from the southern lowlands, she tidies up our cabins. Alfrigga is also the personal attendant to our female visitor."

"Welcome, Marster Hoonter," Alfrigga said in a high-pitched voice. Her black hair was styled in a beehive hairdo with a blue bow pinned to the front. "The youn' lassie 'tis lookin' furward to meetin' you. Aye, an' I knuw she'll not be disappoint'd."

"Thanks, Alfrigga, that's nice of you to say."

No sooner had I spoken then, all at once, Gog stood. Then, Pendragon and the half-orcs stood.

Seeing Morph push his chair back, I followed the sage's lead. Dropping my white napkin from my lap, I rose to my feet.

In the opposite corner of the banquet room, a door swung open. Everyone clapped and cheered.

Captain Gog yelled, "Ya, dat be a beauty, ohhh, ya."

I clapped my hands, straining to see who I applauded.

The massive bodies of Balder and Lycus blocked my view.

The applause stopped.

Morph announced, "Evol, how delightful you can join us for dinner."

She walked past the standing half-orcs to her place setting.

I stood there, stunned. It was her.

She looked beautiful, like a goddess. Awestruck, my mouth became dry. I felt a funny sensation in my stomach.

Morph stepped around the corner of the table, bowed and pulled her chair out.

She looked at the sage and grinned, but she did not make eye contact with me.

Her ebony-black hair flowed over her shoulders and down her back. A long braid of hair ran down her chest onto her tunic. She acted confident, not shy.

Morph had it right, her eyes *did* look like two green emeralds. She had the largest eyes I had ever seen on a girl.

Her flawless olive bronze skin shone under the glow of one hundred candles. Revealing a shapely figure, a human figure, she wore a blue tunic with gold, embroidered trim.

A gold medallion, Triamulet, hung from a ruby necklace around her neck. The red gems sparkled in the candlelight.

Evol took her seat.

Morph returned to his chair and sat down. The remainder of the dinner party guests took their seats. She kept her eyes down, looking at the

Eve

91

place setting. She maintained a serious look on her face. Her high cheekbones accentuated her green eyes. Her curved, black eyelashes blinked with controlled excitement.

"Evol," Morph said, "I would like you to meet Hunter, our most recent visitor to Millennium."

She looked up, straight into my eyes.

Speechless, I knew I had to say something, anything. So, I moistened my dry lips.

She looked up, straight into my waiting gaze.

I sat, tongue-tied.

No one spoke.

Evol's olive skin turned flush. She grinned at me. A coy grin.

The room remained quiet while the dinner party guests watched Evol and me stare at each other.

Finally, I snapped out of my infatuated grin to say, "Nice to meet you, Evo...Eeeee...um...Eve?"

I couldn't believe how I had screwed up her name.

She got this serious look on her face and said, "You may call me Eve if you wish."

Her voice sounded as perfect as her face.

"All right, Eve," I said. "Nice to meet you."

I held out my trembling hand in friendship. She extended her hand with five slender fingers and grasped my hand. Felt a rush of energy shoot through my body, a feeling I had never experienced with a girl.

Eve continued to make eye contact.

Her green eyes sparkled under the candlelight.

"Ah-hemmm."

Captain Gog cleared his throat, impatient for dinner to begin. Place settings rattled from the vibrations.

The girl from another world let go of my hand.

"Now that our guests have been formally introduced, I shall make a toast in their honor," Morph announced as he stood up.

He raised his crystal goblet high with his right upper arm while he held his scepter in his lower left hand. The group raised their goblets in honor of Eve and me.

The sage cleared his throat and said, "May both Eve from Epiphany and Hunter from Earth enjoy inner peace during our voyage. May they discover freedom within, the highest truth, on their journey down the Open Road, The Great Way."

Morph smiled, saying, "Hunter and Eve, we welcome you to Millennium."

Applause and cheers erupted in the room while the two of us, both from different worlds, stared at each other.

Morph sat in his chair, picked up a silver dinner bell from the table and rang the bell three times.

The corner dining room door swung open again. Three gnomes scurried into the dining room with pewter trays filled with food and drinks. Festive music played. The frog faeries accompanied the piano-playing toad faerie.

Spontaneously, the *Skipbladnir's* crew broke into joyful chatter. Andvari and Alfrigga nodded to each other.

I sat there, tongue-tied. Eve looked down at her place setting, emotionless.

Metamorphosis and Pendragon grinned and winked at each other across the long banquet table.

Out on deck, the crew navigated through the swirling fog. A half-orc, high in the crow's nest, held a horn at his side, ready to signal the crew of danger.

A steady cadence, "Rrooowww! Rrooowww! Rrooowww!" bellowed from the bowels of the royal ship.

Forty-eight oars simultaneously broke the surface of the inner sea while three moons cast their eerie reflections on the Sea of Circles.

The *Skipbladnir* would dock at Fog Harbor within one daynight. Time Island had long since disappeared in the primordial darkness.

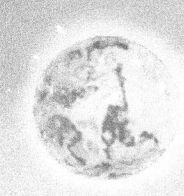

The Paralus

DAYNIGHT OF THE CROCODILE

Aries the 9th
Year of the Dragon

*"Fulfill the needs of others
and your own needs shall be fulfilled.
Rather than putting yourself first,
put yourself last and you shall end up ahead."*
—Metamorphosis

Chapter 7
Maps & Treasures

Sat up in bed and rubbed the sleep from my eyes. My cabin was illuminated by the Millennium sunrise shining through my portholes. It was the morning after my encounter with Eve. If I told you that all I could think about was her, would you be surprised? Actually, my thoughts were negative, how I wished I'd dated more girls on Earth. Maybe then I would have known how to impress her. She hardly talked at dinner. She acted different than any girl I'd ever met.

I gazed out the cabin porthole to find a blue sky peeking at me through the patches of grey fog swirling on the Sea of Circles. The cadence calls of forty-eight half-orcs could be heard two decks below me. In unison, four dozen wooden oars slapped the water's surface.

Climbed out of bed and walked across the cabin to the ticking clock. Almost 3:00 o'clock. I remember the clock struck twenty-four before I fell asleep. I realized I'd slept only three hours, but I felt wide awake, full of energy.

The evening before, the wall clock next to the door read 22 o'clock when Andvari escorted me back to my cabin. The gnome called the clock a weary wheel. The clock had an hour hand, a minute hand, and a red second hand, but the faceplate looked like a military clock. Displaying the numerals 1 to 24, the faceplate had four equal quadrants: two blue, one black, and one red. The upper-right blue quadrant displayed the numerals 1 to 6 o'clock; the lower-right red quadrant displayed the numerals 6 to 12 o'clock; the lower-left blue quadrant displayed the numerals 12 to 18 o'clock; the upper-left black quadrant displayed the numerals 18 to 24 o'clock.

Washed my face, combed my hair, and dressed myself in the same black pants and boots I had worn the night before. Put on a red silk tunic instead of my white one. Stood in front of the full-length mirror, making sure I looked my best for Eve. Caught myself grinning and feeling ashamed for being so happy. I knew that my parents, my entire family, had to be in turmoil.

In the mirror's reflection I spotted a leather-bound book setting on a marble podium. Walked to the podium and read the embossed, gold-leafed letters on the cover:

Thicker than any of the dictionaries in my father's home library, cloth ribbons of various colors divided the worn, parchment pages of the magnificent *Magnum Opus*.

I carefully opened the book.

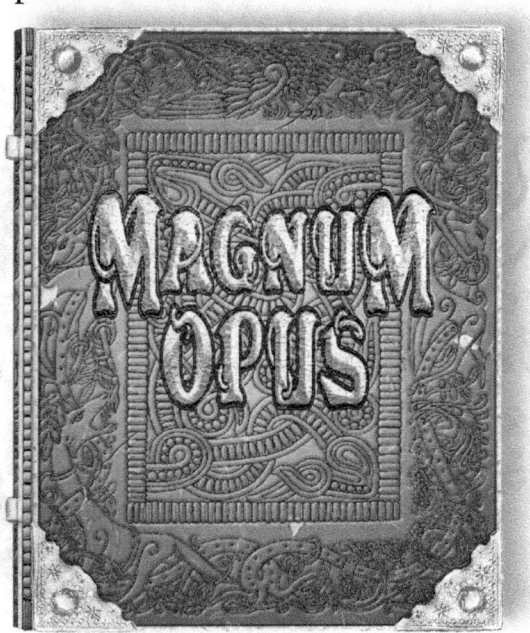

The table of contents revealed:

Turning the pages, I stopped at the section:

Gods & Goddesses: Compendium of Deities

Divided in four subsections according to the empire each deity inhabited, northern, southern, eastern and western, I studied the descriptions, learning that the gods and goddesses lived and breathed on Millennium.

- Odin: Father of the northern gods, ruler of Asgard.
- Tezcatlipoca: Smoking Mirror, southern sol god.
- Zeus: King, ruler of the western gods and Olympus.

I flipped through the parchment pages of deities. Professor Johan had been correct. The gods really *did* exist on Millennium.

Grabbed the black ribbon dangling from the center of the book and turned to the section titled:

Extractor Compendium

Several pages of illustrations revealed the Extractors.

Ex

Vulcan

Fascinated by the drawings, I continued to read about the dysfunctional behavior of the Extractors, followers of Ex.

Barbus

Bodvar

Tarantulana

Marax

Ignorious

Karkinos

Captain Kraken   Tyrannus

After looking at all the Extractor illustrations, I closed the *Magnum Opus* and stretched my arms.

Walked across the cabin to the Millennium parchment map hung on the wall.

Millennium Upperworld

I scanned the Upperworld map to find my exact location, moving my index finger over the parchment. Millennium was one big super continent. The trail my father talked about, The Open Road, wound its way around the map.

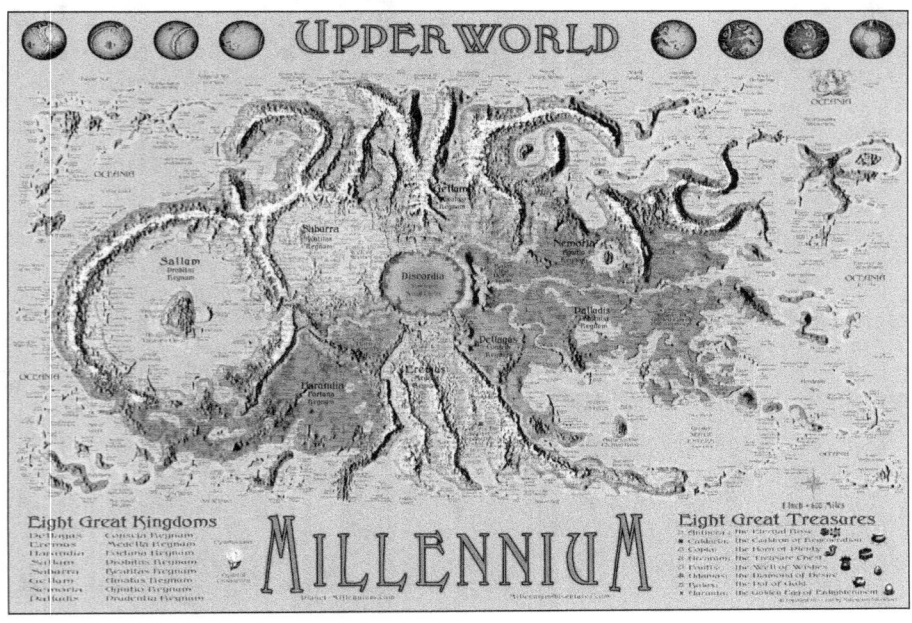

In a clockwise direction, I read the names of the four empires and the eight kingdoms:

SOUTHERN EMPIRE
* Eremus: Kingdom of Medella,
  Home of Caldaria cervina,
  the Cauldron of Regeneration

* Harundia: Kingdom of Fortuna,
  Home of Copia epula,
  the Horn of Plenty

WESTERN EMPIRE
* Sallum: Kingdom of Probitas,
  Home of Arcarum lapis,
  the Treasure Chest

* Saburra: Kingdom of Beatitas,
  Home of Fontis risus,
  the Well of Wishes

NORTHERN EMPIRE
* Gellum: Kingdom of Amatus,
  Home of Adamas fulgor,
  the Diamond of Desire

* Nemoria: Kingdom of Agnitio,
  Home of Balux binaria,
  the Pot of Gold

EASTERN EMPIRE
* Palludis: Kingdom of Prudentia
  Home of Auranta mentis,
  the Golden Egg of Enlightenment

* Pellagus: Kingdom of Conscia
  Home of Anthera amonis,
  the Eternal Rose

"Here it is," I mumbled. "In the middle of the planet, the Discordia Crater."

Taking a closer look, I found the Sea of Circles. Time Island was marked with a red X. Just below, to the southwest, was Fog Harbor, our destination.

Sea of Circles
Time Island

On the bottom legend, I found the map scale.

1 Inch = 600 Miles

The map was about 30 inches long. I multiplied 600 by 30 and got 18,000 miles in circumference. Since the Earth measured 24,000 miles in circumference, Millennium was about seventy-five percent the size of Earth, just like Morph told me. No wonder I could jump so high and felt so strong. The gravity was lighter.

Scanning the map, I recognized many geographical locations as mythological names.

Camelot...Atlantis...Sleepy Hollow...

Tree of the World...Gametasia...Kukuanaland...

Wonderland...Xanadu...Doubting Castle...

Laputa Island...Jotunheim...Ruritania...

Delightful Haven...Mountains of the Moon...

Sea of Green...Portal of Metamorphosis...

Delectable Mountains...Dogworthy Castle...

Bimini Island...City of Apes...Cockayne...

Land of the Greater Gods...Land of the Lesser Gods...

Sleeping Beauty's Castle...Enchanted Wood—

Some of the places originated from myths and fables, some were fable and fairy tale lands.

Wild Wood...Woodman's Hall...Yggdrasil...
Never-Never Land...Vanity Fair...Tree of Knowledge...
South Crater Trail...Mu...Treasure Island...Oz...
Mountains of Mystery...Lilliput...Celestial City...
Bridge of Words...Hermopolis...Escalot...
Ice Falls...Fire Falls...Fog Harbor—

Placing my index finger on the parchment map, I measured the distance from Fog Harbor to the Isle of the Eternal Rose.

When I pushed on the parchment, I discovered a second map underneath the Upperworld. Three rivet holes mounted on three wall hooks supported the two maps; so, I unhooked the top map and placed it on my bed.

Millennium Underworld

The second parchment map, titled Underworld, revealed a supercontinent that had the same perimeter outline as the Upperworld, but it showed different names.

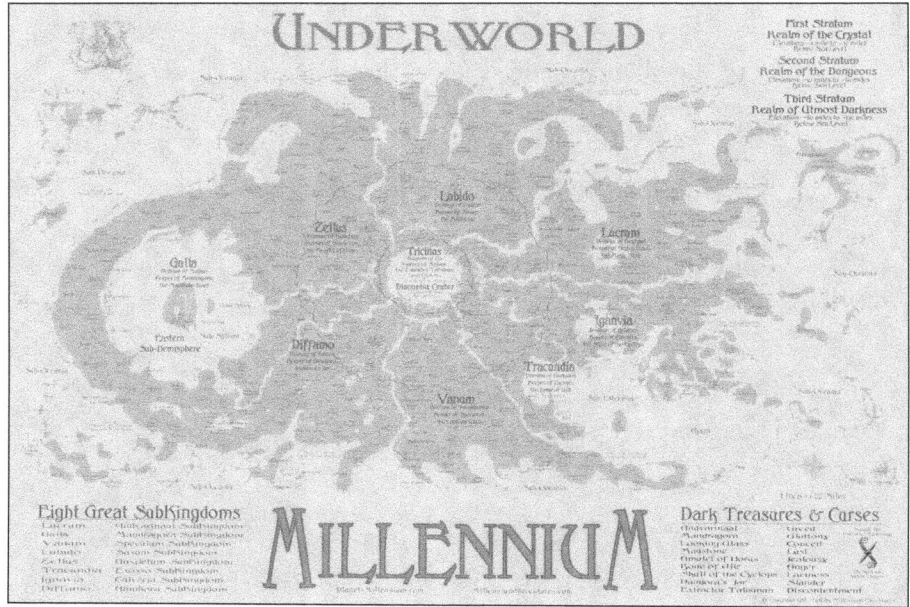

Eight sub-kingdoms were listed, all eight with an Extractor Keeper who guarded the Dark Treasures:

- *Tricinus: Domain of Ex,*
Keeper of Malum, the Extractor Talisman

- *Lucrum: Domain of Reynardo,*
Keeper of Andvarinaut, the Magic Ring

- *Gulla: Domain of Mobius,*
Keeper of Mandragora, the Mandrake Root

- *Vanum: Domain of Tarantulana,*
Keeper of Speculum, the Looking Glass

- *Lubido: Domain of Furcas,*
Keeper of Saxum, the Madstone

- *Zellus: Domain of Rodanna,*
Keeper of Amuletum, the Amulet of Horus

- *Tracundia: Domain of Karkinos,*
Keeper of Exosso, the Bone of Ullr

- *Ignavia: Domain of Brontis,*
Keeper of Calvaria, the Skull of the Cyclops

- *Diffamo: Domain of Kratos,*
Keeper of Amphora, the Pandora's Jar

The map legend also defined three main realms: according to depth of the strata:

First Stratum: Realm Of The Crystal
Elevation: -1 to -30 Miles Below Sea Level

Second Stratum: Realm Of The Dungeons
Elevation: -30 to -80 Miles Below Sea Level

Third Stratum: Realm Of Utmost Darkness
Elevation: -80 to -130 Miles Below Sea Level

I reviewed the First Stratum and discovered eight major underground rivers and a network of trails and circular tunnel loops. Many of the tunnels and subterranean rivers connected to the central Discordia Crater. I read more names, written in blue ink, of the First Stratum—Realm of the Crystal:

Pools of the Three Graces...Avernus...
Realm of the Elves...Pacari-Tambo...Chicomoztoc...
Faerie Cave...Echoing Bridge...Mirmirs Falls...
Land of the Restless Dead...Crystal Cave...
Eridanos River...Erawan Tunnel...Woden's Passage...
Lethe River...Nine Underworlds...Green Room...
Portal of Metamorphosis...Labyrinth...
Erlik's Prison...Wode Land...Arabian Tunnel...
Caves of Kor...Lethe Tunnel...Ginnungagap...
Persephone Palace...River of Darkness...Cocytus River—

Looked at the red-lettered names on the map of the Second Stratum—Realm of the Dungeons:

Knockmaa...Isle of the Blest...Snow Catacombs...
King Solomon's Mines...Valhalla...Annwn...Lis Ard...
Styx River...Dungeon of Fire...Lava Caverns...
Fire Falls...Oxus River...River of Ice...Ice Falls...
Subterranean Loop...Crater Tunnel Loop...
Otherworld...Tunnel of the Eternal Rose...
Dungeon of Ice...Miru Trail...River of Fire—

Continued to read the mythological names, written in brown ink, of the Third Stratum—Realm of Utmost Darkness:

Ogo Hole...Tartarus...House of Bats...City of Dis...
Castle of Chaos...Teshub...Rhadamanthus...
Afterworld...Dark Caverns...Acheron River...
Xibalba...Emerald Falls...Spiritland...Mictlan...
Nudd Tunnel...Tophet...Abyss of the Nothingness—

It became clear that each layer, each stratum, had different geography and different cities from the stratum above and below. There were three other worlds below the surface of Millennium.

Hanging the maps back to their original positions with the Millennium Upperworld on top, I relocated the Discordia Crater on the map. I used my thumb to measure the distance from Fog Harbor to Time Island.

Before I completed my measurement, someone knocked on the cabin door.

"Who is it?"

"Marster Hoonter, 'tis your 'umble servant, Andvari. Aye, I 'ope you slept well. Don't fret, jus' lettin' you knuw that breakfust 'ill be in a 'alf 'an 'our, at 5:00 o'clock. 'Tis a gude mornin' fer eatin' up on deck."

Without opening the door, I said, "Thanks, I'll be ready."

The sound of Andvari's clacking clogs faded down the corridor.

Walking past the Millennium wall maps to the porthole next to my canopied bed, I opened the latch and took a deep breath.

I smelled bacon cooking, mixed with other unidentifiable fragrances. The strange scents reminded me again of just how far away from home I was.

Admiring the blue sky, I listened to the cadence calls below deck, "Rrrooowww! Rrrrooowww! Rrrrooowww!"

Through the patchy fog, white clouds nestled against the distant cliffs. The cliffs looked taller, twice as tall. A radiant red sky lurked on the opposite horizon. Exotic birds swooped and dove into the Sea of Circles, fighting for the morsels thrown overboard by the crew.

Scanning the horizon, I saw no other ships. We had indeed, left the *Paralus* behind us.

Sat on the bed and reached for the feather-quill pen and ink bottle sitting on the night stand. Found white parchment paper in the top drawer of the night stand table.

I jumped up, pulled a chair to the table and sat with the feather quill in my right hand. Dipping the pen in the indigo ink, I began my first of many illustrations depicting the characters and landscapes of Millennium.

My first artistic subject—Metamorphosis.

As I drew the illustration, my thoughts drifted to Carmel, then Eve, then my mother, then my family, then Eve.

I still believed I had made the right choice, my decision to stay.

Feeling more alive on the *Skipbladnir* than at any other time in my life, I knew a great adventure awaited me, a fantasy come true.

My mother often told me, "Follow your dreams, Hunter".

What better dream, than to be on Millennium? I thought.

Satisfied with my first drawing, a portrait of Morph, I signed my initials, *HW*, at the bottom.

Returned the quill to the ink bottle and stood to gaze out the oval porthole. The Sea of Circles remained calm as the *Skipbladnir* surged onward in her southwesterly direction. A warm mist blew through the porthole in my face.

Closing my eyes, I fantasized about being with Eve.

Hungry for breakfast, I followed Andvari across the deck of the *Skipbladnir*. Between the patches of swirling grey fog, rays of amber light danced on the calm Sea of Circles. The twin stars, Helios and Sol, burned brightly in the blue Millennium sky. The mighty *Skipbladnir* surged forward at full speed. Feeling the powerful thrusts of the oared ship, I couldn't believe how fast we were moving.

Awestruck, I stared through the patches of fog and tapped Andvari's shoulder.

"Wow, look at those mountains," I yelled, pointing.

"Nooo, laudy. Them be crater cliffs."

The cliffs stood taller than any mountains I had ever imagined. Gigantic, they had to be taller than Mt. Everest. Half the sky was missing, replaced by the crater's colossal granite walls. On the opposite horizons, a red sky emerged from the east and a black sky emerged from the west, silhouetting the upper rim of the Discordia Crater.

Andvari grabbed my hand, pulling me forward. "Cum on, Marster Hoonter, we'll be seein' them crater cliffs sooon e'nuf. Aye, ta'moorow moornin'."

While we walked across the deck, Andvari complimented me for being clever.

I asked the gnome what he meant by clever. He explained that I had bestowed Eve with a palindrome, a name that reads the same forward and backward, a magical name. I considered telling Andvari the truth, that I had no knowledge of any palindromes, but I enjoyed being called clever by the gnome.

Suddenly, I realized Eve's real name, Evol, written backward, spelled l-o-v-e.

Maybe I was even more clever than I thought.

Shouts came from the crow's nest. "Kraken!"

Looking up, I saw a winged creature diving through the foggy haze. Someone rode on the back of the beast.

"Hoot mon," Andvari tugged on my pants leg, saying, "It be

Kraken n' Tyrannus."

The two Extractors, who I had just seen illustrations of in the *Magnum Opus,* flew over the ship. Kraken held a long spy glass to his eye and, I swear, he looked right at me. He pulled out his saber, circled the ship, and dove at Andvari and me.

By this time, four half-orcs had surrounded us, pointing their long bows at the Extractors.

When Kraken saw the bow with arrows drawn, he pulled up on the reins, turning away from *Skipbladnir.*

"Pay nooh attention to them buggers," the gnome said, as Captain Kraken flew his minion, Tyrannus, in a southwest direction. Within seconds, they were out of site.

The crew quickly resumed their duties. I followed Andvari up the stairs to the forecastle deck and exchanged greetings with Morph and Pendragon. We sat at a round deck table.

"We seem to attract a lot of uninvited guests for breakfast on these beautiful Millennium mornings," the sage said, chuckling.

Although the two Utopians smiled and made light of our visitors, Kraken did not look like anyone to mess around with.

The aroma of bacon and ambrosia toast made my mouth water. Inhaling the smell of breakfast, I remembered my mom's home-cooked meals.

Andvari waddled to the table and lifted my pewter plate cover. A huge egg laid sunny-side up on my plate.

"Goo a'head, Marster Hoonter, enjoy," Andvari said. "'Tis time you eat your dodo egg b'fore your breakfust gets culd."

I cut into my egg with my pewter fork and took a bite. It tasted delicious.

Sitting on a wood deck stool, Pendragon propped his

furry knees above the table. The Utopian's green dorsal scales shimmered in the morning light.

Morph kept his wings folded behind his purple tunic. The sage used more than two hands to eat and drink. The wise sage held a mug of orange juice in his upper right hand, a piece of ambrosia toast in his upper left hand, a fork in his lower left hand and a knife in his lower right hand.

Morph and Pendragon discussed the Millennium weather. Small talk. I noticed that the table lacked other place settings.

"Will Eve be eating breakfast with us?" I asked.

"She has decided to skip the morning meal," Morph replied. "She told Alfrigga that she is not hungry."

The color must have drained out of my face because Pendragon said, "Do not look so dejected, young man, Eve shall be joining us for dinner."

"I believe she is spending time with Fundin in the ship's game room," Morph said. "After breakfast, perhaps we can go below and see if she would enjoy some company."

"Great. I'd like that," I said, biting the corner off my toast, scanning the horizon. I had grown accustomed to the twin suns and the tri-colored sky. In the distance, the low-lying fog crept along the base of the crater.

"So, my son, what do you think of Millennium so far?"

"I love it here."

"Excellent. Pendragon and I, as well as the other Utopians, hoped you would say that."

"Other Utopians?"

"Yes, there are seven more of us; eventually you shall meet our companions."

I raised my hand. "Can I ask you a couple of questions?"

"Ask me anything you wish. That is why you are here."

"I was wondering, do people from Earth live on this planet right now?"

While Pendragon chuckled under his breath, Morph replied, "Yes. You shall meet them, depending on how long you decide to stay."

"Do I know any of these people?"

"Most likely, no. They have lived here for quite some time.

Many of these humans have accepted The Great Way and completed their Open Road odyssey. They have decided to stay with us, not return home."

Swallowing my second mouthful of dodo egg, I said, "Many of the names carved in the surface of Time Island are famous people on Earth."

Morph asked me, "Do you know why the names of the humans have been memorialized in stone on the sacred obelisk?"

Having read the *Planet Millennium Report*, I answered, "They've all been here, on Millennium, but decided to return to Earth."

"Very good," Morph said.

Pendragon said, "Many of those Earth visitors, our guests, stayed for extended periods of time. Some longer than others. They believed that once they acquired one or more of Octilogy's Eight Great Treasures here on Millennium, that they could take the treasures back to Earth and influence people to change. They wanted to improve the human condition, save the human race."

"How did they take the treasures back to Earth?"

"They did not take the physical treasures. They took the essence, the positive, life-changing *energy* of the treasures," Pendragon said. "They took the power of thought and the Secrets of Time & Space—the Universal Truths—to help their fellow man. They returned to Earth with the power to change thoughts. Realizing that the *Extractor Virus* had infected their planet, they returned home to share the cure for Earth's emotional diseases before human beings destroyed each other and their own planet."

Morph said, "I believe our first Earth visitor arrived approximately sixty years ago. Oh, excuse me. For you, that means 3000 Earth years ago."

I replied, "So, that's why the names on Time Island begin with men like Socrates, Plato, Pythagorus. A bunch of older guys."

"Ahhh, older guys." The Sage of the Ages chuckled.

Thinking about all the famous people who had returned to Earth: Lao Tzu, Aristotle, Leonardo da Vinci, Galileo, Shakespeare, the Grimm Brothers, Dante, Lewis Carroll,

Descartes, Mozart, Thoreau, and Jules Vern, I looked at the sage and said, "I understand the origin of the names on Time Island, but I have another question."

Morph gestured, *continue.*

"You've mentioned Octilogy several times. Do you mean the Eight Great Treasures?"

"That is correct. Octilogy *is* the embodiment of all eight treasures. The word Octilogy means, Eight Great Treasures."

"Are those the same eight treasures that my father talked about?"

"One and the same."

I grinned and wiped my mouth with a napkin. "I looked at the maps on my cabin wall and I saw eight kingdoms with eight treasures listed on the map. Those are the ones, right?"

Morph and Pendragon nodded, *yes.*

"So, this rose I'm traveling to see is the first treasure?"

"Right again. In fact, while we are on this subject, I am going to ask Pendragon to explain Octilogy, the Eight Great Treasures."

The dragonram nodded. "Go ahead, my son, finish your breakfast while I explain Octilogy. You need to know why the journey down the Open Road, The Great Way, is critical for your enlightenment."

I bit into a piece of crisp, salty bacon and nodded, *go ahead.*

"I shall make this brief," Pendragon said, setting his pewter mug of draconian tea on the table and holding up his right hand with his four fingers spread open. "Four empires exist in the Millennium Upperworld. Each empire is divided between two kingdoms. Each kingdom reveals one of the Eight Great Treasures, Octilogy. Eight Utopians guard the eight treasures. The Great Way, also known as the Open Road, forms a global, circular path around Millennium's super continent, connecting all eight kingdoms, and therefore, the eight treasures. There are also eight Zodiac Paths connecting the Open Road, the high road as we call it, to each treasure. Each trail forms a loop with a treasure located at the halfway point. Six Zodiac Paths must be traveled by land and two paths by sea, one by way of the Sea of Esteem in the kingdom of Pellagus and one by way of the Sargasso Sea in the kingdom of Sallum."

Pendragon stopped and asked, "Are you with me so far?"

I nodded, *yes*, enjoying the sea breeze in my face.

"The reason he asks," Morph said, "is because you shall have to travel the looped Zodiac Paths to locate each treasure."

Shutting my eyes, I wondered, *How long should I stay on Millennium?*

"I shall describe the four empires and eight kingdoms in a clockwise direction," Pendragon said, "around the central Discordia Crater, with north pointing toward the top of the Millennium map. The Eastern Empire is comprised of two kingdoms, Palludis and Pellagus. The Southern Empire has two kingdoms, Eremus and Harundia. The Western Empire also has two kingdoms, Sallum and Saburra, as does the Northern Empire, comprised of Gellum and Nemoria."

Pendragon tapped his black finger nail on the table. "Right now, we sit *here*, in the center of Millennium, in the Discordia Crater."

"I figured that out this morning when I looked at the map," I said, proudly.

"Good," Morph said, brushing bacon bits off his white beard. "I am glad you enjoy maps."

"Now, as for Octilogy and the Eight Great Treasures," Pendragon said, "I shall begin with the first treasure, then proceed in a clockwise direction, ending with the eighth treasure. Keep in mind, each treasure reveals a life-changing reward. The eight treasures bring you the bliss of eternity, contentment, the ability to know yourself. Your *Self.* Who you truly are.

I nodded, *I understand,* not knowing what to expect.

"The first treasure, located in the southeastern kingdom of Pellagus, is Anthera, the Eternal Rose, emitting the Fragrance of Awareness. Upon inhaling the aroma of the grand red rose, your reward is true Awareness, the ability to know yourself, who you truly are."

I interrupted. "Is the first treasure on the island we're going to visit?"

"Correct," Morph said. "The Isle of the Eternal Rose is located in the Sea of Esteem. Look on the map, you shall see it."

Pendragon continued. "The second treasure, located in Eremus, is Caldaria, the Cauldron of Regeneration. Filled with the Broth of Longevity, drinking the magic brew offers the gift of health. Freedom from illness, for those who are sick of being sick. Marduk the Utopian guards the second treasure."

"Guards the treasure?" I asked.

"The treasures must be guarded by our loyal band of Utopians. For example, with the help of island elves and southern giants, I guard the red Eternal Rose."

"Guard the treasures from whom?"

Morph and Pendragon looked at each other, their expressions solemn.

"What do you know about the Extractors?" Pendragon asked.

"I saw illustrations this morning," I replied. "Professor Johan talked about them. I'm not sure I understand who Ex is."

Pendragon said. "Allow me to explain Ex and his following of minion Extractors. Then, I shall return to the treasures."

"This morning," I said, "I read the Extractor pages, their descriptions in the *Magnum Opus*."

The sage smiled. "We are pleased to hear you spent time reading our sacred Book of Wisdom."

"Allow me to expand your knowledge of the dark forces, the Extractors and how they arrived on Millennium," Pendragon said, taking a deep breath.

"The Extractor Invasion began during the Age of Consciousness, in the Year of the Dragon, 1 A.E., when a gigantic asteroid ascended upon our peaceful planet of Millennium. What appeared to be a natural catastrophe soon unveiled itself as a plot of global domination by an invading enemy, Ex and his Extractors, who had abandoned their dying dimension, known as the Tennibris Dimension. You see, for thousands of years, the Extractors had destroyed their own dimension by spreading their contagious virus and draining all living souls of their essence. Ex hungered for more.

"The Master Extractor planned the destruction of his own dimension by destroying the Dark Star. This plot enabled him to spread his dark energy, his weapon of mass destruction, throughout all the surrounding galaxies.

"Using his evil powers, Ex planned a dimensional explosion of such magnitude that when the dimension blew apart, the Dark Star split into nine vectors of force, each fragment carrying the deadly *Extractor Virus*, as well as the essence of the evil Extractors, the Dark Essence.

"The infected vectors rocketed through stellar space. Ex used the last of his power to form the vectors into asteroids, eight of which collided with planets inhabited by intelligent life forms; specifically, Earth, Leda, Triton, Metis, Phaethon, Phobos, Deimos, and Epiphany.

"Leading the assault himself, Ex targeted the largest asteroid to strike Millennium, knowing that the ninth planet had the highest concentration of soul energy, as well as the grandest prizes within the dimension, the Eight Great Treasures.

"As Ex had planned, the asteroids impacted nine different

worlds in different dimensions, allowing the infected fragments to form dimensional shift bridges between worlds. Each of the cosmic paths, the Astral Highways connected to Millennium, gave the Extractors a way to travel among the nine planets sowing their dark energy, hate and discontent.

"When the Extractor Asteroid struck the center of Millennium, it created a colossal impact crater in her surface, the Discordia Crater, measuring 150 miles deep and 1800 miles wide. Upon impact, the asteroid caused a global chain reaction of unimaginable magnitude. The deadly Extractoroid, as we call it, left everlasting scars and global pandemonium in its wake as evidenced by the crater you're in, the red and black gyroscopic rings orbiting the planet, and the release of the pandemic *Extractor Virus*, the Dark Essence. The Extractor Invasion unleashed the horrific battle between good and evil.

"At the beginning of the Extractor Invasion, all went well for Ex and his minions comprised of forty-six Extractors. Their success was due to their surprise tactics and their aggressive, power-hungry natures.

"We Utopians alerted the inhabitants of Millennium that they had been invaded by a race of dark and malevolent spirits, growing and thriving by feeding on the negative emotions of sentient species, carriers of a contagious, deadly thought virus.

"Hate, anger, greed, jealousy and primal fear, dysfunctional behaviors generated within the life force and the souls of beings everywhere, enabled the Extractors to manifest and spread their negative energy throughout the universe."

Dragon pointed at Morph and said, "Ex, however, had underestimated the power of our great sage Metamorphosis, who combined his invincible will with his understanding of the

Octilogy, the total comprehension of the Eight Great Treasures. By providing leadership for me and the other seven Utopians, he has been able to establish three defense mechanisms against the invading Extractor forces.

"First, we have succeeded in using our Eight Great Treasures to lock down the dimension shift bridges so the Extractors could not directly use them. Unfortunately, the evil creatures were still able to project their dark thoughts across the cosmic paths to the other eight planets because the colliding asteroids had spread the Extractor Virus, infecting and weakening the population of each world. The Extractors were still able to influence the souls in the other eight worlds to follow darker paths in life.

"Second, we have created magical gold Triamulets, made from the shards of the Dark Star material, *Prima materia*, that had been scattered throughout the Discordia Crater.

"These empowered medallions allowed souls, under certain circumstances, to travel between the nine worlds. After arriving on Millennium, souls could be strengthened and reinforced by acquiring the Eight Great Treasures, and then return home to their own world to resist the insidious spread of the Extractor's dark will.

"The Extractors responded by creating the Net of Screams. Should an otherworld soul be killed during its Millennium trials, a portion of the soul will be captured by the magic net and the Extractors can feed off that power. It is believed that a soul that suffers too many deaths shall be lost forever.

"Third, we Utopians have managed to fight the Extractors to a virtual standstill on Millennium. Being the grand masters of knowledge and wisdom, we have formed a plan to protect the souls in the other eight worlds, yours being one of them.

"As Morph continues to remind his loyal followers, 'The fall of each soul to the Extractors may only be countered by the rise of Heroes who face the challenges of the Eight Great Treasures.'"

"Heroes?" I asked.

Morph replied, "We consider all Amalgamation visitors Heroes, for they possess the potential for greatness."

"I'm a Hero?"

"Yes, my son. And so is Eve."

Morph held up his lower left hand. "Please, let Pendragon finish his explanation of Ex."

Nodding, I motioned, *go ahead.*

"Now, as for Ex, the Master Extractor," Pendragon said, "he is the one entity who strikes the most fear in the hearts and minds of Millennians. Before Ex arrived, the most negative of emotions, fear, did not exist on this planet. Nine millennia have passed since the Ex's arrival and no one, not even we Utopians, have been able to stop his reign of terror and chaos. His underground fortress, the City of Dis, lies in the Realm of Utmost Darkness under the Subkingdom of Tricinus. From the bowels of Millennium, Ex rules over his Extractor forces."

I raised my hand. "Why is this creature, this Ex, so hard to stop. You know, so impossible to defeat?"

Pendragon set his mug on the table. "Try to imagine the difficulty in dealing with an evil entity no one can see. Ex exhibits two devastating powers, invisibility and flight. To remain invisible, Ex wears the Helmet of Darkness. After the Extractor Asteroid disaster in the Year of the Dragon, 1 A.E., Ex stole the dog-skin helmet, the winged Cap of Invisibility, from the god Hades, ruler of Avernus. Soon after that, the fabled Feathered Cloak was pillaged from Asgard. Guarded faithfully by Fenris the Wolf, no one knows how the cloak turned up missing."

The winged Utopian grimaced. "The creature wearing the falcon-feathered cloak, a magical garment, can fly. Ex has both the winged Cap of Invisibility and the Feathered Cloak, making him appear invincible."

"Wow, invincible?" I asked, wiping my mouth with a napkin.

"No. We know he is mortal, just like the rest of us," Pendragon said, pointing at the Sage of the Ages. "We have discovered that Ex avoids Morph. We believe the astral glow

Ex

from Morph's scepter, *Joyease*, the pulsating ultraviolet rays, have a negative effect on the Invisible Villain. The rays have also exposed his appearance, so at least we know what he looks like."

"So, Ex *can* be defeated?" I asked Pendragon.

"Yes. As explained earlier, we plan to stop Ex and his Extractors from wreaking havoc and chaos throughout the eight kingdoms of Millennium. Their sole purpose is to destroy the Eight Great Treasures—Octilogy—so that The Great Way, the source of all positive energy, is lost forever."

"How can this be paradise if you've got an invisible maniac running around plotting the destruction of eight treasures, everything that is good?"

"Great question," Morph replied. "But we have gotten way off track. I shall answer that paradise question after Pendragon finishes his explanation of the Eight Great Treasures."

The sage nodded at the dragonram, "Go ahead, my majestic friend, continue."

"More about Ex later," Pendragon said. "Now, where was I? Ahhh, yes, the third great treasure.

"Copia, the Horn of Plenty, is found in the jungles of Harundia and is guarded by Durga the Utopian. The horn overflows with Epula, the Contentment Food. Upon tasting the feast, you are rewarded with the eternal wealth of body and spirit.

"The fourth treasure, the Treasure Chest called Arcarum, is found in the kingdom of Sallum and is guarded by Argus. The sacred chest contains the Lapis, the Truth Jewels. Holding the jewels awards the Open Road traveler with ethics, eternal honesty.

"Treasure five, guarded by Scorpigo, is found in the deserts of Saburra. It is the Well of Wishes. The stone well offers Risus, the Laughter Water. Upon drinking the cool, refreshing liquid, you are bestowed with eternal happiness.

"The sixth treasure is found in the glacial realms of Gellum. Managarm the Utopian guards the Diamond of Desire

122

nestled in the majestic Eye of Fire Volcano, high in the Mountains of the Moon. This treasured gem rewards you with Fulgor, the Love Radiance, eternal love, the ability to love yourself and therefore, love others.

"Treasure number seven is the Pot of Gold, located in the forests of Nemoria within the Cosmic Cave. Cernunnos,

the great stag, guards the golden Coins of Intelligence. The sacred pot, named Balux, is alive. Upon holding the gold coins, one is bestowed with Binaria, eternal knowledge.

"The eighth Open Road treasure is found in the swamps of Palludis. Cradled in the Cosmic Nest, it is the Golden Egg of Enlightenment. Upon basking in Mentis, the Glow of Reason, one is rewarded with eternal wisdom. Nyx the Utopian guards the golden egg from Extractors."

I tried to memorize all eight treasure names and kingdoms. I found it difficult to concentrate; I could not get my mind off Ex and the Extractors. I raised my right hand to get Pendragon's attention.

"Ask your question," the Utopian said.

"Why does evil exist in the universe in the first place?"

Metamorphosis grinned. "My son, please be patient and I shall share all the Secrets of Time & Space, the Universal Truths, in due time. For now, please allow Pendragon to finish his explanation of our beloved treasures."

"Sorry, I guess I'm getting ahead of myself. I have so many questions."

"We understand completely. Please relax and enjoy my fellow Utopian's story."

I nodded in agreement.

Smiling at me, Pendragon's massive wings moved laterally to cool the deck air. The temperature had risen due to the intense rays from Millennium's two daystars, Sol and Helios.

"Now that I have explained each of the eight treasures, you need to know that there is one final treasure, the grand prize, the ultimate reward, that puts all the other treasures in perspective, completes the cosmic circle, and unifies that which sits in the center and knows. The ultimate treasure, guarded by Metamorphosis, is found in the Crystallum Cave. It is Lumen, the Crystal of Consciousness. The white crystal's radiance, the Light of Insight, provides you with life's grandest reward.

"As Morph tells all our visitors, 'Whomever bathes in the warm, radiant glow of the sacred Crystal shall obtain the final step toward greatness.' Your final treasure is, of course, Self-Actualization, to know who you truly are."

My eyes opened wide. "My father talked about self-actualization. He told me that it takes years, sometimes a lifetime, to acquire such a high state of mind, to see the light. He told me only a handful of people attain such a perfect emotional awakening."

"Insightful indeed," Morph said. "Few human beings on your planet know how to attain any of Octilogy's eight treasures, let alone the ultimate treasure, life's grand prize. On your planet, only a few Sages and Masters have attained such bliss."

"Will I experience self-actualization during my stay?"

"Patience my son, your journey has just begun. Self-actualization, freedom within, is yours if you desire it. Let us work on self-awareness, the first treasure. What do you say?"

"You're right. I'll study the map in my room and try to remember all the treasure locations that Pendragon described."

"Excellent, young man. That is the spirit."

"Can I ask one more question that's bothering me?"

The sage grinned. "Go ahead, ask your question."

"This morning I read some of the *Magnum Opus*. The book described gods and goddesses as if they are real, living here on Millennium. I overheard my father and Professor Johan talk about how the gods really exist on Millennium."

I stopped and waited for an answer.

"What is the question?" Morph asked.

Embarrassed, I grinned. "Sorry, I wasn't very clear. I want to know if Zeus exists. Is he real?"

"Before we answer your question," Morph said, "Please share with us what you overheard your father and the professor discuss about the gods and goddesses."

I took a deep breath, looked straight into Morph's eyes, and told him about the conversation I listened to during one of my secret spying sessions in the library. I began with:

> It was last year, when I had turned sixteen, Professor Johan came to visit. I made my way down to the library and into the secret hiding place under the aquarium. For some reason, Julia wasn't with me that time. It didn't take long before I heard footsteps. The library doors swung open and in walked Professor Johan with my father.
>
> "I wish I had stayed longer," Father said. "I might have seen some of the gods and goddesses, like you did."
>
> "I saw one, just one god," Professor Johan replied.
>
> "If there wasn't such a huge time difference, I'd have stayed longer. But, if I'd have stayed as long as I wanted, Gloria would have been an old woman by the time I returned. My kids would have grown up without me around."
>
> "That's right, Wayland, you did the right thing by coming home."
>
> Father patted Professor Johan on the back. The same back that had the most beautiful tattoo I had ever seen.
>
> "I need to talk to you about is my *Planet Millennium Report*," father said. He stepped to the wet bar and poured two scotch on the rocks. "I just wish the report could be completed properly."

Father handed a drink to his best friend.

"Come on, Wayland, you're not going to start begging me again to get involved in this thing, are you?"

"Johan, you've been there. You're an awakened survivor. You're world famous. You are my only reliable mythology connection."

"I will not be interviewed," Professor Johan said, gritting his teeth. "Sorry. I don't want my years of respected work to be discredited."

"Don't worry, your work will always be revered."

"As I've promised, if you can convince the world that Millennium is real, I'll consider coming forward. Other than that, end of conversation."

Father threw his hands in the air. "I give up. You win. I respect your decision. I won't ask again."

"Much appreciated." Professor Johan held his drink in the air, toasting my father's surrender. "I see you have all your mythology and fairy tale books out on the table."

My father grinned. "Since you refuse to get involved with my media event, I do need your expertise on mythology. I'm considering adding it to the report, even if I don't have you as a witness. Don't worry, you won't have to write anything. I'll do the report myself."

"I thought your foundation staff doesn't believe the mythology evidence is solid enough for the report, especially the fables, folklore and fairy tale study."

"Those guys are great scientists and medical doctors, but they've overreacted about mythology. They're paranoid that something's going to go wrong."

"Well, you have to admit, it will be the most amazing announcement of all time. There are going to be negative reactions, radical responses to your Millennium declaration."

I remember wondering what the professor meant by radical responses. His comment bothered me. I had a feeling that something bad was going to happen by the tone in his voice.

"I'll deal with all the negativity as it comes," Father

said, confidently. "Now, let's get down to business. Tell me what myths and legends and fairy tales to put in this report and what to omit. I'm a bit overwhelmed."

"Keep it simple," my friend, the professor said. "First of all, focus on the fact that all mythological information is accurate, that every myth described since the beginning of human history is real. Second, you must make people understand that the gods and mythological creatures, that the fairy tale characters and the fantasy lands exist on another planet. Third, you must explain that over the centuries, people returning to Earth from Millennium brought back factual information that became the myths, legends, fables and fairy tale stories that have become so ingrained in our culture. Myths are real."

Father walked to the conference table in the middle of the library. Ran his hand over the stacks of mythology books and ancient maps covering the cherrywood table.

He pointed to the color map on the wall. "Thank God you had your tattoo done so we have accurate geographical information."

My father picked up a pen and yellow pad from the table. "Please, help me decide what mythological names to put in my report."

The professor said, "During my brief visit with the great sage, Metamorphosis, I learned a lot about Millennium."

"Brief? You were in a coma for more than two months. You stayed a lot longer than I did. I only got to see Time Island and visit with Morph for a few hours. You sailed the Sea of Circles and saw Poseidon, a real god."

"I got lucky when the old sea god surfaced next to the *Skipbladnir*. Unfortunately, Poseidon taught me very little. Most of my mythology knowledge came from their sacred Book of Wisdom, the *Magnum Opus*. I wish I had a copy of that fabulous text."

"If only I could have spent as much time with Metamorphosis as you did."

"I sense jealousy in your voice."

The professor was right. Father *did* act jealous. He never got over his decision to leave Millennium. Throughout my childhood, I heard him complain about, what he called, "his horrible decision to leave."

"Can you blame me?" My father shrugged his shoulders. "Sorry, Johan. Go ahead. I'll stop whining."

The professor nodded and continued. "The wise sage allowed me as much time as I needed to study the *Magnum Opus*. As I turned the sacred book's parchment pages, it became clear that all the mythological history on Earth, all the gods and goddesses, all the legends and fairy tales, all of our grandest myths originated on Millennium. In fact, we need to thank Metamorphosis for our entire cultural heritage. Our language. Our customs. Our knowledge of the sciences. Our philosophical beliefs."

Father scribbled on his yellow pad while the professor talked.

"Wait until people realize that our roots, everything human, came from Millennium. The great sage, Metamorphosis, also taught our spiritual masters, the prophets. Before I went to sleep on Time Island to return home, I'm glad I had the foresight to study the names engraved on the rock platform's surface. I was blown away by all the great explorers and writers and poets and philosophers who had visited Millennium before me. People like Socrates, Lao Tzu, Homer, Galileo, Dante, Shakespeare, the Grimm brothers, Leonardo Da Vinci, Thoreau, Emily Dickinson, and so many more."

While my father lit a cigar, I tried to comprehend what I had just heard. No wonder people were calling Dr. Wainright a lunatic, was my first thought.

Father blew three smoke rings into the library air and said, "The media is going to go crazy when I announce this stuff."

Professor Johan sipped from his glass of scotch. "As for the gods, they are alive and well on Millennium. In their sacred Book of Wisdom I saw descriptions and drawings of all the gods and goddesses. Zeus, Hades,

Odin, Freya, Thor, Osiris, Isis, Brahma and Manitou. Hundreds of them, all alive on Millennium. I was dumbfounded when I studied the Millennium maps and discovered the locations of Atlantis, Wonderland, Enchanted Forest, Sleeping Beauty's Castle, Camelot and all Arthurian legends and fairy tale lands and fantasy kingdoms. Even Aesop's fables are there."

My father opened a wooden humidor and offered his friend a cigar. "I wish I had boarded the *Skipbladnir* so I could have seen the *Magnum Opus* and the maps of Millennium."

"I should have stayed long enough to see the first Great Treasure of Octilogy, the Eternal Rose," Professor Johan said, accepting the cigar from my father, who flicked open his chrome lighter and lit the havana.

The professor rolled the cigar between his lips and blew a puff of blue smoke into the library lights. "I loved the fabulous illustrations of the mythological beasts and creatures in the *Magnum Opus*. The gryphon, unicorn, pegasus, cyclops, centaur, faeries, dwarves, dragons and hundreds more described in perfect detail."

Father pointed to the map on the wall. "We need proof that all our myths originated from Millennium. We need a volunteer, an eye witness who everyone trusts."

"I'm not sure about your Millennium volunteer idea. If I were you, I'd be patient and wait until one of your Coma-X patients awaken."

"I can't wait much longer."

"All right, have it your way. I've spent my entire career proving that myths are important to our civilization. Not once have I confused the issue with my own Millennium experience."

"Well, it's time to clarify the origins of myth. Clear the air. Let the world know the truth."

"I'm not sure the world wants to know the truth," Johan declared, frowning at my father.

I sensed the professor knew something that my father could not comprehend.

Father stared into the professor's eyes, turned and walked back to his desk. He gulped down his drink, opened the lower desk drawer, and pulled out a grey metal box.

My father opened the metal box and took out a Triamulet by the gold chain and held it up to the light.

From my hiding spot, through the louvers, I watched the shiny medallion gleam in the amber lights, swinging back and forth between my father's fingers.

I felt an attraction to the sacred Triamulet. Like a moth to a flame.

I was drawn to its golden glow.

"This is the undeniable evidence that will prove Millennium exists. All I need is one volunteer, someone with the potential for greatness, and we can prove the origin of myths, legends and fairy tales."

"Be careful," the professor said. "Select the right person for the journey or people will think it's a huge hoax."

"Don't worry, I know what I'm doing."

Father placed the gold medallion and chain back into the box and closed the lid.

Without warning, the library doors opened.

Father turned and yelled, "Who is it? Who's there?"

"For God's sake!" my mother shouted. "It's your wife!"

"Oh. Sorry, darling."

"Dinner in ten minutes," she said. "Let me guess. The professor will be joining us?"

"If you don't mind," Father said, smiling at the professor, "Johan just loves your home-made beef stew."

I watched Mom roll her eyes and storm away in the middle of my father's sentence.

His face flushed with embarrassment, Father turned off the lights and shut the mahogany doors behind them.

After the footsteps disappeared down the corridor, I snuck back to my bedroom and...well...that's about all I can remember.

I motioned to Morph with my right hand, *that's all I have.*

"You are fortunate to have two Millennium visitors in your life, especially Professor Johan," Morph said. "Now, please repeat your question."

"I want to know if Zeus exists. Is he real. Alive? Was the professor correct?"

"Zeus?" Pendragon chuckled. "That old god has never been the same since the Extractor Asteroid hit."

"Then, he *is* alive?"

Morph grinned and held up his hand to prevent Pendragon from answering. "Several of our recent Earth visitors have questioned the existence of the gods. We have been told by humans that the concept of gods and goddesses have become controversial on their planet, that most people refuse to believe in their existence *anywhere* in the universe."

I interjected, "That's right. They're all mythological on our planet. Legends. Fantasy."

"That is unfortunate because they are alive and well here on Millennium," the sage said.

"Wow, that's incredible. Where do they live?"

"All over the planet. On Mt. Olympus, at Asgard, in Elysian Fields. Sky World, the Palace of Immortality. In our forests, mountains, deserts, oceans, within every kingdom and empire. Everywhere."

"Many reside in our Underworld," Pendragon said.

"Will I get to see some of the gods while I'm here?" I asked.

"That shall depend on how far down the Open Road, the high road, you travel," the sage replied. "On how long you decide to stay."

I've been here two daynights already, I thought, *that means another one hundred Earth days. Over three months!*

"Any other questions?" Morph asked, interrupting my thoughts.

Pendragon cleared his throat, a purposeful cough. "Ahhh-hemmm."

Morph knew the signal as Pendragon said, "Master, I believe we have discussed enough for now."

Waving my right hand, I said, "I have a question about One World Government. I read in the *Magnum Opus* that—"

"I understand your curiosity," the sage said, interrupting. "Please be patient. All your questions shall be answered, all in good time."

Shrugging my shoulders, I replied, "Okay, Morph."

The Sage of the Ages stood. "What do you say we go below and visit the game room? Eve is down there with Fundin, Andvari and Alfrigga."

My heart rate increased. Eve, beautiful Eve. I would get to see her again.

Pendragon stood and lumbered past the teak table. His hooves resonated off the wooden planks. I found myself engulfed by the shadow of the massive Utopian.

Morph and I followed Pendragon down the steps of the forecastle. I skipped down the stairs, dreaming about seeing Eve.

From the crow's nest, Balder the half-orc waved to me. I waved back.

Millennium's two daystars cast their double shadows on the deck of the *Skipbladnir* as I squinted under the glare of the fiery-red sky.

Pendragon stooped down to enter the doorway. Smiling, I stepped below deck with Morph, anticipating my meeting with the mysterious girl, Eve of Epiphany.

Chapter 8
Gametasia

Below the top deck of the *Skipbladnir*, I followed Pendragon down a lamp-lit corridor. Bent over so his horns would not scrape the ceiling, the winged Utopian hummed an upbeat tune. His shiny hooves clopped on the polished plank floor to the rhythm of his own melody.

Deep in thought, I stepped on Pendragon's tail.

Be careful Hunter, I told myself. *Stop stepping on his tail, that's twice you've done it. Pay attention.*

Metamorphosis chuckled while Pendragon curled his scaly-blue tail around the front of his furry legs. The dragonram stopped humming and moved against the wall, motioning for me to walk past him. Squeezing past the dragon, I heard laughter and high-pitched giggles at the end of the corridor. I recognized the voice of the teenage girl.

"Straight ahead. Down the hall," Morph said, pointing to the end of the corridor.

Ran my fingers through my hair and hurried to the door.

I looked back at the sage, who motioned with his lower left hand, *open the door.*

The carved wooden sign above the entry read:

Gametasia Room

I quietly opened the door and peeked in.

The walls displayed rectangular parchments—scrolls. Each of the hanging scrolls displayed directions to eight game titles named: Sweet Surrender, Quest for the Crown, War of the Four Kings, Bonanza, Gametasia Chess, Battle of the Blue Bloods, Turnaround World, and Open Road.

Two wall paintings depicted game artwork. One painting displayed a chess board with blue cards along each border. The second painting displayed a map of Millennium with a trail of card suits: diamonds, clubs, hearts, and spades, winding over the game map. I would soon discover there were two game boards,

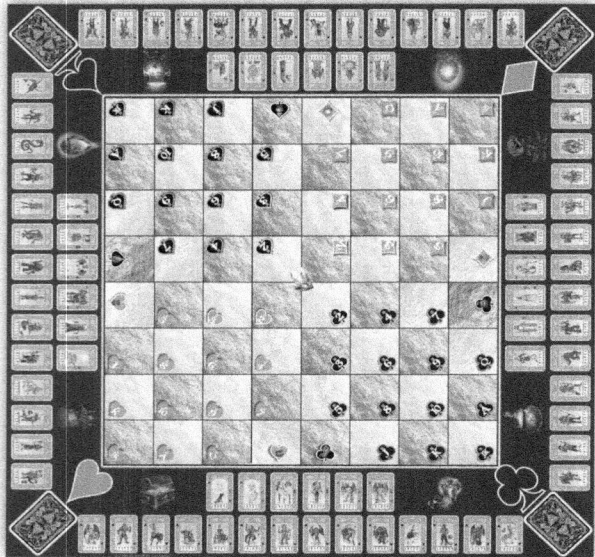

one with a map trail and one with a chess board.

In the far corner of the room, the pudgy toad faerie played his piano while the trio of frog faeries played their violins and cello.

With his claw-like fingernail, Pendragon tapped me on the shoulder motioning, *go inside.*

So, I took a deep breath and walked to the oak banister surrounding the sunken game area. Below a gold chandelier fitted with brightly burning oil lamps, Eve sat with Fundin, Alfrigga, and Andvari. The foursome focused on the game, rolling the red and white dice and moving their

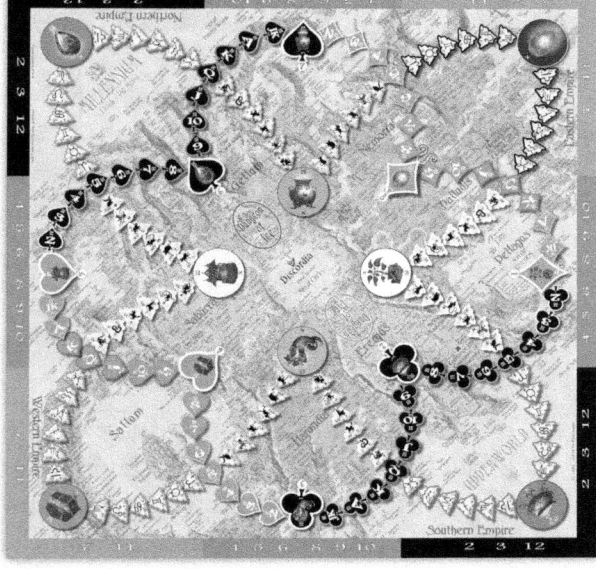

chess pieces. Eve sat quietly, while the gnomes and the faerie gamemaster chatted and discussed strategy.

Andvari looked up and spotted me, an unexpected guest.

"Marster Hoonter, gude to see you. Cum down 'n join us."

While Eve remained seated, the two gnomes jumped out of their chairs. Fundin, a good foot shorter than the gnomes, stood in his chair to greet me. I nervously stumbled down the steps to the game table area. I felt my face turn flush the moment I saw Eve. She kept her head down, ignoring me while Alfrigga and Andvari giggled uncontrollably. Fundin fidgeted in his chair, eager to resume play.

Morph entered the room while Pendragon remained stooped over in the doorway.

"Hello," the sage said. "I thought Hunter might enjoy a rousing game of Gametasia Chess."

"We just finished Open Road," Fundin said in his squeaky voice. "I'd luv to teach 'em some of our tabletop games."

"Excellent, Fundin," Morph said, winking at Eve and me. "I shall see you two youngsters at dinner."

I replied, "Sure…dinner…we'll be there…I mean…I'll be there…I mean—"

As I stumbled over my words, Eve did not respond or acknowledge me.

"We shall see you this evening," Morph said, smiling while he exited the game room. Pendragon ducked under the door jamb and yelled, "Have fun," shutting the door behind him.

"Let the games begin!" Fundin shouted.

The game master's outfit looked wilder than the night before. Fundin's shirt displayed a gaudy checkered chess theme adorned with metallic purple and orange squares. When he spoke, the copper bells dangling from his jester's cap jingled.

"Let's teach Master Hunter Open Road. I know he'd luv the game," Fundin said, standing in his wicker chair.

"Aye, e'cuse us," Alfrigga said. "Andvari an' me gotta' lotta' wurk to do."

"Hoot mon, 'Frigga, whut 'n bloody blazes are ya—"

Andvari stopped abruptly, realizing Alfrigga's suggestion had nothing to do with work.

"Aye," Andvari replied. "Ya be right as a 'ighland rain."

Andvari winked at me while the two gnomes jumped down

from their chairs, waddled up the steps, and giggled all the way out the game room door.

"Master Hunter, b'fore you get comfortable in your chair, tis a gud idea that you review the rules to Open Road. They be right o'er there." Fundin pointed to a parchment hung on the wall.

"All right," I said.

Smiling at Eve, I asked her, "Do you know how to play Open Road?"

Emotionless, she said, "I have played several times."

"I don't have to read all the game directions, Fundin. Eve can help me," I said, grinning at her.

She did not respond, shrugging her shoulders.

"Fine," Fundin said, "but you need to read the Games In Brief section to getta' feel fer the game rules."

"Sure, I'll do that," I said.

Fundin jumped down from his chair and made his way up the steps. I followed him, tripping on the first step, almost falling on his face.

"Whoops. I'm not used to these boots." I looked back at Eve as I walked toward the parchment scrolls.

She did not look amused by my clumsiness.

Eve excused herself. "While you read the directions, I must go to the ladies' latrine."

Fundin

The beautiful Epiphanite glided out of the game room. She wore a black leather skirt, white chemise, and red bodice with matching sandals.

I turned and looked at the main game table. Elaborate, hand-carved chess pieces stood upright on the colorful game board.

Red, white, blue and black kings, queens, knights and pawns waited to be moved along the game's main trail—the Open Road. I figured out that chess originated on Millennium and was brought back to Earth by previous visitors. Fundin confirmed my theory. Adjacent to the game table, a leather-bound book laid on a wooden podium. The leather book with the chiseled gold-colored letters read: Gametasia.

"If I get confused, I can read that book over there, right?" I asked, pointing to the Gametasia rules book.

Fundin smiled. "Tha's why she be 'ere. Even me, the game master, has'ta read the boook ev'ry once in a Millennium mooon."

Fundin climbed up onto the seat of his wicker chair.

Intrigued by the deck of Gametasia Cards sprawled on the table, I walked back down the steps. The blue cards looked like a standard poker deck with diamond, club, heart, and spade symbols, only more decorative. Each card displayed character illustrations, titles, and six chess emblems with numbers along the bottom.

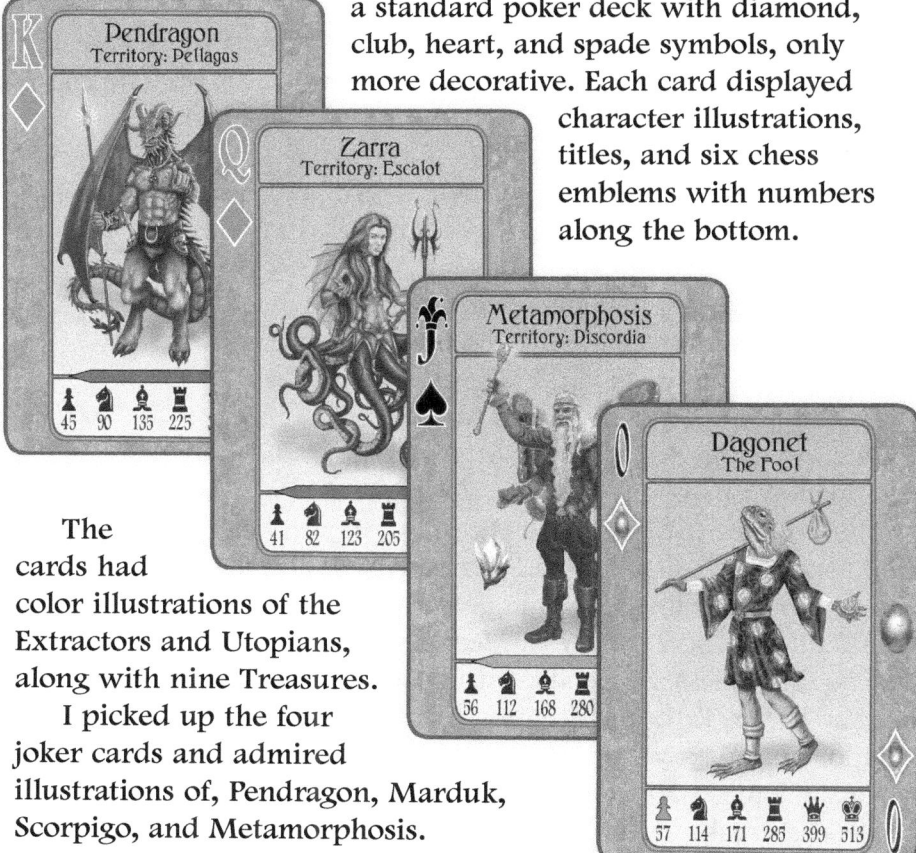

The cards had color illustrations of the Extractors and Utopians, along with nine Treasures.

I picked up the four joker cards and admired illustrations of, Pendragon, Marduk, Scorpigo, and Metamorphosis.

I threw down the joker cards when Eve walked back into the game room.

"I'm ready to play now," I said, jumping down the stairs to pull out Eve's chair. I admired her curved, black eyelashes. Her ebony hair shone under the game room lights.

Took my seat opposite her and fumbled with the playing cards. In my attempt to shuffle the deck, the cards flew out of my hands, all over the table.

She rolled her eyes.

Have you ever felt so embarrassed you can feel yourself blushing, turning red?

Fundin collected the scattered Gametasia Cards, shuffled the card deck, and placed a pair of red and white Fire & Ice Dice on the table. Eve moved all the chess pieces to the edge of the game board and re-stacked the colored treasure coins.

The game master handed me his treasure coins and asked, "What color would you like? The chess piece colors are red, white, blue or black."

"Let Eve choose first."

"Blue is a good color," she said, picking up the blue queen.

Studying the hand-carved chess pieces, I said, "Red is a masculine color; it matches my shirt."

Eve snickered, glancing at my tunic.

Fundin showed me how to position my chess pieces. After drawing three Gametasia Cards, I placed my three red dwarve pawn pieces on three matching game trail spaces—diamonds, hearts, and clubs. I positioned my red king and queen along my border.

Eve rolled the Fire & Ice Dice first, moved her blue queen, and the game of Open Road began. Although I needed helpful hints from Fundin, the game progressed quickly. I found it difficult to concentrate; I wanted to get to know Eve better. She moved her chess pieces and sat in silence. I wondered what to say to her. Father told me that small talk is important when you meet a girl for the first time. Don't try too hard to impress her. Just be yourself. Unless she asks, don't talk about yourself too much.

138

As usual, I ignored everything my father told me, interrupting Fundin several times with self-accolades. I bragged and boasted about my intelligence, my surfing, my music, my lifestyle in California, anything I could think of to impress Eve.

Unlike the girls on Earth, she did not react as I expected. She acted inattentive and unimpressed with the self-serving stories of my teenage exploits.

Eve's silence made me feel awkward. Her mathematical skills surprised me. She displayed greater intelligence than I believed possible. Whenever multiplication of dice rolls, card combinations, or treasure coin totals required a tally, she knew the answer instantly. Instantly. Her math skills frustrated me; I felt inferior. I considered myself excellent in math, that is, until I watched the girl from Epiphany add, subtract, and multiply faster than a calculator.

Angry with myself for letting her upset and intimidate me, I allowed my own emotions to get the best of me. During the game, I blurted out incorrect amounts. Wrong answers. Fundin had to correct me.

My thoughts turned negative. I hated myself for being so stupid around girls. Nervous, I dropped my red king on the game table.

"Are you all right?" she asked, waiting impatiently for me to roll the Fire & Ice Dice.

I gathered myself, rolled the dice, and drew a card. I picked up my red king, moved it, and asked her a personal question.

"So, what is the planet Epiphany like?"

I sensed my question took her by surprise.

She fidgeted in her seat, then answered, "Epiphany is in a state of global reconstruction."

"Where do you live?"

"Here."

I blushed, knowing I had asked the question incorrectly.

"Does your planet have an ocean?"

"Our Sea of Epiphany is the largest body of fresh water, but it is polluted, making it uninhabitable and undrinkable."

I bit my tongue, wanting to tell Eve about Carmel, about the Pacific Ocean. About *my* ocean, teaming with fish and seals and jellyfish and whales and millions of living organisms.

"Hunter, do you want to tell me something?"

"Do you miss your mother and father?" I asked.

Eve's face turned pale. She looked down at the game table and pursed her lips.

I knew I had upset her.

"I'm sorry. It's just that I know how lonely it can be away from home, away from your family," I said, nervously squeezing the red queen between my fingers.

"I am *not* lonely!" she shouted, defiantly staring into my eyes.

Unwilling to maintain eye contact with Eve, I looked at Fundin for emotional support. The faerie game master, who had been quiet except for game-related comments, cleared his throat and handed Eve the red and white dice.

"Is it my turn?" she asked, frowning.

Fundin nodded, *yes.*

Decided to redeem myself with a compassionate comment. "No matter how excited I am to be here, I miss my mom and dad, and my brothers and sisters."

She squeezed the red and white Fire & Ice Dice in her hand, giving me a cold stare.

I looked away, toward the porthole.

You idiot, I thought. *Eve does not want to talk about her family. Maybe she doesn't have one. Maybe she's an orphan. Things are probably different on Epiphany. Stop upsetting her.*

Lost for words, I remained silent.

"Lady Eve," Fundin said in his squeaky voice, "it's your move."

She rattled the Fire & Ice Dice in her left hand and threw the dice violently across the game board onto my lap. Chess pieces flew off the table, bouncing on the plank floor.

Unsure of how to react, I half-grinned at her.

With a scowl on her face, she pulled back her chair and ran out of the game room. The faeries stopped playing their instruments.

Dead silence.

"What did I say wrong?" I asked Fundin.

The game master's pointed ears turned red with embarrassment. He shrugged his tiny shoulders and remained silent. My heart sank.

Feeling terribly alone, I stood and walked to an open porthole. An ominous black sky crept over the crater cliffs, ready to swallow the blue sky. In the opposite direction, a red sky, speckled with pulsating stars, loomed on the horizon.

I clenched my hands, thinking, *Maybe the whole thing was a mistake. I need to get back home before something bad happens. Go back to Time Island.*

Staring at the Sea of Circles, I unclenched my fists to calm myself. I realized my thoughts had become scattered and unfocused. Remorse and negative thoughts turned to frustration; my frustration turned to anger.

Why was I letting a stupid girl upset me? I didn't even know her that well. I needed to have fun, enjoy my journey. I had plenty of time for girls when I got home.

So what if she's beautiful, she's cold and stuck up, I thought.

Turned around and looked at Fundin. The game master smiled from ear to ear. Returning to the table, I sat in my wicker chair. "What other games do you have?"

"Maybe Gametasia Chess 'ill take your mind off things fer a bit," Fundin said, reaching into his pants pocket and holding a

141

gold Millennium pocket watch. "Dinner's not 'till 18 o'clock. We gotta' few hours to play a game o' card chess."

Looked at his weary wheel watch and said, "Okay, teach me to play."

While Fundin prepared the Gametasia chess board, cards, and treasure coins, the musicians resumed their soothing music. I felt calmer as the game master positioned the royal kings, royal queens, dragon rooks, wizard bishops, noble knights, and dwarve pawns on the chess board.

As he shuffled the card deck, I inhaled deeply and tried to imagine, visualize, my upcoming adventure.

After we moved our first dwarve pawns, Fundin drew the king of diamonds, Karkinos, Keeper of the Bone of Ulrr, and could not move his black queen. The faerie gamemaster paid me a Right of Passage Tax in gold and silver treasure coins.

I drew a Gametasia Card from the deck, the two of hearts with an illustration of Tyrannus, and moved my second red dwarve pawn two spaces forward on the chess board.

I fumbled with the chess pieces, unable to stop thinking about Eve, unable to stop feeling guilty for abandoning my family.

My thoughts turned negative. *Stop worrying about Eve, she's not worth it. I miss being home. I miss my dog, Pooh. What am I going to tell Mom when I get home? She's going to know I could have come home sooner. One hell of a lot sooner.*

The mighty *Skipbladnir* surged forward under the power of forty-eight half-orcs manning four dozen oars.

I knew that Millennium, nowhere else in the universe, held my destiny, my purpose for being.

Nowhere but Millennium.

Chapter 9
Millennium Moonlight

Sparkling white stars danced on the vast stage of the cosmos. Through the billowy patches of fog, three moons illuminated the deck of the *Skipbladnir*. The red glow of Fire Falls pulsated against the crater's granite cliffs. A silver mist encircled the royal ship, caressing her body while she moved steadily in a southwesterly direction.

Walking from the ship's banquet room toward the upper forecastle deck, I enjoyed the cool sea breeze on my face. I wasn't sure if Eve enjoyed anything. We had just finished dinner and Morph suggested that I take her for a walk on deck, breathe some fresh autumn air.

During dinner, Metamorphosis told me, "When you awoke on Time Island on your seventeenth birthday, the date on Millennium was Aries the Eighth, Daynight of the Crab."

I learned I had arrived during the Autumn of Sol, in the Year of the Dragon, 9001 A.E..

When we reached the forecastle deck, Eve stopped at the balustrade. She behaved in her usual way, mysteriously silent. I couldn't seem to start a meaningful conversation. Not knowing what to say, I didn't want to upset her like I had earlier in the game room.

Eve had not uttered two sentences the entire evening.

Shifting from one leg to the other, I brushed crumbs off my red tunic, feeling anxious and unsure of myself in the presence of the girl from Epiphany. She acted so confident, so intelligent, so aloof, so emotionally distant.

Gazing at the shimmering Sea of Circles, I struggled to gain my composure, my confidence. She seemed upset with me and I had no clue of what I had done wrong.

To break the silence, I said, "Tonight's dinner reminded me of my mom's home-cooked meals. All thirteen of us would sit around the dinner table and we'd laugh and talk about—"

I cleared my throat.

"I guess what I'm trying to say is, I really miss my family, and—"

Tears welled up in my eyes.

Eve did not respond.

I must have looked pathetic.

My conversation was interrupted by the sound of Metamorphosis walking up the forecastle stairs. The heels of the Utopian's boots clicked on the wooden steps.

Wanting to reach out and hold Eve's hand, I instead turned to greet Morph. The sage walked toward us with a guitar strapped over his shoulder, a double neck guitar. Following Morph, Pendragon climbed the wooden steps; his hooves thudding loudly.

Standing in front of us, Morph's white beard glowed in the Millennium moonlight. His wings remained folded behind his back.

The Utopian Master asked, "Well, my children, what shall we do on this beautiful autumn evening?"

"This morning at breakfast, and tonight at dinner," I replied, "you promised to share some more Secrets of Time & Space. You know, explain some of the stuff I read in the *Magnum Opus*."

The sage laid his guitar on the forecastle bench. "What is your question?"

Eve folded her arms to warm herself, waiting for me to respond.

"I read a section in the *Magnum Opus* on the League of Kingdoms: Self-Government. My mom's a Democrat and my dad's a Republican. They argue all the time about government and politics."

"What is the question?" Morph asked.

"Sorry. How is it possible to have just one world government for an entire planet?" I asked.

"Ahhh, excellent question. The answer is simple. But before I explain the justification for governments and the politicians who run them, dominate them, I must explain civilizations and societies."

Eve stared straight out across the water, in the direction of the red lava falls.

"Within the universe," the sage said, "two types of civilizations exist, primitive civilizations and enlightened civilizations. Intelligent creatures develop civilizations and societies based on the evolution of their personal Triangulum: body/mind/spirit. Each of us, every intelligent life form, must balance our body, mind and spirit, our Triangulum. The majority of creatures in primitive societies are unbalanced. They tend to focus on the pleasures of their body and mind, ignoring their spiritual nourishment.

"Primitive civilizations create dysfunctional societies. Enlightened civilizations create functional societies. At the bottom of the evolutionary scale, primitive civilizations produce primal beings. Because these creatures have failed to evolve properly in body, mind and spirit, they live in a state of organized chaos and fear. They do not understand true love and the importance of spirituality, how to share their planet's abundant resources, how to care for one another."

Morph arched his white eyebrows. "Primitive societies live in constant fear. Fear of themselves and fear of each other. In primitive civilizations, a select group of greedy, dominating creatures benefit, while the majority of their populations live in poverty, hunger and a state of hopelessness, without the basic necessities of life: water, food, clothing, and shelter. If the primitive beings happen to be technologically advanced, they use their knowledge and technology improperly. Primal beings are always on the verge of destroying themselves with the technology they have created. All primitive civilizations, no matter how scientifically advanced, are hostile to other civilizations. This hostility often results in a galactic catastrophe when an unfriendly civilization that has developed space travel attacks alien civilizations in neighboring solar systems."

"Do you mean UFOs?" I asked.

"You humans seem fascinated with unidentified flying objects, as you call them. May I suggest we focus on your original question and discuss the enlightened creatures that have visited Earth another time?"

"Okay," I said, grinning.

When the sage said that space creatures had visited Earth, I *knew* UFOs *did* exist. Extraterrestrials were real.

The sage asked me, "Can you name an intelligent life form that has developed a primitive civilization?"

I looked at Pendragon. Then Eve. Then, I looked back at Morph.

"The Extractors?"

"Excellent response, my son."

I grinned, impressed with my correct answer.

Morph asked, "Any other primitive societies that you can think of?"

I shut my eyes to think. "No, I can't."

"What about humans?"

I frowned. "No way, we are *not* primitive on Earth. We are advanced," I said, knowing that Morph's planet didn't have electricity, or cars, or computers, or smart phones.

"I see," Morph said. "Do you consider Earth's history of revolution, civil unrest, and wars to be enlightened behavior? According to what your father told me, the majority of your planet's population experiences poverty and hunger, the masses are denied the basic necessities of life. I believe you call this the 'war of the haves and the havenots'. Your intelligent life forms are just one fearful decision away from engaging in nuclear war, annihilating one another. Human beings continue to destroy the Earth's natural resources at an apocalyptic pace and they are on the verge of allowing pandemic diseases to wipe them out. Humans are unwilling to change their own world."

"That does not make us primitive. It's just the way things are."

"Have things improved on Earth since I last talked to your father?"

"Listen, Morph. We can't worry about all the starving people in the world and we can't help it if war breaks out all the time. It's not our fault. My country's doing the best they can to help the whole damn planet, and all we do is get attacked by American-hating terrorists."

"It sounds as if things have gotten worse since Wayland and I talked on Time Island."

"Yeah, we're under constant attack by inferior countries."

"Why do these inferior countries hate you?"

"They say we're arrogant."

"Are you?"

"No, we just happen to be the best damn country on Earth."

"I see."

Thinking about my response, my face turned red. Eve looked at me and rolled her eyes. I felt defensive, like I was being interrogated by my father at home.

"So, my son. How do you feel about people going hungry on your planet, starving to death?"

"Hunger? My parents say that the starving and the homeless need to help themselves, find a job."

"Do you believe that?"

"Yeah, we can't help everybody that's homeless and hungry, they got themselves in their own mess. Those people need to get a job, make something out of themselves, quit making excuses."

"Interesting concept."

"My parents work hard and pay taxes. They can't spend their time worrying about all the homeless people in California, or all the starving people in Africa or India, or, you know, all those third-world countries that have corrupt regimes. My mom and dad can't decide the fate of the homeless. I mean, what other choice do working people like my parents have?"

"My son, life is all about decisions, choices. Your parents can help the homeless any time they choose. Your planet can end hunger tomorrow if people decide to make it happen. It is obvious that your primitive human race lacks compassion. Love."

I folded my arms, perplexed with Morph's statement. The sage continued.

"What I find disturbing is that the solution is so simple. All you humans have to do is agree, make the compassionate decision to stop hunger."

"Agree on what?"

"Agree to change your primitive views. Humans must agree to help the less fortunate, stop starvation."

"But, I don't think it's that simple."

"Whether you are willing to admit it or not, it *is* that simple. Your planet is in utter chaos because of the choices unenlightened human beings continue to make."

"My mom says it's difficult to change the way things are in the world, that suffering is part of life."

The sage ran his fingers through his white beard. "The Earth's health is in total decline because the human race makes greedy, primitive decisions, or conveniently fails to make any decisions, mostly in the name of greed. Failing to decide is simply an excuse."

"Okay, I admit, some of your points make some sense."

"Are you aware that your own life is a direct result of your personal decisions, the choices you have made, you now make, or you fail to make?"

Avoiding eye contact, I looked up at a half-orc in the crow's nest. Morph leaned over, placing his upper right hand on my shoulder.

"All intelligent beings create the consciousness that makes all things possible. For instance, humans can make a conscious decision to give less fortunate people the dignity they deserve, now, not later."

I rolled my eyes. "How can that happen on Earth?"

"Humans must end the discrimination and hatred that prevent the majority of people on your planet from having the simple necessities of life: water, food, clothing, shelter. Dignity."

"It's not that easy, Morph. People back home *do* try to help the homeless."

"Try?"

"Poor people are just unlucky. You know, bad stuff just happens."

"My son, that is false. There are no coincidences in the universe."

Looked defiantly at Morph, I said, "Hey, what about bad luck, accidents? Like being struck by lightning, or getting run over by a truck. Or hit by a train?"

"Allow me to offer you the second Secret of Time & Space, 'Nothing, no thing, happens by accident.'"

"I don't believe that."

"Of course not. You have been taught differently by your parents, by teachers, by government, by the leaders of your primeval society. You have been guided down the wrong path."

"Accidents happen from bad luck."

"Do you realize that your beliefs regarding bad luck come from fear?"

"I'm *not* afraid," I said, pointing my right index finger at the sage.

"Young man, you have been raised by parents, teachers, and governments that teach fear and total dependence. You have been raised not to ask questions.

"I'm not in the mood to talk about this right now." I looked away and caught Eve staring at me.

"I understand how difficult it is to accept the truth, especially the supreme truth."

Feeling embarrassed in front of Eve, I frowned and gritted my teeth as the sage continued.

"Greet each event, every moment in your life, as a special part of the grand plan, The Great Way. What you refer to as accidents always come together at exactly the right time and with exact outcomes. Unfortunately, you, like most humans, seem to believe these outcomes are accidental, blind luck. Your own thoughts deceive you because you are fearful of the truth."

I shrugged my shoulders, staring at the sage. "I am not afraid of the truth."

Morph grinned. "Every event, every action, may not be as unfortunate as you think."

"Give me an example."

"People come and go, in and out of our lives, at exactly the right moment."

I thought for a moment and realized that I'd lost my family but new people *had* come into my life. Eve was one of them.

"Okay," I said, "I'll think about what you've said, but I am not afraid."

The sage patted me on the shoulder. "I understand, my son."

"Ah-hem." Pendragon cleared his throat to get Morph's attention. "Master, I believe you were about to explain the

Discordia Crater

concept of self-government for our guest. However, you might want to explain enlightened civilizations first."

"Of course," Morph said, wiping his dinner's ambrosia crumbs from his white moustache.

"Enlightened civilizations have evolved for the benefit of all, where a oneness, a collective consciousness, exists. Enlightened societies with advanced technology use their knowledge so that all creatures benefit. This occurs because enlightened beings balance the needs of their Triangulum: body, mind, and spirit. Love and spirituality, eternal bliss, is the way of life for all enlightened societies. No violence or anger exists in an enlightened civilization. No one goes hungry or homeless."

"Do you Utopians consider yourselves members of an enlightened society?"

"Yes. Utopians enjoy an enlightened civilization."

I smirked. "How can Millennium be called enlightened if Ex and the Extractors exist?"

"Ah, excellent question. Extremely logical," Morph said. "I shall answer that when the time is right. It is time I explain self-government. Government is unnecessary in an enlightened society. Since enlightened beings live the supreme truth, they require no rules, no laws, no organized rituals, no governing body of politicians. Enlightened beings live life as leaders. Before the dark forces of the Extractors arrived, no government or politics existed on Millennium. Prior to the Extractor Asteroid event in the Year of the Rat, 1 A.E., our planet enjoyed an enlightened society, abiding by Universal Laws.

Morph opened his four arms. "After this Discordia Crater was formed, the Extractor invasion, that I explained earlier, began. Primitive tribes emerged from the chaos. As the dysfunctional Extractors conquered more lands, wars broke out and famine crept across small territories throughout Millennium. Soon, our disease-free planet experienced small outbreaks of the emotional virus, the Dark Essence. The low self-esteem diseases infected the thoughts of healthy creatures, turning them into dysfunctional beings, Extractors. Primitive civilizations with dysfunctional societies spread throughout our eight kingdoms, and much faster than we anticipated. Eight new subkingdoms were formed in the Underworld by the dark forces. Many Millennians, peaceful and non-violent, became slaves to the greedy and power-hungry Extractors, carriers of the emotional virus. Even the gods became quarrelsome."

"Yeah, I read in Father's mythology books where the gods and goddesses argue a lot," I said.

Eve placed her index finger to her lips, *be quiet.*

"We Utopians found it necessary, in the Year of the Dragon, 41 A.E., to form one world government and develop a plan to protect Octilogy, our Eight Great Treasures. We organized relief for Millennians oppressed by the alien invaders, the Extractors. We organized a League of Kingdoms, with representatives from every kingdom in the Upperworld and the Underworld. In addition, we formed a Court of the Four Empires. A world court to settle inter-kingdom disputes, as well as Underworld disputes. So far, our world-wide organizations have been effective and the Extractor advancements are under control. Eventually, we shall eliminate the dreaded *Extractor Virus.*"

At the stern of ship, Captain Gog shouted orders to the crew. The *Skipbladnir* picked up speed as I asked, "Who rules the League of Kingdoms?"

"Philosophers and sages provide leadership," Morph replied.

"You mean, *you* guys?" I looked back and forth at Pendragon and Metamorphosis.

"We Utopians are the most qualified to govern."

"Who's in charge? You know, who's the top politician? Your president?"

"A philosopher king provides leadership."

"Who is the philosopher king?"

Pendragon looked at Morph and grinned.

"You?" I pointed at the sage.

"Correct," Morph replied.

"But, don't you need professional politicians to run your government?"

"Since the only politicians on Millennium are Extractors, that would be illogical. This is because the main interest of most politicians is self-interest. They fail to provide leadership. This has been proven by primitive civilizations all over the universe."

I lowered my eyebrows. "Where I live, the greatest country on Earth, we have natural born leaders who have become great politicians."

"Who told you that?"

"My parents. My teachers. History books."

Morph raised his eyebrows. "I have learned that on Earth, most human beings lack the knowledge and wisdom needed to govern; therefore, those drawn to political aspirations are dominated by low self-esteem, egocentric motives such as fame and fortune. Once in office, the politicians are easily seduced by greed and power. These characteristics make them unfit to govern, yet they end up in public office, voted in by millions of uninformed people who, obviously, desire manipulation."

"My father cannot be manipulated politically."

The sage grinned. "Voters know that political speeches are designed to manipulate them, but they *want* to be manipulated. Known as the ignorant masses, voters share a collective consciousness, a faulty mindset of, I'll vote only for who I *like*, not for the person who is wise, ethical, and the most qualified. Public elections have become a popularity contest. Your professional politicians accuse each other of anything, including stretching the truth or outright lying, to manipulate potential voters.

"Your political figures are experts in disputes and arguments. What I mean is, they have no commitment to moral ideas, they only wish to argue against a verbal opponent. They become so skilled in fighting and arguing, refuting whatever is said, that no one can stand up to them. They argue anything, no matter if the issue is true or false, merely for the sake of victory. Your primitive society is unjust and corrupt because it is run by politicians appealing to the ignorant masses."

I frowned, shaking my head, *no way.*

Captain Gog paced back and forth, squinting through a brass spyglass.

"I see doubt in your eyes, my son. Allow me to give you an excellent example."

I gestured with my hand, *go ahead.*

"When a serious problem arises, do the people of Earth seek

out the advice of a specialist, an expert? Or, do they seek the advice of an untrained citizen?"

"The trained specialist, of course."

"When you humans suffer from illness, do you not seek the most competent medical specialist you can find?"

I nodded, *yes*.

"Or, do you go about asking everyone you meet for advice? Do you take a vote among as many people as possible to determine your illness?"

"No, that would be stupid."

"Exactly. So why is it then, with regard to the political health of your government, your nation and your world, you allow untrained, unqualified, self-interest politicians to rise to power, voted in by uninformed and easily-manipulated citizens, the ignorant masses?"

"Somebody's got to run the government."

"You are correct. In a primitive society that requires laws and government, people fight, lie and cheat to be in charge, to be the leader. Often, the power-hungry leader becomes a tyrant, a dictator."

"Okay, so what's your solution to bad leadership?"

"Politics and philosophy must be united in the same person. A suggestion might be that your planet begin a specialized training academy for future politicians so they may wisely navigate the ship of state."

"Ship of state?"

"Yes, your ship of state. On your planet, when you build a ship, you seek a shipwright. When you build a house, an architect does the job. But when it comes to building something much more important, like a society of wise and happy citizens, you humans ignore the experts on government and entrust the job to anyone who succeeds in achieving favor with the voters. How is this accomplished? Politicians flatter the citizens' prejudices and make promises about what he or she will do for them once they are elected to power. In other words, your ship's captain knows nothing about navigation."

"Ship's captain?"

"Allow me to use an allegory," Morph said with a grin.

"Visualize a grand, sea-worthy ship docked in the harbor. A captain is needed. The ship owner is elderly, hard of hearing, poor of sight and lacks sea-faring knowledge, navigation skills. Knowing that the owner desperately needs a captain, all the sailors on the ship argue, fight and quarrel over who shall be the captain. However, these sailors know nothing about navigation or the operation of a ship. Because they have no skills or training or experience, they use brute force, intimidation, lies and deception to win the favor of the elderly ship owner. Whoever succeeds in persuading the owner to choose him is immediately recognized as a navigator, the captain, a person who knows how to navigate a ship. Everyone else is considered inferior and useless.

Morph pointed toward Gog. "The true captain, the one person who completely understands the craft of navigation and how to steer the ship properly, is called a worthless stargazer. The ship sets sail, navigated by a clever, unethical captain, a person of trickery and fraud. A shipwreck is inevitable."

I smirked. "Okay, I get the point. We should have an expert, a philosopher king, run our government. Oh, excuse me, navigate our ship of state."

"Excellent idea. Do you know of any on your planet?"

I scratched my head and thought. I failed to think of anyone's name, but offered a response.

"All right. I admit our government officials might not be perfect, but that doesn't mean we don't have great civilizations on Earth, especially with all of our advanced technologies."

"You believe your society is so advanced, but the first indication of a primitive society is that it believes itself advanced. Unfortunately, beings of primal consciousness believe they are enlightened."

I thought for a moment, watching Lycus climb the main mast to secure the lower yard's rigging. Pendragon stretched and moved his dragon wings back and forth. The circulating air felt cool on my face while I asked my next question.

"So, if we trained politicians to be wise, ethical and honest, would a one-world government solve our problems on Earth? Would that make us advanced?"

"The Earth's population requires a total shift in consciousness," Morph replied. "A new, enlightened global consciousness. A world government, world court and an international peacekeeping force would help, but your primitive society requires a radical change. After all, you have not yet found a way to stop human beings from starving to death, much less stop killing each other."

"Why can't we change?"

"Because you humans do not care enough. You must decide to simply have compassion for each other, to love your brothers as yourself, as one of your Masters so eloquently put it. You claim you love your family, unfortunately, you all share a limited view of who your family members are. You are *all* members of the one, great human family. This means that the problems of the human family are all your problems. Ignore the plight of others, and chaos occurs. Just like the Extractor societies here on Millennium, human societies' greatest problem is their desire to be separate from one another. They cannot seem to grasp the concept of brotherly love, oneness. Simply put, what you do to others, you do to yourself. What you fail to do for others, you fail to do for yourself."

I folded my arms in defiance. "It's not our fault. We need more government programs to help feed all the starving people."

"My son, what your planet needs is a growth in collective consciousness. More love, not a growth of your governments and government programs."

"Okay, how do we grow our consciousness?"

"For fifty thousand Earth years you humans have attempted to cure bad behavior caused by the emotional virus. You have not been able to properly diagnose, let alone cure, these low self-esteem diseases. Like an alien invader, the plague that corrupts and confuses and controls your thoughts has gone undetected on your planet for centuries, eons. You humans have become so accustomed to your own bad behavior that anger, jealousy, hatred and fear are now considered normal behavior. Fighting and killing each other is commonplace. Wars are glorified and politically justified. Yet, you have attempted to solve your problems through governmental action and political means."

156

Time Island
Galactic Portal

Morph raised his index finger. "You actually expect politicians to save you. This, of course, is the blind leading the blind. Before you can grow your consciousness, your planet's emotional virus must be cured. Eliminated. The *Extractor Virus*, destroyer of positive thoughts—the killer of dreams—has created stinking thinking and thereby, destroyed the human spirit. You cannot grow your collective consciousness until you change your thoughts. What you humans have failed to realize is that the change you seek, your dream of a peaceful, loving society, must be made in the hearts and minds of the people as one unified family of man, one world. Separatism always leads to failure and ruin."

The sage pointed skyward. "Nothing exists in the infinite universe that is separate from anything else. Everything, every thing, is connected and intertwined into the grand web of life, The Great Way."

"I *do* understand the concept of how organisms and ecosystems are interdependent," I said.

"Your view of the natural world needs to be applied to governments, to the human condition. You humans view the world as a collection of nation states, separate and independent of each other. Through intimidation and war, you have developed what you call super powers, who consider most other nations inferior. As far as the super powers are concerned, the inferior nation's problems: starvation, war, genocide, and denial of human civil rights, are viewed as internal problems. For example, your nation, the United States, does little for other nations until your own interests are threatened, or until your politicians and captains of industry decide that an inferior nation has a so-called *problem*, or valuable natural resources to exploit for profit."

I flexed my jaw muscles, frowning.

"When your country's investments or security are threatened, you immediately rally your citizens and politicians and armed forces to put down the uprising, or annihilate the corrupt regime. The justification for the action is always a humanitarian reason, to enlighten and educate the oppressed peoples of the world on the benefits of democracy. The truth is, your nation, all super powers, all governments, protect their own self-imposed interests."

"I don't believe that."

"The proof is obvious. When and where your nation has no political or economic interests, you show no concern. You have failed to learn that you are the family of man, what happens to one, happens to all. If you would truly apply your famous slogan, 'One nation under God,' to your entire planet and to all nations, your world would change immediately."

I sat speechless, my eyebrows arched. Captain Gog bellowed orders to the half-orc crew as the red sky crept overhead, casting a sullen glow on the Sea of Circles.

"You separate yourselves from one another. Your Earth's underprivileged live in poverty while your privileged, the elitist few, create new laws for their corrupt governments, exploit the weak, hoard money and material wealth. Their selfish lifestyles cannot be maintained unless they cut down millions of acres of magnificent trees each year, destroy the protective ozone that covers their planet, and pollute the Earth's rivers and oceans so their industries can produce more products. More and more unnecessary actions. Your society suffers from the horrible disease of more. Greed."

I hung my head, admitting to myself that the sage had made some valid points. "Now that you put it that way, I'm kind of ashamed of being a human."

The sage nodded. "Your world's greatest tragedy is discontentment. Your worst of faults is wanting more, always. Contentment alone is enough. Indeed, the bliss of eternity may be found in your contentment. The *Extractor Virus*, the killer of dreams and curse of the universe, is an interplanetary epidemic. Earth's civilization is not the only planet to have experienced the destructive thought-disease pandemic."

Morph pointed at Eve. "Her planet, Epiphany, has experienced the unnecessary destruction of their civilization three times because of the *Extractor Virus*, the Dark Essence."

"Wow, that's incredible," I said, staring at Eve. She made eye contact but quickly turned away.

"The only hope for your planet, the one path to change, is for humans to discover The Great Way. Love is the answer. All you need is love."

I stood expressionless, worried about the uncertain future of my beloved planet. I really believed our civilization was advanced, not primitive. If a great society does not need rules or laws, our government isn't so great after all. I thought about how politicians *are* power-hungry, self-interest liars. I told myself that when I got home I would help the homeless, do something about the people dying of starvation, change the way things are. But first, humans needed to cure their emotional diseases, the *Extractor Virus.*

Morph interrupted my thoughts when he held up his right lower hand and said, "We shall end our philosophical discussion for this evening."

Raised my right arm in the air. "I still have more questions."

"Patience, my son, patience."

Frowning, I sighed and gave Morph the impatient, *I'll wait but I'm frustrated,* nod.

"Let us relax our minds," Pendragon said. "How about some music before we retire for the evening?"

"What a beautiful evening to sing a song," Morph said, smiling.

Pendragon suggested that Eve sit on the forecastle bench. She agreed and I sat next to her.

Morph picked up his guitar and pulled the leather strap over his white, flowing hair. Familiar with guitars, the instrument impressed me. The sage held a double neck, butterfly-shaped guitar. The sunburst finish gleamed in the bright moonlight.

The sage smiled and said, "Pendragon shall accompany me in one of our favorite songs, written for us by a human."

Before I could ask the songwriter's name, Morph looked at me and asked, "Andvari tells me you play harmonica."

Pendragon held out a gold-plated harmonica in his hand.

Startled, I blushed and did not answer.

Why did I tell the gnome about the harmonica? I thought. *What if I make a mistake? Play a bad note while Eve is listening.*

I convinced myself it was my chance to impress her, so I said, "Okay", accepting the shiny gold harmonica from Pendragon.

"I shall sing a ballad called "Open Road," the sage said.

"Sure, go ahead," I mumbled. "I'll follow along."

Eve sat up straight to adjust her black leather skirt. Her gold and silver arm bracelets jingled as the sage strummed the opening guitar chords.

Morph finger-picked the upper-neck strings of his double-neck guitar with two hands, while he strummed with his other two hands on the lower-neck strings. I couldn't believe how well he played guitar with his four hands working in perfect unison. The guitar sounded fantastic, like two guitar players.

Pendragon played a tambourine in his right hand and shook a cabasa in his left hand.

I wet my lips on the reeds and played a short harmonica riff. The mouth harp sounded great.

Morph sang to Eve and me.

"Open Road, always something leads me to you,
    So many times I thought I knew you,
    If I only did, I'd take you down."

Morph's singing voice sounded youthful. To my surprise, Pendragon sang the second verse in his low, resonating voice.

"Open Road, you're always winding and unfolding,
    There's always something new you're holding,
    That takes away all that you give."

Morph and Pendragon harmonized.

"In spite of everything you've shown me,
    I can't believe all that you've told me,
    You're always running away, into your distant getaway,
    Open Road, there's always something there that leads me,
    So many times I felt the needing,
    That leads me to your free and Open Road."

Morph played an acoustic solo on his double-neck guitar; all four hands and fingers moved in perfect unison. I joined in with an impromptu harmonica solo.

Morph and Pendragon grinned at each other while I played the melody. The two Utopians harmonized again.

"In spite of everything you've shown me,
I can't believe all that you've told me,
You're always running away, into your distant getaway,
Open Road, there's always something there that leads me,
So many times I feel the needing,
That leads me to your free and Open Road,
Leads me to your Open Road."

The final guitar chord faded away on the quiet forecastle deck of the *Skipbladnir*.

I clapped my hands, saying, "That song sounded wonderful. That's a great ballad where I come from."

Pendragon grinned. "Your harmonica sounded perfect."

"Thank you," I said confidently, beaming with pride.

"Excellent mouth harp, young man," Morph said, chuckling. "Maybe next time, we can get Eve to sing with us."

"I will have to think about that," she said.

"Do you sing?" Morph asked her.

"Sometimes."

"Can we play a song, so Eve can sing?" I asked.

Before Morph answered, the *Skipbladnir's* bell rang three times.

Captain Gog stood on deck, next to the ship's bell, yelling, "It be 21 o'clock on yonder weary wheel und vee best get below deck. Veer gonna' dock at Fog Harbor in zee mornin' und vee better be vell rested."

Half-orcs scurried about the top deck, securing the *Skipbladnir's* riggings and sails.

"We should retire to our cabins," Morph said. "Maybe Eve can sing us a song during our journey. I'll bring my guitar."

Eve looked at me and said, "Do not count on that."

She stood and straightened her leather skirt, greeting Alfrigga, who had climbed the forecastle stairs.

I jumped to my feet and put my harmonica into the pocket of my breeches. Emotional thoughts filled my head. I decided it was my chance to hug Eve. *Go ahead,* I told myself, *just one, friendly hug. Wait! She'll get upset. Not now. Hug her later.*

While I hesitated to move, Alfrigga waddled to Eve's side and tugged on her hand, signaling, *time to go.*

"Thank you, Morph and Pendragon," Eve said. "That song sounded beautiful."

The two Utopians nodded their heads in gratitude. Eve turned and walked down the forecastle steps with Alfrigga.

Seeking recognition, I yelled, "See you in the morning, Eve." I smiled and waved at her.

She looked back, but did not acknowledge me. The girl from Epiphany disappeared down the stairwell.

My smile turned to a frown. *What about complementing me, Eve? Wasn't my harmonica good enough?*

Andvari walked up behind me and tugged on my breeches.

"Marster Hoonter," the gnome said, "twas a pleasure to hear your ootstandin' harp playin'."

Ignoring Andvari, I said, "Good daynight," to Morph and Pendragon and followed the loyal gnome down the forecastle steps.

The chilly, swirling wind blew my hair in my eyes. I brushed the locks off my forehead and gazed at the starry Millennium sky, taking one last look at the three moons, who seemed to be staring at me.

Walked below deck with the slow-moving Andvari, remembering how Eve had acted upset in the Gametasia game room. Her sudden, unexplained anger bothered me. I could not understand her lack of compassion for her family. And, she had ignored me at dinner. I decided that for being so beautiful, Eve had become an emotional force to be reckoned with.

Told Andvari, "Good daynight," and shut my cabin door. The weary wheel struck 21 o'clock. Turned off the oil lamps in the cabin and got undressed. I could not stop thinking of my mom, my twin sister, Julia, my home on Earth, my own bedroom. I missed my collection of stuff, my car, computer, surf board, games, guitars and smart phone. Thought about my plans to

163

hike the Pacific Crest Trail with my best friend at school, Kirk, knowing I would not be home in time for our trip.

Closed the two porthole windows by my bed, shutting out the damp air and muffling the loud rowing cadence. I crawled under the covers and blew out the flame to the green candle sitting on my night stand. Bright-blue moonlight poured into the cabin through the two portholes.

Lying in bed, I tried to get my family off my mind, tried to get Eve off my mind, tried to get politics off my mind, tried to get the Extractors off my mind. Out of my thoughts.

I wondered if I was at the hospital or at home, thinking, *Mom has to be going crazy with me lying in a coma...I can't allow Eve to upset me any more...Morph might be correct on some of his political views...they seem so different...but, they do make sense. I can't wait to step on dry land tomorrow morning. I wonder if we'll see any of those Extractors at Fog Harbor?*

Transfixed on the Millennium parchment map mounted in the shadows, my mind continued to spin with frustrating, negative thoughts.

The weary wheel struck 23 o'clock by the time I finally closed my eyes.

Annn's
Falls
Lethe River

River of Ice
Harbor

Manitou
Falls

Ice Falls

Cocytus
River

Web
Fate

Sec
Wo

urth
orld

Discordia

Beast
Cov

lo
ls

Time Island

E

xus
iver

Sea of Circles

Lupercal

Crater
Bay

Fog Harbor

Emerald
Falls

styx
iver

Forest Primeval

aron
lls

Kukulcan Trail

Fire Falls

Acheron
River

Cel

Place of Emergence

Embryo Grotto

River of Fire

n of
on

Ogo
Hole

South Crater Trail

Bridge of
Wishes

Tree of Ambrosia

yra

Southern Deep Sea
Southern Grand Canyon

Open Road
The Great Way

en
iac
il

Tree of
Life

City
of the
Kings

Mancy

Pygmy
Kingdom

South Caravan Trail

Badlands

Fantasy
Falls

Waste Castle

Waste City

Palace of
Immortality

Dalay
River

of
o

Marcoisa
River

DAYNIGHT OF THE DOG

Aries the 10th
Year of the Dragon

"Must I fear what others fear?
Should I fear desolation when there is abundance?
Should I fear darkness when that Light is shining everywhere?"
—Metamorphosis

Chapter 10
Fog Harbor

Breakfast had to be eaten in my cabin. Andvari served dodo eggs and bacon while he explained that the *Skipbladnir* had made better time than anticipated; therefore, Metamorphosis had canceled the traditional morning meal on deck. The gnome told me that during our journey we would have to sleep on the ground in bedrolls, but that once the party arrived in the Upperworld at Escalot, a castle fortress overlooking the Sea of Esteem, we would enjoy comfortable feather beds.

Camping sounded like fun. *Anything* sounded like fun as long as Eve was with me.

Peering out the porthole of my cabin, I watched anxiously for Namo's Lighthouse to materialize through the grey mist.

Overhead, the blue sky remained hidden by the patchy fog.

Sea gulls squawked while they followed the *Skipbladnir* into Crater Bay, into the mouth of Fog Harbor.

For the first time on the voyage, I smelled the scent of pine trees, the rousing fragrance of virgin forest.

Balder inhaled deeply and blew the foghorn; the blaring note cut through the damp morning air.

The *Skipbladnir's* oars lifted out of the water. The Sea of Circles' voyage had ended.

Inhaled a breath of harbor air, walked to my bed, and finished stuffing my clothes into a brown leather backpack. Looking in the mirror, I admired my blue tunic with brown breeches and black knee-high boots. My reflection raised goose bumps of excitement on my neck and arms. I felt invincible.

Eve and I were about to embark on an adventure that few people in the universe get to experience.

The ship's bell rang while Balder shouted, "Land ho!"

Without warning, the cabin door swung open. Andvari burst into the room, panting, out of breath.

"Marster Hoonter...aye...we be 'ere. Foog Horbur...'tis cummin' up. We best...put 'ur spurs to tha' nags...laudy."

"I'm almost ready," I said, dropping a pair of wool socks on the floor.

"Aye, 'tis aboot time to get your bloody things t'gether."

"All right, I'm coming," I yelled, biting my lower lip, trying to maintain my composure.

Clogs clacking, the dwarve waddled out the cabin door, leaving it open. I finished packing, ran down the corridor and up the stairwell. Andvari opened the deck door.

Looking up—straight up—my jaw dropped. I couldn't see the top of the gigantic cliffs. Visible through the patchy fog, the crater's grey granite rock disappeared into the scarlet red sky. Half Dome looked puny compared to *those* crater cliffs.

The scene reminded me of my childhood vacations at Yosemite National Park with my family. I remembered that my fear of heights began when my father took me to the top of Half Dome and held me over the cliff's edge. That's where I became scared to death of high places.

If you've ever been afraid of heights, you know what I mean.

Looked to my left, straight up. Fire Falls, five hundred miles away, poured red, molten lava down the face of the cliff, from the heavens to the crater floor.

Directly in front of me, fifty miles away, Charon Falls, fed by the River Styx, exploded from the crater cliffs, like a river falling from the sky.

With Charon Falls roaring in the distance, the *Skipbladnir's* top deck shook with activity. Half-orcs lumbered about in organized fashion.

The relentless rowing had ceased, allowing the ship to coast toward the shore.

"Fog Harbor, seventy yards," a half-orc yelled from the crow's nest.

The harbor sounds of shouting voices and medieval horns came from just beyond the swirling fog.

I wonder if I'll see any humans at Fog Harbor? I thought.

Andvari told me that Fog Harbor was the largest port on the Sea of Circles. He called it a seaside fortress.

I spotted Eve standing at the forecastle, talking to Morph and Captain Gog.

Threw the backpack over my shoulder and ran toward the prow of the ship. I couldn't believe how much faster I could run. My strides were twice as long as they were on Earth. The powerful acceleration excited me. Felt so light, like I was flying across the deck.

Climbed the forecastle stairs, four steps at a time.

Eve glanced my way. She wore black leather breeches and a white silk chemise with a black bodice.

Skidding to a halt, I smiled and grabbed her hand to shake it. Her soft skin felt hot in the cool morning air.

Eve pulled her hand away.

"Sorry. My hands are cold," I said, blushing.

Eve turned away, looking up at the towering cliffs.

There she goes again, I thought. *Why won't she talk to me?*

"Good morning, Metamorphosis," I said.

Morph held a telescope to his right eye as he smiled.

Captain Gog approached me, patting me on the back, hard. "Ya, vatch your backside when your out yonder in der crater und der forest."

"Of course, Captain. I will."

"Und vatch der princess for us," Gog said, pointing at Eve.

Gog chuckled, winked at Eve, and stomped down the stairs.

Morph held a parchment scroll in his lower right hand. "Are you ready to begin your land journey?"

Eve and I looked at each other and nodded, *yes*.

"Good. Let us review our route." The sage rolled out a map of the Discordia Crater. Held it with his two lower hands while he pointed at the map with the index finger of his upper right hand.

"We shall travel from Fog Harbor, right here," Morph said, "to the edge of Forest Primeval. This is where the Kukulcan Trail begins. At this location we shall meet our crater guides and scouts, Galar and Idun, two swamp elves familiar with the terrain. Prior to entering the forest, Pendragon shall fly ahead to make arrangements for your safe journey from the South Crater Trail to the Upperworld. Our expedition shall include Balder and Lycus, who shall assist us with our supplies."

The sage waited for a response. He noticed me admiring Eve, instead of the map. "Any questions?"

"Do you mean we're going to climb *those* cliffs?" I asked, pointing straight up at the sky.

"Yes, it is a lovely hike. Quite scenic."

I swallowed and tried to look confident and fearless in front of Eve. As I told you earlier, I hated heights.

To my surprise, Andvari waddled up the steps wearing a backpack and hiking boots with pointed toes. Holding a spyglass nearly as long as his body, the gnome waited silently by the deck's gangplank entrance, glancing at his weary wheel pocket watch. Andvari never mentioned he'd be going with us.

I felt someone pull on my pants leg.

Fundin and Alfrigga held out their tiny hands. "Marster Hoonter, gude luck to you, laudy."

"I'll see you when I return." I bent over and shook their hands, thanking them for their hospitality.

While Eve and I finished saying goodbye to the crew, a rock-lined jetty and pier could be seen through the fog. In awe, I looked up. To my left, Namo's Lighthouse stared down at me. Constructed of granite stone, the landmark rose majestically from the rock jetty at the mouth of the harbor.

As the *Skipbladnir* docked along the cobblestone pier, Eve pointed at two wooden ships anchored in the harbor. The crews were unloading cargo onto the docks.

The harbor bustled with activity. Many of the figures looked human from a distance. Well, at least they walked upright, on two legs.

Fog Harbor *did* look like a fortress. Beyond the docks, a cobblestone road led to massive walls of wood and stone block that surrounded the seaport town. Beyond the walls and main gate, two-and-three-story-tall buildings rose up, silhouetted by the majestic evergreen trees soldiering the rocky hills.

A half-orc stood on the pier waving at us. Andvari told Eve that his name was Thrud, a half-orc guide who offered his services to travelers. He carried a bow, arrows, and a huge axe.

Balder and Lycus hoisted a gangplank from the ship's port side to the dock. Pendragon spread his wings and glided from the ship to the cobblestone pier. He and Thrud secured the gangplank and stood on the wooden dock, alert, craning their necks and sniffing the damp air. They signaled to our group, *come ashore.*

Eve, Andvari, Morph and I walked down the gangplank carrying our leather backpacks. Balder and Lycus followed, balancing the bulky supply packs on their shoulders. The sound of clogs and boots and hooves and toenails tapping and clicking and clattering on the wooden planks reminded me again of my unearthly location.

Stood on the cobblestone dock, feeling good about walking on solid ground again. Excited to see Millennium.

Fog Harbor

Quiet Lady Inn

Thrud shook Morph's hand, saying, "Mayor Dagan and the Utopian Council welcome you to Fog Harbor. You are invited to a grand dinner at Town Hall."

Morph smiles and said, "Please give Dagan, Fergus, Govad, Jove and Remus my regards. Unfortunately, we will not be staying long. And if you see the town scryer, Thadius, please tell him we shall play Gametasia Chess on my next visit."

Thrud nodded with a grin, *okay*, and Pendragon lifted his divine staff, signaling, *go*.

The half-orc guide led our group down the cobblestone pier.

The Fog Harbor villagers avoided us. No one approached.

Eve walked in between Morph and me as we turned right, entering the main dock area, then turned left up the main cobblestone road to the main gate.

Pendragon signaled, *open the gates*, to the half-orc guards stationed in the entry towers.

Morph warned Eve and me not talk to anyone and to stay close to Balder and Lycus.

The massive wood and iron gates creaked open, revealing the main street of the bustling seaport fortress—Mudfog Lane.

Fog Harbor looked like a medieval village described in

my role playing books at home. The beige and grey buildings displayed walls of plaster over twigs with brown thatched roofs. Town Hall, topped by a glass dome, stood at the end of Mudfog Lane. To our right stood a two-story building with a red roof, its stone chimney belched grey smoke.

Groups of dwarves, elves, and human-looking villagers scurried about the main cobblestone street. Some of them stared at us, while most went about their business, ignoring us.

Eve told the sage that she thought some of the villagers were Epiphanites. I told Morph that several of the strangers looked human. Morph explained that, like most settlements in the Upperworld's Eight Great Kingdoms, small populations existed, all of them originating from the other eight planets of the Amalgamation.

He pointed at several groups, calling out the their planetary names. "Those are three Tritons. That group over there includes Phaethons and Ledanites. And over there are some Metites, Deimosians, and Phobosians."

Then he grinned. "Yes, and there *are* a few Epiphanites and Earthlings moving about."

To me, most of them could have been humans from Earth. Other than their larger eyes, or pointed ears, or taller heights, they looked human to me.

I wanted to talk to all of them and hear their stories, but I followed Morph's orders and stuck close to our group.

We stopped at the red-roofed building on our right. The wooden sign next to the road read: Quiet Lady Inn.

"Thrud and I will be right back," Morph said. "Do not talk to anyone."

He and the half-orc entered the building while our group waited outside, just off Mudfog Lane.

By now, a red sky had risen over the eastern horizon, giving the town an eerie, crimson glow.

Across the street, I studied the Blue Boar Inn, a two-story structure with a blue roof. Two men dressed as pirates entered the building. Before you ask, they were *real* pirates, according to Andvari. When the front doors opened, we heard yelling and screaming, what the gnome called, "A blooody pirate party."

Viviana & Corwin

On the raised front porch of the inn, a tall woman and man waved at us. Without thinking, I waved back. The woman, who looked human, had silvery white hair, a red tunic with a grey skirt, and leather sandals with straps that wrapped up around her ankles and calves. She held a long saber in her left hand. The medieval, dark-haired man carried a round shield and a bow with arrow pouch over his shoulders.

"Ignore them," Balder said. "That is Viviana, a pirate, with Corwin, commander of the *Ringhorn*. We believe they might be loyal to the Extractor cause."

Andvari said, "Aye, Marster Hoonter, you can't trust any o' them blooody characters."

Just as I was about to talk to Eve, she turned to greet Morph and Thrud, who had emerged from the Quiet Lady Inn.

The seven-foot-tall half-orc guide took Balder and Lycus aside, opened a parchment map, and discussed the route through the Forest Primeval.

The three shook hands and Thrud held up his right hand and said, "Good journey, my friends."

He turned and walked toward Namo's Lighthouse.

I watched the sage stare across the street at Viviana and Corwin, who, after seeing Morph, quickly disappeared into the Blue Boar Inn.

Thrud

Morph led us back through the main gate and to the end of docks. He turned left in an easterly direction.

Soon, we found ourselves on the outskirts of Fog Harbor, at the edge of the Forest Primeval.

Our group walked in single file as we followed a winding trail that led us through a soggy marsh shaped by thickets of waist-high deer grass and tangled willows.

We hiked until we arrived at a fork in the trail. A wooden sign, nailed to a rotted cedar stump, read:

The sign's arrows pointed toward the southeast.

In single file, our group entered the meandering trail. Morph led the way, followed by Eve and me, then Andvari, Pendragon and the two half-orcs. From behind, the sage looked trim and fit, younger than his age. His green tail, curled up most of the time, protruded through the back of his black breeches. Emerging from two slits in his leather vest, his membranous wings remained folded on his back.

The red sky crept overhead, illuminating the fog, giving the landscape a surreal pinkish sheen. The smell of willows reminded me of my childhood adventures at a riparian stream near my Carmel home.

I soon forgot about Fog Harbor and studied the lush, prehistoric scenery. Giant cycads, tree ferns, ginkgoes, and lycopods framed the perimeter of the marsh. The plant life reminded me of the illustrations in the dinosaur books in our home library.

No matter how beautiful the scenery looked, I found it impossible to take my eyes off Eve. She seemed to glide over the trail with her incredibly long legs.

We arrived at a clearing, a green meadow with foot-tall grass waving in the breeze. Morph raised his upper left hand, stopping our group. He turned around and said, "Before we continue, I have gifts for Eve and Hunter."

The sage signaled to Balder, who ran to Morph holding a beige canvas sack. The half-orc untied the sack.

"Do you youngsters remember what I told you about keeping alert on your journey?"

Eve replied, "You told us paradise is an emotional state of mind, that the physical world is unpredictable."

I replied, "Just because this is paradise doesn't mean we can't be eaten."

"There must be physical challenges to life, or it is not worth living," Morph said with a stern look on his face.

The sage reached inside the canvas sack and pulled out a knife, a bow with arrows in a leather pouch, and a sword. He raised the weapons with all four hands.

"I shall bestow these protectors upon both of you before we enter the Forest Primeval, path to the Upperworld," Morph said, holding up a knife encased in a sheath. The handle sparkled with jewels.

"Eve, I want you to carry *Arthame*, the mystical knife. Use her wisely and she shall protect you."

The sage handed the knife to the Epiphanite.

She strapped the leather belt and sheath around her thin waist.

"Also, you mentioned your mastery of the bow and arrow; therefore, you shall have our finest bow, *Gandeeva*, hand crafted by the master archer, Arjuna."

Morph handed Eve an ashwood bow with a leather grip and a fur-lined leather pouch stuffed with painted, silver-tipped arrows.

"These are beautiful. I will treasure them," she said.

Eve slung the pouch of arrows over her left shoulder. She grinned at me, as I admired the jewel-handled knife hanging from her belt.

"Hunter," Morph said, "both Pendragon and I feel you are worthy of carrying the sacred sword, *Aroundight*. The ancient weapon of defense shall protect you on your Open Road journey."

I stepped forward and accepted the steel-bladed sword with the bronze, engraved handle. The gleaming blade displayed a gold Triangulum etched in the crafted metal. Held the sacred sword, grinned and said, "Awesome."

"Here are the scabbard and belt for *Aroundight*," Morph said, handing them to me.

Buckled the belt and slid the long sword into my scabbard. I admired the weapon hanging on my left hip. Now, I *looked* like a real Hero.

"Use them wisely," Morph said. "They must be used for defensive purposes only, never for aggression, anger, jealousy, or revenge."

"Understood," I said, clutching the leather-wrapped handle of my prized sword.

"One more item." The sage reached into the bottom of the sack. "Andvari tells me that you are quite the artist. This is for you."

Morph handed me a red leather loculus with a buckled shoulder strap. I opened the flap of the satchel and grinned. My own artist pouch. I reached inside the loculus and pulled out a quill, ink bottle and sheets of white parchment paper. The satchel included hand-crafted wood pencils, charcoal and a bone-handled pocket knife for sharpening the charcoal and lead.

I shook Morph's hand. Smiling, I looked at Eve, saying, "I'd like to draw your face."

She frowned. "Whatever you draw, it better *not* be my face."

I felt my cheeks turn red with embarrassment.

She did it again, I thought,

Eve

slinging the artist satchel over my head and left shoulder while I looked to the sage for moral support.

Morph winked at me and announced, "Follow me," leading our group down the winding Kukulcan Trail in a southeasterly direction.

Fog Harbor, the *Skipbladnir*, and Time Island had disappeared behind us in the primordial mist. The red sky peeked through the patchy fog, turning the prickly pine needles a salmon color.

Whenever the fog thinned, I gazed up at mountainous cliffs that reached for the crimson sky. The aromatic smell of pine trees reminded me of the Monterey pines outside my bedroom window.

After hiking one hour through the haze, a solid wall of towering trees appeared—giant sequoias. The trees stood much taller than the redwoods back home.

I smelled smoke, but saw no flames. I recognized the odor of burning wood.

"There they are," Pendragon said, pointing ahead.

Straining to see the trail ahead, I peered over Eve's shoulder and Morph's folded wings. Farther up the trail, two figures stood next to a campfire. The flickering fire silhouetted their short, stocky bodies. They waved. The sage waved back.

"Hello, Galar and Idun!" Pendragon shouted, startling Eve.

"They are the swamp elves, the guides that shall accompany us on our journey up the Crater Trail," Morph said.

Andvari moaned and spit on the ground. He told me that he and the swamp elves did not get along.

High-pitched squeals and laughter came from the two elves while they smothered the fire, kicking soil on the dying flames.

By the time our party entered the campsite, blue smoke rose from the smoldering coals.

"Ain't you all a sight fer sore eyes," Idun said. Her raspy voice matched her looks.

The swamp elve, two heads taller than Andvari, had dark, wrinkled skin. She wore a buckskin and leather outfit. A coonskin cap covered her black, tangled pigtails. They looked like frontiersmen—Daniel Boone or Davey Crockett.

Galar grinned. "Lookee thar, two lovebirds from outer space."

His voice sounded raspier than Idun's. The two swamp elves laughed hysterically at their own humor.

I grinned. Eve rolled her eyes.

Galar kicked more soil onto the smoldering fire. Dressed like Idun, he carried a knife in a buckskin sheath strapped to his belt. His scruffy, black beard hung to his waist. His beady brown eyes and reddish nose gave his wrinkled face a rugged, wild look.

"Please excuse Galar, he loves to joke around," Pendragon said.

"Aye," Andvari said, "a coople o' blooody misfits."

Galar gave Andvari a cold stare and looked at the sage.

"Golly wampus, you're lookin' fit as a fiddle, Morph."

"Thank you, Galar," the sage responded. "It is good to see you two again."

Pendragon raised his divine staff, pointing to the cliffs. "I shall scout ahead and make sure the trail is safe for our journey."

"Go ahead," Morph said. "We shall see you at Ogo Hole."

Before I could say goodbye, Pendragon sprang into the air. Leaves and dried brush swirled up and into the trees as the Utopian flapped his dragon wings and rose steadily into the foggy red sky.

I whispered to myself, "Look at that, a flying dragon."

After Pendragon disappeared above the tree line, Morph introduced Eve and me to the swamp elves.

Galar and Idun gathered their gear and our group resumed our journey on the Kukulcan Trail.

Andvari, normally happy and talkative, remained agitated and silent in the presence of the swamp elves.

After a seven-mile hike, our group stopped at a living wall of soldiered giant sequoias, the entrance to the virgin forest. A wooden sign, nailed to an abandoned, dilapidated wagon read:

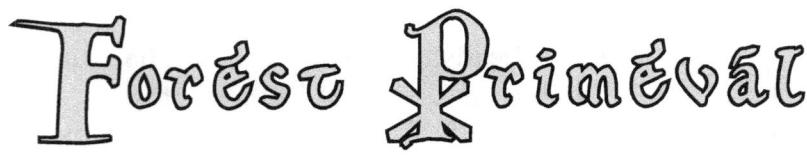

Forest Primeval

Our group entered the shadowy realm of the Forest Primeval. The gloomy woods devoured the Kukulcan Trail. The two elves hiked ahead of our group, scouting for any signs of danger.

The groves of ancient oak trees lining the trail made me feel uneasy. The twisted branches seemed to reach out and grab me while I hiked. Spreading tree roots seemed to trip me whenever I took my eyes off the narrow path.

The muddy trail snaked deeper into the dark Forest Primeval, toward the Crater Trail to the Upperworld. The dark forest gave me the feeling I had been swallowed by a wildwood monster.

The humid fog covered the twisted oak trees like a gloomy grey veil. Visibility, less than twenty yards, made me feel nervous, not able to see the surrounding landscape.

Morph used hand signals. No one spoke.

Besides crickets and frogs, unidentifiable animal cries erupted from the shadowed groves and thickets, causing me to flinch and grab my sword handle. I prayed we'd get out of the creepy woods soon.

Eve hiked with long, steady strides. The girl from Epiphany did not seem to tire, or perspire. The elves, who took two steps to every one of hers, did not seem fatigued from hiking. Andvari, unable to keep pace, had hitched a ride on Balder's shoulders.

Our group arrived at a clearing littered with fallen tree trunks, where the trail widened.

Morph held up his two right hands and said, "We shall take a break here," the sage said.

"Great idea," I told Eve.

We removed our backpacks and sat on a log.

Andvari joined us. "Aye, we'll soon be out 'o this blooody heat," the gnome said, wiping his forehead with a red handkerchief.

The half-orcs sat on their supply packs, swatting craterflies with their huge hands. Galar and Idun rested on two giant toadstools. Morph leaned against a hemlock tree on the opposite side of the trail, drinking from his leather water bag.

Placed my artist satchel on the log beside me, wiping the sweat from my face on my sleeve. I opened my canvas food sack and offered Eve a piece of my bread.

"Here, have some ambrosia."

She thanked me, taking a bite of moist bread.

It became difficult to eat the ambrosia. Pesky craterflies buzzed about our heads, darting on and off the honey bread. Other insects joined the attack. Many looked bizarre, especially the glowing bugs with blue, blinking bodies.

"Sorry about the pesky arthropods," Morph said. "Soon, we shall be out of this forest and you shan't have to tolerate them. We have but a few miles to go."

"Dang me, these 'er varmints ar' headin' fer a woopin'," Galar yelled, covering his stick of squirrel jerky from the diving craterflies.

The red sky bathed the primordial mist in a crimson hue. Charon Falls roared in the distance. Whenever the swirling fog parted, the sheer crater cliffs seemed to be falling on top of us.

The fragrance of pine trees reminded me of home—Tuesday evening—lying in my bed—wearing my father's gold necklace, the Triamulet—inhaling the fresh night air of Monterey.

Swallowed my last bite of ambrosia and drank amrita from my water bag. I felt confident enough to ask Eve a question when I noticed Balder and Lycus jump to their feet.

Both of them drew their wooden clubs from their belts. The half-orcs sniffed the air. Agitated, they circled in place, growling.

The swamp elves stopped whining about the insects, slid off the giant mushrooms and sniffed the air.

Andvari grabbed his spyglass and stood on the log, scanning the surrounding tree line. The wild cries from the Forest Primeval had abruptly stopped. A sudden crater wind bent the tree tops, causing the crimson fog to swirl in circles.

Eve grabbed my left arm and asked, "Is something wrong?"

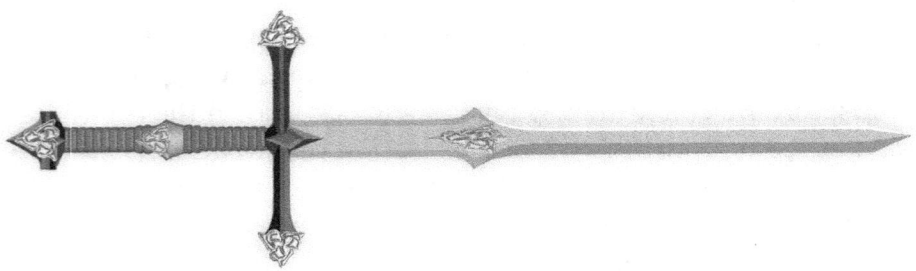

Chapter 11
Kukulcan Trail

Raising his scepter, *Joyease*, above his head, the sage stood in the middle of the Kukulcan Trail, signaling Eve and me, *get up, now.* Morph frowned, an expression I had never seen before. He gave hand signals to the half-orcs and swamp elves, who circled in place, agitated and sniffing the air.

Andvari slid off the redwood log and peered through his spyglass, yelling, "Hoot mon, the blooody fooog 'tis thick as porridge."

The drifting fog made it difficult to see the forest.

Before I sensed danger, bedlam broke out. Wild, crazy screams erupted from the surrounding fog forest.

"Hobgoblin pirates!" Morph shouted.

Jumping to our feet, Eve and I stood on the fallen log.

The sage flapped his wings and lifted off the trail—airborne.

Balder swung his club, intercepting three hobgoblins heading directly for Eve and me. The charging pirates were no match for the half-orc, who battered the hobgoblins senseless.

Two pirates, cutlasses drawn, attacked Lycus. The half-orc knocked them to the ground with his club. He grabbed both stunned hobgoblins by their knee breeches and slammed them against the trunk of a cedar tree, knocking them unconscious.

In front of us, a pirate attacked Andvari. The gnome held up his spyglass and deflected the pirate's blow, breaking the cutlass blade in two pieces. The ugly hobgoblin drew his dagger and lunged at Andvari, who fell backwards behind a log.

A pair of pirates attacked Galar and Idun from behind. Rolling over and over on the muddy trail, the two swamp elves used their sharp fingernails and teeth to scratch and bite the ambushing pirates. Galar scrambled to his feet and drew his hunting knife from his buckskin sheath. The curved, steel blade glistened in the eerie light.

Idun bit a piece of ear off her attacking hobgoblin. Spitting the chunk of bloody flesh at the fleeing pirate, she shouted, "Ya don't even taste gude, you rotten varmint!"

Eve loaded an arrow, pulled back the bowstring and released.

"Arrrggghhh," a hobgoblin screamed, grasping the arrow stuck deep in his thigh. Red blood dripped down the pirate's brown breeches as he limped into the forest underbrush.

I drew my sword, *Aroundight,* when I spotted a pirate waving his cutlass and running straight at me.

Eve screamed, "Look out!" as I braced myself and kicked the screaming pirate in the face. The bewildered attacker crumpled to the ground, his pointed nose broken and bleeding.

As he crawled away, a second pirate charged us. Instead of using my sword, I reacted by jumping off the log, twirling in midair, and roundkicking him in the side of the skull.

He landed flat on his back, dazed and groaning.

Eve shouted, "Hunter, your sword! Use your sword!"

I ran and stood over the pirate, raising *Aroundight* above my head.

He held up both of his hands and begged for mercy, "Sparrre me life."

Go ahead, Hunter, I told myself. *Kill him! Kill the pirate!*

I held the sword above my head, shaking. Seeing the terror in the hobgoblin's eyes, and hearing his pathetic voice, I hesitated.

I couldn't do it.

Lowering my sword, I pointed the blade in the pirate's face, shouting at the wounded hobgoblin, "Get out of here, now!"

He scrambled to his feet and scurried to the woods.

I jumped onto the log next to Eve.

She frowned at me. "You should have killed that filthy pirate when you had the chance."

Insulted, I frowned back at the Epiphanite, thinking, *I let the pirate go. I let him live. I think that's the right decision.*

From above, Morph descended on a pack of attacking pirates, kicking them firmly with his boots and clobbering them on their heads with his glowing scepter. The ambushing hobgoblins proved no match for the diving and swooping Utopian. Tormented by the flying sage, the pirates scattered and ran to the safety of the forest.

 Eve shot two more arrows at the retreating pirates. One hobgoblin took an arrow in the loin, through his waistcoat. The second pirate scurried into the forest with an arrow stuck in his tricorn hat.

Another bleeding pirate limped into the trees after Galar stabbed the hobgoblin with his hunting knife.

"Run, you filthy varmint, or I'll skin you alive!" Galar screamed, waving his blood-stained knife in the air.

The remaining pirates, sensing defeat, scurried into the shadows of the Forest Primeval.

Eve and I stood there, listening to the fading voices of hobgoblins retreating deep into the Forest Primeval.

Within a few moments, everything quieted down. I could hear the sound of Charon Falls in the distance.

Morph descended and touched down on the trail next to Eve and me. Galar and Idun washed off their cuts and gathered their scattered camping gear. Balder and Lycus walked the perimeter, making sure we were safe.

"Are you hurt?" I asked Eve.

"I'm fine."

She touched my hand. "You are shaking."

"I'm okay. I'm just pumped with adrenaline."

I slid my sword back into my scabbard and grimaced in pain. Eve gasped when she saw the blood stains on the left sleeve of my blue tunic.

"Hunter, you are injured."

Feeling weak, I sat down on a redwood stump.

Balder ran to me, inspected the cut and said, "The wound is not serious, Master Hunter."

I drank from my water bag while Balder attended to my arm. The half-orc poured amrita on the gash and dressed it with cloth bandages. The bleeding stopped the instant the mystical water cleansed my superficial wound.

With the pain tolerable, I felt better, especially after Eve expressed her concern for my wellbeing.

Rubbed my left arm and told Eve, "You're some archer with that bow and arrow."

"It comes natural. Archery is a way of life on Epiphany."

She drank amrita from her water bag and slung *Gandeeva* over her shoulder, asking me, "Where did you learn to defend yourself like that?"

"My parents took my twin sister and me to martial arts lessons since I was a kid. Back home."

Held my sword handle while I picked up my leather loculus.

"I must admit, I am impressed with the way you twirled in midair," she said.

Proudly stuck my chest out, enjoying her compliment. "Yeah, that's my Yop Chagi move."

Eve wrinkled her nose and shrugged her shoulders. I realized my Tae Kwon Do terminology confused her, so I remained silent, rubbing my injured shoulder. I scanned the surrounding forest, anticipating another attack.

"I've never seen hobgoblins dressed in pirate outfits, have you?" I asked, half-joking.

She did not grin. "I am certain we will see more strange creatures on this trip."

"Master Morph! Oh no!" Lycus shouted. "Look here!"

Eve and I turned, staring through the mist at Lycus.

The half-orc pointed behind a log.

Morph and Balder ran toward Lycus, as did the two elves with Eve and me following behind.

Eve looked behind the log and covered her mouth with her hand. Dark-red blood covered the forest floor.

Andvari's plump belly protruded through the bed of green sword ferns.

Lycus, fighting back tears, bent over and shook his ship mate's lifeless body.

With the pirate's dagger lodged deep in his chest, the gnome laid motionless.

I stood silent as the reality of death overcame me. Clenching my fists, I stared at Andvari's body.

Andvari can't be dead, I thought. *He's my friend. He wouldn't hurt a fly. This isn't supposed to happen.*

Balder bent down, lifted the gnome from the crumpled ferns and laid him on a flat boulder.

Morph walked over and placed his hand on Andvari's pale forehead, stroking the gnome's silver-grey hair. The sage knelt on one knee beside Andvari. He held the gnome's lifeless hand and mumbled something under his breath.

The sage stood, turned to Balder and said, "Gather some dry wood. We shall return our loyal companion to the universe."

While the half-orcs ran to gather wood, we stood silently around Andvari's lifeless body.

I felt grief, then anger, then fear, thinking, *This isn't what I bargained for. I could be killed myself. We need to turn around and get back to the safety of the ship. God, I feel like a coward. Eve will know I'm afraid. Morph promised me paradise, not hell.*

"Morph," I said, "we need to talk. Alone."

The sage motioned with his hand, *follow me,* and he walked me across the meadow. While we walked, Morph congratulated me on sparing the pirate's life, using the sacred sword as intended, for defensive purposes, not offensive violence.

I nodded, *thank you.*

Stopping in the knee-high deer grass, Morph asked, "My son, what is on your mind?"

Staring at the sage, my lips quivered. "I'm not ready to die at my age. I'm barely seventeen."

With his two left hands, Morph touched my right arm.

"Please, calm down. It is time I share the fourth Secret of Time & Space with you."

"How is another one of your Secrets going to help me?" I asked, wiping the sweat from my forehead with my sleeve.

Morph patted me on the right shoulder, calming me down.

Feeling the sage's positive energy, I took a deep breath. "Sorry. Go ahead. Tell me your Secret."

The sage grinned. "The fourth Secret is, 'All things happen in perfect order.'"

"You're telling me that Andvari's death is part of some perfect order, a grand plan?"

"Yes. His death also confirms the second Secret of Time & Space, 'Nothing happens by accident.'"

I rubbed my sore left shoulder. "Accident or no accident, perfect order or not, I'm afraid to die in this strange place, away from home, without my family."

"I understand your fear. But you have nothing to be afraid of. Death is your friend."

"A friend? I visited my dying uncle in a San Francisco hospital last month. Sam has lung cancer, from smoking. He was in a lot of pain, on life support, fighting for his life. He told us that he just wanted to die, that he didn't want to live any more. He was miserable."

"How sad, your Uncle Sam has lost his dignity."

"What do you mean?"

"I can only imagine that he is emaciated, bed ridden, depressed, and feeling helpless."

"Well, yes, but the doctors are doing their best to keep him alive, beat the cancer. My father keeps telling my uncle, 'Stay strong,' 'Don't leave us,' 'Fight for your life.'"

Morph shook his head in despair. "It is unfortunate that your society, your medical professionals, are trained to keep human beings alive at any cost, rather than allowing the dying to be comfortable, to die with dignity, to die when *they* choose to die."

"America has the best doctors and surgeons in the world."

"My son, according to your medical experts, doctors and nurses, death represents a total failure. Physicians and nurses are trained to keep people alive, no matter what the patient desires."

"Are you talking about suicide?"

"Call it what you will, every creature has the right to die, and with dignity, when and where they wish. I have been told by previous Earth visitors that on *your* planet, death is a negative experience to friends and loved ones. If a dying person tells a relative or friend they wish to die, the response is, 'Don't say that,' or 'Please don't leave me.' Just like your father begged your suffering uncle, 'Hang in there, don't leave us.' You have created a society where it is unacceptable to want to die; therefore, you cannot imagine anyone embracing death, actually wanting to die, looking forward to death, no matter what the person's circumstances or physical condition."

I raised my hands in the air. "All your words of wisdom are not going to help me right now. I have a bad feeling about my decision to stay on Millennium. I need to go back. Now."

"Anything you wish, my son. But first, I need you to understand death. You cannot understand it because you do not like thinking about it. Death scares you because you are unprepared."

"Death *is* scary, but I'm *not* a coward."

"Of course you are not a coward. You are simply unaware of the truth. As for your fear of death, you must never be afraid because there is nothing to be afraid of. Death is merely an illusion. Death is a door opened, not closed. You never really die. Life is eternal; you are immortal. Instead of dying, you simply change your form."

The fog had lifted, allowing rays of hazy light to enter the forest clearing illuminating the blades of yellow deer grass. I looked up at Charon Falls reaching for the blue sky, then turned and looked back at Andvari, lying peacefully on the boulder.

The sage said, "You must understand that Andvari was prepared for his new journey. He had no fear of death. His spirit, his soul, his Self, has been released from his Millennium body, like a butterfly emerging from a cocoon."

"You mean, he's gone to heaven?" I asked.

"Heaven has nothing to do with Andvari's view of death. Andvari has always lived in heaven."

"What are you talking about?"

"We shall discuss heaven another time. Can you grasp the reality that life is eternal, that your physical body is not you?"

"I'm trying to understand," I said.

"Good," the sage said. "Never be fearful of dying; there is nothing to be afraid of. Your personal energy, your divine spark, your Self, what you humans know as your soul, never dies."

"Are you talking about my soul going to heaven, or maybe hell?"

"I am always fascinated how you humans have become so obsessed with getting to heaven, and so fearful of hell. As I have promised, we shall discuss heaven and hell another time. Allow me to focus on death, the path of the soul, so you may understand your destiny, that all things happen in perfect order."

I listened to the sage while the half-orcs gather branches and twigs along the forest's edge.

"My son, nothing in the universe is permanent. All life is ever-changing, forever and ever. You are your spirit. You are not your body; therefore, the passing of your physical body should be of no concern to you. More importantly, you cannot live life without embracing death. When you become a true spiritual being, an enlightened being, death shall no longer frighten you. I want you to remember one thing. You are not your body."

"That doesn't make sense. Of course I'm my body."

"Allow me to give you the best possible example to help you understand you are *not* your body. You are spirit, first and foremost."

I nodded, *go ahead*, thinking, *I can't imagine the sage will be able to explain the mystery of death.*

"Do you remember when you were in grade school?" Morph asked.

"Yes."

"Can you remember how old you were when you realized you existed? When you were aware of your own, unique thoughts."

"Hmmm. Probably five or six. Maybe younger."

"Did you think like you do today. I am not talking about your intelligence, I'm talking about your awareness. That voice in your head that always talks to you."

"I know what you mean. Yes, I still think the same as I did when I was in the first grade. Now that I think about it, I knew it was me. And, I *still* sound the same to myself, I mean, I have the same voice in my head."

"Excellent. So, tell me, do you remember becoming a teenager?"

"Yes, of course. I was a lot older, and smarter."

"And what was your body like?"

"Much larger. More mature. You know, a teenager."

"And do you remember your body on your seventeenth birthday, just before you arrived on our planet?"

"Of course. What's your point?"

"Before I make my point, imagine I showed you a photograph of you when you were one year old, six years old, ten years old, fifteen years old, and one of you now. Then I asked you, 'Who are all these people?' I'm sure you would answer, 'That is me.'"

"That's obvious," I said, smirking. "So what *is* the point?"

"My point is, you have been in many different bodies since the day you were born, but all those different bodies were the same you. All you. Therefore, you are *not* your body. You are spirit."

Speechless, I knew the sage had made a undeniable point that I could not argue with. I *had* been in many different bodies, and all those bodies *were* me. What I mean is, I remember my thoughts, knowing it was me, inside each different body.

The sage said, "Although your body changes constantly, your spirit, essence and thought energy always remains the same."

"Say that again?"

"For instance, take someone your grandfather's age, who has been in many more bodies than you. He can *still* remember having the exact same thought awareness, the same spirit, being his unique Self, throughout his entire life."

"Okay," I said. "You've convinced me that I'm not my body. That I'm spirit. So, why I'm afraid to die? Can you help me to stop being afraid?"

193

"Your fear of death, all your fears, shall disappear when you embrace spirituality as part of your journey down the Open Road, The Great Way. When you realize and accept that you are not your body, death shall no longer bother you. Another way of putting it is, you shall dwell in a place that death cannot enter."

I looked down at the swaying deer grass, biting my lower lip. I glanced at Morph and said, "I'm so sorry for acting like a coward."

"Nonsense, my son. Your honesty has helped set you free. As you begin to understand yourself, you shall begin to understand the universe. When you experience peace within yourself, freedom within, you shall embrace death as part of your life. As we Utopians like to say, 'It is a great daynight to die.'"

I looked over my shoulder at Eve. She stared back at me across the clearing. The sage cleared his throat. "Now, let us turn around and get you back to the *Skipbladnir*, so you may return home to your family."

Grabbing the front of Morph's purple tunic, I closed my eyes and said, "Wait."

Letting go of the sage, I ran my fingers through my hair, wiping the sweat off my forehead. Taking a deep breath, I opened my eyes and looked up into the crimson haze.

Looking directly into Morph's eyes, I said, "I don't want to go back. I need to keep going forward. I'm sorry for causing you problems."

The sage nodded and said, "Our conversation has been a joy, not a problem."

Morph turned and walked toward our group. Calming myself, I followed him across the meadow, staring in awe at the raging waterfall and granite cliffs above me.

Rejoining my companions, I stood next to Eve.

Balder lifted Andvari's body, wrapped in white linen, from the boulder to the top of a wood pile. The wood logs, branches, twigs and dry grass had been stacked in a triangular pattern. Morph instructed our group to form a circle by holding hands.

I stood between Idun and Eve, reached out and held their hands. The swamp elve's hairy hand felt cold and clammy. Eve's hand felt warm and soft.

My heart beat increased as I squeezed the Epiphanite's hand. She did not respond, her grip remained relaxed, limp.

Come on, Eve, I thought, *squeeze my hand, please like me.*

Without warning, the wood pile burst into flames. The red, yellow and blue flames created intense heat, but no one broke the circle. My face felt hot, causing me to squint and look up into the Millennium sky. The smell of burning flesh and hair made my stomach upset. I felt like vomiting, but I controlled my gag reflex by holding my breath. My eyes watered as the belching black smoke swirled above the trees.

Eve began choking. Coughing, she gripped my hand, tightly.

Andvari's body soon incinerated, his gnomish bones turned to hot embers mixed with smoldering white ash.

Morph said, "All is well. Andvari has returned to the infinite cosmos. Our beloved friend lives on, forever."

Our group dropped our hands when Morph announced, "Gather your supplies; we shall continue our journey."

Turning to Balder, the sage said, "Make sure you retrieve Andvari's ashes so we may give our beloved companion a proper burial on the Sea of Circles."

The half-orc collected the gnome's ashes in a black clay urn and kicked soil on the smoldering fire.

My thoughts ran wild. *Calm down, Hunter, everything is going to be all right. You're lucky Morph didn't send you back to the ship. I hope Eve doesn't disrespect me. I'm not a coward like she thinks I am. I kicked that hobgoblin's ass. Maybe I should have killed that pirate, but his eyes looked so human, and when he spoke, I just couldn't do it. I can't believe Andvari is dead. Eve is so beautiful, but is she worth dying for, here on Millennium, 200 million light years from home?*

Morph gave the signal, *move out.*

Our group followed the sage down the trail, through the grassy meadow, and into the heart of the Forest Primeval. Under the panorama of the towering crater cliffs, filtered light penetrated the army of moss-covered conifer trees. The swamp elves scouted the winding Kukulcan Trail ahead. Watching for signs of another ambush, the half-orcs brought up the rear, looking for movement in the dark maze of twisted tree shadows.

Chapter 12
South Crater Trail

Having emerged from the dark Forest Primeval, our group had hiked another five miles up the steep, winding path to the end of the Kukulcan Trail. Below me, towering monkey-puzzle trees poked their prickly heads through the swirling sea of grey and white mist. The west wind, Zephyrus, blew a vaporous mist from Charon Falls into the crater sky. Wave after wave of water droplets gave birth to a vibrant rainbow—bands of red and orange and yellow and green and blue and violet.

To the east, five hundred miles away, the red and black lava of Fire Falls plummeted to the crater floor. Plumes of hot, volcanic vapors mixed with cool air rising from the Sea of Circles created the layer of perpetual fog.

From my five-mile-high vantage point, I spotted Time Island in the distance, staring back at me through the crawling patches of fog. For the first time, I saw the entire rim of the Discordia Crater that formed a three-hundred-sixty-degree circle.

Just like Morph said, it was a colossal crater in the middle of the planet.

The sage stood with Balder at the entrance to the crater trail, path to the Upperworld. Lycus guarded the bottom of the trail with Galar and Idun, who wiped sweat from their hairy brows. Morph pointed upward, discussing the route. Next to the sage, a sign had been chiseled in the granite rock.

South Crater Trail ⇗
Elevation: − 145 Miles Below Sea Level

I sat on a cypress stump, enjoying the blue sky and absorbing the rays of warm solshine on my face while I stared out across the vast Discordia Crater. It felt good to get out of the dreary fog. The air smelled fresh, like pure nature, like those times Father took us camping. Eve sat next to me, drinking amrita from her leather water bag. Lifting the v-neck collar to my blue tunic, I examined my shoulder wound. It was sore, but looked like it was healing. No infection.

The roar of Charon Falls, fed by the River Styx, made it difficult to talk. Morph had requested that we remain silent while hiking the treacherous Kukulcan Trail. Now that I *could* talk to Eve, the deafening noise from the raging falls made it necessary to shout.

Looking up through the arch in the rainbow, the South Crater Trail disappeared into the mist. The steep pathway seemed to climb forever as it hugged the crater wall. Chiseled from the sheer granite cliffs, the trail ascended in an easterly direction, away from Charon Falls, toward Fire Falls. The trail looked steeper and narrower than I had anticipated.

Have you ever been afraid of heights?

A war of emotions raged within me while I stared up at the crater trail ahead. *How was I going to hike that narrow trail on the side of that cliff? I was afraid of heights. Eve would know I was scared. For some reason, I believed she might laugh at me. I considered turning back while I had the chance, before I made a fool of myself, before I got hurt, or killed, or—*

Eve interrupted my negative thoughts. Over the roar of Charon Falls, she shouted, "I need to see your calendar!"

Opened my leather artist satchel. The top flap of the loculus had a Millennium calendar etched into the leather. Eve studied the calendar while she leaned over me. Her soft hair, black as a raven's wing, fell in my lap. Her ruby necklace sparkled in the solshine. I inhaled her pheromones. She smelled wonderful.

Pointing to the calendar, I shouted in Eve's ear, "What daynight did *you* arrive on Time Island?"

She pointed to the fifth of Aries, Daynight of the Monkey.

Pointing to the eighth of Aries, Daynight of the Crab, I shouted, "Here's when I arrived!"

Millennium Calendar

Aries ∞ Taurus ∞ Gemini ∞ Cancer ∞ Leo ∞ Virgo ∞ Libra
Scorpio ∞ Sagittarius ∞ Capricorn ∞ Aquarius ∞ Pisces

01 Daynight of the Dragon	02 Daynight of the Ram	03 Daynight of the Buffalo	04 Daynight of the Snake	05 Daynight of the Monkey
06 Daynight of the Lion	07 Daynight of the Goat	08 Daynight of the Crab	09 Daynight of the Crocodile	10 Daynight of the Dog
11 Daynight of the Bear	12 Daynight of the Butterfly	13 Daynight of the Bat	14 Daynight of the Spider	15 Daynight of the Wolf
16 Daynight of the Scorpion	17 Daynight of the Boar	18 Daynight of the Jaguar	19 Daynight of the Raven	20 Daynight of the Rat
21 Daynight of the Tiger	22 Daynight of the Frog	23 Daynight of the Rabbit	24 Daynight of the Shark	25 Daynight of the Beaver
26 Daynight of the Octopus	27 Daynight of the Horse	28 Daynight of the Rooster	29 Daynight of the Moose	30 Daynight of the Elephant

She nodded, *I know*, and she held up three fingers, pointing at me. I knew she meant that I had been on Millennium for three daynights. I grabbed a stick, scratched some figures in the loose soil, and realized I had been gone 150 Earth days.

Gone five months already! School had started and I'd missed the beginning of my senior year. I'd also missed my hiking trip to the Sierras with Kirk.

I told myself how this would all be worth it. I'd be famous when I returned to Earth. I'd be wealthy and could do whatever I wanted. Get rid of the stupid sports car Father bought me and buy myself a 4x4 sports utility vehicle, and a new guitar, and a new surfboard, and a new computer with upgraded graphics for my games and artwork. Yeah, I could buy all sorts of stuff.

"Ah-hemmm." Morph cleared his throat and yelled, "We have rested enough. We must begin our journey up the South Crater Trail. Gather your gear, we shall hike until the black sky is overhead."

Galar grumbled and yelled, "I reckon we'd better getta' move on 'afor them youngins commence to courtin' an' a sparkin'."

"Shut your yap," Idun yelled, placing her hairy hand over Galar's bearded mouth. "Quit your teezin'."

Eve and I scrambled to our feet, put on our gear, and lined up behind Morph. Lycus and Balder lifted the heavy canvas supply sacks onto their broad backs. We stood at a fork in the trail. Before us, a wooden sign read:

Place of Emergence

"What's *that* place?" I asked Morph.

The sage told our group to remain in place while he led me and Eve up the fork in the trail. He stopped and pointed to the gigantic cliffs ahead.

Fifty yards away, at the end of the trail, two arched doors made of brass and iron loomed on the face of the granite cliff. Each of the six-foot-wide doors displayed gold Triangulums. Two armored soldiers, Vanir giants, stood guard outside the entry.

Morph waved at the guards, who acknowledged our presence by raising their lances.

"The Place of Emergence is one of our most sacred caves," the sage said. "The bodies of all our Millennium visitors rest there until their return."

"What are you talking about?" I asked.

"Should either you or Eve decide to leave us and go to sleep on Time Island, your limp and spiritless body is taken to the sacred cave." Morph pointed to the copper doors.

"Are you talking about *this* body?" I asked, tapping my chest with my index finger.

"Yes. We take your Millennium body from Time Island to the sacred Place of Emergence, a cave leading to the vast Underworld. Your body remains there in a perfect, ageless condition, awaiting the return of your soul."

"What if I never come back here?"

"Your Millennium body dies when your Earth body perishes. Only your soul survives."

"And if I decide to return here? Let's say I die *here* of old age."

"Then, your Earth body dies when your Millennium body perishes."

"That means I would be in a coma for decades on Earth."

"Exactly. This is why many humans leave early. They do not want to return home and find their parents and brothers and sisters and friends long gone. Physically dead."

"Are you telling me that my father's body is in the Place of Emergence? That he's in *there* right now?"

"Yes, as is Professor Van Campbell's body, and all the other Earth visitors. Eve also has relatives in the cave."

Eve turned her head and looked at Morph, saying, "I will never be at rest in that cave because I will never leave Millennium."

Stunned, I rubbed my Triamulet between my fingers, contemplating the reality of being in two bodies on two planets, one alive and one in a coma. Returning to Earth meant my Millennium body would be laid to rest behind those brass and iron doors in that cave.

I tried to imagine *my* Millennium body lying next to my

father's body in a cave in the Underworld.

"Do you understand the Place of Emergence?" Morph asked me.

I nodded, *yes*, still stunned by the revelation that Father's body was but a short distance away. For some reason, I wanted to *see* my father's body, see what he looked like.

Wouldn't *you* feel the same way?

Morph led Eve and me back to the fork in the trail. He pointed skyward with the index finger of his upper right arm and said, "Up we go."

We began our hike up the South Crater Trail, having to climb another fifteen vertical miles before we reached our next destination, Ogo Hole, located at the Third Stratum, Realm of Utmost Darkness.

Still perplexed by the Place of Emergence, I tried to enjoy the solshine on my face while I listened to the distant animal cries from the Forest Primeval, five miles below us. Opposite us, condors with white feathers and bald red heads rode the thermals of the Discordia Crater.

Metamorphosis led our group in single file. The narrow South Crater Trail, engineered and built by cave elves, boggarts, knockers, and a team of giants with pack animals, averaged six to twelve feet in width. Not designed for two-way foot traffic, turn-out caves had been excavated along the trail every 300 feet. The higher the elevation, the stronger the crater winds blew. Charon Falls, miles behind us, no longer roared in our ears. The black sky crept steadily over the northwest rim of the crater.

Under a cloudless turquoise sky, Galar and Idun scouted ahead. To the rear, Balder and Lycus hiked behind me.

Ahead of me, Eve walked confidently, unaffected by the swirling winds and dizzying heights, some twenty-five thousand feet above the crater floor. I admired her confidence as she took graceful, steady strides.

Looking down into the abyss, I tried to calm myself. The ascending crater trail got narrower, and narrower, and narrower. Stepping cautiously, I sensed the trail might collapse under the weight of our group. During the ascending hike, rocks crumbled from the outer edge of the trail and plummeted straight down into the foggy abyss. The eroding trail looked twice as narrow from my sky-high vantage point. I felt as though I walked on the ledge of the world's tallest skyscraper. I knew the heights did not scare Eve. She grinned whenever she looked down.

Not only is she smarter than me, I thought, *she's braver. Morph has wings, he doesn't have to worry about falling off this narrow trail.*

When the trail narrowed to five feet wide, my fear of heights caused me to panic. With the wind whistling in my ears, I felt unstable—dizzy.

Negative images entered my mind. Numb terror overcame me. Couldn't get the negative thoughts out of my mind. *I'm going to fall,* I thought. *I'm going to die. Will I have a heart attack before I hit the bottom?*

Looked down at the trail's sharp edge, down into the abyss, and froze. I felt the color drain from my face as I immediately dropped to one knee and grabbed the side of the rock cliff with both hands.

I remember mumbling, "Please, we've got to go back. I can't do this, the trail's going to crumble, the wind's too strong. I'm going to fall. God, please, get me off this cliff."

Balder whistled. Morph stopped.

Eve looked back at me. I know she saw the fear in my eyes.

Breathless and embarrassed, I tried to act as if I had experienced heat exhaustion, not a fear of heights. Panicked, I dug my fingernails into the cracks of the cliff. Sweating profusely, my heart pounded in my chest.

Eve walked calmly back to me and put her hand on my left shoulder.

"Stop looking down," Eve said. "Look straight ahead. Keep your eyes on *me*."

Her words calmed me. She grabbed my sweaty hand and helped me to my feet.

"Stay right behind me; hold on to my arrow pouch." Eve turned and placed my hand on her leather pouch.

"Ready?" she asked.

I took a deep breath. "I'm sorry," I said, trembling. "I'm not good with heights. I don't know if I can do this."

She turned and looked into my eyes. "You *will* do this, Hunter. We are not turning back."

Told myself, *Look straight ahead. Don't let go of her pouch. Keep your eyes on Eve's arrows and try to relax.*

"Here we go. Watch me. Do not look down," Eve said, stepping forward.

I kept my right arm extended, grabbing her arrow pouch.

"Take it slow and easy," Morph yelled. "No talking."

Resuming our hike, I focused on Eve, following her up the trail in a southeast direction. My breathing relaxed while I walked behind the girl from Epiphany. Her black hair swayed back and forth in the swirling crater wind.

To my relief, six miles above the crater floor the trail finally widened. For the first time I could walk side by side with Eve and Morph. Hiking the wider path, I walked closest to the cliff walls, with the sage in the middle and Eve on the outside.

"We can talk now," Morph said.

Taking a deep breath, I said, "Sorry. I'm kind of afraid of heights."

"My son, I understand. The fear of falling is a human's worst nightmare. Soon, you shall grow accustomed to the heights and know there is nothing to fear on these solid granite cliffs."

I nodded, telling myself to believe in the wisdom of the sage.

The trail cut deeply into the crater cliffs, forming a rock bridge over a narrow stream of rapidly running water. When we had crossed the half-way point of the bridge, Eve pointed toward the center of the crater and said, "Look, hang gliders."

Two gnomes rode the thermals on gliders made of feathers.

Morph nodded. "We shall ride the gliders on our return trip to Fog Harbor."

"I'll have to think about that," I said, knowing that I had to somehow get over my fear of heights.

A wave of apprehension swept through me while we hiked the trail. *Why was I so afraid of dying? I never used to think about death back home. Maybe I'm afraid of—*

"Is something else on your mind?" Morph asked, interrupting my thoughts.

"Can I ask you something?"

"Certainly," Morph said.

"I have a question about the Discordia Crater," I said, as the gusting winds blew my hair in all directions.

Morph nodded, wiping the perspiration from his forehead with his purple handkerchief.

"You said that an Extractor Asteroid from the Dark Star hit the Earth and spread the emotional virus."

"Correct. In fact, your crater and this crater were formed about the same time."

"How is that possible?"

"The Dark Star's orbit was located half way between Earth and Millennium when the supernova exploded."

"When did the asteroid hit the Earth?"

"About fifty thousand Earth years ago."

"That can't be the asteroid that killed off the dinosaurs. It crashed about sixty million years ago."

"I believe you named your asteroid's impact area the Meteor Crater."

"Is that the one in Siberia?"

"No. Earth visitors have told me that the asteroid has created an enormous crater in the southwestern section of your beloved United States of America."

Grinning, I said, "Oh, I know. The Meteor Crater is in the Arizona desert. It is called the Barringer Crater. My father calls it the Diablo Canyon debris field. He goes there a lot."

"I have another question," I said. "It's about death."

The sage motioned, *go ahead.*

"How will I know if my Earth body dies?"

"You shall feel it, deep in your soul. Believe me, you shall know immediately if this event happens."

"You never told me that."

"You never asked."

"I need to start asking more questions."

"Wise decision, my son."

I scratched my head, contemplating the sage's explanation.

"Let me repeat," Morph said, "when you go to sleep on Time Island, only your soul, along with your Triamulet, travels the Astral Highway."

"Then, where does my soul go when I return?" I asked. "You know, if I'm dead on Earth?"

"Where it always goes. All souls exist in the Spirit World. *Both* your bodies shall eventually die. But your soul lives forever."

"Now," Morph said, "we must continue our hike upward."

"Wait." I stopped and reached inside my tunic and pulled out my Triamulet. "Where does *this* go if my Earth body is dead? Does my medallion travel with my soul?"

"I am impressed with your logical thinking. Without the Earth body available, the Triamulet always materializes at the original connection point of the Astral Highway. For Earth, this would be your Meteor Crater in your beloved United States."

"Why at the meteor site?"

"Triamulets are made from the astral gold, *Prima Materia,* found at all the Extractor Asteroid impact craters. No other metal will work. Eve's planet, Epiphany, mines their astral gold from the Alphonsus Meteor. That is the crater impact site where Epiphanites mine the precious metal to make *their* Triamulets."

At that moment I realized *why* Father and Professor Van Campbell were always traveling to Arizona to visit the Canyon Diablo debris field located at the Meteor Crater site.

Staring at the Triamulet between my fingers, I said, "So, if I'm alive in a coma on Earth when I return home, this medallion and chain materializes on my neck again?"

"The instant you awaken."

I dropped my Triamulet and chain down the v-neck collar of my tunic and continued walking with Morph. "It does make sense, my soul being in *this* body. I'm beginning to understand."

"The sage held up his lower right arm. "We shall continue our discussion later. Now, we must hike several more miles before the zenith of the black sky."

The crater trail narrowed and Morph yelled, "Single file."

Eve ran ahead of me, turned her head and said, "Remember, keep your eyes on *me*."

As beautiful as she was, that was easy to do.

Andromeda constellations carved their sparkling formations into the pitch-black sky. The streaking white tails of comets and shooting stars disappeared beyond the rim of the Discordia Crater while three moons illuminated the cliffs.

Twelve miles above the crater floor, we had stopped to set up camp in Embryo Grotto, a shallow cave sheltering us from the gusty winds. Galar and Idun made a fire. The red and yellow flames sent popping sparks swirling into the black sky.

Eating our evening meal of citrus fruit, hemp seeds, ambrosia, and salmon jerky, we enjoyed the warmth of the campfire on our faces. I felt confident I had overcome my fear of heights. With Eve's help, I no longer caused our group to slow down, or stop. Really felt confident I could make it all the way to the top of the Discordia Crater.

The Epiphanite sat to my left, peeling the skin from a juicy orange, guarding her silence. Swallowing several gulps of amrita, I stared at the starry night sky.

Pointing up at the constellations, I asked Morph, "Where is the Sun?"

"Do you mean the Earth's daystar?"

"Yeah, our Sun."

Morph chuckled and said, "Sorry to disappoint you. Your Sun is too far away to see with the naked eye."

"How far?"

"Your daystar is more than 200 million light years away."

I grinned and looked at Eve. "Wow, I traveled all that way through space."

Eve glanced at me, so I continued bragging.

"I know most of the constellations, how the stars align in the heavens," I said, pointing at the river of sparkling stars above us. "I own a huge telescope. I know the twelve zodiacs, the horoscopes."

"Horoscopes?" Eve asked, her tone impatient.

"Yeah, sun signs. I was born in July, so my sign is Cancer."

Morph raised his upper right hand. "My son, your birth sign, your zodiac sign as you refer to it on Earth, is actually Gemini."

"No, that's wrong, I'm the sign of the crab."

"Unfortunately, your sun signs were invented over two thousand Earth years ago; therefore, all the constellations have moved, shifted one full Earth month. You are a Gemini, based on the star locations in your Milky Way."

Eve rolled her eyes while I thought about being a Gemini. *Hmmm, maybe that's why I'm a twin!*

I blushed. "Okay, sorry I brought up horoscopes. They don't matter anyway, because these Andromeda constellations are totally different, since I'm not in the Milky Way any more."

"So, what are the Earth horoscopes for?" Eve asked.

"The zodiac sign you're born under determines your future, your destiny."

"Do you believe the astrology signs indicate your true destiny?" Morph asked.

"Nah, I know better, My destiny is already decided."

"By whom?"

"A higher power."

"May I offer you a different possibility?"

"Sure, go ahead," I said.

"Many humans believe their destiny is completely out of their hands. They think they have no control whatsoever regarding their fate. Humans have two different views of destiny, both incorrect. Billions of humans are convinced that a higher power determines their fate.

Eve sighed, raising her hand. "Morph, is there something besides horoscopes and destiny by a higher power we can talk about?"

I shrugged my shoulders and said, "Okay, I'll shut up. My thoughts are a little scattered."

The sage grinned. "Speaking of thoughts, perhaps we should discuss the power of thought, it shall help you understand your destiny and how you control it."

"Tell me about the power of my thoughts," I said, chewing on a piece of salmon jerky.

"Allow me to enlighten you, my son."

Morph drank amrita from his leather water bag and began the philosophical discussion.

"As you might recall, I promised to explain the third Secret of Time & Space, that is, 'Thoughts are the most powerful force in the universe.' Our thoughts are like radio signals. They send out energy waves like a transmitter. Thought energy. These signals travel out into the vast universe. Right now, the thoughts we are having meet halfway between us. The air, the space between us, is filled with this thought energy, like a matrix, or grid. Do you feel the energy?"

"Thoughts are the most powerful force in the universe."
—Metamorphosis

"Yes, I think I *do* feel the energy in the air," I said.

Morph nodded. "The closer you are to another person, the more intense the energy."

I glanced at Eve. She did not acknowledge me.

"Thoughts have tremendous power," Morph said. "They are pure energy, lasting forever. Forever is happening right now. All thoughts transmit an energy; this energy is known as thought force and—"

I interrupted, "My deep thoughts are pure energy?"

"Not just deep thoughts. *All* your thoughts. These include your inner dialogue, the constant chatter in your head."

"Chatter?"

"Yes, your self-talk. All intelligent life forms talk to themselves."

"I don't talk to myself. Only crazy people talk to themselves."

Eve frowned at me and said, "Shhh."

I motioned to Morph, *continue.*

"In fact, throughout the universe, primitive beings average one thought every two seconds, that is thirty thoughts per minute and 1,800 thoughts per hour, totaling 43,200 thoughts per daynight. On Earth, human beings have a thought almost every second, and most of the thoughts are negative."

I could hear myself thinking at that very moment.

"Right now, as I speak, *your* thoughts are running wild. The more primitive the creature, the more thoughts per minute. The thoughts of primitive beings are quick, scatter-brained and confused, mostly negative. In contrast, enlightened beings average one pure thought per minute. Their positive thoughts are focused, not scattered."

"Why are human thoughts so negative?" I asked.

"An emotional virus, prevalent in primitive societies, causes negative thinking."

"But *my* thoughts aren't that negative."

Morph lowered his chin, raised his eyebrows, and grinned.

"Okay, I guess I do talk to myself a lot," I said. "Maybe some of my thoughts are a little negative."

"I shall discuss negative thinking in a moment. Allow me to continue with the power of thought."

"Sorry for interrupting," I said.

Balder and Lycus stood outside the mouth of the cave guarding the trail while shooting stars blazed across the night sky. The fire crackled, sending orange and yellow sparks into the air. The smell of the fire reminded me of my camping trips to Yosemite National Park with my family.

"Every thought you have ever had never dies," the sage said. "Thoughts are pure energy; they last forever. Once your thought energy leaves your body it begins its journey outward into the vast cosmos, traveling forever. Thoughts know no distance and never perish."

"Wow, that's hard to imagine."

"Thoughts comprise the most irresistible living force in the universe. As living things, they have substance: shape, form, and color. Your thoughts travel faster than light."

"Light travels at 186,000 miles per second," I proudly announced, glancing at Eve.

The Epiphanite remained expressionless.

Morph responded, "Thoughts travel in no time. Infinite speed. Faster than you can say the word. Thoughts travel by ethereal vibrations."

"Ethereal?" I asked.

"Do you know what ether is?"

"No."

"Ether is the medium that transmits light, electricity, and heat, among other things. Think of it as the air itself, the ether of space. Ether is also the medium through which our thoughts travel through space and time. Thoughts are finer than ether. Like a glowing candle sending out ethereal vibrations of light and heat waves in all directions, our minds transmit vibrating thought waves in all directions. We are surrounded by a universal sea of thoughts. We absorb some, and reject some. Thoughts are transmitted from creature to creature, creating a universal World of Thought. Or, as we like to call it here on Millennium, the World of Self."

"Can my thoughts reach my mom on Earth?"

"They already have, faster that you can say the word."

"I've been thinking about Mom a lot."

"Good, she feels and senses your thoughts."

I grinned, watching the campfire's flickering flames cast shadows on the fissured rock walls. The smell of burning wood reminded me of our fire place at home.

"Nothing occurs in your life, no thing, which is not first a thought. Thoughts are your life magnets, drawing positive or negative effects to you. Our thoughts never die, even when we cease to be. All that is and ever was is but a thought away. When a thought, good or bad, crosses your mind, it creates vibrations that travel around the world and then out into space, into the universe. Thoughts travel faster than light, infinite speed, entering the minds of others and producing similar thoughts. For instance, a creature with hateful, jealous or violent thoughts sends out those negative vibrations, which in turn, enter the minds of millions of other creatures, stirring up the same negative thoughts. Good thoughts help others, bad thoughts harm others. It is that simple."

The sage grinned. "Thoughts change the world. They can work wonders. Heal the sick, cure depression, create miracles. When your thoughts are noble, loving thoughts, their vibrations enter all sympathetic minds. They send out similar thought vibrations, resulting in pure love."

I sipped amrita from my water bag as a blazing comet with a streaming white tail streaked across the black sky.

"Thoughts create this world, every world. Thought brings everything, every *thing*, into existence. Thoughts are like objects. Just as you can hand Eve an apple, you can also hand her your powerful thoughts. And guess what?"

"What?"

"Without speaking, she can hand those same powerful thoughts right back to you. This is, in fact, telepathic in nature."

"Like attracts like."
—*Metamorphosis*

I looked at Eve and grinned.

She nodded her head at the wise sage.

"Thoughts pass between and among all creatures. A creature of powerful thoughts can influence a creature of weak thoughts. When you learn to control your thoughts, you shall become as one with the Source, and the universe. As the greatest force in the universe, thoughts are the most powerful weapon in the armor of a Utopian."

"Powerful weapons?"

"This is why you must be careful with your thoughts, my son. Every thought you think always comes back to you. If you send hateful thoughts, hate shall come back to you. When you think and send loving thoughts, love shall come back to you. This brings me to the fifth Secret of the Universe."

"The fifth?" I asked.

"Do you remember the four Secrets I have bestowed upon you so far?"

I felt my expression change when I tried to recall the first Secret of Time & Space and I couldn't.

"Hunter, they are easy to remember," Eve said. "One, 'Like attracts like.' Two, 'Nothing happens by accident.' Three, 'Thoughts are the most powerful force in the universe.' Four, 'All things happen in perfect order.'"

"Yeah, maybe for *you* they're easy," I said, frowning, realizing the Epiphanite made me look stupid again.

"Do not worry, my son, you shall soon learn, and live, the ten Secrets, the Universal Laws."

"You get what you think about whether you want it or not."
—Metamorphosis

The fire cast shadows on the sage's face while gusts of wind whipped more red sparks into the night sky.

"The fifth Secret of the Universe is, 'You get what you think about, whether you want it or not.'"

I glanced at Eve and said, "I get it. Whether my thoughts are negative or positive, they will come true."

"Correct," Morph said. "Your thoughts manifest your destiny. Think you are worthless; worthless you shall become. Think you are ugly; ugly you shall become. Think you are patient; patient you shall become. Think you are loving; loving you shall become. If all creatures lived by the fifth Universal Law, it would change their lives immediately. Unfortunately, the emotional viruses cause chaotic, negative thinking. Dysfunctional creatures, like the Extractors, cannot control their own thoughts. They always behave out of control. They reject the Secrets of Time & Space. Speaking of Secrets, now is an excellent moment to tell you. There is a secret about the Secrets."

I frowned. "What do you mean?"

"Getting what you think about whether you want it or not has never been a secret to enlightened beings. The ten Secrets, the Universal Laws, are not mysteries, they are simply the highest truths. These truths are the supreme physical, Universal Laws. All enlightened beings live by these laws."

"Then, why do you keep calling them the Secrets of Time & Space?"

"I use the term secret for my guests visiting from primitive civilizations."

"You mean, Earth?"

"Yes. Primitive beings that live in primitive civilizations are unaware or refuse to accept the basic Universal Truths. They live in darkness."

"Why don't they accept the truth?"

"Their thoughts are infected by the *Extractor Virus*, the Dark Essence They cannot think straight, logically."

Chirping spiderbats darted outside the cave entrance as I tried to imagine who on Earth had the emotional virus.

"But I tell you this. Just as darkness cannot stand before the light, the dark thoughts of these low self-esteem invaders, the Extractors, cannot stand before the light of positive thoughts."

"What's the *Extractor Virus* got to do with thoughts?" I asked.

"Everything. The emotional viruses infect a creature's thoughts and cripples their mind. This is how the viruses spread, from creature to creature, through ethereal vibrations, creating an epidemic, a collective consciousness of ego-driven, negative thought waves.

"As I have mentioned, on your planet most humans experience more than 40,000 thoughts per day. Of those thoughts, nine out of ten are negative. Negative! Is it any wonder that your society, your world, is in such a state of confusion and decline? When primitive beings interfere with The Great Way, the sky becomes filthy, the world becomes depleted, the equilibrium crumbles, the creatures become extinct."

"Nothing happens by accident."
—Metamorphosis

Listening to the crater wind whistle by the cave entrance, I closed my eyes and thought about the behavior of humans, that people *were* greedy and selfish. They kept destroying the environment. The world was always at war. My intuition told me that things were getting worse on Earth.

"When love is the like thought, the shared thought, miracles happen. When humans share a collective consciousness of negative and fearful thoughts, bad things happen."

"You mean, bad birds of a feather flock together?"

"As I have told you, like attracts like. Your planet's salvation shall occur only when people share unconditional love. Loving thoughts. The perfect message, 'All you need is love,' has been ignored or misunderstood by the majority of human beings."

"Why are humans so negative?" I asked.

"As I just told you, because the contagious viruses have infected your primitive minds, your fragile egos. Although born from perfection, your youthful thoughts have been altered by your parents, teachers, politicians and leaders, all of them infected with the emotional virus. You are made to believe everything but the truth."

"Lies?"

"Worse than lies, you are taught to never think for yourself, to never trust your own thoughts. As I have said, thought waves are extremely contagious. The prime example is the pandemic emotional virus, the Earth's epidemic, the contagious Dark Essence brought on by the *Extractor Virus*."

"Contagious like the flu?"

"Highly contagious, like an emotional cancer. When you think a negative thought of anger or revenge or jealousy, you produce a similar thought in those who surround you. Your moods infect others. Your diseased, low-self-image thoughts leave your mind and they enter the minds of the people nearest you; then, the minds of others far away, on the other side of the world, on the other side of the universe. Positive, cheerful thoughts within your mind work the same way, producing positive thoughts in others. Good thoughts are extremely contagious, traveling great distances. Great minds think alike."

"Doesn't good always overcome evil?" I asked.

"Good versus evil is merely an attitude, a state of mind. When you suffer from low self-image, when you lack enlightenment, there is a constant battle in your mind between two hungry wolves. A good wolf and a bad wolf. Do you know which wolf wins this battle?"

"Hmmm, I don't know. Who wins?"

"The wolf you feed."

"If I think positive thoughts and not feed the bad wolf, I'll be happy?" I asked.

"Yes, it is that simple. Please remember that good and bad do not exist in the universe. Your imagination makes it so. Your mind creates the world of good and bad, happy or unhappy, according to your own thoughts. In other words, nothing can make you happy, happiness *is* the way. Your mind, your total intelligence, exists within each of the millions of cells in your physical body."

"But, my mind is in my head," I said, tapping my right temple.

"Your *brain* is in your head, your skull, not your mind. Your mind exists within all your cells."

"Every cell?"

"Every single cell in your body is endowed with intelligence. Every thought you have is conveyed directly to your cells, reacting to your present state of mind. When you are confused or depressed, your thoughts transmit a negative message throughout your nervous system to every cell in your body. Your cells become weak; they can no longer function properly. You soon suffer from physical weakness and diseases. Your intelligent cells, experiencing unhappiness and hopelessness, produce inharmonious vibrations. The mind of each intelligent cell fills with fear and anxiety."

"All things happen in perfect order."
—Metamorphosis

Galar leaned against the cave wall, puffing on his dragon-bowl pipe. The smell of tobacco in the cave air reminded me of my father's cigars. Idun sat next to him, whittling a piece of wood with her hunting knife.

Morph signaled to Galar, *bring more water.*

"If just one thought cell in your brain becomes infected with the emotional cancer, it spreads to all the other thought cells and eventually your entire thought process is destroyed. You die emotionally. Your cancerous emotions eventually kill your physical body. Mental health is more important than physical health. Intelligent beings produce powerful chemicals based on thoughts alone."

"Chemicals? Like adrenaline?"

"Adrenaline is one. Our glands secrete chemical messages. I shall not name all the various hormones, they are unimportant for our discussion. The reason I mentioned chemicals is that they determine your health and happiness."

Morph brought his upper right and left hands together, forming a triangle with his thumbs and index fingers. "I ask you to memorize this mantra."

I nodded, thinking, *I've always been bad at memorizing. I hope I can remember what he's about to say.*

The sage said, "Positive thoughts, release positive chemicals, creating happiness."

I said, "Positive thoughts. Positive chemicals. Happiness."

The sage raised his hands and looked at me through the triangle. "A triad. Positive thoughts cause your mind to release positive chemicals, resulting in happiness. It is a cycle. Positive thoughts, to positive chemicals, to happiness. Happiness produces more positive thoughts and the cycle continues. A happy mind results in a happy and healthy body. Unfortunately, unhappiness rules your planet. Negative thinking causes negative chemicals, toxins that attack the body resulting in unhappiness. Unhappiness results in more negative thinking. An endless cycle of misery, depression, and illness."

"Do you mean sickness?"

"Physical illness is a result of negative thoughts."

"I hate when I'm sick. Do you ever get sick?"

Morph shook his head, *no.* "Only when we are sick of our sickness shall we cease to be sick. The sage is not sick but is sick of sickness. This is the secret of health. To think a sick thought is to allow illness to arrive."

"Then, we make ourselves sick?"

"If you have a happy mind, you shall have a happy body. A healthy mind promotes a healthy body. All your human illnesses and depressions and anxieties and fears come from negative thoughts. In fact, stress does not exist in the universe, only you thinking stressful thoughts."

"I'm always stressed out about something. How can I stop thinking negative thoughts?" I asked.

"Ahhh, that is the question I have waited for you to ask."

I grinned, feeling I had impressed the sage.

"Before I answer your question, please remember that all evil thoughts form a triad of negative energy. First, they harm the thinker. Secondly, they harm the creature being thought about. Third, they harm all creatures by filling the ethereal realm, the air between us all, with negative energy. A triple curse. When you radiate thoughts of revenge, you injure the person to whom you direct the hateful thoughts. It is, in fact, your own suicide, for the revengeful thoughts come back to destroy you. As you humans so wisely say on Earth, 'What goes around, comes around.'"

I frowned, not sure how to respond.

Morph paused while Galar pushed Idun out the cave entrance. Agitated and shoving each other, the fighting swamp elves had to be separated by the half-orcs.

"To answer your question," the sage said, "the way to stop your negative thoughts, your stinking thinking, is to catch yourself thinking a negative thought. During your internal conversations, when you talk to yourself and hear yourself think a negative thought, *stop,* and immediately tell yourself, 'Stop. I'm not like that,' or 'Stop. That's not like me.' Then, immediately exchange the bad thought for a positive one. Your life changes that instant. Changing your thoughts changes your life."

"What's a good, positive thought?"

"The best ones are affirmations."

"I've heard of those. What do they sound like?"

"They come from within. An affirmation is what you believe to be true, now, not in the future. You cannot think, 'I want happiness,' you must think, 'I *have* happiness.' 'I am happy.' Appropriate affirmations are, 'It is easy for me to control my emotions.' 'All things come into my life at just the right time.' 'My present thoughts determine my future.' 'I deserve love.'"

Loud, high-pitched voices came from outside the cave. The

swamp elves argued, spitting at each other. Balder picked up Idun and Galar by their buckskin collars and carried the yelling swamp elves down the trail, out of sight.

"Please excuse our guides' behavior," Morph said, staring at the cave entrance.

Ignoring the ruckus, I asked, "You're telling me that by saying those phrases, affirmations, my life will change?"

"Absolutely. Affirmations force you to think positive thoughts. You must believe the affirmations to be true. Affirmations are energized messages to the universe. Your positive thoughts become reality. You always get what you think about."

Morph raised his white eyebrows. "My son, your happiness is a thought away. Freedom is but a thought away. Physical health is just a thought away. Contentment and bliss are a thought away. Another person's love for you is but a thought away."

I looked at Eve and blushed. "That sounds too good to be true."

She lowered her black eye lashes, ignoring me.

Morph wrinkled his forehead. "Does the thought of being constantly happy sound unattainable?"

"How do you know whether I'm happy or not?" I asked.

"I *do* know."

"No way, you can't read my thoughts. Can you?"

Morph pointed at me. "No, but I can read your face, your eyes."

I glanced at Eve, who stared back at me, irritated.

Moths with gold and purple-spotted wings fluttered around the crackling fire. The silhouettes of unidentifiable night-flying creatures streaked across the three moons.

"What does my face say?" I asked, smirking.

"My son, it is not important that I read your face this evening. I only wish to remind you that every thought a being thinks is instantly etched into their face and can be seen in their eyes. Over the years, negative thoughts, like a chisel on stone, cut grooves in their face. It does not take long for the face to be covered with scars, deep wounds caused by the vicious thoughts of anger, revenge, jealousy, hatred, racism, and fear. These scars tell us the being's state of mind."

"I'm not sure if I believe that."

"Maybe an example shall help. A happy, positive thought brightens the face. Negative thoughts darken the face. All creatures feel opposing energies; they know the difference between a smile and a frown. Facial expressions are true indicators of your inner state of mind. Your face reveals the truth about your thoughts. Your thoughts produce emotions, which in turn produce strong impressions on your face. Your thoughts are not as secretive as you humans imagine."

I wondered if my face showed how upset I was at that moment.

"Eyes are the window to the soul. The eyes telegraph messages of hatred and fear, as well as messages of love, peace, and harmony. Learn to read the signs on a face and you can read thoughts."

Morph grinned. "Whatever creature believes he can hide his thoughts is an innocent fool of the first order."

Holding up my right hand, I said, "Okay, I've heard enough about thoughts. I get it."

"Get what, my son?"

"That I can change my life by changing my thoughts."

"Excellent, well said. As you think, so you become. As within, so without."

The sage stood and stretched his arms and wings. "I suggest we retire for the evening. Tomorrow, Daynight of the Bear, we must arrive at Ogo Hole by the zenith of the red sky. Pendragon shall meet us there."

Morph looked at me and said, "Become the knower of the truth, my son."

The wise sage walked to the edge of the crater trail and sat, motionless, in a full lotus position with his four arms lifted to the night sky. The swirling winds blew his white hair and beard back and forth to the rhythm of the night.

With an exhausted sigh, Eve laid back and pulled the beige blanket over her body and closed her eyes.

I quietly pulled off my black boots and looked down at my torn, blood-stained blue tunic. Reached inside my backpack for new clothes. Draping a gold silk tunic over the backpack for the morning, I sat on my bedroll and gazed out into the Millennium night, admiring Fire Falls, the great southern landmark, 450 miles to the east. Her glowing, red-hot lava flowed down the face of the southern crater cliffs.

Morph returned to the cave, laid on his bedroll, and covered himself with his grey wool blanket.

While the half-orcs stood guard, we huddled in a circle, enjoying the warmth of the fire. Eve rolled over and pulled her blanket up and over her head. Galar and Idun, finally asleep, snored in opposite rhythms.

Morph's leather boots sat upright by the fire. The tip of his green tail stuck out from under his grey blanket.

I could not sleep. Thinking about the philosophical discussion on the power of thoughts kept me awake. I admit, the curve of Eve's body under her beige blanket became a distraction.

Restless, I grabbed my artist satchel and pulled my bedroll next to the bright flames. I sharpened the lead of a wooden pencil with my pocket knife and took out a piece of white parchment paper.

Listening to the whistling wind blow past the cave entrance, I moved the pencil across the page. Imagining all the fantastic landscapes and creatures I had encountered so far, I decided to draw Morph's entire body.

Domain of Purcas
Keeper of Saxum,
the Madstone

River of Ice

House of
Cold

Gjoll
River

Echoing
Bridge
Gjallarbru

Northern Deep Sea

Great Northern Grotto

Fimbulthul
River

Erlik's Pri.

Snow
Catacombs

Place of Xiuhtecutli
First Lord of the Night

Centrum Terrae

Dungeon
of Ice

Ice Falls

Cocytus

imirs
alls

Svol
River

Cocytus

Manitou
Falls

Tricinus

Crater
Tunnel
Loop

Fjorm
River

Ea

Domain of Ex
Keeper of Malum,
the Extractor Talisman

Eastern
Deep Sea

Great
Eastern
Grotto

Cavum Crystallus

Crystallum Cave beneath Time Island Obelisk

Erawan
Falls

Leipt
River

Discordia Crater

Cave of
Daydreams

Green Room

Ea
Ext
P

Elevation: ~ 150 miles
Below Sea Level

Emerald
Falls

Lupercal Cave •

Place of Emergence
• Embryo Grotto
• Ogo Hole
• Den of Shadows

Fire Falls

Vid
River

• Tartarus

Nudd Tunnel

Bridge of the Separator

Mira Tunnel

Telos

#Portal of
Metamorphos

Lis Ard

Black
River • Knockmaa

Dungeon
of Fire

Shamballa •

Isle of the Blest

Bridge of the
Secret

Lava Caverns

Lake
Avernus

Chicomoztoc

Avernus •

Woden's
Passage

Caves
Naga

Southern Deep Sea

Pools
of the
Three Graces

Great Southern Grotto

Tartarea
Regna

McDougal's
Caves

Gunnthra
River

Slid
River

Montesino's
Caves

House of
Fire

• City of Dis

Mira
Tunnel

River of Fire

Arnhein

River
Phlegethon

• Palace of
Hades

Caves of

DAYNIGHT OF THE BEAR

Aries the 11th
Year of the Dragon

"Therefore, the sage knows himself
but makes no show of himself;
loves himself, but does not exalt himself.
The sage prefers what is within to what is without."
—Metamorphosis

Chapter 13
Ogo Hole

Metamorphosis announced we had arrived at Ogo Hole, entrance to the Third Stratum, Realm of Utmost Darkness. We had reached our destination during the zenith of the red sky, Daynight of the Bear. Wiping the perspiration from my face with the sleeve of my gold tunic, I realized had made it all the way to Ogo Hole without freaking out. I had completed the hike without incident. Still couldn't look down, but I was much better with heights.

Twenty-five miles above the crater floor, we stood at a cave entrance exposed by the crater cliffs. Next to Ogo Hole, a cascading waterfall spilled into a rock pool. Ferns and purple orchids grew on the surrounding rocks. A pool of sparkling water overflowed into a stream that crossed the trail and poured off the cliff's edge down into the crater. A wooden foot bridge spanned the fast-flowing water.

Eve and I removed our backpacks and filled our water bags from the waterfall. We sat at the edge of the rock pool and ate hemp seeds with ambrosia and fruit. Biting into a green alligator pear, I felt the cave's cool, subterranean air on my face. The odor reminded me of my basement at home.

Took a deep breath and stared into the mouth of Ogo Hole. Forty feet into the opening, the triangular cave turned sharply to the left, to the east.

Muffled noises and animal cries came from the depths of the ominous tunnel.

The sage crossed the foot bridge with Balder and Lycus to discuss the next campsite up the trail.

The swamp elves rested, sitting at the mouth of the cave.

"Dag nab it. I got me a blister," Galar said, rubbing the bottom of his buckskin boot.

"Complain' ain't gonna' cure nothin'," Idun yelled, dusting off her ring-tailed cap.

Sitting there, I sensed Eve's fear of the cave. Her curved eyebrows formed a frown while she stared into Ogo Hole. I couldn't blame her. No telling what lived inside that creepy cave.

"Are you feeling all right?" I asked her.

She unclenched her fists and turned away.

"Okay, be that way," I said. "I'm only trying to be nice."

Looking back at me, she said, "I'm afraid of the dark. I will not go in there."

"Don't worry, Morph's taking us up the trail, not in the cave."

Before Eve could respond, grunting noises resonated from Ogo Hole. Staring into the cave, we spotted a figure emerging from the shadows. A hunched, stocky creature wore a tattered russet cloak with a hood. He stood with his back toward Eve and me, pulling on taunt leather reins, one in each paw. Something on the other end of the reins refused to come out of the cave.

The cloaked stranger tugged and snorted, digging his clawed feet with sandals into the gravel floor of the dark cave.

Galar and Idun jumped up and stood on the trail, hissing and bearing their sharp yellow teeth.

"Grimnir, is that you?" Morph asked, crossing back over the foot bridge.

Byelobog

Grimnir

224

"Yes~sth, Mathster Morfff, 'tis I, loyal Grimnir, your sth~ servant and humble guide," he yelled, pulling harder on the reins. He leaned backward and dragged two grunting creatures from the tunnel.

I gawked at the disgruntled beasts with saddles strapped to their backs. Dust blew into the air with each snort of their whiskered snouts.

Eve frowned. "I'm not sure if I like those things."

The two moleipeedes, sumpters is what Morph called them, possessed cylindrical, segmented bodies divided into rows of shiny copper~red plates. Four feet tall at the saddle, they looked like gigantic millipedes with rodent~like faces. Rows of stubby legs with furry paws protruded from under their hairless plates. Their faces resembled furry moles with red eyes and pink, fleshy snouts with a mouth full of fangs. Spikes covered their heads. Their tails ended in flailed spikes.

A single, curved antenna protruded from their foreheads. The bulbous end, glowing with a luminous white light, dangled directly over their noses. Antennalanterns is what Morph called them. Their antennae look like the lure of a deep sea angler fish that lights up in the dark ocean depths.

I admired their saddles and saddlebags, including the horse~ like bridle fastened over each moleipeede's head. Leather reins stretched from the bridles to the horns of the front saddle.

Morph entered the mouth of the cave and shook the aardvark's paw, who said, "Sth~sorry, Mathster Morfff. Them moleipeedes~sth are sth~sensitive to light." He pulled back the hood off his head. The dark aardvark's donkey~like ears popped straight into the air. Mangy brown fur covered his face, accentuated by an elongated pink snout with white whiskers. Prickly, black hairs covered his thick tail.

Drooling, he blinked his beady black eyes at Morph. The front of his tattered sorrel cloak and vest, covered with wet saliva, had become a crusty vest of mud. The sumpter guide carried a wooden club, or staff, almost as long as his body.

Flies and gnats buzzed around his head and body.

"Sth~settle down," Grimnir yelled, patting the spiked heads of both sumpters.

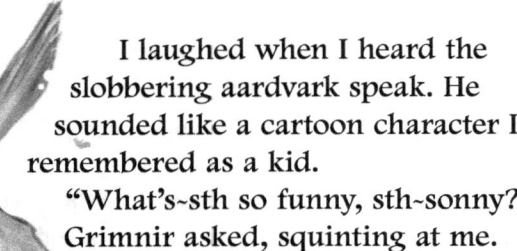

I laughed when I heard the slobbering aardvark speak. He sounded like a cartoon character I remembered as a kid.

"What's-sth so funny, sth-sonny?" Grimnir asked, squinting at me.

I stopped grinning and shrugged my shoulders.

Grimnir spit on the ground in my direction. From that moment, I knew I didn't like him, and he didn't like me.

"Do the sumpters have names?" Eve asked.

"Of cours-sth, me lady," Grimnir replied, bowing and tipping his ears to Eve. The aardvark guide pointed to their saddles. "Their name-sth 'er on their sth-saddles-sth."

Eve read their names. "Byelobog. Chernobog."

Morph pointed at the beasts, each measuring over twelve feet long, and said, "With their bright antennalanterns, these sumpters are one of the few domesticated animals capable of navigating through the Underworld. Their low profiles allow them to crawl through tight tunnels and passageways."

"Those antennae on their heads provide light?" Eve asked.

The sage nodded affirmatively. Then, he asked Grimnir, "What brings you to Ogo Hole?"

Wiping the dripping drool from his black lips, the slobbering aardvark replied, "Sth-simply a coincidence-sth. I came to water the pack animals-sth."

"Come, join us for a bite to eat. We await Pendragon's arrival before we continue our journey."

"Thanks-sth, Mathster Morfff, but I'm gonna sth-sit fer a sth-spell."

The dark aardvark, squinting from the glare of the red sky, pulled his stubborn moleipeedes to the stream. After they slurped up water, Grimnir tied their reins to an iron ring mounted on the cave wall.

Galar and Idun marched over the foot bridge and up the trail to join the half-orcs. Cursing under their breaths, they wanted nothing to do with Grimnir or his two sumpters.

Morph offered the guide a piece of ambrosia. "You seem a bit distracted since the last time I saw you. Is there something bothering you?"

"Sth-certainly not, Mathster Morfff," he replied. The dust-covered guide grabbed the ambrosia with his curved claws and waddled back into the cave. His scabby, bristle-haired tail dragged behind him. He squatted on the ground next to his snorting pack animals, licking the ambrosia with his slender, sticky tongue.

Morph dipped his purple bandanna in the clear water, wrung out the excess moisture, and laid it on a nearby rock to dry. The sage sat on the pool's edge between Eve and me. Shielding his eyes with his hand, he looked up into the crimson sky, waiting for Pendragon's arrival. He kept his wings folded behind his back while his curled tail touched the surface of the rippling water.

"I see you have overcome your fear of heights," Morph said.

"Yeah, I wasn't really that scared in the first place," I said, "just a little nervous."

Eve looked at me and rolled her eyes.

"Of course, my son. Perhaps a bit of an overreaction."

"While we wait for Pendragon, may I answer any questions?" Morph asked.

"Last night I tried to think positive thoughts," I replied, "but my first thoughts were always negative. I'm worried about my family. I couldn't remember any affirmations."

"Until you acquire enlightenment, the first thoughts that enter your mind are usually negative. You humans have a term for this, you say, 'My mind is in a rut.'"

"So, how do I get my mind out of this rut?"

"First, be patient. Change does not happen instantly. Until you learn to stop thinking like that, I have another method besides affirmations that might help. Close your eyes and think of your favorite thing to do."

I closed my eyes, feeling the cool spray from the waterfall on my face, and thought, *Surfing...no...playing guitar...no...drawing... hmmm...I'll choose surfing.*

Nodding, I opened my eyes.

"Now," the sage said, "think of that word again as the first thought that enters your mind."

Grinning, I imagined surfing near Monterey Bay.

"How do you feel when you hear that word?"

"Happy!"

"Now, close your eyes and see the action of the word in your mind's eye. Visualize your thoughts."

I glanced at Eve and closed my eyelids. I'd caught a perfect wave in Hawaii...the weather was gorgeous...all my friends and family were there on the beach...Eve stood on the white sand in a blue bikini and—

"How do you feel?" Morph asked.

"Great," I replied, opening my eyes.

"This is because your mind, every cell in your body, is enjoying the release of positive chemicals. Most humans experience this euphoria when they hear their favorite song."

"So, do I just start off every thought with something I like?"

"Close. You must learn to change your thinking. When your first thought is negative, simply change that thought to something positive that you can visualize and feel. Right now, close your eyes and think of something negative that truly bothers you."

Eve doesn't like me, was my first thought.

"Now, think the exact opposite thought. A happy thought."

Eve loves me and wants me.

I nodded with a look of satisfaction on my face.

"Feel that, Hunter? Feel the happiness flowing through you?"

"Yeah, I do. It feels great."

"The grand feeling you have right now must be remembered and relived in your mind over and over again until it becomes part of you. These grand thoughts are manifestations to the universe. Visualize positive feelings in your mind until you learn to use affirmations. When you make affirmations your mantras, your life shall change."

"Thanks. Now I know how to get that feeling. You're right, my thoughts *do* control my emotions."

"Once your thoughts become more positive, there is

something else you shall learn. Action. You must act your thoughts out. Action is required, not just thoughts. The words are not enough. You must do something about your positive thoughts. Thinking compassionate thoughts are wonderful, but until you treat someone compassionately, your thoughts are nothing but ideas, good ideas, but not yet reality. You must experience the act of compassion to be truly compassionate. Words themselves are ineffective. Do not just think loving and generous thoughts, *be* loving and generous."

"I understand," I said, grinning at Eve.

The Epiphanite looked away, gazing into the cave entrance. The sage put the last handful of dried huckleberries in his mouth and looked up, searching the red sky for his fellow Utopian.

While he chewed his food, he patted me on the back. "Any other questions?"

"Time," I replied. "On Time Island, you promised to explain time."

"Ahh, time. An excellent topic." Morph swallowed his last mouthful of huckleberries before he began the discussion of time and space.

"What do you recall from our first meeting that took place on Time Island?"

"I remember you saying that there is no such thing as time, that all things are happening right now."

Morph nodded, *yes.*

"I don't understand what that means," I said.

"It is a challenging concept. Allow me to add to your limited understanding of time and space. There is no time but this time, right now. All things exist simultaneously, all events occur at once, in the eternal moment of now. Once you understand and embrace this truth, that *you* move and not time, your mind shall come to rest, relax, and not worry about yesterday, or tomorrow, or later on. You shall learn to live in the now. Everything that has ever happened, or is going to happen, is actually happening right now. Now! With your limited intelligence, you are not consciously aware of this time warp."

"I still don't understand."

"We all move through space at a given rate. When you

change the amount of space, or the rate of speed between objects, you alter your perception of time. For instance, your long journey from Earth to here has caused a warp in the time-space continuum. The farther you travel from Earth, the more you have warped space and time. This is why, in regards to relativity, a fifty to one ratio exists between Earth and Millennium. While you age one year here, people age fifty years on Earth."

Fifty years, I thought, *I needed to get home soon or I wouldn't recognize anyone.*

"My apologies, I see I have upset you."

"I'm not upset. The time loss, the aging difference, is hard to believe."

"I understand." Morph patted me on the shoulder and asked me, "Has time ever stood still for you?"

"Hmmm. Time stood still when I almost drowned off Time Island. Underwater, everything looked in slow motion."

"Now is all there is; live in the moment."
—Metamorphosis

"I was hoping you would share a more positive, magnificent experience in your life. Like falling in love."

I immediately looked at Eve. She lowered her curled, black eyelashes. I looked back at the sage, thinking of a clever response.

"Do not worry, my son. You shall have a life-defining moment and time shall stand still. As you say on Earth, 'It is only a matter of time.' Because time is a state of mind, I have another example. Have you noticed that when you do something fun, something you love, have a great time, that time flies by?"

"I know that feeling."

"And when you do something you dislike, have a miserable time, the time drags on and on and on?"

"I *really* know that feeling."

"Remember those feelings and know that time itself is only in your mind. *You* move, not time."

My thoughts reeled in confusion. *The hands of a clock move. I see the sun come up every day. Time moves, I feel it move.*

"Now, right this moment, I shall share the sixth Secret of Time & Space."

Opened the flap of my artist satchel. "Maybe I should write all these Secrets down." I reached inside my leather loculus for a pencil and paper.

"That shall not be necessary. The sixth Secret is easy to remember. It is often recited on your planet, but few humans embrace its wisdom."

Closed the leather satchel and asked, "What's the sixth Secret?"

Morph replied, "Now is all there is; live in the moment."

"Yeah, I've heard that a lot. It means, seize the moment."

"Excellent. What do you think *that* means?"

"Don't worry about the past or the future."

"Why would you worry about anything?"

"Maybe I meant, expectations."

"Why do you humans place unrealistic expectations upon yourselves? You seem to beat yourselves up for failing to obtain your goals and desires soon enough. You seem to expect immediate gratification. You are always in a hurry."

I stared at the horizon.

"My son, are *you* in a hurry?"

"Yeah, I guess I am. This trip is taking too long."

"Please, stop. Think for a moment. Your present anxiety is caused by your thoughts about the future. Relax, breathe deeply and enjoy *this* moment."

"I'm not sure I can do that."

"Of course you can. Stop trying to get somewhere. When you get there, you shall just start running to somewhere else. There is nowhere to go. There is nothing to chase. Just be. Learn to leave the past behind and allow the future to unfold."

"But, it's hard not to think about the past; I have all these memories."

"Memories of what?"

"Some good. Some are bad."

"And what are some bad memories?"

"Being punished. Put on restriction. Arguing with my control-freak father all the time. Stuff like that."

Eve stared at me.

"I don't want to talk about this any more."

"You have given away all your energy to someone else by blaming your father. Holding on to your past memories has caused you to be angry and resentful. Blaming your father has caused you to lose control of your thoughts. You have allowed someone else to control your feelings."

I glanced at Eve and said, "I'll stop thinking about home."

The Epiphanite turned her head to gaze out into the crater, refusing to look at me.

The sage cleared his throat. "Being in a big hurry to get where you are going also causes you to lose your energy."

"What can I do about the way I feel?" I asked.

"Relax. Breathe deeply. Calm all that chatter, that noise in your head."

"You make it sound so easy. I wish I had what you have."

"What is that?"

"Your calmness."

"You already have what I have. You must find it within yourself. You cannot feel calmness, embrace it or understand it, because your thoughts are confused. Your mind is in constant chaos. By learning to focus on now, this moment, your thoughts shall slow down and you shall discover inner peace, freedom within."

I closed my eyes, listening to the gentle waterfall behind me.

"You must learn to live in the moment. You shall know this magic feeling when you stop worrying about past things and future events, when you stop being attached to outcomes."

"You mean, like getting back home before I don't recognize anyone or anything?"

"Yes, let that thought go. Simply focus on the task at hand, this moment. Just be. There is no time but this time, this moment. There is nothing else to think about but now. The past and the future are merely illusions within your mind. They exist because you create them in your imagination. You imagine the past and future, but they do not exist outside the now. Nothing, no thing, exists outside this present moment. The choice is yours, either seize the moment or focus your thoughts somewhere else and suffer the consequences."

"I'm *not* suffering." I closed my eyes and bit my lip.

"Suffering seems to be a human condition. Instead of living in the present moment, you humans choose to live in the past, or you spend your time dreaming of some wonderful future. Your lives are spent anxiously waiting for that right time to make something happen, some *thing* that will supposedly bring you instant happiness. Then, you never obtain happiness when the future does finally arrive. Why? Because happiness is only available right here, right now, in this moment."

I stopped biting my lip, admiring the sage's calm demeanor.

"As for time, you humans ask yourselves, 'Where did my life go? Where did the time go?' You fail to realize that you spent all of your time dreaming about your future, or, even worse, thinking negative thoughts about your past, living in the past. Remember, a majestic tree that fills a man's embrace grows from a seedling. A towering building starts with a single brick. A journey of a thousand miles begins with one step."

"I hear Father say that when I get impatient with my school projects."

"Enormous projects seem small when you begin small, one step at a time. Whatever the task, simply begin from right here, right now. Everything is possible from here because now is all there is. Do not worry about the result. Why? There is always a new journey awaiting you. There is a time for everything. To everything, turn, turn, turn. Just as you breathe in and breathe out, there is a time to be ahead and a time for being behind, a time for being in motion and a time for being at rest, a time for being vigorous and time for being exhausted, a time for being safe and a time for being in danger."

I felt calmer just listening to the sage.

"Live in the moment and free yourself from the chase. Stop striving for more and searching for something better. You already have everything you need to be completely happy, right here, right now."

The sage handed Eve a green alligator pear and grinned. "There is no time, only the eternal moment of now."

"I'm beginning to understand time," I said, grinning at the Sage of the Ages.

Morph chuckled. "To understand time, you must comprehend space, they are interconnected."

"Do you mean the space between us, right now?"

"Yes, and no. By space, I mean all things, everything from the macrocosm to the microcosm, all things. Every thing you can imagine, visible and invisible, is simply energy waves. Vibrating waves of possibility. The universe, from the infinitely large to the infinitely small, is comprised of pure energy. This pure energy is made up of sub-atomic particles, the building blocks of the universe. Are you familiar with atoms?"

I shook my head, *yes*.

"The stuff that makes up atoms, sub-atomic particles, energy waves, appear to be solid, but they are mostly empty space. Actually, 99.99% empty space to be exact."

"Then, why is *this* solid?" I asked, picking up a speckled, granite rock.

"It is not solid."

Without warning, I threw the rock against the face of the cliff. The rock shattered into pieces.

"It looks solid to me," I said, chuckling.

Eve flinched and sneered at me.

The startled moleipeedes grunted and jerked on their reins. Grimnir snorted, jumping up to calm his sumpters.

I bowed my head and shrugged.

Trying to justify my misplaced energy, I held my hand out, offering an apology to Eve.

She ignored me.

"Great throwing arm, young man," Morph said, signaling to Balder and Lycus, *everything is all right*.

Metamorphosis picked up a smooth, black rock, held it in his lower right hand and said, "The reason this rock appears solid is due to the forces that bind the atoms of the rock together. When my hand touches the rock, the force fields of atoms in my hand meet the equally strong force fields of the rock, causing mutual repulsion of the billions of microscopic, but incredibly strong, force fields. This force prevents my hand from penetrating the rock. The rock only has the appearance of being solid, just like our bodies appear to be solid. But we, like this rock, are all 99% space."

"I'm having trouble grasping this concept," I said, shaking my head back and forth.

"In reality, this rock I hold in my hand is moving, just like everything in the universe. It contains countless atoms, protons, neutrons and subatomic particles that race around so fast that the rock appears still, motionless. The pattern of the movement creates the shape of the rock. The rock moves and does not move, all at the same time. We, like the rock, move and do not move, through time and space at incredible speeds."

"That rock is made of pure energy?"

"All things, broken down to their most primal form, are all made of the same stuff, pure energy. This prime energy, the oneness, is the substance of all things in the universe. All things. An endless ocean of energy, never ending, connects us all."

"But aren't there different kinds of energy?" I asked. "You know, electric, solar, the energy that fuels our bodies."

"In their purest form, they are all the same energy, the one energy. Thoughts, sound, color, your dog, rocks, water, your body, even the stars, are all the very same energy."

"Everything?"

"Anything, everything, all things. Both seen and unseen."

"Unbelievable," I said, staring at the red sky.

"The entire cosmos consists of a vibrating frequency of energy. Energy joins together with other energies of the same harmonious frequency and forms the physical world."

Morph asked Eve, "Do you know what this same energy implies?"

"We are all made of the same stuff," the Epiphanite replied, flipping her black hair back off her shoulders.

"Excellent answer. All of us, everything, is a vibrating mass of pure energy and we are interconnected to all other things in the universe. We are one. We call this the World of Self. You, your Self, exists in everyone else, and they exist in you. We are all one world, one universe, one energy. We all live in a World of Self, inseparable from one another. I am you and you are me and we are all together means all the Worlds of Self are one. One world; therefore, we must all live as one."

"Why haven't I heard all this before?" I asked.

"When I speak of the World of Self, it is a realm where everything, every *thing*, is interconnected. I speak of both the seen, the physical, and the unseen, the metaphysical.

"Unfortunately, most of your teachers, your parents, most humans, lack the awareness to share such valuable information. Sadly, they believe it is not important to know. This is why you were never taught this universal concept. I believe you refer to the Universal Truths, the ten Secrets, as quantum physics on your planet."

"My father has a quantum physicist on his foundation staff."

Morph grinned. "I recall a young physicist named Albert displayed intense enthusiasm during my explanation of time and space. He stayed long enough to grasp the concepts and—"

"Wait. Who is Alb—"

"Stop interrupting," Eve said, frowning.

I looked at Eve and said, "Sorry."

"Young man, do you understand the space-time continuum?" Morph asked.

"No," I said. "How can everything be happening right now, right this instant?"

"Allow me to explain space and time in human terms."

The sage stood, walked eight paces toward the cave entrance, looked over his shoulder and said, "What have I just done?"

"Walked away," I said, staring at the sage's green tail and wings.

"Would you say I just moved?"

"Sure."

"What are *you* doing at this moment?"

"I'm sitting here next to Eve."

"Do you consider yourself in motion, moving?"

"No, I'm sitting still."

"That is incorrect. You *are* moving, right now, at the speed of light."

I smirked and squinted.

"By sitting there, you are moving through time, but not through space. In other words, time and space change according to how you move."

"But, I'm *not* moving."

"You might not feel it, but you are. You are moving at the speed of light through time. Time."

Before I could speak, Morph said, "Stand up and walk toward me."

I stood and walked toward the sage. After five paces, Morph told me to stop.

"You have just moved through space. Space and time. However, you moved at such a slow speed that you just moved mostly through time, not space. My point is, the faster you travel, the more you move in space. The slower you travel, the more you move in time."

"Say what?"

"You can move through space without moving through time, and you can move through time without moving through space."

"I don't get it."

"Please, sit back down and I shall enlighten you."

I returned to my seat next to Eve. I told her, "This is fascinating."

She agreed by nodding her head. I wondered if she really understood the concepts.

"My son, allow me to recite the twin paradox."

"Twins? I'm a twin."

"Congratulations. How does it feel to have an identical sibling?"

"I have a sister, Julia. She doesn't look like me, I mean, we're not identical. She's my father's favorite. Julia can do no wrong. That's why my mom treats her so mean."

"I would like to meet her sometime."

"That will never happen."

"Never say never."

"Okay, I won't. Now, tell me about the twin paradox."

Morph raised his upper right arm and pointed to the sky. "Imagine that you leave the Earth in a space craft and your sister

Julia remains home. You travel at the speed of light and you are gone for ten years. Upon your return to Earth, Julia shall have aged ten years. You shall *not* have aged."

"How's that possible?"

"As I told you, the faster you move in space, the less you move in time. When you move at the speed of light through space, for instance, you do not age because you have not moved through time, just space."

"I get it! I see what you mean!" my mouth curved into an unconscious smile as I listened to the sage.

"Time and space change according to how you move. For your comprehension, I speak of how fast you move, the speed. So far, I have referred to the speed of light, but there is another speed which creates the ultimate oneness. Infinite speed. If you and I moved at infinite speed, we would only move through space, not through time."

"So," I said, "when you say in no time, you really do mean, instantly?"

"Yes. All the vibrations of the universe, the waves of possibility, move at infinite speed. Thoughts move at infinite speed, also known as superluminal speed. I know this is hard to understand with your human intelligence, but infinite speed allows things to be in several places all at the same time. All things happen at once, everywhere. All things are connected, even though they do not appear connected. This is what I refer to as the vibrating grid, the matrix of energy that connects us all. Everything, every *thing*, is connected. All things in the universe are connected at infinite speed. All things happen in no time. This leads to my universal declaration, 'Everything is happening now.' Now!"

The smiling sage walked back to Eve and me. He sat between us while the half-orcs patrolled the trail, silhouetted by the red skies over the crater.

"I'm starting to get this," I said.

"Eve, do you understand?" Morph asked.

She nodded and said, "By sitting here I only move through time. By walking, running, flying, or traveling in a space ship, I move through both space and time together. The faster I go, the

238

more I move in space and less in time. This is how I will not age when I move, travel at the speed of light. If I could move at infinite speed, no time, there is no time and I only move through space."

"Excellent analysis of time and space," Morph said.

God, there she goes again, I thought, *making me look ignorant.*

I raised my eyebrows. "I might have more questions later."

"Of course, my son. However, to challenge your thoughts, I have even more exciting knowledge to share with you."

I raised my left hand.

Eve stared at me and placed her index finger to her lips, "Shhh."

Embarrassed by her gesture, I lowered my head and allowed Morph to continue speaking.

"There are no accidents in the universe. Things do not just happen randomly, or by a higher power's intervention. The supreme reality is that observation, thoughts and beliefs, cause energy waves to take shape. Energy waves turn into particles based on the individual thoughts and the beliefs of the observer."

"What observer?" I asked.

"Anyone. Any creature may observe. You are an observer. Eve is an observer. I am an observer. Energy waves act and respond to our thoughts and beliefs at the moment of observation. This supreme truth brings us right back to the power of thought. Your thoughts are also creative. When observing, your thought energy directly transmutes wave forms into subatomic particles which, in turn, take form in proportion to what you, the observer, believe. Thoughts take on physical form based on the perception of the thinker."

"This is mind boggling."

"There is more, as you say, mind-boggling information."

Morph stretched his wings while ruby-throated sparrows and bluebirds landed on the rocks of the waterfall, drinking and bathing themselves in the cascading streams.

"Energy does not need to travel through space and time to communicate, it is already interconnected with all the other energy in the entire universe."

"Everywhere?"

"All things in the infinite universe, the entire cosmos, are interconnected. Everything is a galactic vibrating ball of infinite energy communicating with no regard for space and time, traveling at infinite speed. When this energy joins together it forms one, individual thought. One. The communication between energy waves happens at precisely the same time, instantly, no matter how far away they are from each other, anywhere in the cosmos. The cells of your Earth body, your DNA, reacts to your thoughts here on Millennium."

"Wow, this is great stuff, but how can it help *me*?"

"Always thinking of yourself, Hunter," Eve said, shaking her head.

Morph got Eve's attention by raising his lower left hand. "There is no question that is unworthy or undeserving of an answer."

Eve blushed and bowed her head.

"To answer your question, my son, it has *everything* to do with your health, happiness, and success. Energy waves do not need to travel, they are interconnected to all other energy in the vast universe. A matrix, a vibrating grid of energy, exists throughout the cosmos. Your thoughts and beliefs and intuitions regarding all the events of your life, the way you think, determine exactly how your life shall unfold in your physical world."

My eyes moved up and to the right. I raised my hand, motioning for time to think.

Waiting for a response, Morph looked up, searching the crater skies for Pendragon. Resting in the cool shadows of the cave, Grimnir and his restless moleipeedes snorted and grunted.

"Do you mean I'm not a victim of circumstance?" I asked.

The sage grinned. "You are the creator of your own reality. Your thoughts are determined by your beliefs. You broadcast these thought waves out into the infinite matrix of energy."

"Like a radio transmitter!"

"Correct. Your thought waves are transformed from the spiritual realm, the invisible, into particles of the visible, material realm. These join with similar energy waves that all vibrate at the same harmonious frequency and collectively join. Unite. This union is what you come to see, feel and experience in its pure physical form as your physical world. You create and shape your own life. No one else does it but you—you and your thoughts."

"By controlling my thoughts, I create my own world?"

"Yes, my son. You create your destiny. Remember, an object cannot exist independently of its observer. The act of observing an object, or an event, or a condition, or a circumstance, causes it to be there. All outcomes are based on our decisions, our choices, and how we observe it."

"Say that again?"

"What you think about an object, event or circumstance, anything, and believe it to be true, determines your life path. The real truth or the perceived reality does not matter. All that matters is what you think and believe to be true. If you believe that love is hard to come by, consciously or subconsciously, this projected thought energy is transmitted, broadcast, and harmonizes with similar thought waves. These transmute into particles that attract like particles, like attracts like, and your belief that 'love is hard to come by' shall materialize into absolute truth."

"I get it," I said, gazing into the sage's tranquil eyes. "It works the same with money, or health, or success, or anything I believe in."

"As you think and believe," the sage said, "so shall your life unfold in perfect order, and—"

"Look, he's here," Balder yelled, waving his arm.

Morph stood and waved. Eve and I jumped to our feet. Riding the warm thermals of the Discordia Crater, the mighty Pendragon soared toward us, holding his blue-grey wings straight out, preparing to land. The dragonram navigated from a headfirst dive to a level flight pattern. Using his powerful tail as a rudder, he turned his draconian wings vertically, gliding toward Ogo Hole.

Galar and Idun clapped their hands and threw their coonskin caps into the air.

Eve and I ducked when the dragon-winged Utopian swooped

down, curled his tail back above his horns and landed hard on the South Crater Trail. His hooves shook the trail when he landed in front of Ogo Hole. He slid into the cave, dragging his tail behind him. Dust swirled and rocks rolled off the edge of the path down into the Discordia Crater.

While the dust settled, Morph said, "Welcome, my fellow Utopian, come and sit by the waterfall. Your timing is, as always, impeccable."

"Greetings," Pendragon said, sniffing the cave air, "I am glad to see you are all safe and sound."

The giant Utopian walked to the pond, cupped his hands under the waterfall and drank the spring water. He folded his dragon wings and sat on a granite outcropping. Morph offered his fellow Utopian a red apple and asked, "How do things look in the Upperworld?"

Pendragon bit off a piece of the fruit and said, "Earlier, I spotted Karkinos hiking the East Crater Trail, near Erawan Falls. I flew in to talk with the hypocrite liar. The goatcrab bragged that he had just met with Ex in Tracundia and that the Invisible Villain is planning the capture of the two intruders. He pointed his red pincer skyward and told me that Leyak the Blackguard waits in ambush at the top of the South Crater Trail. When I asked him if he was being truthful, he smirked and said, 'I yam lyin.' He pointed the Bone of Ulrr at me, then he ran off before I could ask another question."

"Sounds like Karkinos," Morph said. "We have no choice but to take a different route."

"How long will that take?" I asked, throwing my arms in the air.

"Excusssth me," Grimnir said, standing at the entrance to Ogo Hole. "Ridin' me moleipeedes-sth can get you to the Upperworld fas-sthter than walkin' that crater trail. Me guide services-sth will cost you one oodle an' two sth-scruples-sth an' five frugles-sth fer each of ya."

Morph looked at Pendragon, who nodded his head, *yes*.

Grimnir snorted and smiled with his rotten teeth, wiping the drool from his tiny mouth. I saw the fear in Eve's eyes while she stared into the entrance of Ogo Hole.

"Wait a minute," I said. "How do we know this Karkinos character is really lying?"

"It is the same as if a human tells you they are lying," Pendragon said. "This is known as the liar paradox."

"What does *that* mean?"

"The liar paradox means, if it is true, it is false. If it is false, it is true."

I put my hands on my hips. "What?"

"Karkinos has told us he is lying about the ambush," Pendragon said. "The logical conclusion must be, if his claim that he is lying is true, then he *is* lying, in which case what he says about the ambush is false. If this is true, then we are no better off, because if Karkinos' claim that he is lying is false, then he is *not* lying, in which case what he says is true. His

statement gives rise to logical contradictions. The statement is both true *and* false. This is why you should take a different route."

"Okay, okay. But why do we have to go in *there*?" I asked, pointing at Ogo Hole.

"It is our only option," Morph replied. Then, he looked at Eve. "Would you prefer to turn back?" Eve walked over to Grimnir and the moleipeedes. The aardvark guide smiled with his decaying brown teeth.

Karkinos

243

"Pleas~sth, me lady, We'll be sth~safe, I promis~sth."

The girl from Epiphany turned and said, "I am fine. I will go in the cave."

Morph asked Balder and Lycus to transfer supplies to the saddlebags buckled to the moleipeedes' saddles. The half-orcs carried the canvas supply sacks into the cave entrance.

Galar tugged on Morph's breeches. "Idun and me ain't no underground guides."

"My friends, you may return to the Forest Primeval. We now have Grimnir to guide us through the Underworld."

"I reckon we'll help Balder an' Lycus move them thar supplies."

"Greatly appreciated," Morph said.

The swamp elves helped Balder and Lycus finish stuffing supplies into the saddlebags. The two half-orcs hugged Metamorphosis and Pendragon. Then, they smiled at me and Eve, bowing at the waist.

Surprised, I asked, "Why aren't they going with us? Don't we need them for protection?"

"The half-orcs are too heavy for the moleipeedes and too large for many of the tunnels. Do not worry, we shall do fine without them."

Cernunnos

Balder and Lycus saluted, turned and lumbered back down the South Crater Trail to rejoin the crew aboard the *Skipbladnir*, docked at Fog Harbor.

"Don't fret, you're in good hands with Morph," Galar said.

He turned and gave Grimnir the evil eye, spitting and hissing at the dark aardvark. Then, he and Idun followed the half-orcs down the trail. Eve and I waved to our loyal companions. The dust settled as the four Millennians disappeared around the curved trail.

Pendragon told Morph, "I shall meet you at the portal. But first, I shall fly to Nemoria to assist Cernunnos at the Cosmic Cave. Bodvar and his Grizzsects have laid siege to the area. The stag needs my help."

Eve gasped when she heard the Utopian's announcement, putting her hand over her mouth.

"Wait a minute," I said, my face red with anger. "Let me guess. You're not going with us because *you're* too big for the tunnels."

"You shall be fine without me," Pendragon replied, "As I said, Cernunnos needs reinforcements to protect Balux, the Pot of Gold. The Cosmic Cave is under siege by the Extractors."

"What if *we're* attacked by Extractors, or, God knows, whatever else lives in that cave?" I asked.

"Stop worrying about the future," Morph said. *What if* does not exist. Do not fear what you have no control over. You have *Aroundight*. Eve has *Arthame* and *Gandeeva*. You have youth, your health and each other's positive energy. I shall be with you. What else could you possibly need?"

"I don't know about this," I said, frowning.

Eve glanced at me and walked over to the agitated Chernobog. She knelt down and petted the sumpter's head. The moleipeede stopped fussing when the Epiphanite scratched her furry head. Rows of razor-sharp rodent teeth gleamed in the light while the pack animal grinned in pleasure. Eve placed her other hand under Chernobog's antennalantern. In spite of the glare from the blazing-red sky, the ganglion bulb shined brightly, illuminating her hand.

"With these lights, we can see in the dark caves," Eve said.

Not sure how to respond, I shrugged my shoulders.

"Riding the moleipeedes, we shall be able to travel an average speed of twenty-five to forty miles per hour," Morph said, pointing at their rows of paws. "Over rugged terrain, these animals are deceptively fast, just look at all those legs."

"It is time we saddle up and get on the subterranean trail," Morph said, unfolding his wings and stretching his membranes. "The Millennium Underworld shall offer a grand learning experience. You shall soon appreciate the simplest of pleasures, like solshine."

"See you soon," Pendragon yelled, waving at Eve and me. He took two giant strides, leaped off the edge of the trail out into the crater, spread his dragon wings, and disappeared over the ledge. Straight down.

Eve and I gasped. It took a few moments for Pendragon to reappear. The magnificent Utopian steadily flapped his wings, taking him higher and higher. I waved, watching the dragonram soar in a northeasterly direction, fading into the red crater sky. On the opposite horizon, pink and purple clouds blazed in the blue sky, like a northern California sunset.

I blurted out, "What if we get lost?"

Morph chuckled. "What if? 'What if' is one of your human excuses. Do not worry about the future, live in the now. Enjoy your journey, my son, each and every moment of it."

I turned red with embarrassment. "I'll try."

Grimnir squinted at Eve and me. The aardvark walked over to Byelobog and grabbed the pack animal's reins.

"The pretty printhcess-sth 'ill ride with me, an' Mathster Morfff 'ill ride with the—"

The sage raised his hand to silence the aardvark guide. "Thank you for your suggestion, but I prefer to ride with you on the lead moleipeede."

"Offf courseth, Mathster," Grimnir said, bowing. "I jus' wurry 'bout the young boy fallin' offf the sth-sumpter an' hurtin' hisssth-self."

He called me a boy, I thought. *I'm twice the man he is. That ugly aardvark pisses me off.*

Morph distracted me by pointing to Chernobog. I walked

to the moleipeede and ran my hands over the sumpter's smooth plates. I admired the embroidered leather saddle designed for two riders.

"You get on her first," Eve told me.

Nodding, I grabbed the reins and mounted the moleipeede. Eve put her boot in the stirrup and swung her leg over the rear saddle. She straddled the saddle behind me, clutching the rear horn with both hands. Grimnir adjusted Eve's stirrups.

I looked down at my stirrups. My boots almost touched the ground.

"Are you going to be okay with this?" I asked Eve.

"I am ready," she replied, taking a deep, nervous breath.

Wondering why Eve was so afraid of the dark, I stuck my chest out, grabbing the handle of my sword. "Don't worry, I'm not afraid of the dark. I'll make sure nothing happens to you."

He waited for a response from Eve.

"Sth~son offa' gun, where's~sth that sth~stupid map?" Grimnir yelled, stuffing his claws inside his saddlebag and removing a rolled parchment.

The slobbering aardvark unrolled the yellow tattered map, a miniature version of the parchment that hung in my *Skipbladnir* cabin. After studying it, Grimnir rolled up the map, stuffed it back in the saddlebag and crawled up onto the snorting Byelobog. The aardvark pulled a leather knocker's cap over his pointed ears while Morph mounted the moleipeede. The sage preferred the rear saddle because of his tail.

Grimnir tightened the reins and whispered to Morph, "All them concepts~sth 'bout time 'n sth~space is~sth really hard to grathp."

"I understand. Shall we depart?"

"Of cours~sth, Mathster Morfff."

Grimnir slapped the reins of his moleipeede and screamed, "Let's~sth go sth~sumpters~sth. Yawww!"

Eve and I lunged backward as Chernobog dashed for the dark security of Ogo Hole. The beast of burden followed directly behind her mate, Byelobog.

I held the reins tightly while Eve gripped the rear saddle horn and closed her eyes.

Above the ominous tunnel entrance, I read a wooden sign:

Third Stratum
Realm of Utmost Darkness
Elevation: −125 Miles Below Sea Level

To enter the cave, I pulled the leather reins hard left. A blast of cool air hit me in the face. I sniffed the darkness. The cavern smelled stale, a combination of eroding minerals, fungus, and subterranean moisture. My eyes adjusted to the dark Underworld as the Realm of Utmost Darkness swallowed us whole. I gripped the reins, knowing I had entered the world where the light ended and the blackness began.

The voice inside my head whispered, *there is no turning back.*

Chapter 14
Millennium Underworld

The light from the bobbing antennalanterns cast rippled shadows on the moist limestone, causing the cavern walls and ceiling to look like the ribs of a sleeping giant. The moving shadows on the cave walls played tricks on my mind as I tried to anticipate the herky-jerky motion of the moleipeedes. The distorted shadows loomed larger, then smaller, growing, then shrinking, like a group of weird creatures waiting in ambush. The surreal subterranean route had taken us through a labyrinth of ever-ascending tunnels. The cavern walls revealed twisted cylinders of helictites and mineral veins sparkling with specks of silver and copper and gold. Like undersea coral, formations of fluorescent-white gypsum crystals hung from the cave's ceiling. Water droplets echoed from the abyss of darkness while a steady subterranean breeze blew through the maze of caves and tunnels.

At least we could see where we were going. The light from Grimnir's knocker's cap shone on the underground tunnels ahead.

I glanced back at Eve.

Her face revealed a gaze of wonderment, combined with fear. Her almond-shaped eyes looked larger in the shadowy light.

She motioned to me, *keep your eyes on the tunnel ahead* and shouted, "Look out!"

Turning in my saddle, I ducked my head, nearly smashing my forehead on the jagged stalactites.

Embarrassed, I raised my right thumb in an *I'm okay* gesture.

"Pay attention," Eve told me as I sat up straight.

The moleipeedes moved fast, really fast.

Below my stirrups, the moleipeede's paws, all sixty of them, moved in perfect unison.

The moleipeedes jerked to a stop.

Eve lunged into my back. She put her arms around my waist, trying to regain her balance. Her arms felt comforting as they wrapped around me. She didn't hold me for long.

"Sth-sorry, we gotta crawl thru them tunnels-sth," Grimnir yelled, wiping the slobber from his lips. "I guess-sth I took the wrong turn back yonder."

While the aardvark shined his knocker's cap head lamp on his parchment map, Morph walked back to me and said, "The tunnels and passageways have become too restrictive to ride the pack animals. You go with Grimnir. Eve and I shall follow."

"How are these sumpters going to fit through those low tunnels?" I asked.

"Their body plates unhinge, then flatten out," Morph said, placing his spectacles in his vest pocket.

I jumped off the moleipeede, helped Eve dismount, grabbed Chernobog's reins, and waited behind the aardvark.

Grimnir signaled with his index claw, *follow me,* and sent his moleipeede ahead of him. Within moments, I had to stoop down to navigate the shadowy passageways. The moleipeede's antennalantern provided enough light to see the tunnel get smaller, and smaller, and smaller.

The aardvark turned and said, "We'ff gotta' crawl on our bellies-sth. Drop her reins-sth, she'll folla' ya."

I released Chernobog's leather reins and got down on my hands and knees. Despite the artificial lights, the passageways grew darker. The cold cave floor felt wet and slimy as I crawled behind the aardvark guide.

Morph calmed Eve.

She gasped and panicked, taking shallow breaths.

Told myself I'd never go into another cave as long as I lived.

The howl of the underground wind and the steady drip, drip, drip of water droplets sounded magnified in the abyss of endless tunnels.

Crawling on my belly, I panicked. The tight, clammy spaces made me feel claustrophobic. My breathing became labored due to the lack of oxygen. Worse yet, Grimnir gave off a stench. He smelled like dirty socks. The flat cave crevice narrowed to where my chest felt crushed when I tried to squeeze through the horizontal rock opening.

Smothering a groan, I gasped for oxygen. I couldn't breathe. It felt like my ribs were breaking.

"I'm stuck," I said, "I can't move. Grimnir...aggghhh...help me...I can't...breathe."

The aardvark looked around. Snorting, he crawled backward.

"Sth~silly boy. Grab me tail."

Grabbing the clammy, rat~like tail of Grimnir, I thought my lungs were going to collapse when I felt myself dislodge from the rock crevice.

The aardvark dragged me through a shallow pool of cold, stagnant water.

"Pleas~sth, let go," the aardvark said, grunting.

My pulse pounding, I released his prickly tail and regained my composure.

Breathe deeply, I told myself, *keep calm, Hunter, don't panic.*

Behind me, I listened to Eve's moans of distress while Morph pulled her through the narrow crevices.

After crawling through pools of slimy water and a labyrinth of tight crevices, a light shined on my face. Through a round opening ahead, I saw Grimnir standing inside a cavern.

The aardvark's head lamp turned toward the darkness.

I slid through the hole at the end of the tunnel that emptied into a spacious cave. Finally, I could stand up straight.

While Chernobog, Eve, and Morph entered the cavern behind me, I did not turn around to acknowledge them. I stood, awestruck by the surreal landscape.

With the antennalanterns glowing, I looked up at the massive stalagmites the size of redwoods rising from the cave floor, towering into the darkness. A rust~colored stream gurgled past them, disappearing into the depths of the colossal cavern.

A breeze brushed my face while I sniffed the air. It smelled like the soil from Mom's garden. Like sweet mulch.

I looked down at my saturated gold tunic. The front had been stained a wet, rusty brown. My shirt was totally ruined.

"This~sth way," Grimnir yelled, squinting at his parchment map as he pointed into the black abyss.

Morph patted me on the shoulder, "Please, saddle up. We have a lot of underground to cover."

Eve sat on the sumpter with her arms above her head, pulling back her soaked black hair into a pony tail. The front of her blue silk chemise, sopping wet, clung tightly to her body.

I stared at her breasts.

Eve arched her eyebrows at me and asked, "Is something wrong?"

Caught off guard, I blushed. Looking down, I shook my head, *no*, and grabbed the sumpter's reins.

My first thought was, *Apologize, tell her you're sorry for staring at her.* Hoping the shadows would hide the flush in my cheeks, I mounted the moleipeede.

Before I could apologize, Morph announced, "Until we reach the Nudd Tunnel, please remain silent."

The sage gave the *move forward* signal with his upper right arm. I decided I would tell her I'm sorry the first chance I got.

Moving rapidly, the moleipeedes navigated their way through the mineral forest of red and orange and maroon stalagmites, so tall they disappeared into the sky-like blackness above them.

Chirping spiderbats and black dragonflies the size of crows flew above my head. Besides the sound of the subterranean wind, strange nocturnal cries echoed from the darkness.

From time to time, Grimnir would shine his bright head lamp from side to side, revealing structures: stone houses and towers and rock stairways built into the cave walls—inhabited dwellings. I looked for signs of life, in or near the structures, but no movement could be seen.

Our group had traveled nineteen miles across rugged terrain when I spotted hundreds of flickering lights in the far distance. The smell of burnt, smoldering wood in the cavern reminded me of my fireplace at home, after the logs had burned to ash.

"What's that?" I yelled, sniffing the air and pointing at the lights.

Morph held up his two right hands. "Grimnir, stop the sumpters. Time for a break."

After dismounting, Grimnir and the moleipeedes drank rusty-orange water from a subterranean stream. We stood next to a stalagmite column, drinking from our water bags.

"It feels good to stand and stretch for a while," Morph said, smiling, fully extending his four arms and wings.

Eve nodded. The warm underground air had dried her clothes.

Pointing to the distant lights, I asked, "What are all those lights?"

"Those are the torches of Rhadamanthus." Morph reached inside his saddlebag and pulled out a spyglass.

Recognizing Andvari's telescope, it reminded me of how much I really missed the gnome. I wished he was with us instead of Grimnir.

Morph handed me the spyglass. "Here, take a look."

Pulled out the telescopic lens and lifted the narrow end to my right eye. Through the darkness, the subterranean city of Rhadamanthus looked familiar to me. The stone city had been constructed vertically on the side of the sheer, limestone cliffs. A network of switchback stairways and ladders connected the buildings, hundreds of smooth-textured structures standing twelve stories tall, built one on top of the other. The buildings reminded me of the Anasazi villages I visited in junior high school. Thousands of lights, mostly torches, flickered inside the oval, arched windows and passageways, illuminating the copper-colored cliffs of the distant underworld metropolis.

"Are those people?" I asked, seeing bodies move about the structures.

"No, they are Barbegazi," Morph replied, "a mutant, dwarve-like race who inhabit Rhadamanthus."

I refocused the lens and studied the creatures. The Barbegazi stood upright and had squatty bodies with elongated feet. White, snarly hair covered their ugly, unclothed bodies.

"Are they friendly?" I asked, handing the spyglass back to Morph.

"Unfortunately, no. They have been infected with the *Extractor Virus* for centuries. They have been known to surface at the Mountains of Apes in Eremus. They hunt and kill prey to replenish their meat supply."

"What kind of meat?"

"They are not particular."

Couldn't understand why Morph called Millennium paradise when it was so dangerous.

I grabbed the handle of my sword and looked at Eve.

She glanced over her shoulder. "Can we leave now?"

"Of course. Here comes Grimnir now," Morph said.

"Sth-say, how's-sth the boy doin'?"

"I'm *not* a boy," I yelled, giving the guide a menacing stare.

"Justh kiddin', young fella'. Pleas-sth, keep your baggy breeches-sth on."

I pointed at the aardvark and started to say something when Eve grabbed my sleeve. "Do not let him bother you. We have more important issues," she said.

Mumbled under my breath, "I hate that donkey-eared flea bag," as Grimnir waddled to the lead moleipeede.

We mounted the moleipeedes and resumed our journey.

After following the stream bank for two miles, we crossed over a stone footbridge.

Suddenly, Grimnir shouted, "Sth-stop!"

He pulled his map from his saddlebag, shined his head lamp onto the parchment and said, "Nudd Tunnel is-sth *that* way," he said, pointing to the west with his index claw.

Morph asked, "May I please see the map?"

"There's-sth no need fer you to sth-see the map! I know my directions-sth!" the slobbering aardvark shouted.

The sage dismounted and walked into the stalagmite forest, disappearing into the darkness.

I couldn't believe the sage had left us alone in the cavern.

Eve asked me, "What is going on?"

"I don't know. Morph just vanished into nowhere."

Soon, a neon glow approached from the darkness. A pulsating, blue light shone on Morph's face while he walked toward us. He held his scepter, *Joyease*, above his head.

"I am disappointed in you, Grimnir," the sage said. "Nudd Tunnel is to the east."

"Sth-sorry, Mathster Morfff," Grimnir said, turning his map from left to right. Then, he flipped the parchment upside down.

"I guess-sth I had the sth-stupid map upsth-side down."

Morph slid his scepter back under his belt and swung his right leg over the saddle. He requested silence and gave the *move forward* signal with his upper right hand.

After a silent two-hour ride in the dreary, cavernous landscape, Grimnir shined his head lamp on a metal sign.

Fastened to the cave wall with iron spikes, the tin sign read:

Nudd Tunnel
Realm of Utmost Darkness
Elevation: −102 Miles Below Sea Level

We had arrived at an entrance to Nudd Tunnel, a major foot-path route connecting the Southern Sub-Hemisphere with the Discordia Crater.

According to Morph, the tunnel ran in a southwest direction, intersecting the Crater Tunnel Loop and the Southwest Subterranean Loop, both major transportation corridors for the Underworld.

"We shall camp there, in the Den of Shadows," the sage said, pointing to a dark grotto.

Grimnir turned his knocker's cap and shined the beam of light into the sheltered cave.

We set up camp in the grotto.

Grimnir tended a roaring fire while Morph, Eve, and I ate our evening meal of hard boiled eggs, dried dodo jerky, almonds and ambrosia.

With his sticky tongue, Grimnir slurped up dried molasses ants out of a crusty canvas feed bag. He wiped the ant-filled saliva dripping from his snout, burped, and waddled over to his moleipeedes. He fed them each a bag of molasses roachmash.

After they ate, Byelobog, Chernobog, and Grimnir dug shallow burrows in the ground and went to sleep. Within moments their antennalanterns dimmed, leaving the crackling campfire as the only source of light.

Eve told Morph she did not feel well, that the dark caves had upset her. She turned over on her side and pulled her blanket over her head.

The Epiphanite murmured, "Good daynight."

Realized that her and I wouldn't be talking that evening. I wondered when we'd *ever* talk. I needed to apologize, tell her I was sorry for staring at her.

I sighed and pulled my bedroll next to the fire, closer to Morph. "Can I ask you a question?"

"This is a good time to talk," the sage replied.

"I've been thinking. I'm bothered about the people in charge of everything back on Earth."

"In charge of what?"

"You know, the people that run the government."

"What is your question?"

I moved closer to the sage and said, "Sorry, I'll get to the point. I'm beginning to agree with you that the President of the United States should be a philosopher."

"Thank you. But my suggestion is that *all* humans in positions of leadership must have philosophical training, not just political leaders. In other words, all humans require enlightenment. First, you must cure the viral epidemic, the *Extractor Virus*; otherwise, philosophical wisdom shall fall on deaf ears."

"Why should everyone, all humans, become leaders. Don't we need just a few, good leaders?"

"Because leadership begins at the most basic level of all, parenting. Parents must be philosophers. Philosophical training must be taught to all the parents and teachers and politicians of your primitive societies. Keep in mind, within enlightened civilizations, the wise and patient elders provide philosophical training, as well as education. Philosophy must be taught at a young age and reinforced into adulthood."

"That probably won't happen where I come from. That's reality."

"Reality? You humans have no sense of reality."

"Sure we do."

"Then, why do you resist enlightenment, the highest form of truth, the supreme reality?"

"What do you mean?"

"When an enlightened leader rises to popularity on your planet, often a sage with a message of wisdom, love, and peace; you eliminate him or her."

"Are you talking about assassination?"

"That is one method. I have learned that many of my earlier guests who returned to Earth to become great sages and Masters have been poisoned, crucified, tortured, burned at the stake, hung by the neck, shot, and assassinated."

I grimaced and swallowed hard. "Why do all our great leaders get killed?"

Morph pointed at the cave wall. "See your shadow dancing on the cave wall?"

I looked over my shoulder and nodded, *yes*, while the shadows on the cave wall swayed to the rhythm of the fire.

"Imagine a group of human beings who have lived their entire lives trapped in a subterranean chamber, a cave. Imagine the cave looks like this cave, with the fire as its only source of light. Imagine these humans are permanent cave dwellers, chained and held immobile since childhood. Not only are their arms and legs chained in place, but their heads are also fixed, making them stare at the cave wall in front of them. As for their bizarre existence, they are unaware of any other way and they offer no complaints.

"Behind the chained humans a blazing fire burns brightly. Between the fire and humans is a raised walkway. On the walkway are puppets shaped like animals and plants and mountains, moved by an observer. A manipulator. A tyrant. The humans are forced to watch the shadows on the cave wall. The shadows are the only objects the humans have seen since infancy. Noises echo off the cave walls from the walkway, their only reality of sound."

Morph's eyes glowed with the fires of wisdom. "Do you think the humans would believe the shadows to be real things, or just reflections of reality?"

"Probably real things," I said.

"Imagine most of the human beings content with the lights and shadows, while the most clever among them become highly skilled observers and question the reality of the shadows. In either case, they cannot comprehend what they see. Their chains prevent them from seeing the true source and nature of the ghostly images on the wall. Imagine one of the clever humans breaks his chains and climbs through the bleak underworld to the surface of the Earth."

"Escapes?"

"Yes. And with his eyes accustomed only to the dim light of the cave, what would happen to him when he emerged into the upper world?"

"He'd be blinded by the bright light."

"At first, he is only able to gaze upon shadows and reflections of the real world. But, with some time and effort, as his eyes become accustomed to the light, this former cave dweller discovers the real world, gazing in awe and wonderment at the living trees and animals and rivers and majestic mountains. Finally, he looks upon the Sun itself. Imagine this escapee, witness to the Sun, returning to the cave. What do you think he would do?"

"Tell the others about the real world. Inform them they'd been looking at a bunch of stupid shadows on the wall."

"What would happen when he tells his former friends and family what he has seen, that there is a better world in which to live, not the world in which they have been content to dwell? He announces he shall free them from their chains of ignorance. How do you think they would respond?"

"They would all agree."

"Are you sure?" Morph asked, raising his eyebrows.

"Yes. Why would they want to stay in the dark?"

Black spiderbats dove and captured the fluttering moths hypnotized by the light of the dancing flames.

"The imprisoned humans notice how their former companion, who has seen the bright world above, now acts inept and clumsy in the dark realm of the cave. They doubt his word, believing he is mad, crazy, out of his mind. They mock him and name him the 'enlightened one,' the human blinded by the divine light of the Sun. They remind him that nothing is wrong with their dark existence and they are content; they lack nothing."

"People would not stay in the cave. No way."

"Even if some people agreed with the enlightened one and visited the surface, many would be immediately frightened and return to the cave. To their familiar, safe existence in the dark. Many would never journey to the surface. Frightened of the truth, they would feel safe, be content and happy to remain in the shadows. Only a few would be willing to journey to the upper world and look at the Sun, the light, and see the world as it truly exists. A few would realize that their cave life had been a total farce and a shadow of the truth. They would know they had been taught incorrectly, misguided, lied to."

"Maybe you're right. That does makes sense."

"Many of them would want to return to the cave and free their family and friends from bondage, but would discover that they are also the focus of scorn and ridicule and persecution."

"I can see how that might happen."

"Would it not have been in the best interest of the cave dwellers to entrust their lives to the enlightened one, the human with the most knowledge and wisdom?"

"Yeah, for sure."

"And what else might happen to the enlightened humans who return to the dark cave to help their fellow humans see the light?"

I bit my lip, shrugging my shoulders.

"Imagine the paranoid cave dwellers declare that the enlightened one's eyes have been corrupted by the light. 'Beware of his lies,' they scream, 'It is not worth trying to go to the surface.' Vicious rumors begin. They warn each other, 'Do not follow the madman's teachings.' They scorn and ridicule him. And when they discover that the enlightened one plans to unchain and release humans from their shackles, lead humans up to the light, do you think that the fearful and ignorant masses might possibly plot to kill the enlightened one?"

"Murder him?"

The sage nodded, *yes*.

"You mean, because they believe he's crazy, out of his mind?"

"Correct. Out of his mind. They realize that the madman, the radical thinker who speaks only of the one, true reality, has won favor with the masses. His popularity has grown. Jealousy erupts as the cave dwellers realize how many people have actually dedicated their lives to follow the enlightened one out of the dark and into the light."

I raised my right index finger. "I know what you're getting at," I said, glancing over my shoulder at Eve.

"What might that be?"

"That humans are afraid of change," I said. "They like the way things are. Anyone who thinks differently is crazy and must be silenced, or eliminated."

"Excellent response."

I grinned. "They will do anything, even murder or imprison the enlightened one, if they believe he is trying to change them, or their society, with a new idea."

"My son, you *do* understand my allegory."

"Thanks," I said, proud of my answer.

"Now, what is the message of my story?"

"Ummm, that a philosopher should be our president?"

"Close."

Shrugging my shoulders, I shook my head, *I don't know.*

"The meaning of my allegory is that the enlightened one, having seen the Light, the truth, the supreme reality, is now capable of philosophical thought. With proper thought comes leadership. Therefore, philosophers make the best parents, teachers, and leaders. Philosophers live life as leaders. Anyone willing to see the light, change their thoughts, shall become a leader; that is, they shall become an enlightened being who leads by example, not by force or deception or corruption or control."

"That makes sense."

"The Underworld, like the initial path to enlightenment, lacks illumination. Darkness prevails. Patience and persistence guides all beings from the darkness into the Light."

I stared at Eve's beautiful face glowing in the firelight.

"Tell me, my son. What would happen if humans actually embraced philosophy and became enlightened by it?"

Looking into Morph's tranquil eyes, I replied, "The world would change for the better."

"What would it take for this enlightenment to happen?"

"People would have to be made aware of the truth?"

"Excellent answer. Awareness! Two groups of humans exist on Earth: aware and unaware."

"Unaware of what?"

"You just had the answer. Truth. The majority of humans are unaware of the truth and unable to think for themselves, allowing others to create their thoughts for them. Their thoughts are created by lying politicians and governments and ritualists and negative books and all those media devices your technology has provided you."

"Sounds like brainwashing." I drew a deep breath. "Why don't we do something about it?"

"It is easier to let others make your decisions for you, let them create your reality."

"Like a bunch of robots."

"Yes. You humans allow others to do your thinking for you, preferring the easy way out. Someone needs to get the word out, think for yourself. Somebody needs to wake up the world. Perhaps *you* shall be the one to perform such a noble deed."

"Maybe." I glanced at Eve, who remained asleep.

"An ancient axiom is, 'Think your own thoughts, not the thoughts of others.'"

Metamorphosis smiled and rubbed his four hands over the fire. "I believe we have discussed enough for this evening. Excuse me, while I meditate. When there is silence, one finds the anchor of the universe within oneself."

Morph turned around, removed his boots, folded his wings and crossed his legs in a full lotus position. He curled his tail and raised his four arms skyward, remaining still.

I stared at the sage's shadow on the opposite cave wall, a shadow that few people on Earth would understand or accept as reality. Quietly dragged my bedroll closer to the fire, opened my artist satchel, and pulled out a piece of parchment paper and a pencil.

In the glow of the crackling flames, Morph lowered his four arms, turned around and grinned at me. The sage placed his spectacles in his vest pocket and crawled under his wool blanket.

Alone with only my thoughts, I hoped that we'd arrive at the Open Road soon. The trip was taking longer than I planned. I needed to get back home so I could graduate. Graduate? Why was I worried about that? I'd be a billionaire after I told my story and released my books and video games.

But it also meant I wouldn't see Eve ever again. I wondered if she could somehow visit Earth with me. There was something about her I really, really liked. I convinced myself that she had begun to understand me a lot better. I was glad she was afraid of the dark. Maybe if the lights went out, she'd want me to hold her. Hug her.

Wide awake, I drew an outline of the Millennium map. While I fantasized about Eve, I penciled in names on the map— names of all the kingdoms and castles and towns and waterfalls and rivers and mountains and treasures and trails that I could possibly remember.

DAYNIGHT OF THE BUTTERFLY

Aries the 12th
Year of the Dragon

"Surrender yourself humbly; then,
you can be trusted to care for all things.
Love the world as your own Self;
then you can truly care for all things."
—Metamorphosis

Chapter 15
Bridge of the Separator

Proudly wearing the red tunic that Andvari had tailored for me, I pulled the reins of Chernobog to the right, through the entrance to Nudd Tunnel. Having left the smoldering campfire at the Den of Shadows behind us, we had entered the ascending subterranean route. By the light of the two antennalanterns and Grimnir's knocker's cap, I could see that the tunnel had been engineered and excavated like a mining shaft. Twenty feet wide and twelve feet high, the tunnel route looked different from the previous caves and caverns. Wooden posts, beams and rafters stretched the entire length of the tunnel. Rails two feet wide—iron tracks—ran down the middle of the tunnel. The warm, damp air smelled earthy, like my basement at home.

Grimnir and Morph rode Byelobog, the lead moleipeede. The aardvark hollered commands, coaxing the subterranean sumpter to climb the steady incline as fast as possible.

Wearing a gold silk chemise, Eve sat behind me. The Epiphanite had eaten her breakfast in silence and had not spoken since the Daynight of the Butterfly began.

This was a perfect time to talk. Just as I thought of something clever to say, the girl from Epiphany surprised me by tapping me on the shoulder and asking *me* a question.

"What did you mean at Ogo Hole when you said your father is a control freak?"

Caught off-guard by the question, I said, "Why do you ask?"

"Please, I want to know."

"Okay," I said, turning my head to the right. "I meant that my father always wants to control everything I do. Ever since I was a little kid, he's told me what I was going to be, that every

Wainright is successful, that I'm going to be a doctor or lawyer or scientist. Stuff like that."

"Then, he fails to ask your opinion?"

"Right."

"Does he become angry when you fail to follow his instructions?"

"Yeah, sometimes."

"Has he ever hit you?"

"No, never." I paused, and said, "But sometimes I wish he would hit me instead of constantly bitching."

"Bitching?"

"Sorry, I mean that he's always harping on me, giving me instructions, telling me how to live my life. I can't seem to please him. I never do anything right."

The moleipeede snorted and slowed down. The tunnel's incline had increased significantly.

"So, what do you want to do with your life?" she asked.

"Before I answer that, can I ask *you* a question?"

"No. Answer first. Then, maybe I will answer your question."

"I'm an artist. That's what I love to do."

"You mean, those drawings you create?"

"Well, sort of. Those are just pencil and ink sketches. When I get back home, I'll remember what I've drawn and recreate them in a different media, paintings and computer graphics."

I turned my torso around in my saddle and grinned at Eve. "Now, you owe *me* an answer."

"It depends on the question."

I nodded and asked, "Why are you so afraid of the dark?"

Turning my head back around I waited for a reply. I snapped the leather reins to make the moleipeede pick up speed, waiting for Eve of Epiphany to answer. Fifty years farther up the tunnel, I turned around again. "Okay, since you won't answer that, can I ask one more question?"

"I am not sure about this, but go ahead."

"Why did you get so upset with me in the Gametasia room, back on the *Skipbladnir*?"

She closed her eyes and sighed. "I apologize for my rude behavior. I do not enjoy talking about my family, but since we

266

are going to be together a bit longer, I will confide in you."

"Maybe it's good to get it off your chest. I mean, your mind," I said, turning forward.

"Perhaps you are wiser than you act. For some reason, I trust you."

"Thanks a lot," I said in a sarcastic voice.

"Do not take it personally. I am not accustomed to your playful behavior."

"Is that because of your childhood? Don't you like to laugh and have fun?"

"Let me explain why I came to Millennium," she said, taking a deep breath. "My mother died when I was eight years old. I barely remember her. When she died, we still lived underground. When we finally made it to the surface, into the light of our daystar, I was thirteen years old."

"Underground?"

"Please, let me finish."

I raised my right hand to signal I would not interrupt her.

"Father treated me extremely cruel. He beat me and yelled at me all the time. My grandfather, who lived with us, tried to save me from the abuse. He was wise, but physically weak. One day, while I traveled with my grandfather through the Great Southern Dome, he told me about Millennium. That night he offered me his gold Triamulet. He had fashioned a ruby necklace, just for me. He told me how he had visited Millennium and made the mistake of returning to Epiphany. He described a magical world where I could be free of my father's abuse, be free of the darkness. So, I wore the ruby necklace and Triamulet, went to sleep and woke up on Time Island."

"God, that's terrible, I mean, about your father," I said, turning to look at her. "I'm glad you're here."

Tears welled up in her eyes as she continued. "I truly love it here. Morph has been so kind and insightful, just like my grandfather."

"Do you mean you're never going home?"

"I am going to—"

The moleipeede jerked to a stop, pushing Eve into me. She put her arms around my waist to keep herself upright. My heart raced when I felt her hands against my stomach and her warm breath against the back of my neck.

Hold me, was my only thought. *Don't let go.*

Eve regained her balance, letting go of me.

Morph raised his upper left arm and made a fist, the signal to remain still, *keep quiet.* A dim light approached from the tunnel ahead. Within moments, the sound of creaking, clacking wheels on tracks echoed in the tunnel.

Grimnir motioned to move the moleipeedes to our right, against the rock walls.

From the darkness, a mining cart filled with copper ore approached at a steady, downhill speed. Two furry animals resembling giant badgers pulled the cart. A knocker stood on the rear of the cart next to a glowing oil lantern, waving to Morph and Grimnir. The miner, dressed in coveralls blackened with sooty dust, nodded at Eve and me. When the cart rolled by, we waved to the dirty-faced miner grinning with white lips and teeth. The steel wheels rattled and clacked against the iron tracks.

Morph tucked his wings behind his back and gave the *move forward* signal with his left upper arm.

The moleipeedes lunged forward, snorting and sniffing the tunnel floor.

"You were going to tell me if you're going home," I said.

"I'm not in the mood to talk about that right now."

There she goes again, not talking, I thought, knowing not to say any more or I'd upset her.

The tunnel snaked toward the southwest. When the pair of moleipeedes made the third twisting turn, a bright light shone fifty yards ahead. As they approached the light, I saw two enormous openings on both sides of the Nudd Tunnel.

Grimnir closed the latch to his knocker's cap and announced, "It's~sth about time. Here she is~sth, the famous~sth Crater Tunnel Loop."

Byelobog and Chernobog entered the lighted opening in the tunnel wall and abruptly turned left. Eve and I clung to our saddle horns to stay upright on the pack animals.

The tin sign nailed to a timber read:

Crater Tunnel Loop
Realm of the Dungeons
Elevation: ~80 Miles Below Sea Level

The tunnel measured forty feet wide and twenty feet high. Morph told us that, as a major underground transportation corridor, the Crater Tunnel Loop encircled the entire Discordia Crater. On the floor of the tunnel, two sets of iron tracks ran side by side.

Grimnir kept the moleipeedes on the right side of the tracks, heading east. On the ceiling of the tunnel, hung every thirty feet, globe-like objects glowed with a white luminescence.

"What makes those round things glow?" I yelled, hoping to get Morph's attention.

The sage turned and yelled, "Luminescent fungi. Those are fungus globes."

"Just be happy we have light in here," Eve said.

Climbing an ascending tunnel trail, the powerful moleipeedes managed to travel at a rapid speed, thirty miles per hour according to Morph.

On three occasions, mining carts filled with coal passed by. A rail handcar, pumped up and down by two elvensmiths, passed us. On the left side of the tracks, traveling in the opposite direction, I observed a parade of underworld creatures. Cave faeries, dwarves, dark elves, leprechauns, knockers, and elvensmiths. Some of the subterranean travelers waved; some paid no attention to our group. After an hour of travel, Grimnir stopped.

Morph gave the signal, *dismount*. Our group walked to an oval opening in the side of the tunnel. I stood in awe at the site before me. The cavern's stalagmites stood hundreds of feet tall. The domed cave's ceiling disappeared into a subterranean night of blackness.

The sage announced that they had reached the city of Knockmaa, a thriving subterranean metropolis of cave faeries. While we drank from our water bags, Eve and I admired the distant city through the opening in the tunnel wall. Grinding noises—the sound of machinery—echoed off the cavern walls. Morph explained that southern gnomes and dark elves helped the cave faeries build Knockmaa, stone by stone.

"Here, take a look," Morph said, handing me the spyglass. "That is the Bridge of the Secret, leading to the Isle of the Blest."

The sage explained that the Black River, a tributary of the River Styx, flowed around the mining city. The Styx emptied into the Discordia Crater as Charon Falls.

I smelled smoke while I focused Andvari's telescope on the underground river that curved around the perimeter of the walled city. An island sat in the middle of a river. Like a gigantic glistening snake, the river wound her way around Knockmaa and disappeared into the dark caverns. A stacked-stone wall, two stories tall, surrounded the city. Guards patrolled the top of the wall. Four watchtowers with pointed spires pierced the darkness, one tower at each corner of the fortress. A two-story gate house soldiered the entry.

Morph pointed to an arched, stone bridge spanning the river, leading to Knockmaa's main entry, a pair of wood and iron gates towering two stories tall. Four mills with thatched roofs stood along the far bank of the river. The water wheels turned in unison. The inner-city buildings, constructed of stone block, brick and mortar, revealed numerous towers with pointed spires, decorative columns, and arched windows. Orange chimney stacks belched blue smoke. A massive domed structure emerged from the center of the city. The dome's ribbed copper roof glistened in the maze of glowing lights, a combination of torches, lanterns, and fungus globes.

I handed Eve the spyglass.

"No thank you, I can see fine," she said.

Her pupils looked larger than I had ever seen them. I was surprised the Epiphanite could see anything that far away.

"The sign reads Knockmaa, City of the Cave Faeries," she said, pointing.

I squinted, but could not read the letters. I could barely see the sign, looking through the telescope and spotting the Knockmaa sign at the entrance.

She had eyes like an eagle. Eve could see twice as far as me.

"Too bad your eyes-sth ain't no good, sth-sonny," Grimnir said as he pointed at me.

"I can see a lot better than *you*. You squinty-eyed son of a—"

Eve grabbed my arm and whispered, "He doesn't mean anything by it. Ignore him. Leave him alone."

"But, that aardvark's made fun of me this whole trip."

Morph turned and smiled. "Come, my son. Let us visit Finvara."

"Who is Finvara?" I asked, following the sage.

Grimnir stuck out his slender tongue at me. I gave the slobbering sumpter master a threatening stare.

We saddled up, and moved on.

Morph requested silence as we approached the Bridge of the Secret. When we arrived, the sage waved to the gate tower guard. The moleipeedes carried us across the bridge that spanned the Black River. We stopped at the entrance.

The wooden sign read:

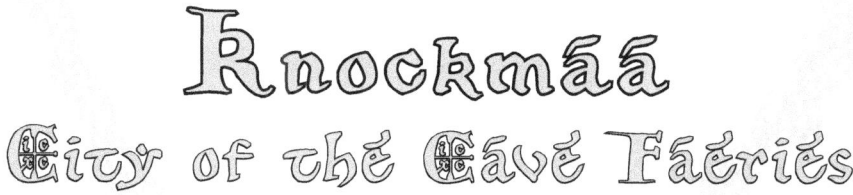

Knockmaa
City of the Cave Faeries

The two-story-tall wood and iron gates creaked open, allowing us to enter the City of the Cave Faeries. Eve and I smiled when they saw the cave faeries cheer and applaud our arrival. The wee folk looked humanoid, about three feet tall at the shoulder. The cave faeries had no wings. Their clothes, dark and dirty, looked like miner's coveralls. Morph told us that for two millennia the industrious miners and metalsmiths had excavated precious jewels, metals, and ore from the Second Stratum, Realm of the Dungeons.

Torches, oil lamps and fungus globes lit the city streets. At the end of the main street, Morph stopped at a three-story building with Gothic-style architecture. I helped Eve dismount and we followed the sage up the stone steps. Grimnir attended to the moleipeedes, taking them toward the stables.

Stained-glass-windowed doors swung open when we reached the top of the stairs.

"Finvara, my old friend," Morph said. "You look well."

"Aye, thank ye, Morph," he replied.

Finvara, king of the cave faeries, invited us into the ancient building. Except for his royal green robe, jeweled scepter, white hair and beard, he looked like the other cave faeries.

Eve and I entered a grand hall. A thirty-foot-long banquet table sat in front of a floor-to-ceiling stone fireplace. Cave faeries scurried about, preparing the table with food and drink. While troubadours played festive music, cave faeries sat at square tables along the perimeter of the stone walls, preparing to play Gametasia board games.

We sat next to King Finvara, who said, "Aye, I'll 'ave the maids get your rooms ready so you can stay a spell."

Morph, seated at the opposite side of the wooden table, grinned. "We appreciate your hospitality, but we must keep moving. Hunter is in a hurry. We must reach the Lava Caverns by this evening."

"Aye, another human visitor in a big hurry," Finvara said, chuckling.

Embarrassed, I glanced at Eve and looked down at the table, choosing not to respond.

"Surely, you can stay for a bite to eat." The king grinned.

Morph nodded in approval.

Before the sage could speak, three wee folk entered the hall with a violin and two guitars on their backs.

"Ya must sing fer your supper, me ole' friend," Finvara said.

"Will you join me, Finvara?" Morph asked.

I raised my hand. "Can I play guitar?"

"The boy cun play guitar?" the king asked.

"I have only heard him on the mouth harp," the sage replied.

"Yeah, I can play," I said, glancing at Eve.

"Aye, give the young man the guitar," Finvara said. "I'll take the fiddle."

The cave faeries handed Morph a double neck guitar, me a six string guitar, and Finvara a violin and bow. On a corner stage, a cave faerie stood with an acoustic bass fiddle, a second faerie stood behind a snare drum holding brushes.

Morph plucked both low-E strings. I plucked my high-E string. We both strummed an E-major chord.

"We're in tune," I said, grinning.

"What do you wish to hear?" Morph asked the king.

"Me favorite song 'tis, 'Love Teaches All'. Aye, it be a grand tune to sing."

"All right, follow me," Morph said, nodding to me.

A hush fell over the room when the sage strummed the double-neck guitar. Finvara played violin. The music sounded great. The hall had good acoustics.

I played guitar by watching the sage's fingers form the chords. Morph sang the first verse.

> "From where I stand, below are Mountains of Mistakes,
> The hardest part, is all the promises we break,
> This gift of life, is not just ours for the take,
> It's what we all pass on, we take so much of life for
> granted, And feel so sure it will be there,
> When nothing goes the way we planned it,
> I say relax, there may be more, know that—"

The king and the cave faeries harmonized with Morph as he sang the first chorus.

> "Love teaches all,
> Patience and calm, to the weak and the strong,
> Love teaches all,
> It's a lesson learned, by a fall, ooh, ooh, ooh."

Morph grinned and sang the second verse.

> "Have this life, I can't hold it in my hands,
> It takes a life, to truly understand,
> That God has ways, of showing us His plan,
> In His own due time,
> So when you feel your journey's over,
> 'Cause you can't put some fight to rest,
> That little voice taps on your shoulder and says,
> The things that come may be the best, know that—"

Having learned the chords, I played guitar confidently as Morph and cave faeries sang the chorus.

"Love teaches all,
    Patience and calm, to the weak and the strong,
    Love teaches all,
    It's a lesson learned, by a fall."
Morph played a guitar riff.
    "Love teaches all,
    Patience and calm, to the weak and the strong,
    Love teaches all,
    It's a lesson learned, by a fall."
Finvara danced and played his violin while Morph smiled and sang the song's outro.
    "Love teaches, always reaches, to where the need is, in us all, Love teaches, always reaches, where our need is, in us all, Love teaches, always reaches, where our need is, in us all, Love teaches, always reaches, to where the need is, in us all, ooh...ooh...ooh."
Morph played a final guitar riff with four hands, fingering harmonic notes on his double neck guitar. When the final note faded into the cathedral ceilings of the great hall, the cave faeries cheered and applauded in approval.
Eve clapped her hands and nudged me, saying, "I like the way you play guitar."
Surprised by her comments, I failed to say thank you. I just sat there grinning.
"Aye, Morph cun sure sing a song," Finvara yelled.
The king clapped his hands and announced, "Time to eat, drink, 'n be merry."
Piano and guitar music played. The hall came alive with wee laughter and giggles. Cave faeries placed bowls of mushrooms, fruit, and ambrosia on the table in front of Eve and me. The tremella had the aroma of buttered popcorn.
Between the music and the faerie chatter and Finvara's laughs, I tried to find the right time to talk to Eve. She sat next to me, smiling at Finvara, but silent. Every time I said something to her, she nodded and looked away, eating her meal. The Epiphanite refused to respond to my conversation.
The silence between me and Eve became unbearable. Nothing I said got her talking. But I knew she liked my guitar playing.

I had barely finished eating when Morph stood and bid King Finvara farewell.

Surprised, I wiped my mouth with my green napkin, jumped up and followed Eve and Morph outside. Descending the stone steps, I spotted Grimnir waiting at the bottom of the stairs feeding his moleipeedes.

"Sth-say Moorfff, it's-sth 'bout time we sth-saddle up," the slobbering aardvark said, wiping the drool from his lips.

I mounted my sumpter after Eve. We waved goodbye to Finvara and rode our sumpters out of Knockmaa, over the Bridge of the Secret, and into the opening of the Crater Loop Trail.

Entering the trail, I pulled the leather reins to my left, easterly. I smelled Eve's vanilla-like body fragrance and felt her breath on the back of my neck.

Focusing my thoughts, I wondered, *How I can I get Eve to talk to me about her planet, Epiphany, like she did earlier? Why is she so cold? At least she complimented me on my guitar playing. Come on Hunter, think of something intelligent to say to her. She's sitting right behind you...Stop! Listen to yourself. Stop thinking negative thoughts!*

Just as I found the courage to speak, Morph gave the *all quiet* signal with his left upper hand.

By the evening of the Daynight of the Butterfly, our group had ascended 280 miles through the Crater Tunnel Loop. The moleipeedes had averaged thirty-five miles per hour on their extended ride. During their ascent up the illuminated tunnel, I tried to talk to Eve twice, but the Epiphanite refused to carry on a conversation.

Having reached the Lava Caverns, we had set up camp near the River of Fire, fifty yards from the main tunnel's route and one hundred yards from the river of molten lava.

While Grimnir fed his sumpters a ration of roachmash, we sat by the campfire, silently eating our meals of dodo jerky, ripe açai berries, and ambrosia. I could see that Morph enjoyed his silence. He looked so calm and relaxed as the River of Fire glowed in the distance.

Eve finished her meal and asked the sage, "Are we going to see the River of Fire in the morning?"

"No, there is nothing to see but lava flow," Morph replied.

Before I could respond, the sage announced, "It is time we retire for the evening. Good daynight."

Metamorphosis stretched his wings and said, "Stillness is the master of unrest," as he turned toward the cave wall, raised his four arms to the heavens and began to meditate.

Eve whispered, "Good daynight," and pulled her wool blanket over her body.

It wasn't long before Morph turned, placed his spectacles in his leather vest and laid under the blanket of his bedroll.

Retrieved my artist satchel and took out my quill pen and ink bottle. I leaned back against a boulder and began to draw by the light of the fire, finishing a drawing of Pendragon.

The sage slept quietly while Grimnir and his sumpters tossed and turned in their furrows. Eve, lying silent and motionless under her beige blanket, had fallen asleep.

I put the finished drawing, along with the quill and ink bottle, back into my artist satchel. Decided that I needed to see the River of Fire. I'd be back before anyone woke up.

Quietly strapping on my scabbard belt and sword, I slung my water bag over my shoulder and snuck away from the campsite.

The glow from the River of Fire lit the cavernous landscape well enough for me to see the trail ahead. The river's pulsating yellow light cast shadows on the forest of orange stalactites and stalagmites. The smell of burning lava permeated the stale air.

Stopped at a trail that headed straight for the glowing river.

I heard a noise behind me. Looking over my shoulder, I drew my sword and stared wide-eyed into the dark shadows. Listening to the pulse pound in my head, I prepared to defend myself.

Out of the shadows, Eve appeared.

"What are you doing out here?" she asked, raising her black eyebrows.

Sighing, I lowered my sword and said, "I want to see the River of Fire before we leave in the morning."

"It is too dangerous out here. We must go back."

"What are you afraid of? The dark?"

Eve frowned. "That is not fair."

"Sorry, I didn't mean it like that."

"Well, how *did* you mean it?"

I shrugged my shoulders. "I'm mad because you won't talk to me."

"If I promise to talk tomorrow, will you return to camp?"

"Come on, Eve. Let's go see the river. We can talk on the way; I'll keep my voice down."

Wiping the sweat from her forehead, Eve looked back at the flickering flames of our campsite. She was wearing cut-off breeches—shorts—that exposed her thin, long legs. Her sandals had leather ties that wrapped around her ankles and calves. Her white tunic had been cut short, exposing her belly button.

She said, "I'm going back to get *Gandeeva*. And my knife."

"Don't worry, I have my sword."

She stared at my hand, holding the handle of *Aroundight*.

"All right," Eve said, blinking nervously, "but just to the river. I *would* like to see it."

I slid my sword into its scabbard. "Come on, let's go."

Held out my arm. To my surprise, she reached out and held my hand. The warmth of her touch shot up my arm and I immediately felt a funny, weightless sensation in my stomach.

"Awesome," I mumbled, grinning.

She grinned and followed me down the trail lined with jagged magma rock formations. When we neared the river, the sound of flowing, crackling lava grew louder.

I couldn't believe she was holding my hand. For the first time, I believed she might have feelings for me.

"Look, there it is," I said, pointing ahead.

Within moments, we stood on the magma bank above the River of Fire. Although the river flowed fifty feet below us, the air felt like a blast of heat from an open oven. The smell of smoke filled the vast cavern. The rumbling lava and popping embers roared past us at a rapid speed, making it impossible to talk.

"Let's go up *there*," I yelled, pointing up the trail.

Still holding my hand, Eve followed me up the steep, winding trail of black, magma rock. When we reached the top of the pathway, the temperature had cooled considerably. We sat on a flat boulder, staring down at the mighty River of Fire. The entire cavern glowed from the river's red, orange and yellow light. The roar of the flowing lava had subsided, allowing us to talk.

"Here, have a drink," I said, offering Eve my water bag. We both drank amrita and stared at the glowing river below.

"The last time we spoke," I said, "you were telling me about Epiphany. I'd like to hear more. I am interested in your life. I really mean that."

"I sense your sincerity. What do you want to know?"

I looked into her emerald-green eyes. The light from the river caused her flawless skin to glow like an angel. Her lips turned up in a relaxed smile. I was dying to kiss her lips, but I knew she won't let me. *Calm down,* I told myself, *don't ruin this moment, just ask her about Epiphany. Don't talk about yourself.*

"Do you have any brothers or sisters?" I asked.

"Although I am not comfortable with your question, I trust you. The answer is, yes, I have a brother. No sisters."

"What's his name?"

"Elbon. He is two years older than I am."

"Your names sound strange."

"So do yours."

I grinned. "You're right."

Eve frowned and said, "I have not seen my brother since I was fourteen years old."

"Where is he?"

"I do not know. My father allowed the military leaders to take him. I found out later that my father sold Elbon to a mining organization."

"That's horrible, I'm sorry."

"My brother is still enslaved in the Great Northern Dome."

"Dome? What's that all about?"

"If you are chosen, you can move from the underground bunkers to a dome. You must be approved by the leaders of the corrupt government. Much of my childhood was spent underground. I remember my mother always being afraid of the dark. I hated the darkness."

"You mean the dome is above ground?"

"The domes, thousands of geodesic domes connected together, allow us to see our daystar, see the sky. Feel alive. Even though the air is grey and dirty and radioactive, it is still better than being below ground, in the dark all the time."

"Morph told me that you've had three nuclear winters on your planet. He didn't explain why, but I have to assume that your planet has had some kind of nuclear accident."

"There have been no accidents. As Morph keeps reminding us, primitive civilizations eventually destroy themselves with their own technology. Weapons of mass destruction have wiped out billions of us Epiphanites."

"So, how long do you have to stay in those domes? When can you breathe fresh air again?"

"It will be at least another two hundred years before it is safe to come out, expose ourselves to the atmosphere."

I squeezed her hand, asking, "Is that why you're never going back?"

"I have nothing to go back to, except my grandfather, and he is not going to live much longer." Eve had tears in her eyes. "Like you, my grandfather was taught as a child that the Epiphanites were advanced, perfect. Although we were overpopulated, we had enjoyed nuclear energy and space travel for several centuries. We also—"

"Wait. Space travel? In a rocket ship?"

Eve grinned. "You have space crafts on Earth. Correct?"

"Yeah, but we've only sent humans to the moon and back, not other planets."

"Well, hopefully you will never need to go to another planet."

Nodded my head, knowing her statement had merit.

"Where do your space ships go?"

"I wanted to leave Epiphany on a space craft. Because of the waiting list, I would not have left until I was sixty years old."

"Where would you have gone?"

"There were several similar planets to choose from. They have environments where we could immediately blend in and adapt without rejection by the native inhabitants. Three of the inhabitable planets are in your Milky Way galaxy."

I swallowed. "Was Earth one of them?"

"Yes. I was told that centuries ago, Earth was the first choice of relocation for most Epiphanites. My grandfather told me that one hundred years ago, Earth had become overpopulated, suffered air quality problems and was on the verge of destroying its own civilization with nuclear weapons and other self-destructive technology."

"You mean, your ancestors landed on Earth?"

"Hundreds of them."

No wonder she looks so human, I thought, *Wait a minute, maybe I look like an Epiphanite.*

"My grandfather could tell you a lot more about the intergalactic migration. He told me that I have distant relatives on Earth."

"This is incredible. Wait until I tell your story when I get home."

Eve grimaced. "You really want to go back home, don't you."

I looked into Eve's eyes and squeezed her hand.

"Yes, and no. I really miss my family. But...ummm—"

"Go ahead. What?"

"I want to stay here and get to know *you* better."

Eve smiled and squeezed my hand.

I don't know what overcame me, but some force inside me made me lean forward to kiss Eve.

Eve let go of my hand and jumped up.

"I have shared enough," she said. "We need to get back to camp."

"I'm sorry, I'm out of control," I said as I stood up. "I like you very much. I won't do that again, I promise."

Eve turned away and tossed her black hair across her shoulders in a gesture of nervousness.

I looked away, trying to control my emotions.

Looking down the back side of the trail, I spotted a stone bridge spanning the River of Fire.

"Check it out," I yelled, "at the bottom of the trail, a bridge."

Eve walked several steps in the opposite direction. "It is time to get back to camp."

"Come on, let's take a look. There's nobody down there."

"No. You are acting foolish. We must go back. Now."

"Just for a moment, stay here and watch me."

I wanted to show her that I wasn't afraid, how brave I was.

"Please, do not go down there," she yelled, running to me and grabbing the sleeve of my red tunic.

"I'll be right back," I said, pulling away from her tight grasp.

I grabbed my sword handle and boldly hiked down the winding trail cut into the side of a black magma cliff.

Beyond the bridge, molten lava flowed from a volcanic cave. The fiery river poured down the side of the rock cliff and erupted into an explosion of crackling red and yellow sparks.

Traversing the jagged rock formations and obsidian boulders littering the trail, I felt the heat increase as I walked closer to the bridge.

Twenty yards from the bridge, I stopped and listened.

Over the roar of the river, I heard voices—cries and moaning. Someone was crying on the other side of the lava river.

Drew my sword from its sheath and looked up at Eve.

She motioned with both hands, *come back, now!*

I wiped the sweat from my forehead and spotted a sign by the bridge. Decided to get closer so I could read it.

Then, I would get out of there and rejoin Eve.

So, I ran to the foot of the bridge, perspiration dripping down my face as the roar of lava echoed off the cavern walls.

Bridge of the Separator

Dungeon of Fire

Engraved in stone, the sign read:

BRIDGE OF THE SEPARATOR

I sensed movement and looked up.

Standing on the other side of the bridge, a pair of glaring red eyes stared at me. Then, the fiery eyes moved straight toward me.

"Holy shit!" I shouted as I turned and ran.

I remember hearing the snap of a rope and found myself lying flat on my stomach, stunned. My sword had flown out of my right hand and landed between two black boulders.

Eve, still at the top of the trail, shouted, "Run Hunter! Get up! He is coming for you!"

Looking back at my boots, a yellow rope was wrapped tightly around my ankles. The rope moved. It was a snake!

I glanced up and saw a blue-skinned monster with a shiny helmet and a scarlet-red cape running toward me.

Swinging a flail with spikes, he shook the ground with his footsteps.

Got to my hands and knees, struggling to scramble to my feet, but the snake tightened its grip around my legs. Then, I felt a boot in my upper back, between my shoulder blades.

"Uhhhh!"

I had the breath knocked out of me as my chest was smashed into the black magma floor.

"I can't breathe...get off me...I can't...breathe."

The pressure from his boot caused me to panic.

I choked, gasping for air.

A cold, clammy hand with the grip of a monster grabbed the back of my neck and pulled me toward him.

Looking up, beyond the monster's glowing red eyes, I saw Eve running up the dark trail toward camp.

I knew it was my fault. I made Eve leave her bow, arrows and knife behind, that she had allowed me to influence her logical decisions, that I had to pay the price for my human stupidity.

Those were my last thoughts before everything turned blurry, then dark, then black.

DAYNIGHT OF THE BAT

Aries the 13th
Year of the Dragon

"A good soldier is not violent.
A good fighter is not angry.
A good winner is not vengeful.
A good leader is humble."
—Metamorphosis

Chapter 16
Dungeon of Fire

Bewildered, I awoke thinking I had awakened from a bad dream, a nightmare. Blurry eyed and dizzy, I found myself lying on a damp stone floor. Propped myself up onto my right elbow and looked through the rusted iron bars.

I heard, "Wake up, alien. Welcome to the Dungeon of Fire. You think you're so damn smart. In a few daynights you'll know that Vulcan is the boss 'round here."

Standing in the torch light, I recognized the Extractor from the illustrations I saw in the *Magnum Opus*. The dungeon master's piercing red eyes gleamed with delight. The muscular Vulcan wore a scarlet cape, knee-high boots with yellow eyes, black loincloth britches, and a silver helmet. His oily, pale blue skin glistened with rippled veins and muscles. Attached to the neck of his flowing cape, an iron key dangled against his flexed chest muscles. His snake rope, hissing, had attached itself to Vulcan's spiked belt.

The dungeon master swirled around; his red cape flowed behind him. Holding a throwing axe, he crossed a stone bridge that spanned a glowing lava river and stomped up a flight of stone steps to a platform scattered with, what looked like, torture equipment.

He yelled at a pair of menacing cave trolls, who held their torches up to reveal a second stone stairway, some fifty feet tall. The steps led upward to an iron door, the entrance to a temple-like stone structure. The dungeon master climbed the stairs and entered his private chambers, slamming the heavy iron door behind him.

I grabbed the dungeon bars to my cell and pulled myself to

my feet, wiping my sweaty forehead with my sleeve. God, it was hot in that dungeon. The stagnant air smelled like sulfur.

Hearing moans and groans from the adjacent cells, I peeked through my prison bars. Strange arms and hands reached through the rusted iron grills. Some arms were covered with fur, some arms were hairless. Some were skeletons with rotting flesh. I wondered if the remains could be human bones.

Smoke rose from the river of smoldering lava as it roared through the Dungeon of Fire. The cavern's domed ceiling, stained black from smoke and ashes, towered three hundred feet above the dungeon floor. The perimeter's rock walls, honeycombed with caves and jagged magma formations, dripped with humidity from the geothermal activity.

Eight stone bridges led from the cells to a central platform, allowing the River of Fire to flow underneath the arches. The prison cells, facing the platform, had been built with massive granite blocks fitted with metal grills. Prison bars.

In the center of the dungeon, a circular wooden platform, one hundred feet in diameter, had been built around a central stone fire pit surrounded by torture racks, spiked chairs, iron maidens, a hanging cage, and the main gallows.

Beyond the platform, the River of Fire flowed under the stone

bridges, winding its way to an opening in the cliffs of Discordia Crater, where it formed Fire Falls.

Darkness prevailed. The only light sources came from the central fire pit, from the torches and oil lamps mounted between the cells, and from the pulsating glow of the lava river.

I spun around, hearing noises behind me. Chains rattled.

"I beseech thee, who goes there?" a feeble voice asked from the darkest corner of the prison cell.

"It's me, Hunter Wainright."

"Come 'ere, me fine lad."

I cautiously stepped toward the back of the dark cave. The cell walls, covered in green moss, oozed with moisture. I noticed two wood racks, bunks, hung from the rock wall by chains. Torn burlap blankets laid on the warped wood planks. Two cast iron waste buckets sat under the bottom bunk. A pewter plate and cup set at the head of each rack. Dungeon roaches, feeding on waste and dead skin, scurried about the cell. I ducked under the dangling spider webs draped from the rock ceiling. The cell smelled like one of those portable toilets at the faire.

The dim light revealed the eyes of a human being. An emaciated man dressed in tattered clothes sat with his back against the cave wall. He had sunken, hazel-colored eyes and a red, full-length beard.

"I be Owain Glydnwr," the man said, extending his filthy hand in friendship. "Greetin's."

"How long have I been unconscious?"

"A few 'ours, me boy."

"Are you from Earth?" I asked, bending down and shaking Owain's cold and clammy hand.

"Thou art correct," Owain said, pointing at me.

"W'ere does thou hail from?"

"The United States."

"W'ere is that planet?"

"Earth, old man. America."

Owain shrugged his shoulders.

"Forget about Earth. Where am I now?" I asked. "What is this place?"

"Aye, ye be in the Dungeon 'o Fyre, Hoonter."

I stared at Owain's ankles, shackled together by a three-foot chain.

"Naught to wurry 'bout me shackles, they be the fashion 'ere," he said, chuckling.

Not amused, I asked, "Is that guy with the silver helmet named Vulcan?"

"Ye be right."

"What does he want with me?"

"Jus' a bit 'o fun."

"Fun?"

"Aye. Betwixt torture 'n interrogations, 'tis a loot 'o fun 'ere," Owain said with a half-crazed look in his eyes. "Hast anyone told ye thou hast a fuuuny accent?"

"I haven't got an accent, *you* do."

The prisoner smiled with his rotten yellow teeth. "I like ye lad. Henceforth, ye shall be me friend."

I looked in the opposite corner of the cave and saw iron shackles bolted to the rock wall.

"Yonder is thine own shackles."

This guy is crazy, I thought, *I've got to get out of here.*

"How did you end up here, old man?"

"Old man? Me thinks ye mistykin'. Me be only fifty-four. Me nyme is Owain."

"Sorry, Owain. Tell me how you got here."

"Tarantulana caught me in her web."

"No, I don't mean *here,* I meant how'd you get to Millennium in the first place?"

"Yer youth reminds me 'o me early years in Wales."

"I know where that is. When did you arrive here from the British Isles?"

"I came 'ere fourteen years ago."

I knelt on one knee and scratched numbers on the dusty cave floor and calculated, fourteen years multiplied by fifty is seven hundred Earth years!

"So, you've been gone from Earth for seven hundred years?" I asked. "Since 1400 A.D.?"

"Twas 1409 to be exact," Owain said, smiling and scratching his scraggly beard. "I lived 'ere in paradise 'till I got caught."

"How long have you been in this horrible dungeon?"

"Only six months hath passed. Aye, Tarantulana, she caught me in 'er kingdom, Vanum is what she called it."

"Is this female an Extractor?"

"Aye."

I didn't remember seeing her picture in the *Magnum Opus*.

"Naught to wurry, ye shalt meet Tarantulana. 'Er seductive beauty shalt—"

"Did I hear my name?"

I turned my head to see an attractive dark-haired woman peeking around the corner of the cell. Owain placed his hands over his eyes as if to hide.

"Fer sure. I think I found me a new boyfriend," she said, smiling through the cell bars.

I scrambled to my feet and asked, "Excuse me?"

"Come over here young man, so I can see if you look good enough to be with beautiful me."

I walked toward the cell bars while the lady admired herself in a hand-held looking glass.

Her flowing black hair fell over her shoulders and down her bare back. Two polished silver cups, strapped around her shoulders with brass rings, supported her breasts.

"Do you think I'm seriously beautiful?" she asked, still smiling and batting her eyelashes in the mirror of her brass-handled looking glass.

"Are you asking me?" I asked, stopping next to the wooden bunks.

"Come over here, darlin'. I won't bite you," she said, motioning with her five-inch-long fingernails.

I stepped to within three feet of the iron bars. Tarantulana's hazel eyes looked hypnotic. Her ruby-red lips puckered when she spoke. "Do you find me attractive?"

"Sure, um, you look great," I said. "Can you help me get out of here? There's been a mistake."

"Oh, there's been no mistake," she said, stepping around the outside corner of the cells, in full view.

I froze, shocked. The light of the fire pit revealed her lower body, a black, fuzzy abdomen with eight jointed legs, like a

Tarantulana

giant black-widow spider.

"What happened to you?" I asked, stepping backward in fear and disgust.

The conceited Tarantulana gave me a cold stare. "Ya humans are all the same. You don't know true beauty when you see it."

I spotted the menacing figure of Vulcan approaching the vain spider woman.

"What are you doin' here?" Vulcan shouted from the platform, pointing his throwing axe. "Get outta' my dungeon!"

Tarantulana sneered at the dungeon master. "Don't order me around. Who do you think you are, you no good son of a—"

"Silence!"

I looked past Vulcan to the spot where the screaming voice came from. I saw no one.

Somehow I knew it was the Invisible Villain. I quickly realized I was in deep trouble.

The cave trolls stood at attention. The moans and groans from the dungeon cells stopped.

Ex had entered the Dungeon of Fire.

"Shhh," Tarantulana said, placing her index finger to her lips. "You'll scare the frightened boy."

"Begone, my bewitchin' beauty!" Ex shouted.

Vulcan stormed down the platform steps and across the stone bridge toward my cell.

The eight-legged Extractor pointed her looking glass at Vulcan. "Not to worry," she said, scowling. "This young boy's ugly, and not my type."

Tarantulana took one last look at herself in the mirror, stuck her nose in the air, and walked past Vulcan and the two cave trolls. Her jointed spider legs moved in perfect unison as she disappeared through a cave-like opening toward the entrance to the Bridge of the Separator.

"Here's the human. Over here, Master," Vulcan yelled, walking toward my cell.

I smelled a foul odor, different from the disgusting air already present in the dungeon. It smelled like rotting garbage.

"Pathetic boy, meet Master Ex," Vulcan yelled.

"Come closer, my boy, so I can see you in the light," Ex said.

Owain whispered, "Stay put, Hoonter. Don't ye move."

"Get over here before I have Vulcan come in there and whip your ass," the Master Extractor yelled.

I swallowed and stepped forward.

"Ahhh, much better," Ex said. "Vulcan, don't you have somethin' to do, some prisoners to torture?"

"Yes, Master, of course."

The dungeon master marched away, screaming at the cave trolls to get the torture rack ready.

"Greetings, Hunter," Ex said.

"How do you know my name?"

"I know everything."

"I doubt that," I said, folding my arms.

"Ahhh, a spirited human, full of defiance."

Although fearful, I stood my ground and stared through the bars, allowing the Master Extractor to talk.

The odor overwhelmed me. Ex smelled rancid.

"I'm willin' to offer you your freedom, an' with it, wealth beyond your wildest dreams. I ask only one small favor."

"What's that?"

"Yer allegiance to me and our noble Extractor cause."

"That's not fair. I've done nothing to harm you or your friends. Let me go."

"Fair?" Ex shouted. "I'm always fair, as long as you keep an open mind."

"No. I don't want anything to do with you, or your Extractors."

Groans and gasps and moans erupted from the other cells.

"Silence!" Ex shouted. "Ta show my fairness an' generosity, I'll give you one more chance to gain your freedom. If you can solve a simple riddle, I'll let you go."

"What if I don't guess the riddle?"

"Then, my alien visitor, I'll have Vulcan put you on the rack to help you get your mind right."

Being pretty good with riddles, I believed I could get it right.

"Ready?"

I nodded and wiped the sweat from my face.

"The Riddle of the Sphinx is an easy one. Your riddle is, 'What walks on four legs in the mornin', on two legs at noon, and on three legs in the evenin?'"

"Four legs? God, there's thousands of choices. What animal loses two legs, and then grows a third leg? This isn't fair. The four-legged thing must be a weird Millennium creature."

"I need an answer, now," Ex yelled. "Ya either know it or you don't."

"It's got to be one of the creatures here on Millennium. I haven't been here that long. Your riddle isn't fair."

"When I tell you the answer, you'll know I'm fair."

I turned red with frustration, searching my memory for a possible answer.

Vulcan

"I don't know, dammit. I give up. What creature has all those weird legs?"

"*You* do, my pathetic Earth creature."

"Me?"

"Humans crawl on all fours as a baby, walk on two legs as an adult, and walk with a cane in their old age."

I blushed. "A human, of course."

Owain laughed hysterically from the rear of the cell.

"Quiet, old man. You're no help," I yelled.

"Well, my boy," Ex said, "what am I to do with you? To be fair, I'm offerin' you your last chance to become an Extractor, pledge your allegiance to me."

Pointing at the Invisible Villain, I said, "No."

"Ya have chosen poorly," Ex shouted. "Vulcan, prepare the rack for our guest. And don't forget the necklace. I need the medallion."

"Yes, Master," Vulcan yelled with a satanic smile on his dark lips, clutching a key hanging around his neck.

Mayhem broke out in the prison. The dungeon captives screamed and rattled their pewter cups against the iron bars.

I ran to the back of the cell and cowered in the corner next to Owain.

"What should I do?" I asked Owain. "Help me."

"Pray, boy. Recite thy prayers."

Reached under my shirt and grabbed the Triamulet around my neck. Holding the charm tightly, I thought how I should have turned back when I had the chance and how I might never get home. I promised myself that if I ever got out of the mess, I would go straight to Time Island, go to sleep and return home.

Suddenly, Vulcan and a green-skinned cave troll wearing a black hood marched straight toward my cell.

"The Earth creature is over there," Vulcan yelled, pointing at my end prison cell.

The voice sounded like it came from the central platform, somewhere near the fire pit.

"Bring the boy here!" an invisible voice shouted.

Vulcan grabbed his key and unlocked the cell door, allowing a cave troll to rush inside. Within moments, the hooded torturer dragged me from the cell by the feet.

"Let go of me, you asshole!" I shouted.

Vulcan locked the cell door while the drooling cave troll dragged me up the platform steps by the back of my red tunic. The other two cave trolls forced me against the torture rack.

"That's fine, do not tie 'em to the rack just yet," Ex yelled.

The two cave trolls held my arms by my side while the hooded troll stood by the central fire pit.

"Since I'm known for my fairness," Ex said, "I'll give you one last chance to earn your freedom."

"I've done nothing to hurt you. Let me go home," I yelled.

My lips quivered as I spoke.

"I have another riddle that you should easily solve," Ex said, his deep, haunting voice three feet from me. "There are two sisters. One gives birth to the other and she, in turn, gives birth to the first. Who are they?"

I told myself, *It's got to be two goddesses who were sisters. All those mythology books you've read, you should know this one. Focus, who are the two goddesses?*

"Your time is up," Ex said. "Who are the sisters?"

"They are Hera and Gaea. Wait, maybe Freya and Hel. Or, they could be Ishtar and Inanna."

"Ahhh, brilliant answers. But wrong," Ex said, chuckling. "Vulcan, tell this human the answer."

"Day and night!" the dungeon master screamed, sneering. His fangs gleamed in the fire light.

"Now, ain't that answer 'bout as Earthly as you can get?" Ex asked, laughing.

The cave trolls laughed with the Invisible Villain.

"Quiet, you fools!" he shouted.

The trolls grunted and hung their heads. Yellow drool dripped down their hairy green chests.

Ex yelled, "Even though you proved your stupidity, my offer still stands. Join me, become an Extractor, and you'll be free. Rich and famous. Millennians will kneel before you. Women will lay before you. Your every desire will be satisfied."

Sweat dripped from my face. I stared in Ex's direction and shook my head, *no.*

"You'll regret your decision!" Ex shouted.

"Hold him tight," Vulcan said. "We'll stretch 'em a bit on the rack."

"Don't forget his Triamulet," Ex shouted. "I want that necklace!"

While the two trolls held my arms, the torturer stood in front of me with crazed, blood-shot eyes set behind the round holes of his black hood. The sadistic troll pointed to the torture rack a few feet away, motioning for them to put me on the rack.

These maniacs are really going to torture me, I thought.

"Wait!" I shouted, closing my eyes. "I'll do it. Don't torture me, I'll do whatever you want."

My entire body trembled. Confused and angry with myself, I hung my head in shame.

"Ahhhrrrgggg."

I heard the sickening sound of ripping flesh and looked up at the torturer.

A silver-tipped arrow, dripping with blood, had impaled the troll's neck and black hood. The beast grabbed the shaft of the quivering arrow and gasped for air. Dark-red blood gushed from his neck wound. He choked and fell to his knees.

"Take the boy back to his cell!" Ex shouted, still on the platform near the trap door.

Just as Vulcan looked up at the cavern cliffs to locate the archer's position, a streaking arrow slammed into the chest of the second cave troll. The green-skinned beast groaned, let go of me and stumbled forward. Writhing in pain, he grabbed the arrow's feathered shaft protruding from his barrel chest and tumbled off the platform.

I looked up just as Eve swung through the air from the rocks above. Clutching an iron chain suspended from the ceiling, she was heading straight for us. Right on target, she collided with the third troll, kicking him on the side of his bald head. The beast released his grip on my arm.

Eve let go of the chain and landed on her feet behind the troll. While she pointed her knife at the bewildered troll, Morph flew down with his scepter in his lower right hand, using the sacred wand to strike Vulcan on the back of his silver helmet.

The confused dungeon master stumbled and backed up, looking for his attacker.

I leaped onto the torture table and assumed my martial arts stance. The angry troll lumbered toward me. I spun around and roundhouse-kicked the beast in the face. Barely fazed by the blow to his nose, the troll drew his saber from his scabbard.

Eve jumped on the troll's back and clung to his neck. When the beast reached back to grab her, Eve took her knife, *Arthame*, and slit the troll's throat.

The green-skinned beast dropped the saber and grabbed his bloody throat while Eve leaped down onto the platform. The moaning cave troll stumbled backward, lost his footing, and fell into the River of Fire. A geyser of flames exploded into the dungeon air while the burning troll screamed in agony.

"Arrrggghhh!"

I smelled burnt flesh and hair as Eve and I ran past the pit and leaped from the platform to the rock floor.

The prisoners had gone berserk, screaming and howling and rattling their pewter cups against their cell bars.

Vulcan shouted, "Ex, do somethin'!"

The Invisible Villain screamed, "The sage brought his wand! Your all on your own, you blunderin' fools!"

Morph heard Ex's voice on the other side of the platform,

next to the river bank. The sage flew over the platform and pointed his wand, *Joyease*, in the same direction.

The sage's scepter radiated with ultraviolet, pulsating waves. The astral glow from the wand exposed the mysterious shape of Ex, the Invisible Villain.

Eve and I looked back and shielded our eyes. Twenty-five feet away, Ex's hideous shape had been exposed by Morph's scepter, *Joyese*.

A ghostly shadow with a glowing, violet-blue outline revealed a two-legged humanoid creature with fiery-white eyes covered with reptile-like scales. Ex wore a feathered cloak on his primordial body and a cap on his head. Foot-long wings protruded from the sides of the magic cap.

"Damn you, Metamorphosis! You'll regret this!" Ex shouted, growling and pointing at the sage with his dagger-like fingernails.

Before the sage could react, the Master Extractor vaulted over the River of Fire, vanishing into the belching smoke and hot ash.

Vulcan cursed, watching me and Eve escape, running over the stone bridge to a cave entrance leading to freedom.

Morph flew behind us. The Sage of the Ages pointed his wand to create light so Eve and I could see through the tunnels leading out of the Dungeon of Fire to the Bridge of the Separator.

"See you soon, Metamorphosis. You got lucky this time!" Vulcan shouted. "Next time we meet, I'll have that ugly head of yours on the end of my axe!"

DAYNIGHT
OF THE
SPIDER

Aries the 14th
Year of the Dragon

*"True knowledge exists in
knowing that you know nothing,
and in knowing that you know nothing,
that makes you the smartest of all."*
—Metamorphosis

Chapter 17
Realm of the Crystal

Byelobog led the way for Chernobog, up the winding Crater Tunnel Loop in an easterly direction. We had traveled all night long and into the morning, ascending 120 miles of subterranean trail without stopping. I rode in silence, emotionally exhausted from my dungeon nightmare, reliving my capture, imprisonment and abuse at the hands of Ex and Vulcan.

My thoughts turned to embarrassment and confusion. *I feel like a coward. Eve acted braver than me. I needed to prove to her that I wasn't scared of anything. Now what am I going to say to her? I know she thinks I acted like a coward and...Stop! I must stop thinking like that. I'm not like that any more.*

The two moleipeedes panted and gasped for air while we climbed the steady grade of the lighted tunnel. Eve's black hair bounced and swayed while she rode the lead moleipeede. I was glad she was riding up ahead with Grimnir. I wouldn't have known what to say to her if she sat behind me.

Grimnir, seated in front of Eve, raised his left paw to signal, *stop.*

A shallow stream of water ran across the tunnel floor, splashing against the moleipeede's furry paws. Having ridden the sumpters at top speed for more than three hours, Grimnir allowed his pack animals to rest and lap up the cool water.

The aardvark guide pointed ahead, at a cave on the right side of the tunnel. The pitch-black entrance measured half the size of the Crater Tunnel Loop.

Grimnir shined his head lamp at a wooden sign mounted above the cave entrance:

Miru Tunnel
Elevation: ~ 33 Miles Below Sea Level

Grimnir squinted, holding the parchment map close to his muzzle. Eve pulled her hair back in a ponytail, turned in her saddle and looked back at me. She grinned and lifted her right hand in a gesture of friendship. Returning the grin, I ran my fingers through my uncombed hair.

Eve wasn't mad at me. I could tell she didn't hate me. She was being nice.

"Prepare to enter Miru Tunnel," Morph said.

Eve's grin turned into a frown when she stared into the bleak tunnel. More darkness. That was the last thing we needed.

"Morph, we need to talk," I said, turning in my saddle to face the sage.

"We shall, as soon as we enter the tunnel. Now, gather the reins."

"Sth~sumpters~sth, let your antennalanterns~sth shine bright," Grimnir yelled.

The guide opened the brass lid to the head lamp of his knocker's cap and kicked Byelobog's sides. Both moleipeedes lunged forward, entering Miru Tunnel in a southerly direction.

Although similar to Nudd Tunnel, a mining shaft with support timbers, Miru had no iron-rail tracks, or lighting. The humid, dusty subterranean passage climbed steadily into a series of zigzag turns.

The sage placed his upper right hand on my shoulder. "How do you feel, my son?"

"Not so good. I need to apologize for acting like a coward, for giving in to Ex's demands."

"No need to apologize. You were traumatized. Your decisions were made under stress."

"I didn't mean what I said. That I would join Ex. I had the torturer in my face and I freaked out."

"Stress always exposes a human's true nature. How a person acts under pressure reveals their level of inner contentment."

"I want to be brave, fearless. How do I do that?"

"Focus on understanding yourself. Do not worry or be distracted by the behavior or opinion of others. No one has power over you. You experience fear because you are still infected with the emotional virus. The disease of low self-esteem causes fear. We must raise your esteem to a higher level."

"How do I learn to have a higher self-esteem. How can I have a healthy ego?"

"You already have it. Remember, all humans who travel here with a Triamulet have the potential for greatness. All you have to do is rid yourself of the emotional virus."

"How?"

"The answer is simple. To cure your emotional illnesses, you must change your thoughts. Then, and only then, shall you find the path to enlightenment, The Great Way."

"Finding The Great Way will make me brave?"

"Correct. Once you discover the path of enlightenment, your life changes. You have been led down the path of confusion during your childhood journey. The people who guided you through your youth had the contagious virus. It was not their fault. Because of their emotional illnesses, they were lost, wandering in a sea of despair. Arrogant and over-confident, they did not realize they were lost."

He made sense. My fear came from my negative thinking. I needed to be patient. I had to keep going, not go back to Time Island because of fear.

Needed to find out if the Open Road, the Great Way he kept talking about, could really give me what I wanted.

"I see that Grimnir found your sword," Morph said, interrupting my thoughts.

"Yeah, I don't remember losing it," I said, glancing down at the handle of *Aroundight*.

In the shadowy lights ahead, I heard Grimnir talk his non-stop-slobberish to Eve. She did not respond, holding a handkerchief over her nose.

"It was a shame that your decision to wander from camp, then, ignore Eve's advice, resulted in such pain."

"I should have known better, it's my own fault," I said.

"Who's that crazy Owain guy?"

"Owain Glydnwr is a human that has been with us for some time. He disappeared a few months ago. Now that we know his whereabouts, we shall negotiate his release."

"Are other people from Earth in that prison?"

"We are not sure."

"Where do the other humans live on Millennium? The people that have decided to stay."

"The people from Earth have created some peaceful settlements such as Sleepy Hollow, Vanity Fair, Rollingstone, Xanadu, and Sherwood Forest, to name a few."

"They must be happy here; they've decided to stay and not return to Earth."

"You shall have to ask them."

The lead moleipeede made a quick turn to the right, southwest. I held the saddle horn tightly when Chernobog whipped around the sharp corner.

"Are there a lot of humans living on Millennium?"

"Several hundred."

"Do any of the humans live with people from other planets?"

"Yes. There is cohabitation between planetary races. Why do you ask?"

"Just curious," I said, staring at Eve up ahead.

"Look," Morph said, pointing at a wooden sign. "We are entering the First Stratum. The Upperworld is only thirty miles above us."

First Stratum
Realm of the Crystal
Elevation: – 30 Miles Below Sea Level

The sage tapped me on the shoulder. "Your prison experience has made you wiser."

"How do you know that?"

"Within misfortune, good fortune hides. You have discovered

the true meaning of good fortune."

I held the reins tightly. "I know one thing, I never want to be in prison again."

"What you experienced was a worldly prison; the loss of physical freedom. The universe has only one true prison."

"Where is that?"

"The prison in your mind."

I searched for the meaning behind the sage's words as I grabbed the saddle horn before our moleipeede made a sharp turn to the left. East.

"So, what do you plan on doing when you return to Earth?" Morph asked.

"I've decided to be an artist and an author and a game inventor. Maybe on top of everything else, I'll become a sage."

"My, you *are* ambitious. Just like your father."

"I am *not* like my father."

Turning my head to the right, I asked, "Do you have any suggestions that might help me?"

"Follow your dharma, your purpose."

"Do you mean my art, my creativity?"

"What else is there?"

I looked down at my artist satchel hanging on the saddle horn and grinned.

"Allow love to flow from your art, your creativity," the sage said. "Let your natural gift touch others. You can change the world with your message."

"I have a lot to say. That's why I'd like to be an artist and a wise sage."

"A grand plan. You shall be great at both."

"Great? I don't know about that."

"There go those negative thoughts again," the sage said. "Do not doubt your ability. Affirm your dharma. Say it to yourself, 'I *am* a great artist. I *am* a great messenger.' Visualize it. Now, feel it. Feel the sensation of helping millions of humans with your art and your books. Now, keep that feeling in your heart and soul always. Never let go of that feeling. Every daynight, with confident humility, say the affirmation, 'I am a great messenger.' It shall materialize. You shall manifest your destiny."

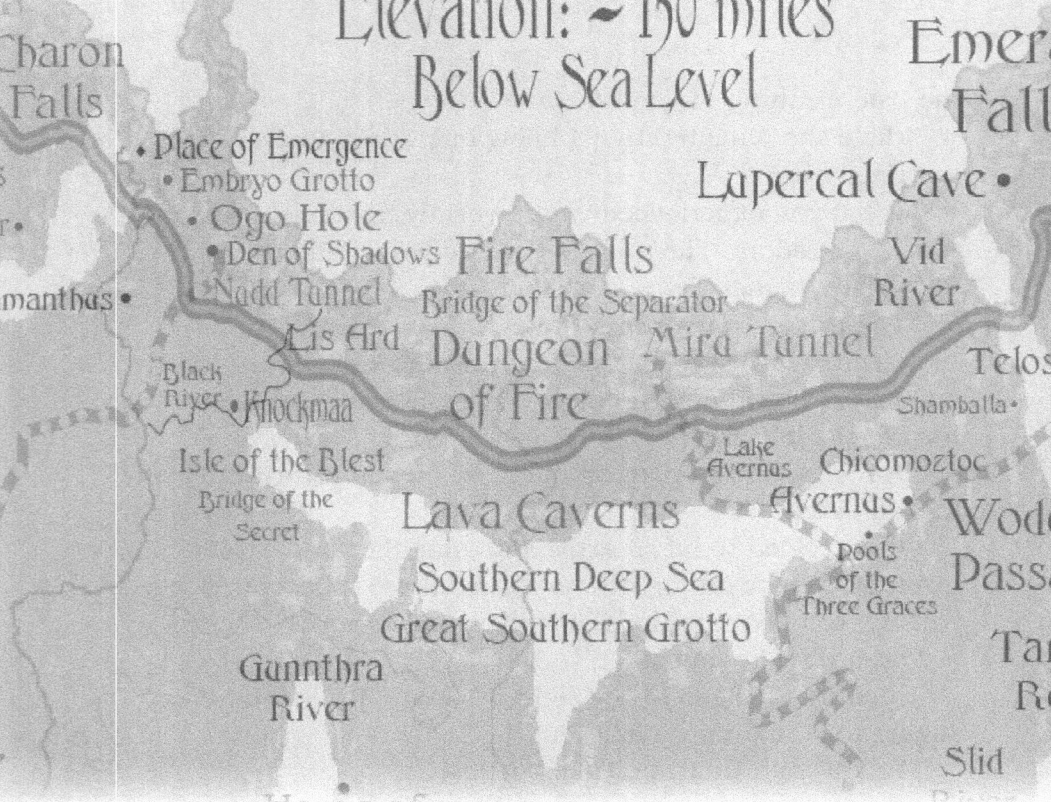

Charon Falls

Emera Fall:

Place of Emergence
Embryo Grotto
Ogo Hole
Den of Shadows   Fire Falls
Nadd Tunnel   Bridge of the Separator
Lis Ard   Dungeon   Mira Tunnel
Black River   Knockmaa   of Fire
manthus
Lupercal Cave

Vid River

Telos

Shamballa

Isle of the Blest
Bridge of the Secret   Lava Caverns
Southern Deep Sea
Great Southern Grotto
Gunnthra River

Lake Avernus   Chicomoztoc
Avernus
Pools of the Three Graces

Wode
Passa
Tar
Re
Slid

"I love art, creating things."

"Whatever you do, love it. It is you. Do what you love doing. Why would you spend a moment doing something you do not like?"

"My father says people have to work for a living, like it or not. That's why he's so determined to send me to Stanford University."

"I understand his statement. In primitive societies, such as yours, humans work a job they dislike because of financial and family obligations. The Extractors have perpetuated the same negative work experiences here on Millennium by creating a slave labor force on their collective farms and in their mines."

"My father already warned me that sometimes you have to work a job you hate just to make ends meet."

"Not true. You do not have to do anything. You choose everything you do. If you decide to work a job you do not like in order to feed your family, then please, love that job, for it fulfills your destiny. It is part of your Self. Embrace whatever you do, no matter what the job. Never complain."

"I need to figure out how I'm going to get my father off my back when I get home."

"I have a premonition that your father is going to allow you to follow your dharma, your grand purpose, when you awaken at home."

"I hope so. I'm sick and tired of arguing with him."

"Follow your dreams, my son. You have nothing to fear."

I nodded my head. Morph tapped me on the shoulder and said, "Pull right on the reins."

Byelobog made another sharp turn to the right, southeast, into a straight section of the Miru Tunnel. The aardvark guide immediately raised his mangy right paw and yelled, "Yo, sth~sumpters~sth, full sth~speed ahead."

"Hold on," Morph said. "With good fortune, we shall arrive at the Southern Deep Sea within the hour."

Chernobog jerked forward to pick up full speed. The light from the two antennalanterns revealed a thick layer of red silt covering the rock walls and tunnel floor. The tunnel air immediately filled with rust~colored dust.

Closed my eyes and pulled my red tunic up over my nose. God, I hated the darkness. I hated feeling claustrophobic. I knew my thoughts were negative, but I really hated the Underworld. I just wanted to breathe fresh air again. See the sky.

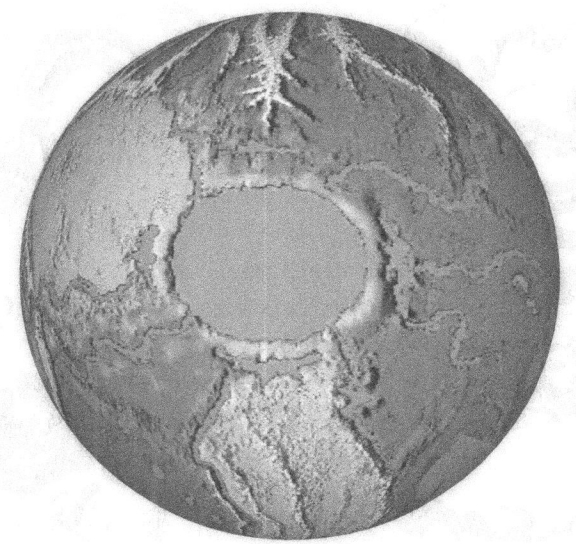

Chapter 18
Southern Deep Sea

Without warning, the sumpters emerged from the darkness of the Miru Tunnel into the southeast region known as the Southern Grand Canyon. I shielded my eyes from the blinding light of the two Millennium daystars. Before me, the vast Southern Deep Sea shimmered like blue glass. Eight miles above the subterranean sea, a colossal opening in Millennium's crust allowed the bright blue sky to penetrate the underground terrain.

"Dis-sth-mount the sth-sumpters-sth," Grimnir yelled, sliding down off his saddle and wiping the foamy slobber from his black lips.

Morph and I dismounted. Eve turned around to look at me. When our eyes met we smiled, staring at each other's face in the bright light of the two daystars. The Miru Tunnel trek had left us covered with a rusty-red dust.

I pointed at Eve and laughed. Eve's white teeth and green eyes looked hilarious behind her mask of reddish powder. Eve pointed at me and put her hand over her mouth. I stared at my rust-colored hands with white fingernails and stopped laughing, realizing that my face looked like hers.

"The boy looks-sth sth-stupid," Grimnir said, pointing at me.

There he goes again, I thought, *making fun of me.*

The aardvark turned, pulled his goggles up on his forehead, and waddled toward a foot path.

Morph vibrated his wings to shake off the red dust. "I shall make sure the path is safe," he said, walking down the trail.

Grimnir fitted leather blinders over the moleipeedes' light-sensitive eyes. The slobbering aardvark waddled down the zigzag path toward the water's edge, pulling his sumpters by the reins.

"It's~sth time to water me moleies~sth," he said, disappearing behind a massive boulder.

"Come on, Hunter. We need to clean up," Eve said. "Let's get out of these dirty clothes."

We slung our backpacks over our shoulders and started down the switchback path to the beach. Following Eve along the rocky trail, I enjoyed the walk.

For the first time during our underground journey, I no longer felt claustrophobic. The open grotto and the shimmering Southern Deep Sea renewed my love for adventure. The squawking birds brought a smile to my face; the gulls made me think of the beach where I always surfed.

Eve stopped and pointed. I ran to her side.

"Flowers," Eve said, smiling. "Most of the flowering plants on Epiphany have died off."

I followed Eve down the path lined with pink and purple orchids, blue bromeliads and yellow ginger. The vegetation smelled like the jasmine vine that grew outside our home.

Grimnir led the moleipeedes down the shoreline. The glassy waves rolled perfectly before they crashed on the white sands of the beach.

"Look at those tubes," I mumbled. "Great waves. I wish I had my surfboard."

Eve ran toward the beach with me following behind her. I couldn't believe how fast I could run. Eve took long, graceful strides toward the water.

When we reached the water we took off our boots and socks, then wiggled our toes in the warm sand. Hundreds of seabirds soared high above us. I stood and absorbed the scenery, shielding my eyes from the light of Helios and Sol.

To my left, the shoreline curved for miles. Palms, jambu, giant tree ferns and cycads grew as far as I could see. To my right, the shoreline disappeared around a rocky point.

Grimnir waddled toward the point, jerking his moleipeedes by their reins. "Them three pools~sth is gotta' be up ahead."

"Come on," Eve said. "I hear waterfalls."

She looked at my red face and covered her mouth, giggling. She turned and ran down the white~sand beach.

"Wait. You forgot these," I yelled, picking up the Epiphanite's black boots.

She even *ran* faster than I did as she pulled ahead of me and disappeared around the rocky point. The girl from Epiphany continued to amaze me.

I wondered, *what couldn't she do better than me?*

Looked back over my shoulder and realized I stood alone on the beach. Looking skyward, the grotto's cavernous rock walls rose straight up, eight miles high.

Overwhelmed by the enormous height of the Southern Grand Canyon, I took off running. I loved the feeling of sprinting in the lighter gravity of Millennium. Rounding the rocky point, I stopped in a cove and gawked in amazement.

Like a vision from a dream, three crystal-blue waterfalls poured majestically into three pools. The terraced ponds had been formed from fissured, chocolate-brown rock emerging from the green rain forest. Like showers of sparkling diamonds, each waterfall glowed in the radiant solshine.

Eve climbed the stone steps to the uppermost pool. She disappeared behind a waterfall. The upper falls gushed from a triangular fissure in the face of the cliff and fell thirty feet into the upper pool.

Morph stood at the middle pool waving at me to come up and join him. The middle falls measured half the height of the upper falls. A ten-foot-tall waterfall splashed into the lowest pond, overflowing into a bubbling blue stream that meandered through the white sand to a rocky tide pool at the mouth of the cove.

I ran up the stone steps to Morph's side. Panting, I asked, "Where...are we?" straining my neck to catch a glimpse of Eve.

"The Pools of the Three Graces," the sage replied, scanning the surrounding rain forest and shoreline.

"Will we camp here tonight?" I asked, watching Grimnir water the moleipeedes at the stream.

"No, we shall bathe, eat, and continue our journey."

"Why?"

"Hades." The sage pointed east, down the shoreline toward an enormous cavern.

"The Greek god of the Underworld?"

"My, you *do* know your gods; however, he is not Greek."

I smirked, looking down the shoreline. Eighty miles to the east, columns of smoke rose from the jungle.

"Does someone live down *there*?" I asked.

"That is Avernus, the underworld domain of Hades."

"So, we need to keep moving because Hades is dangerous?"

"He is unpredictable. Ever since Ex stole the old god's winged helmet, Hades has been extremely hostile. He became uncontrollable after he became infected with the *Extractor Virus*. Since then, he has ruled as a tyrant over the corrupt kingdom of Avernus."

"How did the kingdom get corrupt?"

"After the *Extractor Virus* spread out across the land, Hades became the supreme ruler of Avernus. He rules by dressing magnificently, wearing a sharp sword, stuffing himself with food and drink, and amassing wealth to the extent of not knowing what to do with it. To the citizens, he is a robber. He has created unjust rules. Millennium was once a world where rules and laws did not exist. Without laws, we all lived in peace and tranquility. We knew no hatred or war. Thievery was unknown. The Millennians lived without needing to be governed. Codes of conduct and laws were unnecessary. Anarchy did not exist. Everyone lived life as a leader."

"Where I live we seem to need lots of laws and rules."

"The greater the restrictions and prohibitions, the more the people are impoverished. The more advanced the weapons of state, the darker the nation. The more artful and crafty the leader's plan, the stranger the outcome. The more laws that are posted, the more thieves appear."

"Doesn't that go back to what you said about governments, that we need less government?"

"Truly, the best governor governs least. When the rulers know their own heart, the masses remain simple and pure. When the ruler meddles with their lives, they become restless and disturbed."

"I guess politicians do like to be in charge of everything, tell people what to do."

"They are power fanatics. Once Hades became infected with the *Extractor Virus,* he radically changed the cultural direction for the infected citizens of Avernus. They abandoned The Great Way. Once they lost their way, they needed rules. With the rules came the rulers to restore order. From the order came chaos. The Great Way is very smooth and straight, and yet primitive beings prefer devious paths. That is why the governments are corrupt and the fields lie in waste."

"Do a lot of governments fail?"

"All governments eventually fail. This is because governments base their existence on deception. Lies. Governments lie to maintain stability and to hold the loyalty of the citizens. The leaders of government, politicians, want you to believe that their self-interest is the same as your self-interest, but this is false."

"So, why do the citizens of Avernus allow this?"

"Because it reflects their low self-esteem society, their collective consciousness of negative thoughts. In other words, the ignorant masses have made all the wrong choices."

"You mean, like *my* country?"

"You keep voting for the same politicians year after year, decade after decade, century after century. Your government officials not only represent you, the people, they *are* you, personified. For the past 250 years your citizens have chosen your leaders unwisely. Look at the results."

"I'm not going to argue with you."

"There is nothing to argue about. Truth rules. All governments plunder the planet, destroy the environment, start wars that only benefit them and deny their citizens the basic necessities of life."

"Tell me again; what's the solution?"

"The collective consciousness of your nation, all nations, must change. Only when all of you change your thoughts shall the government change. Only then shall you have less government. Less government is the wisest choice."

"I'll remember that. Less government is the wisest choice."

"Excellent, my son."

"I bet if a philosopher king or a sage ruled Avernus, no one would starve."

"Good point. A sage's crown is in his heart, not worn on his head, not decked with diamonds and stones, nor to be seen. The crown is called content, a crown that kings seldom enjoy."

"With all his wealth, why doesn't Hades enjoy his riches and fame, take care of his people?"

"Hades is power hungry. Those who seek power over others develop unjust rules to benefit themselves. With the unjust rules come laws, and with the laws come government, and with the government comes corrupt politicians, crime, poverty, and high taxes."

"You have high taxes on Millennium?"

"Yes, just like Earth, when self-serving politicians and government officials are in charge of lawmaking, they write rules that benefit them personally. The masses are overtaxed to sustain the bad decisions of politicians and the rule makers' luxurious lifestyles. Rule makers always take advantage of their citizens. But keep in mind, unhappy citizens always rebel. Revolutions have become a predictable part of your world history. Unhappiness starts at the top, with leadership. Hades, Ruler of Avernus, self-proclaimed 'King of the Underworld,' has become an extremely unhappy god."

"If he is the king, a powerful god, why is he so unhappy?"

"Because he has become a tyrant. All tyrants begin their reign as the champion of the poor. Like Hades, tyrants promise to release the citizens from their debts and bring wealth and prosperity to the kingdom. By the end of the ruler's reign, the citizens are over-taxed and enslaved. The tyrant, the master over all, becomes a slave to all that he rules over. The greedy tyrant is ruled by his uncontrollable appetites. He cannot sleep, worried about betrayals and assassinations. The power-hungry ruler lives in fear. I believe your Shakespeare said it best, 'Uneasy lies the head that wears a crown.'"

"Did he get that from you?"

Morph grinned. "Human wisdom originated here, on Millennium, and was brought back to Earth."

I grinned, thinking about the sage's profound statement. I then asked, "So you're saying that Hades is paranoid?"

"Among his other emotional illnesses, yes."

"Are those his ships out there?" I asked.

"They are Hades' slave ships."

Before I could ask more questions, Morph turned and walked away. The sage pointed to a grotto underneath the middle waterfall. "I suggest you bathe up there, in the second pool."

While Morph walked down the steps to bathe in the bottom pool, I ran up the steep rock stairway, dropping my backpack at the middle waterfall.

Climbed the steps holding Eve's boots. The upper pool came into view.

Where's Eve? I thought, looking in the water.

"Hunter!" Eve shouted.

Standing behind the waterfall, the girl from Epiphany waved. I dropped her boots as I realized that Eve had no clothes on.

She ran and dove through the clear waterfall into the pool. Seeing her beautiful figure emerge from the falls confirmed my suspicions. She *was* naked.

"Come on in. The water is nice and warm," Eve said, treading water.

She submerged her head underwater and swam toward me. Her wet ebony hair glistened in the light when she surfaced. The curves of her perfect body glided through the rippling water.

She smiled and swam closer, and closer.

My heart raced while my face turned flush. The red dust on my face concealed my embarrassment.

"Ummm...here's your boots...I better get cleaned up down below," I yelled, turning and running down the stone steps.

I scrambled down the steps and stopped under the waterfall grotto. I picked up my backpack, panting. While I undressed behind the waterfall, my thoughts ran wild.

Am I crazy? She wanted me to swim with her, and I ran away. I should go back up there. Maybe being naked is no big deal on Epiphany. She wasn't embarrassed in front of me. She acts so free spirited. Why am I so shy? What's wrong with me?

I stripped down to my black briefs. Decided that swimming naked with Eve was not right, it was the wrong thing to do. I felt I had done the right thing.

Washed my soiled breeches and rust-red tunic in a separate,

314

smaller pond under the waterfall and laid them over the warm rocks. Stared into the crystal-clear pool.

Ten feet deep, bubbles rose to the surface from the smooth-pebbled bottom. Purple fish the size of minnows darted about. Seeing no strange creatures lurking in the clear water, I dipped my left foot into the pool. Perfect temperature.

I dove in, head first. When I surfaced, the water around me had turned a cloudy red. The water felt soothing. While I swam in the rippling pool, Eve laughed and splashed in the pool above. I stopped swimming and propped my elbows over the edge of the pool, looking up at the incredible scenery.

A fiery-red sky approached from the east, casting a crimson hue on the subterranean sea. In the distance, the rain forest had turned a salmon-pink color.

I gazed out across the Southern Deep Sea and saw that the three ships had vanished beyond the horizon. I imagined the creatures who sailed those vessels.

Reflecting on my incredible journey, I knew I was not turning back. I needed to keep going.

After all I've been through, I thought, *turning back makes no sense. I've been gone a year already, a few more days can't hurt. I wish I didn't miss my family and friends so much and—*

Movement interrupted my thoughts.

Morph stood below, waving at me to come down.

I got out of the pool to get dressed before Eve came down the path. I walked behind the waterfall and spotted Morph, who now stood below the lower pool. Wearing clean clothes, the sage prepared the mid-daynight meal.

Hiding behind the grotto waterfall, I put on my dry clothes from my backpack, brown breeches with a black tunic. I pulled up my wool socks and put on my black boots.

"Your face looks nicer clean than dirty," Eve said, walking down the stone steps.

Surprised, I jumped up and ran my fingers through my wet hair.

Blushing, I smiled, awestruck by her beauty. Her olive skin looked radiant after her swim. Her new outfit, black breeches with a white chemise, fit her perfectly. She had tied her ebony hair in a ponytail. She wore her sparkling ruby necklace with gold Triamulet on the outside of her silk chemise.

The Epiphanite stopped and asked, "Why did you run away when I asked you to swim with me?"

Shrugging my shoulders, I replied, "I didn't run away."

I held up my hand before Eve spoke. "Okay, I admit I got a little nervous up there and, ummm—"

"Are you afraid of me?"

"No. Of course not. I'm not afraid of girls, no way. I'm not afraid of anything."

She raised her eyebrows. "Heights?"

"That doesn't count because I'm not afraid any more."

Eve stared into my eyes. "I want to trust you. If you lie to me, we cannot be friends."

I looked down, clenching my hands, my face flush with embarrassment.

She was right. I was lying about being afraid.

"Come down and eat!" Morph shouted from the lower pool.

I looked up at the Epiphanite. She offered me a smile and said, "Maybe we can talk later. Come on, time to eat."

She hurried down the stone steps.

"Coming," I said, tucking his black tunic into my breeches and following her down the pathway.

Am I hearing things? I thought. *She wants to talk to me.*

While Eve's and my clothes dried in the warm solshine, we sat with Morph on three flat boulders next to the bottom pool. Beyond the waterfalls, exotic bird songs and animal cries echoed from the rain forest. Still intrigued by Eve's display of uninhibited playfulness, I enjoyed my meal of fresh jambu fruit, hemp seed, salmon jerky, and ambrosia.

Grimnir fed and watered his sumpters at the gurgling stream.

Eve seemed preoccupied while she chewed her food, watching the surf crash on the beach.

The more I studied the perfect barrel waves, the more homesick I became.

"I'm going to walk on the beach," Eve said as she stood up.

"I'll go with you," I said.

"I'd rather be alone, if you do not mind."

"Ummm, sure. I've got some things I need to ask Morph."

There she goes again, I thought. *Wanting to be alone and not talk. She was just smiling at me a minute ago, wanting me to swim naked with her. Now this. What is up with this girl?*

"Eve," Morph said, "do me a favor and stay within our sight."

"I will." The girl from Epiphany ran down to the beach and turned right, walking toward Avernus.

The sage gestured to Grimnir, who said, "Yes-sth, Mathster Morfff, I'll keep an eye on 'er."

The slobbering aardvark, still covered in red dust, finished feeding Byelobog and Chernobog. Carrying the wooden club over his shoulder, he waddled down to the beach, leaving a pair of elongated footprints and a tail print in the soft sand.

"Morph, what if I must use my sword to kill someone?"

"Why do you ask?"

"Eve just killed a troll with *Arthame,* but you said our weapons were for defense only."

"Excellent point, well deserving of an answer."

The sage sipped amrita from his water bag. "When you travel the Open Road, the high road, and learn The Great Way, you shall discover that killing is not part of the magnificent universal energy, the Source. This is why I asked you to always use your sacred sword, *Aroundight,* for defensive purposes only, never for aggression."

I grabbed my bronze sword handle, thinking, *Remember, Hunter...defend...do not attack.*

"First of all, keep in mind that you have no enemies. This is because we are all one. One. Harming your enemy harms you. When you believe you have an enemy, you and that enemy exist together and there is no room left for the treasure. The treasure I speak of is peace of mind. Contentment. The bliss of eternity may be found in your contentment. If combat becomes inevitable, as it often does in the worlds infected with the Dark Essence, then defense must be practiced. If you are required to defend yourself or someone in your immediate circle of family and friends, people you dearly love, practice defense rather than offense."

"Did Eve kill the troll because she loves me?"

"You shall have to ask *her* that question."

"As for battles and wars, the killing of another being must be grieved. If injury or death occurs, there can be no celebration. Every battle must be viewed as a funeral with no victory, only remorse. Compassion must rule your heart if you kill because you had no other options. You must have compassion or you shall stray from The Great Way."

"You mean, Eve had no other options?"

"She had other options. The knife, *Arthame*, was her choice. I did not make that decision. She did."

I stared at Eve walking the beach.

"Use your sword wisely, my son."

"But I want to be brave. A hero."

"Well, there is reckless bravery and there is cautious bravery. Reckless bravery leads to death. Cautious bravery leads to life. For instance, by attempting reckless bravery back at the Bridge of the Separator, trying to impress Eve and throwing caution to the wind, you quickly faced death."

I bowed my head, embarrassed.

"Sages behave cautiously. They are vigilant and alert, not reckless and foolish. As for your hero quest, true heroes move cautiously, not foolishly."

"What about warriors?"

"The warrior turns to violence when no other options are available. As a last resort, the warrior uses defense and avoids killing. Great warriors are cautious, peaceful."

Eve ran down the beach with the dark aardvark shuffling in the sand behind her.

Morph motioned to me. "What is on your mind, my son? You still look perplexed. Why do you appear unhappy?"

"This isn't what I expected. This quest is not going as I had planned."

"All your plans, my son, are not you. Plans do not determine your fate. Do not be attached to your plans or their fulfillment. Do not be attached to their results. Whenever things do not go your way, when your plans seem ruined or unattainable, listen to the beautiful winds of change. Accept what comes your way. Go with the flow. Relax, let the dust settle."

Unaffected by the sage's response, I stared straight ahead at the beach.

"I sense there is something else on your mind, a more important issue, beyond your fear of not attaining your expectations. What is it, my son?"

Eve walked the beach, her hair blowing in the breeze.

"Do you think she likes me?" I asked.

The sage chuckled. "Yes, of course she does."

"I really like her, a lot."

Morph grinned. "Would you describe your feelings as love?"

Blushing, I glanced at the sage and replied, "I don't know; I really hadn't thought about it much."

"From the look on your face, it appears you have thought about it quite a bit."

"Okay, yeah," I said, grinning, "I mean, I think I *am* in love with her."

"Excellent. Love is the grandest emotion."

"She's so different from the girls on Earth."

"Yes, Epiphanites have superior intellectual capacity, but often display inferior emotional intelligence."

"She seems cold. Distant. Kind of rude most of the time."

"She is not rude, she is just being herself. Do not confuse her inner peace and quiet personality with negative behaviors."

"Easier said than done. She frustrates me."

"You have placed expectations on her that she shall never meet. You act frustrated because you believe she should give you constant attention. If she doesn't acknowledge your every word, you automatically believes she does not like you."

"Well, isn't that true?"

"Of course not. She enjoys her solitude, her inner peace. That is an excellent trait. You should try it sometime."

"You mean, meditation?"

"That is one way to find inner peace."

The sage drank amrita from his leather water bag, moving his wings back and forth in unison.

"My son, your love for her will only grow. Be patient with her, all things happen in perfect order."

"Morph, I want her really bad," I said, staring at Eve walking the beach, throwing pebbles at the crashing waves.

"Want her?"

"I mean, I want her to like me. To love me."

"Do you remember what we talked about earlier, that your thoughts manifest your destiny?"

"Yeah, I think so."

"By thinking and saying you *want* something, anything, gives you exactly that, just wanting."

"Huh?"

"When you think something, the universal Source shall make sure your wish comes true. Your thoughts, your words, shall always become reality."

"What's your point?"

"Your thoughts are manifested by the universe. When you think 'I want,' that is exactly what the universe hands you in physical reality. So far, your only experience is wanting Eve, not having Eve."

"Say that again?"

"By saying you want Eve, that is as far as you shall ever get, wanting. The creative power of your thoughts, your very words, bring you exactly what you ask for. Therefore, you shall never *have* Eve. By wanting her, you are pushing her away from you. The very act of wanting something gets you exactly what you do not want."

"So, what can I do to change this?"

"Remember our discussion on thought?"

"Change my thoughts and my life changes?"

"Correct. The harder you try, the more resistance you create. Your solution must be to change your thoughts. Stop thinking that way."

"So, instead of telling myself, 'I want Eve,' what do I say?"

"Think and say an affirmation to the universe. 'Eve likes me,' or 'I know Eve is part of my life,' or 'Eve loves me.'"

"It's that easy? Will it really work?"

"Yes. You are your own creator of reality. The power of

thought rules the universe. Your happiness is only a thought away. Freedom is only a thought away. Physical health is just a thought away. Eve's love for you is only a thought away. Bliss is only a thought away. All that is and ever was, is but a thought away."

Shielding my eyes, I watched the white clouds drift across the blue and red skies. My eyes shifted back to Eve walking on the white sand.

"God, she would make me so happy if she'd just pay more attention to me. I know I could make her happy if she'd let me get close to her."

"Unfortunately, that is the primitive way of looking at your relationship with her."

"What's primitive about being happy?"

"May I offer you the ninth Secret of the Universe?"

"Will it upset me? Are you going to tell me I'm not right for Eve?"

"I speak only the truth."

"Okay, what's the ninth Secret?"

"There is no way to happiness; happiness *is* the way."

"What's this got to do with my love for Eve?"

Morph tilted his chin down and looked at me over the rim of his glasses. "You are not capable of making Eve happy. She cannot make you happy."

"There is no way to happiness; happiness is the way."
—Metamorphosis

"That's not true. My mom and dad make each other happy."

"Did they tell you that?"

"Yeah, my mom told me when they were first married, my father would say, 'You make me happy.' She told him the same thing."

"I see. What if I told you that the greatest happiness comes from self-love, discovering yourself?"

"I'd say you were wrong."

I looked at the sage and raised my right hand. "Okay, I'm sorry. But I know with all my heart that I can make Eve happy if she'd just let me."

Morph took a bite of a juicy jambu and chewed slowly, observing Eve running down the beach.

I threw my hands up in the air. "All right, go ahead. Share some of your wisdom. Tell me how I can win Eve's heart."

Smiling, Morph threw the jambu core down to the beach. A pair of speckled gulls fought over the morsel of food.

"There is no heart to win. All things happen in perfect order. Friends and loved ones come and go, in and out of our lives, at just the right time. Your relationship with Eve may remain at its present level of energy, or it may develop into the dance of life."

"The dance of life?"

"More on that later; I need to share more of the ninth Secret."

"No, please tell me about the dance of life."

Morph grinned and ran his fingers through his white beard. "Your request is my command. I shall explain the dance of life, and then, true happiness."

"Great," I said, not taking my eyes off Eve. "Right now, my stomach feels queasy when I look at her."

"That is your lower energy center letting you know how powerful your attraction to Eve is."

"My stomach?"

"It is not your stomach; it is energy concentrated deep within your lower chakra that signals your attraction to Eve."

"Whatever it is, I like it."

The sage grinned. "The dance of life is about energy, combining energies, two beings coming together as one being. Do you recall the power of thoughts?"

"That thoughts are like radio signals," I replied.

"Yes, but not just your thoughts transmit signals. From the center of your Self, your inner being, a pulsating energy source transmits a signal throughout the universe."

"Do we all have this inner signal?"

"Not just us, but everything, every physical thing. All plants and animals and rocks and creatures in the universe emit a vibration of energy waves in a 360° circle. These are the energy waves that begin from inside your body and move through space and time into the infinite universe and keep going, forever. This energy is the most powerful force in the cosmos. According to your moods and your thoughts, your energy field's wavelength, the speed of the vibrations, change by speeding up or slowing down. As you change your thoughts, the ethereal air around you also changes. What this means is, you affect everyone around you. We all affect each other. The closer you are to another being's energy source, the greater the complexity of intertwined emotions."

Morph raised his bushy white eyebrows. "Can you imagine the power generated from this interwoven matrix of energy vibrations throughout the universe?"

I shook my head, *no*, and closed my eyes, inhaling the fragrance of the jasmine vines cascading from the rocks above.

"Your energy is measurable. It is physical. I can feel *your* vibrations right now."

I opened my eyes and stared at the vast inland sea in front of me. A swirling breeze blew my hair in my face.

"Just imagine how complex and dynamic the energy grid becomes when more than two of us gather in a group. All that inner energy, all those signals bouncing off each other. The air fills with incredible vibrations. The exchange of vibrating energy is so complex that it continually affects all things, from two people, to an entire room, to the entire world, to the entire universe. The energy waves become signals of attraction, like attracts like."

The sage waved at Grimnir, who raised his wooden club to signal, *all is well.*

"The manifestation of our inner energy, just like our thoughts, creates physical objects and directly changes events and circumstances. The energy exchange is in constant motion. It never stops. It is happening right now between you and me, but more importantly, between us all. Between you and Eve."

I sat up and stared in Morph's tranquil eyes. "Go ahead, what about Eve and me?"

"Since you and Eve met, you have been transmitting energy that meets midway between you and her. This forms its own energy, a third and separate energy. Whenever your energies unite, you are now connected in spirit. You feel each other's energy metaphysically. This invisible energy source is within the two of you, as it is within all things. This energy is the music of the universe. This music is silent, yet, we all hear it. As the two of you begin to share the same spirit and the same positive energy, you shall be drawn closer. Eventually, you shall be drawn physically closer to match your spiritual energy. If enough energy is created, the two of you shall embrace and enjoy the dance of life."

"Wait a minute," I said, smirking. "Is this about the birds and the bees?"

"The birds and bees?"

"I've already had sex education in school. I know everything I need to know."

"The dance of life is about high self-esteem love, not about misguided sexual energy, or about egos out of control."

"I never heard that before."

"Once your educational system embraces philosophy, teaching you how to think for yourself instead of forcing you to memorize facts and someone else's ideas, your world shall change. I shall enlighten you on how to educate youth when we arrive at the Upperworld. Right now, we should focus on the dance of life because that was your question."

"Okay. So, how do I create all this energy of real love so I can do the dance of life with Eve?"

Metamorphosis stretched his wings, absorbing the solar heat. "It must happen naturally, my son. You cannot force it. Remember, like energy attracts like energy. Both you and Eve must have it together, not just you."

"How will I know when our energies are one, that it has happened?"

"Oh, you will know *exactly* when it happens."

"How? Tell me what it feels like."

"The dance of life happens spontaneously. As I have said, an incredible energy field draws you together. The dance shall begin when you and Eve are no longer satisfied with your invisible, metaphysical connection. Your souls are one, but now you both desire to experience this intense energy between you physically. Your souls know what it is like to be one, but now your bodies want to experience the oneness."

Morph paused and sipped amrita. "You find yourselves moving closer toward each other. The energy field between you and Eve intensifies. The silent music of the universe gets louder, and louder. The closer you get, the more intense the energy waves. As you two are drawn closer, the energy vibrations heat up, becoming hotter and hotter as the vibrations of energy waves speed up, faster and faster as you both move closer and closer. The closer you get, the hotter your energy waves, until both of you are literally burning up with desire."

I closed my eyes.

"You and Eve touch. A red-hot rush of euphoria envelopes you both. Sparks fly from the burning energy field, creating unbearable sensations. The two of you cannot help but come together in an unforgettable embrace, your bodies and souls feeling alive and tingling with passion. You both cannot get enough of each other. In an energetic frenzy of loving passion, your bodies unite. Your energy becomes intensified, urgent and breathless and passionate. Eve and you cannot get close enough as an indescribable union occurs. In a spontaneous explosion of energy and shock waves and vibrating ecstasy, the two of you become one. At that moment, you and Eve experience the ultimate union of body and spirit. Time stands still as your world expands and collapses around you in the ultimate in-and-out-of-body experience."

"Wow, that sounds beautiful. The dance of life must feel fabulous."

"Yes. When the music of the universe plays, the dance of life happens a billion times a second all over the universe. This energized dance has a purpose. When the combined energies are just right, a third and separate energy is created in physical form."

"Babies?"

"Correct. Baby birds and baby bees."

I laughed. "Okay, you got me on that one. I'm sorry for sounding so stupid."

"A little humor never hurts. You are perfect as you are, not stupid."

"Thank you. That explanation was fantastic."

Eve had turned around, walking back toward us.

"Now, all I have to do is figure out how to make Eve love me. Tell me again, how do I make her happy?"

"As I have already said, it is impossible. Nothing, no thing, can make Eve or you happy. Happiness *is* the way."

"You've lost me again."

"Do not act happy, *be* happy. Just be. Do not act loving, *be* loving. Perhaps I can explain this concept better by describing real love. May I use humans as an example?"

"You always use humans for your examples."

"I find your civilization fascinating."

"I'll take that as a compliment."

"I only have love for you humans."

"I believe you. So, tell me about real love."

"Love is the most misunderstood word on your planet. Humans confuse love with lust, infatuation, promises, and obligations. True love is unconditional and asks for nothing. Love has no requirements. Once you discover real love, you shall truly enjoy the dance of life."

"How?"

"Humans enter into relationships for the purpose of getting something from the other person, rather than giving something to the relationship. They believe the other person is supposed to make them happy and secure. For instance, during your brief relationship with Eve you have already displayed human behaviors that can only result in a dysfunctional relationship."

"I just want Eve to listen to me. Talk to me."

"I already know how you imagine Eve responding to your advances."

"You can't read my mind."

"I do not have to."

"Okay, tell me. What are these things that I expect to hear from Eve?"

"You believe it is extremely romantic to hear her say that she was nothing until you came along; that she will change for you; that you complete her and make her life worth living. You imagine her telling you that she worries about your health, your safety and your happiness. That she worries about you and only you. That you are her whole life, all she thinks about is you. That she will die for you."

"What's wrong with all those things?"

"They are not true love, simply a counterfeit version. I can sense that you have been agonizing and worrying about what she is thinking, how she is acting, what her expectations are. You are dying to know whether she loves you or not."

"What's wrong with that? I love Eve. I want to know how she feels about everything. She won't talk to me. I need her to tell me her feelings."

Folding his wings behind him, Morph said, "This is not your fault; you have been trained to love this way. Unfortunately, it is low self-esteem love. You believe by forcing your love on Eve, she will love you and then you will feel lovable and secure. You believe she will complete you. You believe you need her for your own happiness."

"You're right, I *do* believe that."

"This is why you are love sick. This is why you are unhappy with yourself. How would you feel if Eve told you she loved you?"

"I'd be the happiest guy in the universe."

"Yes, for a few moments, maybe for a few daynights. But eventually you would begin to question how long you can keep Eve's love. Whether or not you had to change to keep her love and admiration. You would also expect her to meet your expectations. Arguments or extended periods of silence would be inevitable. Over time, the relationship is lost because you and Eve will have lost touch with your own souls."

"Then, what's considered a good relationship?"

"First, the relationship you have with your Self is the one that must be nurtured and cherished or all other relationships shall fail. It is written in one of your great books, 'Love thy neighbor as thy self.' These six words declare the perfect way to love and respect others. You shall never be able to respect the feelings of others if you do not respect and honor your own feelings, your own thoughts."

"Are you telling me that my love for Eve is not real?"

"The answer lies within you, my son. My message is, 'You must first love your self, before you can love another.' It is such a simple concept. As I told one of my earlier visitors, 'To thine own self be true.' I request that you become self-centered in a high self-esteem way."

I drank from my water bag while the Sage of the Ages continued. "Your enlightenment shall come when you love yourself. Then, and only then, can you truly love Eve."

"But I think I already *do* love myself."

"Of course you do. Everything you do is for yourself. That is your nature, human nature. It is your primitive nature that shall prevent you from obtaining true love. This is because low self-image, an inflated ego, corrupts your thoughts. You think you love yourself, but it is merely your grand feeling of being conceited, narcissistic, self-absorbed, selfish, vain, and blinded by your own self-proclaimed glory. You humans have become legends in your own minds. Your loving feeling is actually the emotional virus producing egotistical thoughts convincing you how wonderful and happy and loving you are. When you suffer from low self-image you believe with all your heart that you love yourself. As I have told you, until the *Extractor Virus* is cured, humans cannot change their thoughts, therefore, they shall never know true love, only the fraudulent version of love, a poor imitation of the real thing."

Watching Eve frolic in the white sand, I said, "I still have the exact same feelings I had a moment ago."

"Because you are infatuated and blinded by love."

"Blind or not, it feels great. What should I do about it?"

"Relax. Be patient with Eve and focus on yourself. The harder you try to win Eve's heart, the more resistance you shall create for yourself. Do not seek the favor of Eve. Do not be concerned about her opinion of you. Do not allow her opinion to affect your life. Do not worry about her feelings for you. Time shall make you the wiser. Allow truth to always be your guide, your inner strength. When you learn to love yourself unconditionally, your relationship with Eve changes instantly. You shall see her in a new light. You shall love her even more than you do now."

"Promise?"

"My words come from the Source. I speak only of love. Do you feel my love?"

"Yes."

Morph smiled and pointed toward the beach. "Here comes your friend."

I jumped to my feet as Eve ran toward me.

She is so beautiful, I thought. *I need to tell her that I love her so we can....Stop! Listen to yourself....relax...calm down...follow Morph's advice.*

I smiled and asked her, "How was the beach?"

"It is wonderful down by the water," she replied, smiling. "Thank you for allowing me my freedom; I just needed some time to think."

"Ummm, sure. You're welcome," I said, looking at Morph, who winked at me as he stood and motioned to Grimnir.

"Grimnir, prepare the sumpters for our journey," the sage said. "Let us gather our gear and be on our way."

The aardvark guide untied his sumpters.

"Eve, would you mind riding behind Hunter again?" Morph asked.

She untied her pony tail, letting her silky black hair fall to her shoulders.

"Not at all, that was my preference," she replied with an adventurous toss of her hair.

She wants to ride with me, I thought. *This is getting better all the time.*

I grabbed the reins from Grimnir, ignoring the guide.

"You take the front saddle," I told Eve, "I'll ride behind you."

"Are you sure?"

"You just saved my life; I think I can trust you with the reins."

She grinned and placed her left boot in the stirrup and swung her right leg over the front saddle. I adjusted my sword and jumped onto the rear saddle.

Chernobog snorted and fidgeted.

"Whoa, steady," Eve said, holding the reins tightly. I gawked at the restless sky exposed by the opening in the Southern Grand Canyon, eight miles above us.

The clouds had turned pink and purple with the coming of the red sky. Rays of solshine pierced the ominous clouds, forming three radiant spotlights on the water's surface.

Grimnir snapped Byelobog's reins. Eve kicked Chernobog's sides with her stirrups. Leaving a trail of perfect tracks in the white sand, the moleipeedes shuffled down the beach and headed east. To our left, the Southern Deep Sea stretched as far as we could see. To our right, the emerald-green jungle hugged the towering grotto walls.

Eve smelled fabulous. I decided it was a good time to talk.

"I'm sorry that I didn't listen to you back at the Bridge of the Separator," I said. "I should have never gone down there."

She turned her head so I could hear her over the sound of the waves. "No need to apologize. I admire your spirit and your energy. I am not used to males acting so playful."

"I like having fun. Sometimes, I get in trouble."

"Yes, you certainly got yourself in *big* trouble at the dungeon."

"Sorry, it won't happen again."

The corner of her mouth turned upward. "I was afraid you would quit and want to turn around, go home. I am glad you have decided to continue forward."

"I am liking my decision more and more each minute. What I mean is, I like being with *you*. I think you're really nice."

"That is sweet, Hunter. You are nice too."

I was dying to tell her that I loved her. But I bit my tongue.

"I am happy we are still together," she said with a coy smile on her lips.

"Yes, as fate would have it," I said.

"That sounds like a Morphism."

"What's that?"

"On our planet, all of Morph's philosophical sayings, his words of wisdom, are often quoted among our people. We call these words of wisdom, Morphisms."

"You mean, like, 'All things happen in perfect order?'"

"Yes, that is one of them. My favorite is, 'You get what you think about whether you want it or not', and—"

The moleipeedes stopped abruptly. I lunged forward into Eve, causing me to put my arms around her waist. My face pressed

330

against her velvety black hair. Eve placed her right hand over my trembling fingers and held them tight to her stomach.

I remember thinking, *I can't believe how good she feels. I could hold her like this forever.*

Eve let go of my hands. I regained my composure, sat up straight, and pointed. "They've found something."

Grimnir had located the tunnel entrance.

"I hope this tunnel has lights," Eve said.

"Me too," I said.

The sumpters climbed the steep jungle trail through the tangled vegetation and stopped at the face of the granite cliff. The blue sky had disappeared. Dark-grey storm clouds moved across the red sky. The humid air smelled like rain.

"This-sth is-sth it," Grimnir yelled, stopping at a cave entrance to remove the moleipeedes' eye blinders.

I read the sign chiseled in the rock:

Woden's Passage
Elevation: ~8 Miles Below Sea Level

"What's-sth wrong, Mathster?" Grimnir asked.

Morph looked skyward and pointed. "It is Chamalcan. He has spotted us."

I looked up. Silhouetted against the crimson atmosphere, a pale, hairless creature that looked half monkey and half bat circled the sky above the cave.

"That thing is really ugly," Eve said.

As Chamalcan disappeared into the swirling storm clouds, Morph explained that the creature was one of Ex's personal messengers.

Rain began to fall while streaks of lightning flashed across the red sky. The crack and roar of thunder hurt Eve's ears.

With rain pelting our heads, Morph gave the *go* signal.

We entered Woden's Passage. As my eyes adjusted to the

light from the moleipeedes' antennalanterns, I noticed that the temperature felt cooler and the air smelled fresher, not as musty and stale as in the previous tunnel systems. The underground passageway had a different appearance than any of the other tunnels. The walls had been built with stacked blocks of limestone.

On top of the ten-foot-tall block walls, a continuous row of twelve-foot-long cedar timbers spanned the tunnel's ceiling. The floor had been constructed of slabs of sandstone with a flat, smooth finish.

The sumpters moved rapidly, shuffling their paws in perfect unison along the sandstone floor. Their antennalanterns cast creeping shadows on the tunnel walls.

I knew it was my chance to talk to Eve. Maybe say something romantic.

"Um, so tell me," I said. "Do you have a boyfriend back on Epiphany?"

"I had a life partner chosen for me," Eve said, turning her head so I could hear her.

"Like a dowry system?"

"Yes. My father has already promised me to a high-ranking officer in the military, an older Epiphanite."

"Is he nice to you?"

"I met him once. I do not care for him, but he has promised to reward my father financially."

"You're being sold to this older guy?"

Eve sighed. "My father always reminds me how valuable I am."

"You *are* valuable. Wait! I'm sorry. I don't mean it like that, I mean—"

"I know what you meant. I sense your feelings for me."

"You do?"

Eve nodded her head, *yes*.

"Then, you know how I feel?"

"I have a general idea."

"So, how do you think I feel about you?"

"I believe you want me to act more playful, not so serious. You think I am boring."

"No way, you are *not* boring."

"You seem intimidated with my intelligence."

"I'm getting used to it."

"So, can you teach me how to play and not be so serious?"

"Sure, my father says I'm really good at playing around."

Eve grinned. "Good. When we get to the Upperworld, you can help me to become playful."

"All right. Maybe you can show me how to add numbers as fast as you do."

"I will try, but it might take some time. I know you need to get back home. I am not sure if I will have enough time."

"Don't worry about that. I'm learning to relax and not be in such a big hurry. Morph's helping me with that."

"Do you mean you might stay longer?"

"Sure."

I told myself, *There you go again, making promises you might not keep. I don't know what I'm going to do. I really want to stay longer and get to know her, but I have to go home. How am I going to handle this?*

A small colony of chirping black bats flew over our heads in the opposite direction, westerly.

Eve ducked and looked behind her. The dark creatures flew toward the entrance of Woden's Passage.

She turned and pointed ahead, saying, "Morph is a great sage. I have learned a lot from him in such a short time."

"Yeah, I've never met anyone like him."

I cleared my throat. "Ah-hem."

"Are you okay?"

"Uh-huh," I said, squirming in my saddle. "Can I ask you a question?"

"That is all you have done for seven daynights."

"Yeah, I guess I have." I chuckled nervously. "I was wondering. Has Morph ever told you about the...ummm...the dance of life?"

"No."

"Well, it's, um...it's about...you know...two people getting together and having the same energy and ummm—"

"What are you trying to say?"

"Nothing," I said with a quiver in my voice. "Let's talk about it later. Tell me about Epiphany."

"Why do you want to know?"

"You mentioned living in protected domes and the dark underground, but your world must still have some beautiful areas that haven't been destroyed."

Eve shook her head, *no*.

"I'm sorry. I thought maybe you still had some distant forests or tall mountains not contaminated by the radiation."

"I have seen photographs of our once beautiful landscapes."

"You have photographs? Cameras on your planet?"

"We have had more technology than you humans have ever dreamed of."

"Okay, I didn't mean to insult you, I just—"

"No, I apologize," she said, turning her head to the right, pursing her lips. "I am extremely upset at the plight of my planet. They could not help but destroy themselves over greed and power. Even though I know the *Extractor Virus* caused all the problems and pain, I am still angry. My beautiful planet has become a wasteland because the emotional virus could not be cured. The Epiphanites refused to listen to the great sages and ancient Masters. The hideous thought diseases corrupted our minds and ruined our civilization forever."

"That's horrible. I can imagine how you must feel."

"You might experience the same pain if you return to Earth."

"What's *that* mean?"

"I have overheard Morph and Pendragon discuss your planet's nuclear problem. My grandfather, Otto, told me stories that the Earth was no longer the best option for migration due to their volatile situation, the human propensity toward nuclear war."

"Yeah, we've had a cold war going on since before I was born. I know we've got a lot of nuclear warheads stockpiled all over the Earth, but I believe they're just for show. No government is really going to use them."

"I hope you are correct. That is exactly what my Grandpa Otto told me about the grand rulers of Epiphany. They promised us that the weapons were necessary for defense only, to keep pace with the enemy governments and galactic invaders."

Chicomoztoc
Cave of Creation

"Galactic invaders? What else did your grandfather tell you?"

"Grandpa told me to never trust humans. Especially men."

Oh, great, I thought, *she's been taught to hate me before she even knows me. No wonder I can't—*

"Whoa!" Chernobog stopped abruptly.

Lunging forward, I pressed against Eve's back.

Wrapping my arms around Eve's waist, my left cheek pressed against her right cheek.

I blurted out, "Did anyone ever tell you that you smell heavenly?"

"Oh, Hunter. You are so playful," she said, holding my hands and giggling.

Before I could respond, Morph turned in his saddle and yelled, "Dismount, we shall spend the evening here."

"Where?" I asked.

"I think he means in *there.*"

Eve and I watched Grimnir tie Byelobog's reins to an iron ring. He turned and waddled to a massive stone door displaying a skeleton with wings. He pushed the creaking door open and shined his head lamp into the pitch-black entryway.

Byelobog's antennalantern dimmed.

Woden's Passage grew darker.

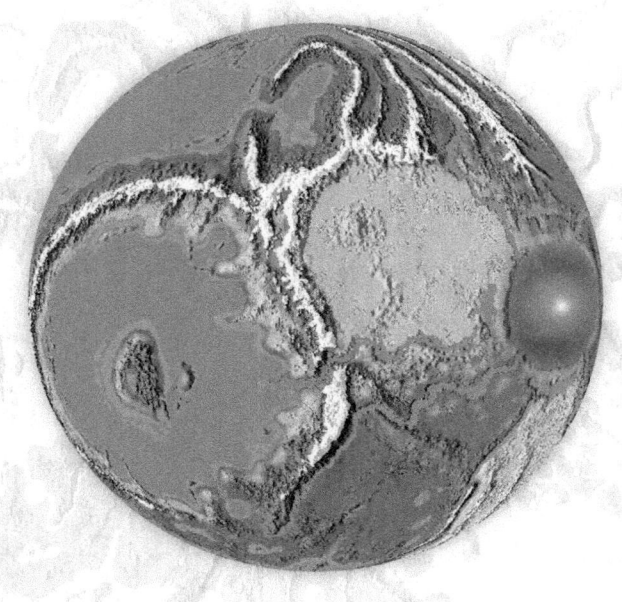

Chapter 19
Cave of Creation

ight shined through the arched stone doorway, casting a yellow glow on the sandstone floor. Chernobog's antennalantern dimmed. I jumped off the restless moleipeede and helped Eve dismount. The beautiful Epiphanite, still afraid of the dark, squeezed my hand.

"Come, this way," Morph said, motioning us forward in the dim light. The sage grabbed the leather reins and pointed to the opening. "I shall secure the sumpter. Please, go inside."

Eve held my hand as I led her through the stone door.

"Wow, this is great," I said, entering the chamber. "Professor Van Campbell would love this place."

Grimnir had lit twenty oil lamps mounted on brass sconces. The round chamber, fifty feet in diameter, had twelve marble columns encircling the perimeter. Each column supported a massive marble beam.

My eyes adjusted to the lamp lights. I admired the colorful hieroglyphics covering the white plastered walls. A stacked-stone fire pit sat in the center of the ancient chamber. Four clay vases, filled with lamp oil, sat by the entrance.

On the far side of the circular room, a narrow stream of water trickled down the limestone wall into a stone bowl.

While Eve and I stared at the symbols adorning the walls, Grimnir lit the oil fire pit. The flames warmed the damp air as Morph entered the chamber.

Slapping the dust off his clothes with his four hands, he smiled and said, "My, this is cozy."

Grimnir stood at the stone bowl, filling two water bags. "I'll be waterin' n' feedin' the moleipeedes-sth. If any of you need me, jus' whissssthle."

"Join us for dinner," Morph told Grimnir.

The aardvark wiped the drool from his mouth on his crusty sleeve. "Thanks~sth, Mathster, but I gotta' put my sth~sumpters~sth to sth~sleep. Besides~sth, sth~somebody's~sth gotta' sth~stand guard."

Thank God he's leaving, I thought. *That slobbering idiot is smelling up the place.*

"See you in the morning," Morph said, as the aardvark waddled across the sandstone floor through the archway.

"Let us gather around the fire and have a bite to eat."

"Before we sit down," I said, "can you tell me who painted all these hieroglyphs? I see Egyptian, Mayan, Aztec, Runic and other symbols."

"We are standing in Chicomoztoc, the Cave of Creation. During the early days of the Extractor Invasion, this secluded subterranean chamber was built by the Telosians for purification ceremonies."

"Where are they now?"

"The Barbegazi wiped out all the peaceful Telosians, exterminated them during the last millennium."

"My grandfather told me that Telosians live on Epiphany," Eve said.

"Correct."

"Are any on Earth?" I asked.

"Yes," Morph said.

"Where?"

"I hear they still inhabit your underworld."

"Can you tell me where?"

"Before we get into that subject, let us sit down and eat. We shall need our energy for tomorrow's ride. We must travel northeast for seven hours before reaching the portal."

I followed the sage's request and, along with Eve, spread out my bedroll and sat by the fire. The temperature had dropped. The fire warmed my face and hands. Enjoying a drink of amrita, I ate my salmon jerky, pine nuts, carrots, ambrosia, and my final piece of jambu fruit.

Morph brushed the bread crumbs off his white beard and smiled. "Before we have our evening conversation, I want to wish you a happy Earth birthday. We shall not have time to celebrate in the morning."

"Who? Me?" I asked, blushing.

Eve smiled and raised her leather water bag.

"You shall turn eighteen on Earth tomorrow morning, the Daynight of the Wolf," Morph said, raising his water bag.

I couldn't believe a year has passed at home. I had missed my high school graduation. I wondered what my mom did for my birthday. Julia was eighteen now. I hoped she had been accepted to Stanford University. That should make Father happy.

"At least I didn't spend my eighteenth birthday in prison."

"Good point. Your birthday shall be celebrated in freedom. May you enjoy many more," Morph said, smiling.

The three of us toasted and drank amrita in honor of my birthday. As always, I felt a rush of exhilaration when I drank the delicious water.

"How old are *you?*" I asked, pointing to Eve.

"I just turned seventeen on the Daynight of the Bear, back at Ogo Hole."

"How come you didn't say anything, so we could celebrate?"

"Because I will not be celebrating my Epiphany birthday any more. I am a Millennian now. My next birthday will be in 356 daynights."

I stared at Eve, expressionless, thinking, *She really is staying here. On her next Millennium birthday I'll be sixty-eight years old on Earth and she'll be only eighteen here.*

"Is something wrong?" she asked me.

I glanced sideways, surprised. "No, I was just thinking about our age difference."

"I am only a year younger than you."

I looked at Morph and shrugged my shoulders. "She's right as usual."

Eve gave me an impatient shrug.

Frustrated, I unclenched my fists, trying to relax.

"Well, my son, what should we discuss this evening?"

"You were going to tell me about the Telosians," I said, staring at the red, blue, and green hieroglyphic symbols painted on the white chamber walls. "Why were they exterminated?"

"For no good reason whatsoever." Morph said, lowering his eyes. "Because their killers, the violent Barbegazi, suffer from the low self-esteem virus, the Dark Essence."

"Low self-esteem doesn't cause people to kill each other."

"This is a good time to discuss self-esteem, young man."

"I would like to hear more," Eve said.

"I already know a lot about self-esteem," I said, bragging. "We heard a self-esteem speaker at our school. She said that all of us would be getting ribbons and trophies and awards for participation that would help raise our self-images."

Grinning, Morph said, "Awards and trophies are not exactly what I had in mind."

Before I could respond, Eve gave me her *be quiet* look. I nodded back to her and motioned to Morph, *continue.*

"Allow me to share some life-changing information that you did *not* learn from your parents or in a school classroom."

"I'm ready," I said, inhaling the fragrance of burning oil that smelled like cinnamon.

"When you have high-frequency thought vibrations, you enjoy high self-esteem, a healthy ego. This is because the fast-moving energy vibrations create your highest thoughts. When your thought vibrations are low frequency, slow-moving energy, you suffer from low self-image. A unhealthy ego. This is because your thoughts vibrate at a low level."

"You mean, negative thoughts?" I asked.

"Correct. You *have* been listening, young man."

I nodded and bit off a piece of salmon jerky.

Beyond the chamber doorway, the outside tunnel turned pitch black. The sumpter's two antennalanterns had burned out.

"As I have mentioned earlier, your negative thoughts are a direct result of the low self-esteem Dark Essence, the *Extractor Virus*. The viral epidemic has infected humans, as well as Epiphanites, for the past 50,000 years. Since the dawn of social awareness, Earth and Epiphany have been plagued by crippling emotional diseases that have infected their populations."

I looked out of the corner of my eye at Eve and asked, "How do I prove to the people back on Earth that this emotional virus, this Dark Essence, really exists? How do I let people know they are infected, that they have an emotional virus?"

"Simple," the sage replied. "The viral thought diseases have recognizable symptoms. Just like the common cold or the flu, you can see, with your own eyes, the infectious symptoms. The symptoms are revealed in your behaviors, how you act and treat one another. Through the power of negative thoughts, you infect each other with the emotional virus. You imitate one another's actions. I believe your saying is, 'Monkey see, monkey do.'"

"That's funny, Morph. Now we're a bunch of monkeys?"

"No, monkeys get along better than humans."

"Touché," I said, making a goofy face for Eve.

She frowned and said, "This is *not* funny."

"Sorry, just kidding." I stopped smiling.

With a wounded look in my eyes, I motioned to Morph, *continue.*

"May I remind you that your primitive civilization on Earth has unintentionally developed hypnotic ways to teach dysfunctional behaviors to your children."

I raised my hand. "Say that again."

"You glorify bad behavior on the electronic screens that transmit images and vocal signals into your dwellings. In fact, all the unacceptable behaviors that you demand that your children *not* do, you show them *how* to do on the screen of moving images. Examples of your deadliest thought disease, *emotionalsclerosis,* is broadcast electronically to the children on Earth. You teach young minds that violence and wars are acceptable. You glorify bad behavior, then demand that your children behave themselves."

"Yeah, television and the movies and video games are full of violence," I said, glancing at Eve.

"How you communicate to each other and to your children is the key," the sage said. "Ancient humans sat around their campfires. Modern humans gather around their televisions."

"Yeah, I guess we *do* sit around our televisions like they are campfires."

"Yes, and until the world's new campfire message is a *positive* one, you shall continue to experience chaos. Until you change your culture of negative thought, bad behavior shall flourish."

"We have the same problems on Epiphany," Eve said, her green eyes filled with tears.

"On Earth, the disease symptoms can be witnessed all around you," Morph said. "Your inherent ignorance lies in the fact you humans believe your egotistical behavior is normal and perfectly acceptable."

"For instance?"

"Anger, depression, jealousy, and lying to name a few. All ego-driven, unacceptable behaviors caused by the Dark Essence, the *Extractor Virus.* Should I go on?"

I sighed and shook my head, *no*, staring at the walls with the hieroglyphic symbols.

"Egotistical personalities rule your planet. If I give them nicknames, you shall recognize them immediately."

"Go ahead. Name a few."

"Intimidators, talkaholics, impatient hotheads, power fanatics, sarcastic assassins, gossip mongers, hypocrite liars, compulsive addicts, miserable misers, show-off braggarts, rebel outlaws, unethical tricksters, complaining pessimists, arguing soreheads, unforgiving avengers, and angry bigots, to name a few."

"How can you remember all those names?"

"Easy. I see them all over Millennium. They are called Extractors. They are the killer of dreams. Earth is crawling with them. You see, the Dark Essence has left a legacy of low self-esteem, preventing humans from changing their thoughts."

"You've lost me," I said.

"Your legacy as human beings is to continue to live dysfunctional lifestyles. You practice emotionally crippling behavior because you believe it is the right way to live. The Dark Essence, low self-esteem, has been passed unintentionally from generation to generation since the beginning of your recorded history, since the Extractor Asteroid struck Earth.

"This legacy guarantees the egotistical thought viruses are passed from parents to children, from generation to generation to generation. The viruses are the perfect infectious life forms, masquerading as love and discipline. It does not take long for the egotistical behaviors to become accepted as normal. This contagious, viral masquerade means that the *Extractor Virus* has the potential to destroy all intelligent life in the universe if the pandemic virus is not cured and eliminated."

Morph held his four hands up to the fire to warm himself.

"What about Epiphanites?" I asked. "You keep talking about humans. What about Eve's people?"

The sage grinned at Eve and said, "Although they suffer from the emotional viruses, the Epiphanites have much better control of their emotions than humans. Unfortunately, the beings from Epiphany lack emotions. Their obsession with logic has caused them different psychological issues."

"I want to hear more about that," I said, glancing at Eve.

She frowned while the sage said, "Perhaps we shall discuss Epiphany another time. This evening I wish to finish with a final thought on self-esteem."

I motioned, *go ahead.*

"Your level of self-esteem is directly related to the law of attraction. Low energy thoughts attract low energy responses from the universe and from other low-energy beings. High energy thoughts attract high energy responses for the universe and from other high-energy beings. True happiness attracts true happiness. Thought energy never lies, so be careful what you think. I pray you Earthlings and Epiphanites learn this grandest of truths so you may enjoy your existence to the fullest. That you always live your bliss."

"Thank you, Metamorphosis," Eve said. Then, she pointed toward the chamber entry.

The sage looked over his left shoulder.

Grimnir stood in the doorway, squinting. "It's-sth gettin' late, Mathster Morfff."

"Yes, it is," the sage replied. "Good daynight everyone. Tomorrow we shall see the Upperworld. It shall be a glorious experience."

Morph stood and walked in a circle around the chamber, extinguishing the oil lanterns. He returned to his bedroll and said, "When you remain peaceful inside, even in the midst of chaos, you have arrived."

He sat, pulled off his boots, faced the wall, and assumed a full lotus position.

Folding his wings behind him, he bowed his head and raised his four arms skyward.

The flames of the central fire pit offered the only light.

Morph's four-armed shadow danced on the chamber wall while the flames moved rhythmically up and down.

"Good daynight," Eve said. "See you in the morning."

She took off her black boots and slid her slender body under her beige wool blanket. Facing me, she closed her eyes.

Eve, beautiful Eve, I thought. *I wonder if she knows I'm in love with her? She really is planning to stay here. I wish I could bring her back to Earth with me. I can't wait to see daylight again, the upper world has got to be better than this dark, dreary place. I wonder what my family is doing right now? I really miss my mom and brothers and sisters. I can't wait to tell my friends about this place. I'm going to write a book and create some great artwork when I get home. Home...when am I going to get home? If I stay here the rest of this month, almost four years are going to pass me by on Earth.*

Interrupting my thoughts, Morph returned to his bedroll, stretched his wings, and crawled under his grey wool blanket.

Opened my leather artist satchel and removed a piece of parchment paper, ink bottle and a quill. While I sketched an ink drawing of Eve with her knife, I thought about my imprisonment at the hands of Vulcan.

The oil fire burned while I continued to draw.

I paused often to stare at Eve's enchanting face illuminated by the orange and yellow flames. Signed my illustration with my initials, *HW,* then put the parchment page back into my leather loculus.

Wide awake, I studied the calendar inside the leather flap.

Tomorrow would be the fifteenth of Aries, the Daynight of the Wolf. Glanced down at my sword, *Aroundight,* wondering if I would have the courage to use the weapon if threatened.

Somehow I knew the Upperworld would change me forever.

Daynight of the Wolf

Aries the 15th

Year of the Dragon

"When The Great Way is lost, there is goodness.
When goodness is lost, there is kindness.
When kindness is lost, there is justice.
When justice is lost, there is ritual.
Ritual is the husk of true faith,
the beginning of chaos."
—Metamorphosis

Chapter 20
Portal of Metamorphosis

One hundred yards ahead of us, blue sky and solshine poured into Woden's Passage. Eve pointed to the natural light at the end of the tunnel. I whispered in her ear, "I feel like I've been in the dark forever." She turned her head and held her index finger to her lips. "Shhh."

I bit down on my lower lip, thinking of a clever response. Didn't say anything. She was right. I'd only upset Morph, who had asked us not to talk. The six-hour-non-stop ride through the damp and dreary tunnel had been frustrating for me.

After our group broke camp and began our final leg of our subterranean journey, Grimnir damaged his head lamp on a sagging tunnel beam. Due to exhaustion, the moleipeedes' antennalantern lights had become dim and yellow. Unable to see effectively, the sage had requested silence.

The silence gave me time to think.

I wondered if I was lying in some hospital bed like a vegetable in Carmel or Monterey? I felt really bad for Mom, I know she was suffering because of me. I hoped my Father was sorry for giving me such a hard time. When I got home, Julia would be half finished with college. Sebastian would be walking. I still questioned if I had made the right decision. My eyes filled with tears. I started feeling sorry for myself.

I thought, *How old will I be when I get home? What if something bad happens and I get killed, or—Stop! Quit worrying about everything. You've made your choice, Hunter, now deal with it. Stop your stinking thinking. Say an affirmation. How about, 'I enjoy making the right decisions'...'I am in control of my thoughts'...'I live in the moment'...'My choice to remain on Millennium is a wise one'...'I know I am loved.'*

347

Believe it or not, the affirmations made me feel better as we approached the portal. A cool breeze blew in my face. The incoming fresh air had replaced the musty odor that constantly reminded me of the root cellar at my Carmel home. Inhaling deeply, I felt a rush of excitement.

Eve's hair swayed to the movements of the moleipeede. I yearned to hold her. She had been a lot nicer since the dungeon experience. Even though we hadn't talked, I felt her positive energy. Morph was right, silence wasn't so bad after all. I didn't care if we ever talked, I just wanted to be near her.

The light became brighter. I looked over Eve's right shoulder at the mouth of the Portal of Metamorphosis. Blue sky. It looked so beautiful.

Squinting, my eyes hurt from the radiant light flooding the tunnel. I hoped my face wasn't covered with red dust.

"Fasthter sth-sumpters-sth," Grimnir yelled.

The exhausted moleipeedes, having climbed a thirty-mile incline, gasped for oxygen while they approached the Portal of Metamorphosis. The portal, a cave-like opening located at the south end of the Druid Hills, provided travelers access between the Underworld and the Upperworld.

"Cover your eyes," Morph yelled, "we are about to enter the wonderful world of light."

Eve and I squinted, shielding our eyes as we emerged through the opening of the portal.

"Whoa, big fella', sth-stop." Upon Grimnir's command, both moleipeedes skidded to a stop. The golden rays of Sol and Helios touched my face while I sat quietly, astonished at the landscape in front of me. White clouds reached high into the blue sky. Evergreen trees covered the surrounding hills. Below us, two castle tower ruins sat beside the Open Road.

Closed my eyes to feel the warm solshine. The inside of my eyelids turned red as I enjoyed the songs of chirping birds.

I inhaled, deeply. The air smelled sweet, a mixture of fresh mountain air and pine trees. The air reminded me of our family camping trips to the Sierra Nevada Mountains. To my left, Sol burned brightly in the eastern sky. To my far right, Helios shone, but with half the size and intensity of its twin daystar.

We had stopped outside the portal on a flat landing overlooking Pellagus, Kingdom of the Eternal Rose. The area had been covered in crushed gravel. Eve allowed me to help her dismount. I looked at my hands; then, Eve's face. No dust. Her blouse was still white. I knew my face looked clean.

"I'm a little saddle sore," I said, brushing off the sleeves of my black tunic.

"What's-sth a matter, you little pus-sth-sy cat? Is-sth your fanny hurtin' ya?" Grimnir asked, snatching the sumpter's reins out of my hands.

"I've had it with your smartass remarks, aardvark," I yelled, pointing my right index finger at Grimnir.

The subterranean guide spat at me and kicked gravel on my black boots. I clenched my fists and stepped forward. Grimnir raised his wooden club in the air. I grabbed the handle of my sword, ready to defend myself.

Eve moved between us and grinned at the slobbering aardvark, saying, "Let me help you with Chernobog."

Grimnir smirked and bowed at the waist. His ears flopped over. "Yes-sth my princess-sth, anythin' you wish."

The aardvark stuck out his sticky purple tongue at me and walked away, arm in arm with Eve.

She turned and grinned at me. "Happy Birthday!"

I tried to grin, but my disdain for the dark aardvark kept the scowl on my face.

"Young man," Morph said. "May I see you for a moment?"

I nodded and walked toward the sage, still staring down Grimnir. My thoughts turned to anger. *That mangy aardvark has ruined my birthday. He needs to be taught a lesson. I know I can beat the crap out of him, he's smaller than me...and— Stop! Listen to yourself, Hunter, you sound like a hoodlum. Stop thinking like that.*

Morph patted me on the shoulder. "Congratulations young man. You have made it to the Upperworld."

My face still red and blotchy, I frowned and looked over my shoulder at Eve and the self-proclaimed sumpter master.

"I see you have allowed Grimnir to rob you of all your personal energy."

"I can't help it, Morph. That guy's been making fun of me the whole trip."

"You must forgive Grimnir. By now, you must be aware that he suffers from the *Extractor Virus*."

"No kiddin', he's one sick son~of~a—"

"Anger is your worst enemy. Calm down. Enjoy the scenery."

I took a deep breath. "Sorry, I'm a little frustrated. I've been thinking about my family and how long I've been gone and I'm dying to talk to Eve and, you know, I'm just...well, a really feeling out of sorts."

"I understand. Things will get better, I promise."

The sage turned and walked toward the edge of the gravel landing. "Come, our ride awaits us."

I followed the sage, trying to calm down.

"Look. Our wagon is at the outpost," Morph said, pointing to a turnout in the trail below.

"There is Blunderbore, feeding the oxen."

Down the slope, fifty feet below us, there stood a log cabin with a thatched roof, a red barn, and a corral.

A decorative wagon sat in front of the cabin. Four black and white, spotted oxen with spiral horns stood hitched to the wagon, grunting while they munched on alfalfa hay.

"Where are we going?"

"My son, there is no need to know where you are going to enjoy the road you are on."

He's right, I thought, *calm down and stop worrying about your destination.*

Blunderbore saw Morph and waved.

The sage yelled, "Hello, my friend. We shall be down in a moment. Allow us to gather our—"

"Mathster Morfff!" Grimnir interrupted. "Will you need me sth~services~sth fer the return trip?"

"Thank you," the sage replied, turning around, "but we shall not require your sumpters upon our return. You may take the remaining supplies with you."

"Sth~suit yourselfff," the aardvark said, smirking. "Ya owe me two oodles~sth, three scruples~sth, an' six frugles~sth fer me sth~services~sth."

Drool dripped from the corner of his mouth while he held out his dirty paw. Morph reached inside his backpack and removed a red leather sack. The sage counted out seventy-five points worth of treasure coins.

He placed the coins in Grimnir's paws and said, "Your services are greatly appreciated. I shall see you again."

"Ya sth-certainly will, Mathster Morfff," the dark aardvark said, winking one of his squinty eyes.

He bowed to Morph and Eve, grabbed the moleipeedes' reins, and disappeared through the portal entrance to Woden's Passage.

"Take care o' that princess-sth, little boy!" Grimnir shouted from the portal.

Good riddance, I thought. *I hope I never see that slobbering idiot again...Stop! Where does all your anger come from? Forgive him, he's suffering from the virus...he can't help himself.*

"Do not mind him," Eve told me. "He is only joking."

"Yeah, he's hilarious," I said, smirking.

"Come," the sage said, "let us gather at the wagon. We are not far from the Open Road."

We followed the sage down a winding stepping-stone path to the outpost.

"Yo. It is gud to see you, Moorf," Blunderbore yelled.

The Vanir giant stood nine feet tall. He wore a scarlet-red tunic with a brown jerkin, baggy black pants and brown boots. A silver-handled saber with scabbard hung from his leather belt. Instead of ox horns, his iron helmet had curving ram horns protruding from the sides. His woolly black beard hung to his Triangulum belt buckle.

"Ya, how is my cousin doin' on der ship?" Blunderbore asked while he shook the sage's hand.

"Fine. Gog sends his regards," Morph replied. "These are my guests, Eve and Hunter."

The giant grinned at me and the Epiphanite. "Oh, ya, some fine lookin' youngins."

Blunderbore pointed at the wagon. "Vee bes' be gettin' in der vardo'. Der oxen 'ave been vaitin' fer a long time."

"I hear the Open Road calling us," Morph said. "We shall eat in the wagon while you escort us down the hill."

"Ya, dat be a gud plan." Blunderbore looked around. "Und ver is der vagon master?"

I heard a commotion in the nearby log cabin. A cackling red rooster flew out the front window. A trail of red and green feathers floated to the ground.

The front door of the cabin burst open.

A gnome holding a hatchet stumbled down the front porch steps and yelled, "The blooody chicken 'tis gettin' away. There'll be noo sooper 'tis evenin'."

Dressed in a blue tunic, beige breeches, and black boots, the bald gnome wore a frizzy red beard. He smiled when he spotted Metamorphosis.

"Hallo, Marster Moorph. 'Tis me, your 'umble wagon master."

"Greetings, Vindalf," Morph said. "I wish to thank you and Blunderbore for making your fine wagon available."

"Aye, we be wurried aboot you; that you got yourself lost."

Vindalf waddled to the sage and shook his hand.

"We had a couple of slight delays. My apologies," Morph said.

Then, he introduced the gnome to me and Eve.

"Where can I change into something more comfortable?" Eve asked the gnome.

"Aye, lassie. You cun use me 'ouse to freshin' oop," the gnome said, pointing to his log cabin.

While Eve entered the cabin and closed the door, Vindalf looked around and asked, "Beggin' your pardon, may I arsk aboot me coosin, Andvari? W'ere in blazes is 'ee?"

"My friend, I am afraid I must share some unexpected news," Morph said. "Your cousin has left his body and passed on to the Spirit World during our journey."

Vindalf stopped smiling and lowered his head.

"T'was it oold age?"

Morph shook his head, *no.*

"Did me coosin die an 'onorable death?"

"Andvari died fighting the Extractors."

"I told that stooburn fool to watch 'is back. Aye, 'is momma's gonna' be cryin' 'er eyes ooout."

"Give my regards to Hiordis the next time you see her. Please tell her I shall visit her when I am up near Midgard."

"Aye, 'ill be lettin' 'er know 'twas a blooody mistyke, nae Andvari's fult."

Morph handed Andvari's gold pocket watch to Vindalf. "He would want you to have this."

Wiping his tears with a red checkered bandanna, the gnome accepted the watch.

"Ya, dat Andvari be a gud lad," Blunderbore said, bowing his head. "Vat in tarnation is der little fella' doin' fightin' dem devils?"

Morph bowed his head. In Andvari's honor, they stood silent for a few moments.

The cabin door swung open and my eyes widened. Eve had changed into a green satin chemise with gold buttons, black leather skirt with belt, and medieval sandals with leather ties that wrapped up and around her ankles.

Grabbing the v-neck leather ties of my black tunic, I asked Eve, "How did you manage to get *real* buttons on your blouse?"

"Special request," she said, walking past me. "Alfrigga also made the skirt, and the sandals."

She looked fantastic in that outfit!

"Vee best load der vagon," Blunderbore said, "before der boy's eyeballs pop outta' his head."

Chuckling, the giant lumbered to the rear of the wagon.

"Hoot mon!" Vindalf shouted, pointing at his cousin's gold pocket watch. "Me weary wheel says it be past 13 o'clock. We best be puttin' spurs to the nags!"

"Time to board the Vindalf's vardo," Morph announced. "Gather your gear."

While Vindalf climbed up to the front driver's box and grabbed the reins, Blunderbore opened the rear door of the polished cedarwood wagon.

I followed Eve up the five wood steps.

A sign carved above the rear door read:

VINDALF'S VARDO

"This is beautiful," Eve said, admiring the inside of the coach, eighteen feet long and ten feet wide.

"Vindalf's Vardo?" I asked.

"Correct," Morph said, closing the lower half of the wagon door and leaving the upper half open. "It is an example of Millennium's finest wagons, suitable for living and traveling."

"Kind of like a recreational vehicle," I said, grinning at Eve.

Not familiar with my description, she raised her eyebrows as she removed her bow and arrow pouch.

Eve sat on a cushioned bench, crossed her legs, and stared out the window.

"Excellent analysis, young man," Morph said, sitting on a bench by the left-front window, opposite Eve.

Vindalf's custom vardo had gold-leafed carved figures and motifs on the seven-foot-tall cedar walls and ceiling. Every inch of the oak wagon, inside and out, had been hand-carved with decorative murals, including the arched roof and the four-spoke wagon wheels. Just like the *Skipbladnir,* most of the carvings depicted gods and goddesses and hieroglyphics.

The coach had four tall windows, two on each side. The top portion of the rear half door remained latched open. The exquisitely decorated coach contained a wash basin, stove, closet, cupboards, and a feather bed at the front end.

A maroon throw rug, embroidered with gold Triangulums, ran down the center aisle. Two guitars and maracas sat in the corner next to a full-length mirror.

The sage wore his leather vest, purple tunic and brown boots.

I removed my scabbard and artist satchel and sat on the same bench as Eve, next to the right-rear window.

Blunderbore stuck his head in the window next to Morph, hitting his curved ram horns on the wooden frame. "Ya, der is gud viddles und fresh vater und juice in dat der cupboard. Help yourselves if you're hungry."

The giant smiled, lumbered to the front of the wagon and climbed aboard. The iron suspension bars squeaked and groaned while the wagon tilted forward.

"Heeeyaww!" Vindalf shouted and snapped the leather reins.

"Hang on," Morph said.

The wagon lunged forward, pulled by the four grunting oxen with spiral horns. The isolated outpost disappeared when we made a sharp turn and headed down the Druid Hills Trail toward the Open Road.

The sage stood and walked down the center isle while the wagon swayed back and forth. Morph managed to keep his balance using his green tail as a third leg. Steadying himself, he opened the cupboard and took down three pewter plates and mugs. He removed fresh ambrosia, alligator pears, huckleberries, and fried dodo legs from an oak storage chest. He prepared the plates and poured three mugs of açai juice.

The gracious sage handed me and Eve our plates. While the wagon rolled down the switchback trail, the three of us enjoyed our food, especially the dodo drumsticks that tasted like turkey.

Eve ate her meal, gazing out the window. She had a grin on the corner of her mouth, enjoying her first look at the Upperworld.

The pine tree forest began to surrender ground to the gigantic firs and redwoods. At the switchback turn, a clearing in the trees allowed me to see the Glittering Plains three thousand feet below us. The amber grasslands, dotted with vast herds of grazing animals, stretched on forever.

Listening to the crunching rhythm of the wagon wheels rolling down the gravel road, I swallowed a swig of juice and asked Morph, "When I return to Earth, how am I going to find someone like you?"

"With wings?" Morph asked, chewing on a bite of green alligator pear.

The sage winked.

Grinning, I said, "Very funny. No, not someone with wings and four arms. I mean someone with your wisdom. A *real* sage."

"Your planet has many sages. You must find them, seek them out."

"Who should I look for?"

"For what purpose?"

"You know, to learn more of what *you* teach."

"There are many sages and messengers and great teachers on your planet. You have Masters who speak of The Great Way."

"How do you know that?"

"You are not the only human to have visited us recently. Several humans have remained here. They have informed me of positive events and about the great work these teachers and sages and Masters have accomplished."

"How many of these human visitors have remained on Millennium in the past six months?"

"Let me think. Six Millennium months, that is twenty-five Earth years. We have had three humans remain with us."

"Are they near here? Can I talk to them?"

"There are two living in Hermopolis. I shall introduce them to you, that is, if you can find the time."

Grinning, I said, "I'd like to hear what they have to say."

"You should know that the Earth visitors have told me of the negative effects of your cultural media. They speak of books and magazines with negative information. They also warn of a greater danger, of hypnotic visual images and messages that are portrayed on screens with moving images. World-wide broadcasts reaching billions of humans on a daily basis."

"We call it the TV and Internet. A better word is media."

"I am told that these images and messages, this media you speak of, controls your minds. I am told that the media is highly revered and worshiped. That humans stare a screens filled with negative information all day long."

"Yeah, it has gotten a little out of control."

"This leads to human ruin. Media can destroy a civilization."

I sighed heavily, pondering Morph's words.

"For seven hundred years," the sage said, "humans suffering from the *Extractor Virus* have not been able to handle media properly. For example, soon after you humans invented the printing press and books became available to the masses, the two most popular publications were The Bible and *The Witches Hammer*, known then as *Malleus Maleficarum*."

Before I could speak, Morph held up his hand to silence me.

"Unfortunately, positive books like your Bible and Lao Tze's *Tao Te Ching* are rare. For every positive book, you print a thousand negative books. *The Witches Hammer* was your first example of negative press, hypnotic media."

"A book about witches?"

"No, a book about innocent women being tortured and murdered. The lowest form of the Dark Essence."

Eve looked at me with saddened eyes.

"Around 1450 A.D., just after Owain arrived, humans experienced their first mass media era, the distribution of books. In your fifteenth century western civilization, the second most popular book printed after The Bible was, as I have said, *The Witches Hammer*. This book, read and revered by educated humans, was an instruction manual on how to find, capture, torture and properly kill witches. Specifically, any women who acted inappropriately."

"Inappropriate?"

"Any woman, young or elderly, who defied men, spoke her mind, or acted too intelligent, came under suspicion. It did not take long for the human media, through the distribution of books, to instigate a witch hunt."

"That's crazy." My face grew hot with humiliation.

"The craziness has continued on Earth for seven hundred years. *The Witches Hammer* was your first warning of how media can destroy a civilization. You have not heeded this profound warning. Your media, no matter what form it is presented in, is worshiped by most of you. It controls your lives."

"Mind control?"

"Yes. In your recent Earth history, a world war started because of a new media technology."

"Bombs?"

"No. Radio. Another media invention."

"Radio? A world war began because of a radio?"

"One small man with a funny mustache hypnotized Europe armed with nothing but a microphone and a radio signal. What saddens me is, you humans did not learn from that negative media experience resulting in the deaths of millions of people. Things have not changed; the media has gotten worse."

Before I spoke, Morph raised his upper right hand.

"I do not wish to review your tragic human history. Let us focus on the subject, media. My point is, your human curiosity for gossip and misery and negative events, *bad* news, is destroying your civilization. Media controls your lives. Your media elects your politicians, judges your innocent prior to trial, determines what you eat and drink, and shows you how to look. The media tells you what is right and wrong. You have allowed your media to run your lives. The saddest part of all of this is, the media *is* you."

Feeling frustrated, I said, "I will do something revolutionary when I get home."

"Say the word, and it shall be done."

"I'm going to create positive media. Positive. I will change the way things are."

"I believe you, my son. Because of your commitment to change, I have a suggestion for your enlightenment when you return home. A simple one."

"Anything you say, Morph."

"Seek out and read the books written by your Masters of wisdom have written their messages in books. One of the greatest gifts we Millennians have given you humans is the alphabet, the written word. Stop abusing the alphabet. Avoid the books with negative words. Find the books with positive words, sacred words."

"How will I know these books?"

"Seek out the books that change your beliefs."

"You mean, on politics?"

"Not exactly. I speak of the books that help you think differently about thinking. The books that help you eliminate your negative thoughts and replace them with positive thoughts. Once you know how to think properly, you shall choose wise books and positive media."

"How about self-help books?"

"That sounds logical, since you humans need help; that is, need to improve your Selves. No one can help you change your thoughts except you. Only you. So, self-help sounds like a good place to begin. Philosophy is also important reading for your growth."

"But, which books are the right ones?"

"You shall know when the book is right for you. Soon after you open the book, the words have an immediate life-changing effect upon you. You are drawn to the book like a butterfly to a beautiful flower filled with sweet nectar. The book, containing *real* magic, becomes your best friend. The words sooth you. The messages of enlightenment create tranquility in your life."

"Thank you, Morph."

"You are most welcome. Next to a living sage, books are your greatest source of positive energy. Treasure them. Relax in total silence. Read often. Fill your mind with positive thoughts."

The wagon picked up speed after Vindalf snapped the leather reins.

Eve gazed out the right-front window at the green hills covered with orange poppies.

I turned my attention to the sage and asked, "So far, who is your favorite Earth visitor? Not counting me." I chuckled at my own satire. Eve did not react, she kept staring out the window.

The sage smiled. "I have no favorites. I have loved them equally, as I love you."

"Then, who did you believe was the most interesting?"

"Shakespeare was quite a fascinating character. He visited Millennium two times. His first visit as Sir Francis Bacon. Then, on his second visit as William Shakespeare."

"Twice? But how? You told me only *one* trip is possible."

"Patience. I shall share his method of visiting us a second time if you remain on Millennium. On his final visit, Willie stayed long enough to learn the Secrets of Time & Space. Like all Europeans of that era, he was in a big hurry. So, I returned him to Time Island for his journey back to Earth. He said he had a lot of writing to do."

"What human visitor stayed on Millennium the longest?"

"Excellent question," the sage replied, closing his eyes.

"Lao Tzu," Morph answered.

"But he was from China. How did you communicate with him when he arrived?"

"Like all our visitors who do not speak Millennish, he chose to learn *our* language. I remember Lao Tzu learned quickly."

"Is Millennish a universal language?"

"No. There are many languages and dialects in the cosmos. I do know, however, that Millennish is spoken on the eight planets connected to us by the Cosmic Force, the Amalgamation. Besides Earth and Epiphany, the other planets are Leda, Triton, Metis, Phaethon, Phobos, and Deimos."

"How do you know that Millennish is spoken on all those planets?"

"Because, like the earliest Earth visitors, I taught our native tongue to *all* our intergalactic guests."

"I remember on Time Island you told me I'm not speaking English, that I'm speaking Millennish, but, ummm—"

"What is your question?"

"If you taught Millennish to early man, why do we have so many languages on Earth?"

"In the beginning, humans had one tongue, one language, Millennish. After the Extractor Asteroid struck Earth and the *Extractor Virus* spread, humans began to quarrel, fight, and kill each other. Eventually, humans migrated to distant lands. As their skin color and facial features evolved due to climate, so did their languages."

"That makes sense. But, when Lao Tzu returned to Earth, what language did he speak?"

"He was bilingual. He spoke his native tongue and he was also fluent in Millennish."

"I'm lucky that I spoke English, I mean Millennish, when I got here. Otherwise, I couldn't have communicated."

"First of all, there was no luck involved. Your destiny has unfolded in perfect order. As for language barriers, none exist. All Earth visitors are welcomed in their native tongue. Like the other eight Utopians, I speak several hundred languages."

"Why did Lao Tzu have to learn Millennish?"

"Most of our population speaks Millennish. Our books are written in Millennish. Lao Tzu was brilliant. He knew exactly what to do."

"You mean, when on Millennium, do as the Millennians?"

"Well said, my son," Morph said, grinning.

"How long was Lao Tzu here?"

"Long enough to visit the final treasure, Lumen, the Crystal of Consciousness. Long enough to become a great sage, a Master. He had the heart of a dragon. When Lao Tze absorbed the Light

of Insight, self-actualization, he discovered who he truly was. When you discover the eight treasures and then see the Light, you shall know who you are."

"How long will that take?"

"As long as you wish."

Scratched my head and looked out the window. A squawking blue jay flew alongside the wagon, then disappeared into the towering trees.

I looked back at the sage and asked, "Who else saw all of the Eight Great Treasures?"

"Only a handful of humans. The remainder suffered from impatience and returned home early. They were still enlightened, but eager to get back home, to their families."

"What humans saw all eight treasures *and* the Crystal?"

"Another human being who completed his divine journey was Siddhartha Gautama. Many stayed for extended periods of time. Socrates, Dante, Jacob Grimm and his brother, Leonardo Da Vinci, Lewis Carroll, Jules Verne, and Thoreau, to name a few."

"So, once I visit the Eternal Rose, or any one of the treasures, I can help people back on Earth?"

"My son, you must first help your *Self*. Focus on you. The longer you stay here, the greater your message shall be upon your return. Each treasure brings you closer to sageness, closer to the Oneness, closer to your Source."

"I think I get it."

"Get what?"

"That if I change and become a sage, people will seek me out."

"They might also crucify you. Are you prepared for that?"

Staring at Metamorphosis, I asked, "How do I prepare for that?"

"If you stay long enough, you shall not have to ask that question."

I took a bite of my dodo leg and gazed at the snow-capped mountains on the western horizon.

Looking at the interior of the vardo, I asked, "Is this wagon the best form of transportation you have?"

"Other than Wotan's Wagon, the royal coach at Doubting Castle, this is our finest means of conveyance," Morph said.

"Wagons? Only wagons?"

"Yes, vardos have become our favorite means of land travel during stormy weather."

I stared out the window at the narrow trail ahead.

"What perplexes you, my son?"

"If you are such an enlightened civilization, why does your technology seem so old fashioned? You know, primitive."

"Technology is not a true measure of civilizations."

"But, how come our civilization on Earth has computers and smart phones and air planes and rocket ships, but Millennium doesn't have electricity or running water or cars that get you around faster."

"We Millennians have what you would consider futuristic technology, but choose to remain close to nature and live a simple existence."

"How's that?" I asked, staring into the dense forest carpeted with green sword ferns.

"We have knowledge of electricity, telephones, combustion engines, nuclear energy, rocket science, and computers. We also have knowledge of technology that you humans can only imagine."

"Tell me, which ones?"

"Teleporters, protective force fields, intelligent robots, and nano-robotics. Epiphany also has these technologies; unfortunately, their scientific discoveries have led to their planet's destruction."

"Wouldn't life be easier if you'd use cars and computers?"

"That technology leads to industrialization, overpopulation, and pollution. Should I go on?"

"Okay, what about electricity?"

"As for the Upperworld, trying to outshine the stars is not our idea of advancement. In the Underworld, you witnessed some of our lighting technology."

"The lights worked okay, but I can't imagine Americans living without bright lights in their houses. You know, light bulbs. Not candles and oil lamps. I can't imagine the world without street lights and head lights and neon signs."

"Maybe you humans should try something different for a

change. Gathering around candle light or a campfire with a billion stars overhead is good for the soul."

"I believe technology is better. Having light bulbs and street lights makes the world safer."

"You just survived without light bulbs on the *Skipbladnir* and the Cave of Creation. Was that so terrible?"

"No. But it was *really* different."

"I understand your feelings and attachment to worldly conveniences. They give you false security. I have been told that you humans enjoy conquering nature, altering day and night. Unfortunately, civilizations in our neighboring galaxies have proven that too much technology leads to self-destruction. All those technological advancements and time savers and gadgets lead to information overload and emotional insanity. Technology always seems to end up in the wrong hands, resulting in pollution of the mind and the environment. The technology that primitive civilizations create to serve them often destroys them. This is why we Utopians choose to avoid industrialization and alternative energy sources, especially nuclear energy."

"Hmmm, maybe you have a point."

"Slow down. Live in the moment and free yourself from the chase. Stop striving for more and searching for something better. You already have everything you need, right here, right now, to be completely happy."

I raised my eyebrows, sipping juice from my pewter mug.

"I ask you to be open minded, my son. Enjoy the simple lifestyle. Believe me, you shall have more time to think. Except for the Extractors' factories and mining operations, we have a quiet world here on Millennium. We enjoy the slow pace of nature, living in the moment."

"If you don't have technology and want to stay the same, what do your kids learn in school?"

"Are you speaking of education?"

"Yes. School. What do you teach the kids here on Millennium?"

"Excellent question. Perhaps I shall let Eve explain her educational system on Epiphany. Before the corrupt government destroyed the planet's biosphere, they had initiated an outstanding educational program, similar to our Utopian methods here. The Epiphanites did this in spite of the *Extractor Virus*. Change had truly begun."

Eve sat up straight and pulled down her short leather skirt. She re-crossed her legs and said, "It is quite simple. I was educated with the new awareness system based on fundamental thoughts and creative methods."

I asked, "What's the difference between that and what I've learned in school?"

"Our education system abandoned competition and trying to outdo each other. We were allowed to move at our own pace according to our abilities. Grading and performance were also abandoned. Instead, the system focused on teaching core values that made us caring and understanding beings. Besides basic reading and writing and arithmetic skills, we were taught critical thinking and logic and problem solving. We were also allowed to let our artistic talents flow from deep inside us. The education system promoted and encouraged music and art and mythology and storytelling. Philosophy was a core curriculum. The best thing I learned, that my father never learned, was to be honest and be responsible for my own decisions."

I had never heard Eve talk so much. I loved her strong, reassuring voice.

"It sounds like a strange school system, kind of bizarre. Radical," I said, looking at Morph.

The sage said, "Eve's teachers never demanded that they memorize irrelevant information that would not improve their future and the future of their planet."

"Like what?" I asked, leaning to my right while the vardo made a switchback turn.

"History," Morph replied. "All the negative things their earlier societies had done were not glorified in books. Eve no longer had to memorize all the dates and historical events her parents had to memorize. She was taught how information can always be evaluated later in life and should only be read with an open mind."

"But isn't knowledge critical to success?"

"Let go of your thirst for knowledge, that is, let go of

the accumulation of information and facts and figures and memorized trivia. Let go and seek wisdom."

"How do I tell the difference between knowledge and wisdom?"

"Knowledge is learning what others think about something. Wisdom is thinking for yourself. Please, do not abandon knowledge in favor of wisdom. Basic education is important, just not *too* much knowledge. Allow your children to discover knowledge on their own. For instance, history books are written by historians from *their* point of view. School books are written for children so they see the world from a specific point of view, which of course, is biased in favor of political indoctrination and ideology. History books seldom describe what actually happened. All information should be totally accurate and unbiased, so the children may come to their own conclusions, to think for themselves."

The fragrance of the virgin forest filled the wagon.

"We were taught to think for ourselves," Eve said, "and not believe everything we hear and read."

"So, why didn't the new educational system save the planet?" I asked.

"What is the question?" Eve frowned and looked at Morph.

As Vindalf snapped the reins, the sage replied, "He wants to know why your planet self-destructed."

"Oh, I understand," Eve said. "My grandfather told me that we waited too long to change. The new educational system should have been put in place a century before the apocalyptic holocaust and we might have been saved. Since our history began, every generation continued to teach the next generation what they believed was the truth. The truth as they believed it to be. They never let the children discover the real truth. They never allowed the children to think for themselves."

"That makes sense," I said. "It sounds familiar, the more you describe it. Do the Utopians have this awareness education system here, on Millennium?"

The sage nodded, *yes*. "Our curriculum has worked successfully for thousands of years. This is because we teach important life skills, how to love and be respectful of others."

"What kind of educational system do the Extractors have for their children?"

"The Extractors have developed a school system based on propaganda. Competition is the main focus. The children who learn and memorize the most information are rewarded the most. The system is about total control. A loud bell rings and the young Extractors are made to sit in the same chair for hours, memorizing pre-determined conclusions devised by their dysfunctional society written in untruthful books.

"Next, they are graded on their competitive performance. The grading system determines how well the propaganda worked. Those who cannot keep up the hectic pace are expelled from the system. Any childish activity such as daydreaming or playful behavior is considered anti-establishment and punished severely. The educational system indoctrinates the children at a young age, dictating how they must function in society, demanding they learn a specific skill or trade.

"The curriculum is designed to prepare the young Extractors for the mining-and-factory-mentality work force. Youth are taught to never question authority, do whatever their boss says, and work for the almighty moolah."

Staring at Morph, I asked, "Those schools are *here*, on Millennium?"

The sage nodded, *yes*.

Listening to the sage, I had to admit, his descriptions sounded like the schools I've attended since first grade. We never had enough art classes or music or the stuff I really wanted to do. I never got the chance to be myself.

"Can I visit one of your Utopian schools?" I asked. "I'd like to see how the system works."

"Certainly. If you stay a bit longer."

The sage was always trying to get me to stay a little longer.

"Why even *have* schools?" I asked. "Wouldn't it be better for our parents to teach us all the things you just mentioned? You know, the courses taught in the Utopian school system?"

"Unfortunately, that will not work on Earth. Proper instruction must take place in a separate school system with enlightened teachers, free from the *Extractor Virus*, who are completely detached from the parents' prejudices and preconceived beliefs. Keep in mind, with few exceptions, parents *are* the problem, because they unknowingly pass down their egotistical, low self-esteem values to their children. It is not the parents' fault, they suffer from the Dark Essence, the emotional virus, making them unqualified to instruct their own offspring. Human parents have taught their children incorrect bad behavior for hundreds and thousands of years, for centuries. The ways of the past have not worked. The solution is memorialized in the song, 'Love Teaches All.' Make this phrase your new mantra and your world shall change."

"Who are the best teachers?"

"The best teachers are elders."

"Old people?"

Morph grinned at me, running his fingers through his white beard.

"Sorry," I said, raising my right hand. "I meant to say the elderly. You know, senior citizens."

"Your country is fighting a silent war. Can you name it?"

"The war on drugs?"

"No, that is a public, government funded effort to fill up your prisons with non-violent human beings who require counseling, not incarceration."

I racked my brain for an answer, then shrugged my shoulders.

"The generation war!" Morph said. "Your great nation worships youth. Elders are considered too old and in the way. You have banished and exiled them from your homes and given them to strangers who fail to care for them properly. You push the elders aside, abandoning them, resenting them as a burden on society. You have cursed your civilization by cursing your elders. Do you know the consequences of your actions?"

"No." I said, glancing at Eve.

"Each and every one of you has denied yourself the richest and most valuable resource available on the planet, the gift of wisdom provided by elders. They are your greatest teachers."

I thought, *He's right about a generation war...elderly people are not respected...I never paid attention to what Grandma and*

Grandpa had to say. All those proverbs they would recite were probably full of wisdom. I just never paid attention to them.

Interrupting my thoughts, Morph asked, "Do you understand why elders make the best teachers?"

"I know. They have the most wisdom."

Metamorphosis nodded, *yes.*

"I need to tell everyone back home about your schools."

"And so you shall."

"I know I could make a difference when I get back home."

The sage grinned at me, nodded, and turned his head to gaze out the window.

Eve finished her meal, placing her plate and mug on the floor.

Before I spoke, the wagon turned sharply to the left. The wooden wheels skidded across the gravel trail.

Eve, thrown off balance, leaned against me. I caught her in my arms. Surprised, we gazed into each other's eyes. Eve relaxed in my arms and smiled.

"Sorry," she said, "I lost my balance."

With an infatuated grin on my lips, I held her tightly while our eyes remained fixated on each other.

"Ah-hem." Morph cleared his throat, continuing to look out the window.

Eve blushed and put her arm around my neck so I could lift her. She sat up, straightened her black leather skirt and composed herself.

The wagon picked up speed while it hugged the descending trail carved into the steep slopes of the Druid Hills. A dense pine forest covered the hills east of the Open Road. Vindalf guided the spotted oxen around a sharp switchback turn. The sweaty bovines struggled to maintain their footing on the gravel road.

"Aren't we going a little too fast?" I asked.

Morph glanced at me and did not answer.

I raised my right hand. "Okay, okay. I know. Stop worrying and trust Vindalf and Blunderbore."

Eve grinned at me. "I thought you liked being in a hurry."

"I like getting a lot of things done. You know, multi-tasking. I don't like wasting time."

"Multi-tasking?"

"Never mind," I said, rolling my eyes.

The sage placed his empty plate next to me on the seat, next to his curled tail. "The more you hurry, the less you get done."

"How can that be true?"

"You suffer from young man's disease. Dis-ease."

"What's that?"

"You are in a big hurry to get nowhere. You are anxious and try too hard."

"Come on, Morph. Aren't you ever in a hurry to get places?"

"The sage does not hurry but all things happen on time. This is known as divine timing. Non-action works magic in your life."

"Is that why you don't carry a watch? Like the pocket watches that Andvari and Fundin and Vindalf carry."

"Weary wheels are worthless to a sage. Time is of no concern to me. Patience has no limitations."

I had to admit, it must feel great not having to worry about what time it is.

"You're probably right. I should try to relax, be patient."

The gravel road had become narrower. Heading south, the vardo hugged the edge of the cliffs. It had be a thousand foot drop off.

"Is something wrong?" Morph asked.

"No. Well, yes. I wish they'd slow down a bit," I said, glancing at Eve. "The wheels are almost touching the edge of the cliffs."

"Vindalf has made this trip hundreds of times. You must trust his skill as a wagon master." The sage stood and walked down the aisle.

"I'll try. But I wish he'd slow this thing down."

Vindalf shouted commands to the spotted oxen. While the wagon traveled down the steep trail, I ate my last bite of dodo leg. Trying to calm myself, I stopped staring out the window and watched Morph pick up two guitars. The sage walked back down the aisle and handed a six-string guitar to me.

"Enough conversation. It is time to play Eve a song."

Morph's double neck guitar had a six-string and a twelve-string neck. My guitar sounded excellent, but I really liked Morph's double-neck guitar better. I wished I could play it.

On the other hand, I didn't want to screw up the song and make a fool of myself in front of Eve.

"Do you have a song you would like to play?" Morph asked, removing his spectacles and placing them in his vest pocket.

Scratching my head, I said, "No, you pick a song. Anyway, I do better with an electric guitar and an amplifier. Ummm, never mind. Go ahead, I'll follow."

"What song would you like to hear?" Morph asked Eve.

"We do not have much music on Epiphany. I like anything that you and Hunter play."

"I believe a song about freedom, personal freedom, might be appropriate," the Sage of the Ages said while he tuned his double neck guitar. "It is a song about the Source. You have a lyric sheet to the song in your loculus. It is called, 'Free Me'."

I grabbed my artist pouch. "In here?" I asked, removing the stack of parchment paper.

"Yes. I asked Andvari to add lyric sheets. Look on the bottom of those papers."

Setting the stack of parchment pages on the seat between myself and Eve, I found lyric sheets on the bottom of the stack.

"Why didn't you tell me these were here?" I asked Morph while I shuffled through the papers.

"I thought you would have found them by now. Besides, we did not need them until this moment."

"Did you draw these?" Eve asked, picking up the pile of parchment illustrations and studying the artwork.

I grabbed for the stack of paper, but Eve pulled them away.

"Those are just rough sketches. I don't want anyone to see them yet."

"I want to see what you have drawn. May I look at them?"

"Okay, but they are just—"

"I know, only sketches," she said, grinning.

The Epiphanite turned page after page of illustrations while I continued to tune my guitar. She stared at the illustrations of herself, then, she handed the stack of drawings back to me. "I love your drawings. They are excellent."

"Thanks." I said. "Wait until I redo these in color, on my computer, and when I—"

"Ah-hem." Morph cleared his throat. "Did you find the lyric sheet to 'Free Me'?"

"Yes, right here," I said, calming myself. "It starts in the key of A." For confidence, I strummed an A major chord.

Morph tapped his boot and played his double neck guitar.

I read the lyric sheet while the sage sang the opening verse of the ballad.

"Free me, take me out of the blue,
Won't You see me, show me the way to get through to
You, Need me, I wanna' let it be known, I need You,
"Free me, take me out of the world,
Won't You see me, show me the way I might be near You,
Need me, I wanna' let it be known, I love You."

Morph sang the bridge.

"Goodbye to things that I once knew,
That took me away from You, and let it be known,
Free me, take me into Your heart,
Won't you see me, please just let me be part of You,
Love me, I wanna' let it be known, I love You,
Goodbye to things that I once knew, That kept me away
from You, and let it be known, let it be known,
Free me, take me out of the world,
Won't You see me, 'cause I wanna' know that You could,
If You'd only love me, 'cause I wanna let it be known,
I love You."

I sang harmony. I was surprised when Eve joined me, singing softly. As she sang the bridge, Eve grinned at me.

"Goodbye to things that I once knew,
That kept me away from You, and let it be known,
Free me, take me out of the blue,
Don't You see me, show me the way to get through to
You, Love me, 'cause I wanna' let it be known, I love You,
I wanna' let it be known, I love You,
"I wanna' let it be known, I love You."

Morph and I finished playing. Our guitars resonated.

Eve smiled at me. "I love that song."

I grinned, pleased with my impromptu performance.

"Your voice sounds beautiful," I told Eve.

"Back home, I always got in trouble for singing."

The sage said, "My dear, you can sing all you want here, in fact, let us sing 'Bridge of Words.'"

"Open Road ahead!" Blunderbore shouted from the driver's box.

Morph laid his guitar on his seat. "We shall have to sing again later this evening, perhaps at the campfire."

Laid my guitar on the seat as the sound of squealing brakes made Eve cover her ears.

"Whoa, big fellas, whoa!" Vindalf shouted.

We hung onto our seats while the wagon came to a stop, sliding on the loose gravel.

"Ya, ve be at Druid Junction," Blunderbore yelled.

Free Me

C#m · F#m · F#m7 · D
Free me, take me out of the blue, won't You see me, show me the way to
E · E7
get through to You, need me, I wanna let it be known, I need You,
C#m · F#m · F#m7 · D
Free me, take me out of the world, won't You see me, show me the way that
E · E7
I might be near You, need me, I wanna let it be known I need You,
D · C#m · Bm · C#m · D · E7
Goodbye to things that I once knew, that took me away from You, and let it be known,
C#m · F#m · F#m7 · D
Free me, take me into Your heart, won't You see me, please just let me
E · E7
be part of You, love me, 'cause I wanna let it be known, I love You.
D · C#m · Bm · C#m · D
Goodbye to things that I once knew, that kept me away from You, and
E7 · E · G
let it be known ... let it be known ...
C · Gm · Gm7 · F
Free me, take me out of this world, won't You see me, 'cause I wanna know that
G · G7 · C
You could, if You'd only love me, 'cause I wanna let it be known, I love You,
Gm · Dm · Em · G7
Goodbye to things that I once knew, that kept me away from You, and let it be known,
C · Gm · Gm7 · F
Free me, take me out of the blue, don't You see me, show me the way to get
G7 · Dm · G7 · C
through to You, Love me, 'cause I wanna let it be known, I love You,
Dm · G7
I wanna let it be known, I love You,
Dm · G7 · C
I wanna let it be known ... I love You.

The wagon had arrived at a crossroads where the Druid Hills Trail intersected with the Open Road. The Utopian River Gorge loomed directly to the west. The Great Way, twenty feet wide and paved with yellow cobblestone, ran north and south as far as the eye could see.

The sage opened the rear door to the vardo.

"Time to stretch our legs," Morph said.

"And our wings," I said, chuckling.

We stepped down onto the Open Road and I read a wooden sign:

Open Road
The Great Way

Mesmerized by the scenery, I turned in a circle and listened to a forest choir of singing birds. To the north, the Discordia Crater chasm loomed in the distance. To the east, a dense forest covered the Druid Hills. I looked straight up into the blue sky, sniffing the air. Pine trees—the smell of home sweet home. The gigantic pines, two hundred feet tall, grew from the edge of the Open Road to the top of the hills. To the south, the snow-capped Melody Mountains stretched beyond the horizon. To the west, the view took my breath away.

"That looks like the Grand Canyon," I said, astonished by the size of the chasm forty feet in front of me.

"This is incredible," Eve said.

"That is our Utopian River Gorge," Morph said, "one of our eight great river systems. The river has created a magnificent gorge measuring eight hundred feet deep and ninety miles wide at the northern end. As we travel south, you shall see the gorge run shallower. When she empties into Souda Bay, she is four hundred feet deep and—"

"Frugles? Frugles for the poor?"

A crippled dwarve, dressed in rags, crawled out of the manzanita shrubs with his hand out, begging for money.

"Skadoodle, you vagabond," Blunderbore yelled, stomping toward the beggar.

Morph held up his right upper hand to silence the giant.

"My friend, how may I help you?" the sage asked, approaching the homeless dwarve.

"If you gotta' frugle to spare, I'd be much obliged, kind sir."

Morph got out his bag of coins and dropped the entire red leather bag into the dwarve's paw.

Stunned, the beggar asked, "Fer me? All these coins, fer me?"

The sage nodded, *yes.* "Go in peace."

As bewildered dwarve crawled away, Blunderbore said, "Ya,

ve best getta' movin'. Vindalf is itchin' to go. Der vagon master is holdin' der big oxen back."

The giant helped Eve up the wagon steps.

Morph closed the door behind him, took his seat and extended his two right arms out the window, signaling, *go.*

Vindalf snapped the leather reins.

The vardo jerked forward. The snorting oxen headed south along the Open Road.

Sitting next to Eve, I told Morph, "You didn't have to give that beggar all your money."

"Why not give it away?" Morph asked, moving his green tail behind him on the cushion seat.

"Because one frugle would have been plenty. That's all he asked for. He didn't expect any more than that."

The sage smiled and said, "The more you give to others, the greater your abundance."

"How can I have more abundance if I give it all away?"

"That which you give away is never lost."

I rubbed my chin, thinking.

"My son, what determines your self-worth? You or what you own?"

"I guess I'm worth more than the stuff I own."

"So, if I said you are worth a million frugles, would that be accurate?"

"No, I believe I'm worth more than that."

"And what would Eve's value be?"

"She's priceless," I said, smiling at the Epiphanite.

She nodded, *thank you.*

Morph asked, "So, why are you concerned that I gave a person in need all that I had to give?"

"I don't know," I said, rubbing my temple. "What are we going to do for money once we get to Hermopolis?"

"Do not be fearful of our future."

"I can tell you never worry about anything."

"Should I fear desolation when there is abundance?"

"My mom has taught me to always save for a rainy day, you know, have money put away for an emergency. She says that you can never have too much money in the bank."

"Humans fear scarcity. They always believe they need more money, more things, more of everything. Accumulation of wealth leads to anxiety, the fear of losing their money. Humans fear not having enough and then, once they accumulate too much, they fear losing it. This is the disease of more. When you realize you have enough, you are truly rich. Stop the chase."

"What chase?"

"The chase for things. Your quest for adoration, power, and money is a waste of energy because there is never enough. Many humans spend their entire existence motivated by not having enough. In the end, this quest for more, always more, drives you all crazy."

"Come on, Morph, don't you have some sort of possessions somewhere?"

"Sages do not accumulate anything. They give everything to others; having more, the more they give. My advice is, if you love something, give it away. The act of giving is an act of love. Serve the needs of others and all your own needs shall be fulfilled."

"I'm going to have to think about this concept of giving everything away."

"Certainly. Give it some thought. Keep in mind, what you gain is more trouble than what you lose. An ancient axiom is, 'The sage gains by losing, and loses by gaining.'"

I listened to the wagon wheels roll on the yellow cobblestone, a different sound than gravel. The sage got up and filled our empty mugs with amrita. I stared out the window at the passing pine trees, thinking about my possessions. *Maybe I do have too much stuff. My bedroom closet is filled with junk. Sometimes I can't find what I'm looking for, but, I'm not sure I want to give away the things I love.*

Morph returned to his seat with the drinks in three hands.

"I don't think people are willing to give up what they have worked so hard for," I said.

"Then, how do you humans plan to end poverty and hunger?"

"We already have a plan in place."

"All your plans have been miserable failures. On your planet, too many people live without the basic necessities of life. Eve's planet, Epiphany, experiences the same problem."

"Okay, I'm listening. What's the best solution to solving all the world's problems? I need some answers to bring back to Earth."

"I offer a two-fold solution for Earth. First, appoint a philosopher as your ruler. Since you humans cannot seem to live without a leader, the least you can do is choose a great one."

"Do you mean one leader for the entire planet?"

"One."

"That will never work."

"With that attitude, you are correct."

"Okay, how do you propose we pull off this one-world leader?"

"Simply begin in your own country with a philosopher and the grand concept shall spread through collective consciousness, through the power of thought."

"I admit, I like the idea. Maybe that philosophy academy you talked about will convince people. Okay, what's the second thing we need to do?"

"Second, impose a humanitarian tax," Morph said. "This would work because you humans cannot seem to survive without government control. Tax is another word for donation as it relates to compassion."

"People don't like taxes in California. My father says we're already over taxed."

The sage handed me a mug of amrita. "I use the word tax because it is a concept you understand. Enlightened beings do not have to be taxed. They share everything. They do not need to be asked. Your Native Americans understood this concept of sharing. Until your world eliminates the emotional virus and learns to share naturally, I suggest you use the magic number eight to solve poverty."

"Eight is magic?"

"Yes. From Octilogy, the Eight Great Treasures, comes the concept of eight. For Earth, it would be an eight percent humanitarian tax. The eight percent donation would solve all your poverty and hunger issues, among other things."

"No more poverty? That doesn't sound realistic."

"If every person on Earth gave eight percent of their income, no more, no less, your entire planet would prosper. All human beings would enjoy the basic necessities of life: food, shelter, clothing. This, of course, would restore your human dignity, which has been lost entirely, except by the elite, who suffer from the disease of more. Once dignity is restored, humans could focus on proper education, productive careers, divine leadership, and living a noble existence."

"We need that on Epiphany," Eve said.

I looked at her. "The eight percent sounds fair. I hear my father complain that he pays forty percent or more of his income to the government. I saw on the news that foreign countries pay fifty percent or more."

"As I've already told you," Morph said, "over-taxation is inevitable when governments are run by self-serving politicians."

"I'll bet my mom and dad are willing to share eight percent of their income with people who really need it," I said. "Maybe more."

Vindalf snapped the leather reins. The spotted oxen grunted while the wagon surged forward.

"Always share with others. Generosity is just one secret to happiness. On Earth, it is your key to salvation. The less you open your heart to others, the more your heart shall suffer."

"Thanks, I'll think about your two solutions," I said.

The sage handed Eve her mug and said, "Compassion and generosity go hand in hand. Helping others shall bring you the greatest joy. Giving is always better than receiving."

Eve took the mug from Morph and said, "I agree with your generosity. Forgive me for changing the subject. May I ask another question that has me perplexed?"

"Certainly." The sage wiped his moustache with his purple handkerchief.

"I mentioned that you told me that the Extractors are evil. My grandfather, Otto, told me that there is no evil in the universe."

"Your grandfather is correct," Morph said. "I remember Otto. He was a fine Epiphanite."

I raised my hand and said, "But the Extractors are evil, you said so yourself."

"My apologies for confusing you. I must use primitive, human words and concepts so you understand me. There is no evil. I only mention the Extractors' low self-esteem behavior so you may understand the consequences of the *Extractor Virus* and its effects on human thought, why people act the way they do."

"You mean, so I can understand why the Earth is in such a mess?"

Morph crossed his legs, nodding, *yes.*

"But I believe good and evil exist."

"Your belief is incorrect. There is no evil. There is no right or wrong. You have created this idea of right and wrong, good and evil, because you want everything to fit into a neat and understandable concept. You seek perfect order. Unfortunately, this is incorrect and confused thinking. Humans require that everything be categorized neatly into a divine order, as if by some superior source. The reality is, two truths can and do exist at the same time. When two truths exist simultaneously, humans automatically believe one of the truths to be wrong. This is incorrect thinking. There is no right and wrong in the universe, only opposing forces."

"Okay, give me an example of two truths that oppose each other," I said.

"Your answer lies in the Law of Opposing Forces. It states that nothing exists without its opposite. These universal forces can never be reconciled. They exist in opposition. The best words I can use are conflict, polarity. To answer your question, opposing forces are fire and ice, hot and cold, up and down, light and dark, left and right, pleasure and pain, love and fear. The favorite on Earth seems to be good and bad, or good versus evil. It is actually *high* self-esteem versus *low* self-esteem. Ego versus *no* ego. Your entire existence is based on trying to reconcile these forces that exist together in perfect opposition."

"I'm confused."

"Listen carefully. You are but a moment away from true understanding. I ask you to stop choosing one or the other. Stop thinking what is and what is not. Change your thoughts to, 'everything just is.' Stop dividing things into right and wrong and then choosing one. A contradiction does not mean something is right or wrong, it just is. Fighting and arguing over right and wrong has destroyed your civilization. You kill each other over the dichotomy of right and wrong."

"Dichotomy?"

"Yes. Dichotomy. Two opposites that contradict each other. Take love and fear, these are polarities that coexist in perfect conflict and opposition, making the universe a grand experience. You cannot know love until you experience not loving, just like you cannot experience cold until you experience hot. You cannot know light until you know dark."

"Yes, I'm getting this."

"The moment you think you are good, you immediately introduce the idea of bad. And when you cannot be good you try to be moral. Morality is merely your self-imposed standards of right and wrong that you try to uphold. I suggest you follow your essential nature. Do not try to be anything; just be. In an effort to be good, just, moral, and loving, you lose your true nature; you lose your Self. Just be."

I closed my eyes and thought, *If there really is no right or wrong, I'd been wasting a lot of time arguing over nothing.*

Opened my eyes and gazed out the window. The wagon had picked up speed and the road had crept within twenty feet of the cliff's edge.

Morph continued his explanation. "The polarities of good and bad, right and wrong, proper and improper, legal and illegal, justice and injustice, must all be abandoned. When they surface, The Great Way is lost. Oneness has no polarity. This supreme truth is difficult to grasp. I have learned that telling humans there is no such thing as good or evil, there is only love, causes confusion. Telling humans that evil is a state of mind causes frustration. Perhaps I shall focus on the Duality Paradox to help you better understand opposites. The Great Way is about opposites. These opposites create the great primal paradox, the Duality Paradox. Listen carefully and expand your mind."

I stared into Morph's tranquil eyes as he continued.

"True words appear paradoxical. When confronted with a choice, that choice always involves opposites. Correct?"

"Do you mean right or wrong?"

"Exactly. I offer you the answer to your dilemma. When faced with a choice or question involving two opposites, always choose the path of least resistance. And if you are not certain, always err on the side of compassion."

"How do I do that?"

"Rather than being forceful, be humble. Rather than grasping, let go. Rather than being rigid, be flexible. Rather than taking action, take no action. Be patient and do nothing."

"That's it? The best action is non action?"

"Yes. I suggest you live the elusive paradox. Whatever you have been conditioned to believe, I ask you to consider the exact opposite view. When you think someone is wrong and do not agree with them, hold your tongue and be silent. Never argue again."

"That's the answer to solving my problems?"

"There are no problems, only solutions. I suggest you embrace every problem as an opportunity for growth."

"Okay. I get it. I'll start looking for the opposites in everything. Stop choosing one over the other. This will keep me from being upset and arguing and worrying about whether I'm right or wrong. I need to share the dual paradox, the duality thing, when I get back home."

Morph nodded, *yes*. "I shall share my favorite paradox. 'Fulfill the needs of others and *your* needs shall be fulfilled. Rather than putting yourself first, put yourself last and you shall end up ahead.'"

"I like that one."

"The path of least resistance can be found on The Great Way, the Open Road."

"The road we're on?"

Morph nodded, *yes*, and swallowed the last drops of amrita from his pewter mug.

"I get it."

"Get what?"

"That I'm all screwed up in my thinking."

"My son, do not be so hard on yourself. You are perfect as you are. Be patient, your journey has just begun."

"If you say so."

Eve smiled at me and said, "You are really smart, Hunter. I feel your energy."

I smiled. "Thanks, I feel better already."

"That's the spirit, my son. When you practice putting yourself last, your life changes. The sage serves. The sage gives, not takes. Give. Ask nothing in return."

"Is that why you gave that poor person all your money?"

Morph nodded, *yes*. The sage stood, unfolded his wings, and flapped them.

The Purpose

Bm   Em   C♯
Too many broken hearts in the promised land,
                               Em
When the things we want become the things we need,
C♯   C
I don't understand, with all the motions we go through,
        C♯   C
I guess I'm waiting just like you, seems the more we do,
                     B+9
The more it's true, I've tried to see it in your eyes.
     Em   Bm   Em
  Give me the plan, for a purpose, give me the plan,
  Bm   Em   Em
  We need to stand, for a purpose, we need to stand.
Bm   Em   C♯
Why we take so much from the very few,
            Em
Then what we've become, shadows what we could be,
      C♯   C
We built a house on sand, no I can't get it out of my head,
      C♯   C
All the noble things we've said, but it's what you leave to your childrens' dreams,
    B+9
That shows what you meant with your life.
     Em   Bm   Em
  Give me the plan, for a purpose, give me the plan,
  Bm   Em   Em
  We need to stand, for a purpose, we need to stand.
You know this could be our finest hour, We can't leave this to chance like so many mistakes,
C   C♯
When you're feeling the need for greed and power, We need to push out the problem,
                B+9
Begin to believe, The power of the purpose and it's just you and me, yeah.
    Em   Bm   Em Bm   Em   Bm   Em
  Give me the plan, for a purpose, give me the plan,, We need to stand, for a purpose, we need to stand,
    Em   Bm   Em Bm   Em   Bm   Em
  Give me the plan, for the purpose, give me the plan, We need to stand, for a purpose, we need to stand.

Our hair blew in our faces. "When I flap my wings, the vibrations can be felt thousands of miles away and out into the universe. Likewise, my act of kindness to that unfortunate soul-in-need sent out high-frequency vibrations into the cosmos. When we get enough vibrations of compassion throughout the universe, change is inevitable."

"I plan to help the homeless when I return to Earth," I announced.

"That is a noble cause." The sage sat back down. "Your life shall have a grand plan. A purpose."

"My father told me I need to find a purpose in life besides my artwork. He wanted me to volunteer for charity work this summer. I mean, last summer."

"He is a wise parent."

"Mom said if other people don't agree with my purpose in life, that I need to make a stand for what I believe in, no matter what other people say."

"That is also a wise statement." Morph held up his right hand. "I commend you on your plan. By helping the homeless, your purpose shall be to heal some of the broken hearts in your promised land."

"Promised land?"

"America," Morph said, removing his spectacles and putting them in his vest pocket.

While I grinned, Morph picked up his guitar from the seat cushion. "I have an appropriate song for you. It is called, 'The Purpose'. Would you like to hear it?"

"Yes," Eve said, crossing her legs and grabbing the stack of song lyrics from the seat.

I picked up my guitar and rested it on my right thigh. Eve flipped through the parchment pages and placed the lyric sheet on the seat.

I nodded, *ready.*

Morph strummed the double neck guitar and sang the opening line.

♪ "Too many broken hearts in the promised land,
When the things we want become the things we need,
I don't understand,
With all the motions we go through,
I guess I'm waiting just like you,
Seems the more we do the more it's true,
I've tried to see it in your eyes."

Morph nodded at me, signaling the beginning of the chorus.

"Give me the plan, for a purpose, give me the plan,
We need to stand, for a purpose, we need to stand."

Morph sang the second verse.

"Why we take so much from the very few,
Then what we've become, shadows what we could be,
We built a house on sand,
No, I can't get it out of my head,
All the noble things we've said,

But it's what you leave to your children's dreams,
That shows what you meant with your life."
Morph and I harmonized on the second chorus.
"Give me the plan, for a purpose,
Give me the plan, we need to stand, for a purpose,
We need to stand."
I anticipated the chord change for the bridge.
"You know this could be our finest hour,
We can't leave this to chance like so many mistakes,
When you're feeling the need for greed and power,
We need to push out the problem, begin to believe,
The power of the purpose and it's just you and me, yeah."
Morph played a solo on his guitar.
Eve sang with Morph and me on the final choruses.
"Give me the plan, for a purpose,
Give me the plan, we need to stand,
For a purpose, we need to stand,
Give me the plan, for the purpose,
Give me the plan, we need to stand,
For a purpose, we need to stand."
Morph and I let the guitars fade away.

"Another wonderful song," Eve said, smiling at me and Morph.

"Good guitar playing, young man."

The sage smiled at me, laid his guitar on the seat and asked, "Any other questions?"

Eve and I looked at each other, shaking our heads, *no*.

She pointed out the window. "Look. The black sky is almost full."

Staring out my window, I became nervous again. Traveling at top speed, the wagon swerved within ten feet of the gorge, the edge of the cliffs. The chasm looked like a bottomless abyss. Looking down, I realized the Utopian River Gorge had to be wider than the Mississippi River. The western shoreline laid beyond the horizon.

Glancing out the opposite window, I admired the moss-covered forest growing along the Open Road. Forest growing right down to the road on one side, cliffs on the other side.

Utopian River Gorge

The scene reminded me of Highway One from Big Sur to Santa Barbara, that time Father took us on vacation.

Restless, I stuck my head out the window to look ahead. In the fading light, I could see the Open Road hug the jagged edge of the gorge.

I looked down into the chasm and the scene took my breath away. Eight hundred feet below me, the Utopian River wound its way along the bottom of the gorge.

Stared into the abyss. Heights still scared me. Pulled my head back inside the coach and ran my fingers through my messy hair.

It seemed like ever since I had arrived on Millennium I was on the edge of some cliff.

"Look. Up there, Doubting Castle." The sage pointed out the left-front window.

Eve and I both moved to Morph's side of the wagon to look out the left-rear window.

"Unbelievable," I muttered, staring up at the wooded hills ahead.

Eve put her hand on my arm and squeezed.

Silhouetted against a rising red sky, Doubting Castle looked exactly like the fairy tale illustrations I had grown so fond of since childhood.

"I've got to capture this on paper," I said, reaching for my satchel.

"You shall have plenty of time to draw; we are stopping here for the evening," Morph said. "Darkness is upon us. It is too dangerous to continue on our journey. The oxen do not see well at night."

"Great, this place looks really awesome."

Eve and I gawked at the castle.

"Whooooaaa!" Vindalf shouted.

The wagon veered left, pulled off the side of the Open Road and skidded to a halt.

Morph swung the wagon door open.

I grasped Eve's hand and helped her down the vardo steps.

We walked into a clearing surrounded by a forest with towering pines.

The wooden road sign read:

We had arrived at the Doubting Junction crossroads, nestled between the gorge and the western slopes of the Palatine Hills. The connecting road to Doubting Castle snaked up the hill and disappeared into the primeval pine forest. The sounds of crickets and tree frogs and owls and strange animal cries came from the surrounding hills.

Inhaling the fragrance of pine trees and cypress, the scene reminded me of Carmel By-The-Sea in the summertime.

"We shall camp here for the evening," Morph said, gesturing to the giant and the gnome.

"Aye, she be a blooody fine evenin' fer a cracklin' fyre," Vindalf said, pulling the brake lever and climbing down from the driver's box.

Blunderbore jumped down and reached below the wagon undercarriage for a gunny sack of oats and barley.

"Ya, I better keep der ox hitched up; dem big fellas 'ill wander off in der dark und fall into der gorge ober yonder."

The giant poured grain on the ground in front of each spotted ox while Vindalf unloaded supplies from his wagon.

Located at the northeast corner of the junction, the campsite clearing measured 150 feet wide with a central stone fire pit. Tree stumps formed a circle of wooden stools around the pit. Massive monoliths, granite boulders taller than the wagon, stood upright, spaced evenly in an elliptical formation along the eastern edge of the gravel clearing. Atop each monolith, rectangular granite slabs spanned the space between the erect row of boulders, giant boulders that looked exactly like Stonehenge.

Across the Open Road, the cliffs of the Utopian River Gorge beckoned us.

"We should look at the gorge," she said, placing her bow and arrows by the wagon.

"Come on, Hunter, follow me."

She took off running. Without hesitating, I followed her.

"Dat boy is sure liken' dat girl, ya," Blunderbore yelled.

It felt great to stretch my legs, still not believing how fast I could run. I loved this lighter gravity. With the wind in my hair, I ran freely behind Eve. I crossed the yellow cobblestone Open Road in two leaps and stopped at a semi-circle of granite boulders perched on the cliffs.

Standing next to the Epiphanite, I read a sign engraved in a granite boulder:

The POINT

In front of us, a flat granite outcropping overhung the gorge, jutting fifty feet out into thin air. We stood on the precarious rock ledge. The scene reminded me of Yosemite.

I remained in place, breathing heavily, afraid to walk closer to the ledge.

Eve walked to the edge of the rock cliff. "Look, the scenery is fantastic."

I stood frozen, unwilling to join her. She looked over her shoulder and smiled.

Eve walked back to me and held out her left hand. "Trust me, I will not let you fall."

Get it together, I told myself. *Be a man, you're not afraid of heights any more. Trust her, she wants you to hold her hand.*

"All right." I placed my right hand in hers.

She squeezed my fingers and my heartbeat increased. My arm tingled all the way up to my arm while we walked to within three feet of the end of the overhang. I held my breath.

"Can you believe how fabulous this is?" she asked, intertwining her slender fingers with mine.

I took a deep breath, looking skyward. The retreating red sky hugged the eastern hills. The black sky loomed overhead while the fading daystars colored the rocks in an orange sunset hue.

"Look. A ship," she said, pointing down into the gorge.

I looked down at the Utopian River, eight hundred feet below us. In the fading light, a ship with red sails navigated north, up the river.

"Come on, we can sit over there." Eve pulled me by the arm and we climbed up on a stone bench in the middle of the semi-circle of boulders. We stood on the bench, looking eastward, toward the Palatine Hills.

"Awesome," I said, transfixed on the grand castle perched on the hill above them.

Doubting Castle towered above the tops of the pine trees. The magnificent six-story stone castle had been constructed from greenish-grey limestone block. I counted eight main towers with conical spires silhouetted against the Millennium twilight.

Four domes surrounded a central octahedral spire. Red, white, and blue flags waved from the tops of the gold finials adorning each pointed spire and pinnacle.

Circular staircase turrets hugged the sides of each tower. Rectangular loopholes accentuated the towers and turrets. Arched stained glass windows sat between stone buttresses, highlighting the pointed gables and the main oculus.

The pitched roofs had been covered in blue-grey slate shingles. The ornate dome roofs had been finished with red fish-scale tile. White smoke poured from the four main chimneys. Battlements and balustrades encircled the tops of the outer walls.

In the fading light, I saw movement behind the battlements. Armored knights walked the walls.

What a great looking castle, I thought, *tonight I'll draw the—*

Eve pulled on my sleeve, pointing across the Open Road.

Morph stood in front of the glowing campfire, waving us back to camp.

"I'll race you," Eve said, giggling.

She leaped off the bench and took off running, past the boulders and across the Open Road.

"Hey, that's not fair, you got a head start," I yelled, trying to keep up with her.

Racing back to camp, I followed Eve straight to the wagon.

White smoke rose from the vardo's chimney pipe. Inside the

wagon, glowing oil lanterns cast yellow shadows onto the camp grounds. Whistling the tune, "Open Road", Blunderbore and Vindalf cooked the evening meal.

"Ya, get der silberware und mugs, vere a eatin'," the giant yelled.

Blunderbore handed Eve and me our copper bowls through the wagon window. Morph sat with us on tree stumps around the blazing fire eating our bowls of porridge. The giant and Vindalf ate their meals on a table at the rear of the wagon.

While I enjoyed the delicious porridge and ambrosia, I stared at the heavens. Overhead, billions of twinkling stars lit the black sky while three multi-colored moons shone brightly over Pellagus, Kingdom of the Eternal Rose.

Finishing my porridge, I swallowed the last drops of amrita and placed my bowl and mug on the ground.

While Eve continued to eat, I told Morph, "Please don't think I'm stupid, but I've been wondering about something."

Morph lowered his chin and looked at me over the rim of his spectacles. "What is the question?"

"Ever since I've been here, Eve and Owain are the only normal looking persons I've actually talked to. I was wondering, how did all these really weird creatures evolve on this planet?" I raised my hands in the air, palms up.

"Weird?"

"What I mean is, on Earth they'd be considered bizarre, really strange space creatures, monsters."

"Does that include me?" Morph asked, grinning.

"Well, you'd be considered a fantastic comic book freak." I held up my hand. "Wait. Sorry, I didn't mean that quite like it sounded. That was actually a compliment."

"I understand; taken as such."

I raised my eyebrows and waited for an answer. Above us, Andromeda constellations revealed their sparkling formations in the starry black sky. Streaking white tails of comets and shooting stars crisscrossed the heavens.

The sage swallowed his amrita and placed his pewter mug on the stump next to me. "Your answer can be found in your question."

"You've lost me."

"You said evolve. Evolution is unpredictable," the sage replied. The reflection of the fire gleamed in my bright eyes.

"So, things really do evolve? Evolution is real?"

"Yes. Always has been; always will be."

"Then, the belief, 'The Creator made the Earth in seven days,' is wrong?"

"My son, did I hear you say *wrong*?"

I looked at Eve and blushed.

"What did we just discuss?" Morph asked.

"I know, I know. Right and wrong don't exist." I sighed.

"You still continue to think of everything as right or wrong."

"Sorry. What is the correct answer? Who is right, the people who believe in evolution, or the people who believe in creation?"

"I believe the correct answer is obvious."

I frowned and shrugged my shoulders while the sage continued. "As with all things, the opposing doctrines of evolution and creation exist simultaneously."

"You mean, they are *both* correct?"

Morph nodded, *yes*.

"How is that possible?"

"If you recall our discussion regarding time and space, all things happen now, in no time. Evolution takes billions of years; however, this is the same as no time. Therefore, a supreme being created it all in the blink of an eye. Creation and evolution both happened simultaneously, as fast as you can say the words."

"That's so simple. It's brilliant. You just answered the whole mystery, solved the problem."

"There never was a problem or a mystery. You have created this incredible tension and controversy because you humans desire all things to be right or wrong. Evolution and creation are not opposing forces. Everything just is. Creation and evolution just are. Evolutionists are not right or wrong, any more than the creationists are right or wrong. There is no right or wrong regarding these two realities. They exist in perfect harmony, simultaneously."

Crickets chirped while the dancing fire light cast eerie shadows on the stone monoliths that soldiered the camp.

"So, humans have been arguing over nothing?" I asked.

"Not just arguing, killing each other. Humans have created this tremendous tension between ritualists and scientists and everyone caught in the cultural crossfire."

"Thank you, Morph. I'm really starting to understand this concept. There is no right or wrong."

"Excellent. You look pleased with yourself, happy."

"I probably ask too many questions."

"Nonsense. Asking questions shows wisdom. Questions are the path to wisdom."

"Where I come from, people don't like being questioned."

"I have noticed many humans dislike Metamorphic dialogue."

"What's that?"

"Discovering the truth through critical thinking. Making other beings think clearly by asking a series of logical questions leading to a supreme and undeniable conclusion. When I use Metamorphic thought, pure logic, humans become fearful."

"Of what?"

"The truth. Logical questions agitate humans. They get too near the truth and they become afraid. Humans fight to be right; they cannot tolerate thinking they are wrong. This is why I choose to limit my questions when humans visit me. I prefer that they ask *me* the questions."

"When I get home, can I learn this Metamorphic dialogue?"

The sage nodded, *yes.* "Some of my earlier visitors embraced Metamorphic dialogue. They loved the idea that the truest knowledge is knowing that you know nothing. For this very reason, questions must be asked to seek the truth. There is no better communication among primitive beings, yet, they seem to dislike logical questions. I am aware that one of my earlier guests wrote several books."

"Who's that?"

"Plato and Socrates both loved Metamorphic dialogue. Read Plato's great books upon your return. I've been told that *The Republic* is an excellent choice."

"Thanks, I will."

Smiling at Eve, I said, "I can tell you already know a lot about this logic stuff."

The Epiphanite grinned and nodded.

I thought for a moment, then said, "I've noticed that all the weapons on Millennium look medieval. I don't see any guns or rifles."

"Do you have a question?" Morph asked.

I arched my eyebrows and said, "What I meant is, I saw an illustration of an Extractor with a musket. They looked like the guns that pirates used. Are there any six guns, like the ones cowboys used in the Wild West?"

Eve raised her eyebrows, curious of my explanation of the weapons—firearms—I had seen in the *Magnum Opus.*

The Epiphanite asked, "What is the Wild West?"

"I am familiar with the adventure stories of pioneers and their Wild West era," Morph replied. "I believe that historical period is when the Americans attempted to exterminate entire races of human beings because they had a different skin color, different cultures, and did not speak the same language."

"I read about Wounded Knee in history class. That was a mistake we are sorry for."

"I am glad to hear that, my son. I have enjoyed the esteemed company of two of your native American visitors. Their civilization seemed highly advanced compared to the invading settlers of the Wild West."

"How is that?"

"Many Native Americans knew about oneness, that what you do to others you do to yourself. They knew how to share. None of their people went without. They divided everything equally. The chief that visited me told me that they would never dream of owning the land, or any other natural resource. I learned that these *savages,* as the European invaders called them, understood the web of life, that all things are interwoven and interconnected. I admired their humble and generous attitudes toward nature and the universe. I believe your settlers of the Wild West could have learned how to live a worthwhile existence from these enlightened beings. Instead, you tried to exterminate them."

"All I know is, the Nazis did a lot worse stuff during the last world war."

"Genocide is genocide, whether you are referring to Wounded Knee or Dachau."

I bowed my head. "Sorry I mentioned the Wild West. I wanted to know about the muskets I saw in the book."

"Why?"

"Because, guns give your enemies an incredible advantage."

"Is our safety your concern?"

"Aren't you worried about those powerful weapons getting into the wrong hands?"

"Obviously, they already have. Fortunately, all firearms are outlawed on Millennium and therefore, difficult to obtain, especially bullets and gunpowder."

"That's good to hear."

Eve looked at me with sympathy in her eyes. "Our history has been the same. We also have experienced genocide on Epiphany. Many races have been wiped out."

I glanced at the Epiphanite and sat silently, staring at the fire. Morph sipped amrita from his water bag, allowing us to contemplate our planets' legacies of war and genocide.

"To answer your earlier question," Morph said, his eyes twinkling in the fire light, "we have a small number of fire arms on Millennium. Bullets are difficult to find. An earlier Earth visitor, that rascal, Samuel Clemens, innocently told an Extractor about the process of making gun powder and fire arms."

Samuel Clemens? That name sounds familiar.

While I thought about how weapons destroy civilizations, Blunderbore walked toward the fire with the two guitars in his huge hands.

"Ya, der gnome und me is gonna' play a Gametasia Chess match und ve'd like to hear some more guitar music."

The giant handed Morph the two guitars.

"Thank you. I shall see what I and Hunter can come up with."

"Ya, ve'll be at der back of der vagon if you need us fer anythin'."

The sage handed me the double neck guitar while the giant lumbered to the back of the wagon.

"You're going to let me play *your* guitar?"

"What is mine, is yours."

"Thanks." I admired the hand-crafted instrument in the fire light. I set the double neck guitar over my left knee and strummed a guitar chord, E-major.

"This thing's way out of tune," I said, turning the tuning pegs and strumming another E-major chord. "Hmmm, I'm still out of tune."

"Allow me to help," Morph said, plucking his low-E string on his six string guitar.

I listened to each of Morph's six strings and properly tuned my guitar.

"Thanks, I'm a little distracted."

"Is something on your mind?" Morph asked.

"Yeah. I wish I knew everything you know."

"Be patient. Your wish shall come true."

"But I want to know it *now*."

"Nature's way is patience. She does not create a storm that never ends. Just like the storm, when your life calms down, wisdom shall enter."

"I feel like there is not enough time to learn all the things you can teach me."

"Stop worrying. Relax and allow things to happen in divine order, without trying to interfere or figure out why they are happening. True mastery is gained by letting things go their own way. It cannot be gained by interfering. Relax. Just let go."

"I have so many things I want to do before I leave."

"The more you pursue desires, the more they shall elude you. Slow down and find the rhythm that suits your nature."

"When I get home, I'm going on TV and the Internet and telling everyone the knowledge I've learned from you. Maybe I'll write a book."

"My son, when you try to explain your enlightenment, few people on Earth shall understand you. Very few, if any, shall comprehend what you have learned."

"They'll listen to me if they believe the world will become a better place."

"The more enlightened you are, the more difficult it is to communicate with humans. They shall not understand your wisdom. They would rather listen to performers, politicians, entertainers, charlatans, and false leaders. Be prepared for scorn and ridicule."

I frowned, thinking about Morph's answer.

Blunderbore and Vindalf moved their black, white, red, and blue Gametasia Chess pieces. Sitting at the back of the wagon under the glow of an oil lantern, the two Millennians laughed, then argued, then laughed, then argued.

"Would you like to play a song together?" Morph asked, cracking the twelve knuckles of his four hands.

Inspired, I smiled and gently strummed a chord on the twelve-string guitar. "Okay, I'm ready to play a song," I said, grinning at Eve.

She returned the grin. Her eyes twinkled in the light of the fire. Eve's lips curled up into a smile as she requested a song from Morph. "Earlier, you were going to play 'Bridge of Words'."

"Excellent choice," the sage said.

I opened my artist satchel and found the lyric sheet to Eve's request. I laid the parchment paper on a flat rock and asked, "Should I play the six string or twelve string neck?"

"I usually begin the song with a twelve-string riff."

Not knowing the song, I decided to let Morph start 'Bridge of Words'. I stood and handed the double neck guitar to the sage. "I feel more comfortable with the six string guitar."

"I understand," Morph said, exchanging guitars with me.

Vindalf stopped playing Gametasia Chess and grabbed a pair of maracas inside the wagon door. He tossed a maraca to Blunderbore.

Bridge of Words

I can't be your keeper, I can help you out of here,
If we build our bridge of words, so we can walk right over fear,
I can lead you through your darkness, should you open up your eyes,
Then it's you who would be seeing, how it looks is your surprise.
Oh, our bridge will not be finished, till our hearts are opened up,
If I could live to see it happen, I'd give all that I have got,
Oh, our bridge will not be finished, till our hearts are joined as one,
But I fear it will not happen, if alone we choose to run, oh, yeah.
If I'm the well of fresh spring water, it's still you who makes us wine,
Should you take and choose to swallow, how it tastes is in your mind,
'Cause alone I'm not no builder, no river has one side,
Are efforts worth the time we spend, we could drown inside our pride.
Oh, our bridge will not be finished, till our hearts are opened up,
If I could live to see it happen, I'd give all that I have got,
Oh, our bridge will not be finished, till our hearts are joined as one,
But I fear it will not happen, if alone we choose to run,
Oh, our bridge will not be finished, till our hearts are opened up,
If I could live to see it happen, I'd give all that I have got,
Oh, our bridge will not be finished, till our hearts are joined as one,
But I fear it will not happen, I fear it will not happen, you know we've got to make it
happen, or alone we choose to run, oh, yeah, run, run, run, run, run, run, run, yeah, run.

"Key of G, young man," Morph said, playing his double neck guitar while I followed his lead. After a harmonic twelve-string guitar riff, the Sage of the Ages sang the first verse.

"I can't be your keeper, I can help you out of here,
If we build our bridge of words,
So we can walk right over fear,
I can lead you through your darkness,
Should you open up your eyes,
Then it's you who would be seeing,
How it looks is your surprise."

The giant and gnome shook the maracas to the rhythm of the guitars while Morph sang the chorus.

"Oh, our bridge will not be finished,
'Till our hearts are opened up,
If I could live to see it happen,
I'd give all that I have got, oh,
Our bridge will not be finished,
'Till our hearts are joined as one,
But I fear it will not happen,
If alone we choose to run...oh, yeah."

Morph's four hands moved in unison on the double neck guitar. I smiled, watching the sage play rhythm guitar and lead guitar at the same time.

"If I'm a well of fresh spring water,
It's still you who makes us wine,
Should you take and choose to swallow,
How it tastes is in your mind,
'Cause alone I'm not no builder,
No river has one side,
Are efforts worth the time we spend,
We could drown inside our pride."

Confident of the chord changes, I looked at the lyric sheet and sang a harmony part for the chorus.

"Oh, our bridge will not be finished,
'Till our hearts are opened up,
If I could live to see it happen,
I'd give all that I have got,
Oh, our bridge will not be finished,

The Open Road

'Till our hearts are joined as one,
But I fear it will not happen,
If alone we choose to run,
Oh, our bridge will not be finished,
'Till our hearts are opened up,
If I could live to see it happen,
I'd give all that I have got,
Oh, our bridge will not be finished,
'Till our hearts are joined as one,
But I fear it will not happen,
I fear it will not happen,
You know we've got to make it happen,
Or alone we choose to run…oh, yeah, run, run, run, run."

As the guitars faded away, white clouds drifted silently across the black sky. The forest remained silent, as if the plants and animals had stopped to listen.

Eve broke the silence by clapping her hands. "You two sound fabulous together."

Blunderbore and Vindalf whistled and clapped as they stomped their feet.

Just as the applause died down, the ground vibrated.

Morph set his guitar on a log and stood.

"You and Eve go to the wagon. Hurry."

I laid my guitar against a stump. Feeling the ground rumble, Eve and I ran to the vardo.

Vindalf grabbed a meat cleaver and stood on the wagon steps. Blunderbore blew out the lanterns, holding his saber by his side.

While Eve pulled an arrow from her pouch and laid the wooden shaft across her bow string, I drew my sacred sword, *Aroundight*, from its leather scabbard.

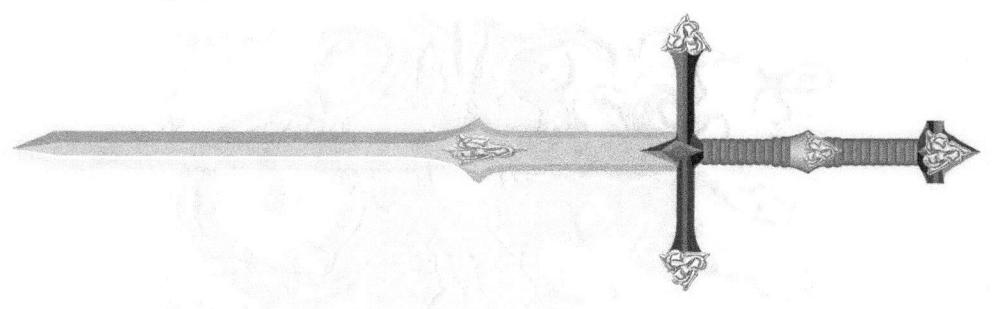

Chapter 21
Battle of Doubting Junction

The steel blade of my sword gleamed in the mystical light of three Millennium moons. The silhouette of a creature with dragon wings soared across one of the full moons. Metamorphosis raised his scepter, *Joyease*, above his head while the sound of thundering hooves shook the campsite.

The sage waved his wand high in the air and shouted, "Have no fear, it is Malagig and his boar soldiers!"

"Look, it's Pendragon!" Eve shouted, pointing to the sky above the galloping horses.

"Yes, it's the Utopian," I yelled. "He's holding his staff."

The blue light from the sage's scepter acted as a beacon for the approaching army. Pendragon glided down and landed on the cobblestone road while the cavalry of boar soldiers galloped into Doubting Junction.

Eve held her hands over her sensitive ears, upset by the thunderous roar of three hundred horses and the clanging of armor and weapons and wagons.

"Greetings," Pendragon yelled, entering the campsite.

Eve and I stood behind Vindalf's wagon, waving to the winged Utopian. He returned the wave.

Malagig the Paladin dismounted his black stallion, Arion. The boar soldier commander chomped his lower tusks and pointed to the dense forest bordering the eastern perimeter of the camp. "Position guards on all roads and along those trees in yonder Palatine Hills," he yelled to his troops. "We shall camp across the road, henceforth, secure the perimeter."

The battalion of armored boar soldiers crossed Doubting Castle Road to set up camp for the evening.

Eve and I ran from the wagon to a spot behind the rock

monoliths. In the darkness, we laid on the ground spying on Morph. I'm not sure if 'spying' is the right word, but as Eve and I laid side by side in the dark watching the meeting, it reminded me of all those times Julia and I hid in the cabinet under Father's aquarium.

Malagig removed his horned helmet, bowed to Morph, and extended his arm.

The sage shook the paladin's hand and said, "It is good to see you again, my friend."

"Thy presence be an honor, Master Morph," Malagig said, wiggling his pointed ears. "I am glad we hath arrived in time."

"In time for what?" Morph asked. "Please, enlighten me."

The commander bowed to Pendragon and said, "I shall let Pendragon tell ye the news. I must rejoin our troops."

Malagig turned and marched across the junction road. Blunderbore and Vindalf followed the paladin, carrying a cauldron of elixir porridge to the hungry soldiers.

Morph shook Pendragon's hand and said, "I shall have Vindalf prepare a meal for you."

"Not necessary," Pendragon replied, standing by the fire, moving his dragon wings slowly back and forth.

"How was your flight?"

"Challenging. I had numerous events occur at the same time."

"Please, update me."

"After I arrived at Nemoria, I received word of a visitor on Time Island. Another human, a young female, had arrived on the Daynight of the Spider."

I nudged Eve's shoulder and whispered, "A human, did you hear that?"

Eve placed her index finger to her lips, "Shhh."

Morph raised his white eyebrows. "Her arrival is not timely. Who was available to greet our visitor from Earth?"

"Before I joined Malagig's army on the Open Road, I flew to Palludis and requested that Nyx greet the girl."

"To take our guest on the *Skipbladnir*?"

Pendragon nodded, *yes*. "Nyx left for Time Island. She flew on Ava, our finest gryphon."

"That is good news."

"You are correct. However, I also have *bad* news." The Utopian grimaced and gazed into the black sky.

Morph studied Pendragon's worried expression. "What bothers you?"

The dragonram looked up at the three Millennium moons. The Utopian lowered his eyebrows and said, "Cernunnos has been wounded at Nemoria."

The light from the blazing fire cast a shadow on Morph's sullen face. The sage wiped his mouth with the back of his hand.

"Do not worry, the big stag shall recover. I have worse news than that," Pendragon said. "Balux has been captured. The Pot of Gold and the Coins of Intelligence are in the hands of Ex and the Extractors."

Morph frowned. "How?"

"Grizzsects. Our Millennian forces were no match for the swarming beasts."

"Then, we have more serious issues with the grizzsects than we thought."

"I have never seen such an organized mobilization of the monsters."

"By whom?" Morph clenched his four hands.

"Bodvar the Berserker."

Morph unclenched his fists and pointed to the hills. "The paladins told me that Bodvar and the grizzsects have gathered in Turnaround World."

"Then, they are just over the Palatine Hills," Pendragon said, looking east.

"They must be heading this way."

"I suggest we break camp and travel farther south."

"That is a possible option. I suggest we discuss our strategy with Malagig."

The boar soldiers had begun pitching their tents and had ignited several campfires. Armored sentries moved cautiously along the edge of the dense forest.

Morph pulled *Joyease* from his belt and walked toward the encampment. Pendragon followed his leader's pulsating blue light across Doubting Castle Road.

While the two Utopians walked across the road, Eve and I hid behind a monoliths, alone. Above us, white clouds grappled with the three moons for possession of the black sky.

Eve grabbed my hand. "They will be busy for a while. Can we take a short walk? I must talk to you."

"Sure. As long as we stay close to camp."

"We are safe, look at all the soldiers," Eve said, slinging *Gandeeva*, her sacred bow, and her pouch of arrows over the back of her green chemise.

"You're right. Let's go," I said, holding out my right hand.

Crickets chirped while we quietly made our way behind the perimeter of the monolithic boulders hugging the edge of the dark forest. Holding hands, we crossed the Open Road and entered The Point, the secluded area we had visited earlier that day. Followed by our two moonshadows, we walked to the end of the narrow ledge overlooking the Utopian River Gorge.

With Eve's hand in mine, I acted confidently. I stood on the edge of the cliff, looked down, and pointed to the red-sailed ship illuminated by deck lanterns.

"Whose ship is that?" I asked.

"Never mind that ship," Eve said, pulling my arm. "Come and sit with me."

We sat on a stone bench chiseled into the granite boulders. Eve laid her bow and arrows below the bench. Hidden from Morph's view, we held hands and stared at the shooting stars crisscrossing the cosmos.

Eve's green eyes sparkled under the Andromeda stars. Her black hair shone under the light of the three moons.

She held my hand, making it the perfect time to tell her how I felt about her.

"My, it is warm out tonight," Eve said, unfastening the top button of her satin chemise. Her gold Triamulet and ruby necklace sparkled under the twinkling stars.

A warm breeze blew in our faces while we gazed out across the gorge.

"I like holding your hand," she said, looking at me with a coy grin on her lips. "Seven daynights ago I did not believe I could trust you, but now I feel differently."

"What changed your mind?"

"I thought you were immature and too playful, but I have learned to enjoy that aspect of your personality."

"That's good. I mean, thank you for liking me. I'm trying to change."

"For me?"

"No, for myself."

"Now you sound like Metamorphosis," she said, giggling. "You really *are* changing."

Eve squeezed my hand. "I need to tell you something."

I nodded, *go ahead*, admiring her ruby necklace and gold Triamulet hanging from her slender neck.

"I wish I had a family like yours," she said. "You are most fortunate."

"Thanks. I miss them a lot."

Eve grabbed my other hand and turned toward me. "I must trust what I tell you remains between us."

"I can keep a secret."

She lowered her eyes and said, "I have never entered into a courtship with a boy before."

"You told me you were forced to date that army general."

"No, Hunter. Nothing like that," she said, trying to suppress her nervousness. "He is not a general. I never knew him. Never will."

"That's good."

"So, have you ever been with a female?" she asked, raising her black eyebrows.

"Not exactly. I have three friends who are girls. You know,

from school. But we never went steady or got serious or anything like that. Just friends."

Eve grinned. "So, what do you think of *me*?"

I looked up at the moons and swallowed. My mouth felt dry from nervous energy.

"Honestly, how did you feel when you first met me?" she asked. "You can tell me your feelings. I am extremely logical. I can handle the truth."

God, she wants the truth, I thought. *I need to be honest, but she might freak out...Stop! Tell her the truth...how you really feel.*

"Well, to be honest," I said, my voice trembling, "I thought you were sort of...well...conceited when I first met you. You acted kind of distant."

She stared at me with her hypnotic green eyes while I struggled to find the right words. "Now you act differently, a lot nicer. As I've told you, I really like you very much."

"I like you, too," she said, squeezing both my hands.

I felt her energy shoot through my body. She moved her leg against mine. A tingling sensation welled up inside my stomach.

"Have you ever kissed a girl?" she asked, her lips curled up in a coy grin.

"No, but I've wanted to."

"So, what happened?"

"I guess the time was never right, or maybe I was too shy. My father says I spend too much time on my computers and hanging out with the guys and playing guitar and surfing and—"

She quickly let go of my right hand and pressed her index finger against my lips.

"It is fine. You do not have to explain."

Eve brushed the hair off my forehead with her hand. My heartbeat increased as she moved her fingers across my temple and down the side of my face, placing her hand on my shoulder.

"I need to tell you how I feel, how I *really* feel," I said, trying to swallow the lump in my throat.

The air between us became electrified.

"I know how you feel," she said, moving closer and tilting her head to the left.

Eve's sweet breath felt warm and moist against my face. In

slow motion, Eve's gorgeous eyes closed. Her curved, black eye lashes shut while she moved her mouth toward mine.

Naturally tilting my head to the right, I closed my eyes as our lips touched. I saw a flash of light when her mouth pressed against mine. The touch of her soft lips sent a shock wave through my body. Time stood still. A sensation I had never felt before, the breathless wonder of the first kiss, burned deep inside my body.

Eve placed her arm around my neck and pressed her body against mine. A faint sound of wonder came from her throat. She gently sighed; her eyelashes fluttered against my cheek. I felt my head spin when Eve pulled her lips away.

She opened her eyes. Her lips quivered while she laid her head on my shoulder, snuggling against my neck.

"You smell wonderful," she whispered.

I touched the side of her face and cupped her chin in my left hand. She looked deep into my eyes.

Gently kissing her cheek, I said, "I love you, Eve."

Reaching up, she pressed her hand against my cheek. "I love you, Hunter Wainright."

She wrapped both of her arms around my neck and kissed me a second time. Our Triamulets pressed together when I put my arms around the small of her back and squeezed.

Eve felt hot to the touch. Her breathing quicken while her heart pounded wildly against mine.

My feelings turned to ecstasy, knowing how much I loved her. I'd never felt that way before. She was everything I'd ever dreamed of in a girl. Just as we were about to kiss again, nearby screams ruined our perfect moment.

"Eeeeeaggghhh-skrrreee-rrraarghhh!"

"What was that?" Eve asked, frowning.

I jumped onto the stone bench and peered over the boulders toward the campsite. Eve slung her bow and arrow pouch over her shoulder and climbed next to me.

Under the glow of three moons, we witnessed hideous creatures emerge from the dark forest.

"We are being attacked!" she shouted. "Look! They're crossing the junction road!"

Bodvar the Berserker stood at the edge of the Palatine Forest. I remembered his illustration in the *Magnum Opus*. The giant bearman roared battle commands. His army of grizzsects, led by Chax, came armed with lances, poleaxes, maces, and flails.

Chax led the charge from the dark forest toward the Doubting Junction encampments. A dozen armed ballistas and catapults had been dragged from the trees and positioned to hurl lethal javelins, rocks, and flaming balls of pine-sap pitch.

The bearman commander had ambushed Malagig and his boar soldier cavalry. Morph, Pendragon, and the paladin stood at the southern end of the encampment next to the herd of war horses. Malagig shouted orders to the troops, sending half the armored boars to the front lines while the other half scrambled to mount their horses. The eastern flank maintained their positions, fighting the first wave of grizzsects.

I had never seen anything like the six-limbed monsters. Each grizzsect stood seven feet tall, had the abdomen and tail of a green praying mantis with the torso of a brown grizzly bear. Their hideous face was part bear and part insect. The grizzsect's two mantis arms had pincer-

Bodvar

paws that extended six feet in front of their furry chests. A dagger-like stinger protruded from the end of their tail.

Eve and I watched Malagig's ground forces grab their weapons and form lines of defense to the east, north, and south. The first defensive rank formed a living barricade with their scutum shields, lances, staves, and polearms.

The second rank prepared to attack, while the third rank released a flurry of arrows from their longbows. The first wave of grizzsects survived the incoming arrows. They would drop to the ground, curl into balls, and cover their heads with their insect arms. The incoming arrows proved ineffective against the armor-like exoskeletons of the seven-foot monsters. Several of the four-legged beasts fell seriously wounded, struck in vulnerable spots, their necks and bear torsos.

Pendragon spread his wings and lifted off the ground in a southerly direction. He circled and flew north toward Chax and the grizzsect ranks. Morph pulled out his scepter and flapped his wings, taking flight.

Hidden behind the rock formations, we watched in horror, listening to the battle cries and screams of the wounded and dying soldiers echo off the hills, down into the gorge. The clanging and thrashing of swords and flails and axes made my heart race.

A dark premonition overcame me, that we were going to die, that both of us were going to be killed.

Without warning, eight flaming balls of burning pitch shot through the air, lighting up the black sky. Eve gasped when the fire balls exploded within the boar encampment, sending flaming bits of burning pitch in every direction. Dozens of boar soldiers rolled on the ground, engulfed in flames. Hot embers ignited entire sections of the camp. The glow of roaring flames illuminated the entire battleground.

Thick dust and black smoke rose into the sky. I smelled burning flesh. Along with the barrage of fifty-pound rocks and fire balls from the catapults, the ballistas launched wave after wave of lethal ten-foot-long javelins into the wild boar formations. The heavy javelins impaled the defenseless boar soldiers as if they wore no armor.

On the other side of the junction, the wild boar cavalry, led by Malagig, charged the advancing grizzsects. The armored horses gave the undersized boars a fighting chance. Charging through the smoke and the battle dust, Malagig killed dozens of grizzsect soldiers.

Eve pulled my arm.

"That looks like Pendragon," she yelled, pointing up at a shadowy figure soaring across the starry sky.

The dragonram spread his wings, swooping and dive-bombing the enemy troops while he paralyzed grizzsect after grizzsect with a disabling lightning jolt from his divine staff, *Caduceus*.

"We've got to do something," I yelled, pulling my sword from its scabbard.

"Let's make it to the wagon," Eve yelled.

"Wait!" I shouted, pointing to the vardo. Blunderbore ran across the campsite.

Eve gasped, holding her hand over her mouth.

Two grizzsects had entered the campsite. Blunderbore the Giant swung his saber at an attacking grizzsect, cutting off the beast's pincer-paw. Vindalf held the reins of the oxen, screaming, "Kill da blooody clooties!"

The giant rammed the wounded grizzsect with his horned helmet, leaving the horns stuck deep in the beast's chest. Blunderbore directed Vindalf to turn the wagon around and face the oxen north.

The giant shouted, "Eve! Hoonter! Come 'ere, now!"

"Come on, let's go," I yelled, grabbing Eve's arm.

"Stay down," Eve yelled, "they are bringing the wagon this way."

Blunderbore climbed up into the wagon. Just as he raised his saber to give the *go* command, a grizzsect climbed on the roof of the wagon, swinging a flail. When the frightened team of oxen lunged forward, the grizzsect struck Blunderbore on the side of his unprotected head with the spiked iron ball.

The giant's blood splattered onto Vindalf's face just as the gnome snapped the reins. Blunderbore fell forward, off the wagon and under the wooden wheels of the vardo.

Swinging his flail a second time, the blood-crazed beast struck Vindalf on the right shoulder.

"Ahhhrrrggghhh!"

The gnome screamed in agony, grabbing his broken arm with his left hand. Vindalf bravely held the reins in his paralyzed right hand, losing control of the four charging oxen.

"Here they come!" Eve shouted.

We jumped down off the stone bench and ran to the north end of the boulder formation. Horrified, we watched the bewildered oxen gallop at full speed, pulling the runaway wagon across the Open Road's cobblestone.

On the west side of the road, the vardo's spoke wheels crushed and splintered when it crashed onto the jagged boulders, launching the crippled coach up and into the air. Seemingly in slow motion, Vindalf's terrified eyes and mine met as the wounded wagon master passed by us, flying through the air.

The wagon slammed into the ground once and hurled off the cliff, down into the gorge.

Eve and I ran to the ledge, watching the oxen and vardo plunged eight hundred feet into the Utopian River Gorge. My fear of falling became a visual reality when I saw the illuminated wagon smash into the rocks below and burst into flames.

In my mind, Vindalf took forever to fall to his death.

Chax

What the hell are we going to do now? I thought. *We've got to find Morph and Pendragon and—*

Eve gasped and grabbed my arm, pointing to the gorge.

In the moonlight, the grizzsect climbed up the sheer cliffs. The murderous beast had leaped off the top of the wagon at the last moment and managed to survive. While Eve pulled an arrow from her pouch and placed it on her bow string, I stood at the edge of the cliff and waited.

I gripped my sword handle with my trembling hands. Within moments, a green pincer-paw appeared. Then, the hideous head of a frenzied grizzsect with bulging, metallic green eyes and white fangs stared me in the face.

Eve aimed her bow at the grizzsect's head. Yellow froth dripped from the beast's iron jaws.

"Now, Hunter!" Eve shouted. "Use the sword! Now!

The beast gripped the rocks with its other pincer-paw. The enraged monster roared as I thrust *Aroundight* through the grizzsect's open jaws, down his throat.

"Rrrroooaaarrr—aaagggrrrgggghhh!"

When I withdrew my sword from the grizzsect's mouth, green and red blood gushed from the fatal wound. The beast grabbed his throat, gurgled, and fell backward.

Eve lowered her bow and arrow as the monster plummeted down the face of the cliff.

My hands trembled as blood dripped down the blade of *Aroundight*.

Eve ran to me and threw her arms around me. I closed my eyes and hugged her tightly.

"Let's find Morph and get out of—"

"Well," a deep voice yelled, "what do we got here? Young lovers?"

I let go of Eve and stepped in front of her, holding my sword high.

"Ex, is that you?" I yelled.

"Were you expectin' someone else?" the Invisible Villain replied. His resonating voice came from behind a group of carnivorous grizzsects. Mashing and crunching their mandibles together, seven of the green-eyed monsters glared at us.

Behind the beasts, silhouetted by the rising red sky, a swarm of growling grizzsects had overrun our Open Road campsite.

Eve laid an arrow on her bow and pulled the string back.

"Seize the girl!" Ex shouted. "Don't kill the boy!"

The growling beasts charged us.

Eve released an arrow past my shoulder. Straight and true, the arrow impaled a charging grizzsect in his eye. The beast moaned and grabbed the arrow, stumbling to the ground.

"Gihap!" I shouted as I jumped seven feet high, twirling in midair. My roundhouse leg kick glanced off the grizzsect's pincer-paws, hitting the surprised enemy in the chest. I continued my Tae Kwon Do turn with my sword swinging, striking the confused grizzsect across the neck. The monster fell to his side in disbelief; red and green blood spurting from his mortal wound.

Before I could raise *Aroundight* again, three grizzsects knocked me to the ground and held my arms and legs.

"Leave her alone!" I shouted, watching two grizzsects overtake Eve before she could release a second arrow.

"Bring 'em over here, Chax," Ex yelled from the secluded, semi-circle of boulders.

Led by their grizzsect leader, they dragged Eve and me by our arms to the stone bench area. Hidden behind the rock formations of The Point, the monsters forced us against a rock wall.

"Don't struggle, children," Ex yelled. "Life's too short."

In the sky above, we saw Morph fly over our campsite overrun with grizzsects.

Ex yelled, "The sage has taken flight; he's lookin' for 'em."

In the campsite, grizzsects ate the flesh from Blunderbore's body, lapping up the giant's blood.

"Cover them aliens. Keep 'em quiet," Ex said, watching Metamorphosis hover above the battle scene.

The grizzsects grabbed our throats with their pincer-paws and shoved us under their insectivorous abdomens. I watched Morph fly directly over The Point, over invisible Ex, over us and the grizzsects.

The sage hovered above the gorge.

His wings flapped at full speed while his scepter illuminated the sky with its ultra-violet, pulsating waves. Ex hid behind a boulder, safe from the astral glow of *Joyease*.

Choking and gasping for breath, I looked between the grizzsect's four legs. Morph held the scepter with two arms and dove head first into the gorge.

He didn't see us, I thought. *He thinks we went over the cliff. He thinks we're in the burning wagon.*

Watching Morph's blue light grow dim, the grizzsects raised their weapons and growled in celebration.

"That bumblin' idiot's headin' down to the wagon!" Ex shouted, laughing. "Chax, stand 'em up. And take that knife away from the young lady. I've seen what she can do with it."

Chax snatched *Arthame* from Eve's belt sheath and forced us against the rocks. The mammalian-insect warriors backed away and formed a semi-circle around us. Eve adjusted her skirt and grabbed my left arm. I put my hand around the small of her back. The sickening sound of clashing weapons and the screams of wounded and dying soldiers rang in my ears.

To my surprise, a familiar face crawled out from between Chax's four legs.

Grimnir!

Our subterranean guide waddled into the semi-circle, smirking and wiping the drool from this mouth. The slobbering aardvark held his wooden club up and pointed the weapon at me.

Grimnir

"Sth-see Mathster, I told you the boy is-sth a sth-scardy cat."

I sneered at my betraying nemesis. "Now I know why I never liked you; you traitor. You slobbering son-of-a—"

"Silence!" Ex shouted.

The Invisible Villain had entered the semi-circle, standing within six feet of Eve and me.

We held our breath. God, there was that awful smell again, the rancid stench of Ex.

"Did you bring the glider?" Ex asked.

"Yes-sth, Mathster. It's-sth tied to me sth-sumpters-sth."

The slobbering Grimnir pointed north. A grizzsect held the reins of the two agitated moleipeedes. The feathered hang gliders had been tied between the subterranean sumpters.

"Outstandin', my clever aardvark," Ex yelled.

"Ya owe me a hundred sth-scruples fer me sth-services-sth," Grimnir said, holding out his dirty paw in the direction of Ex.

"Bodvar will pay you," Ex yelled. "Be gone, lowlife."

The drooling aardvark guide bowed his head and waddled to the stone bench. He spit at me, sat on the bench, and said, "I'll sth-sit here an' wait. I wanna' sth-see you toss the sth-stupid boy off them cliffs-sth."

Ex instructed two grizzsects to bring the hang glider onto the rocky ledge of The Point.

Pointing in the direction of the Invisible Villain, Eve shouted, "Leave us alone! We have done nothing to harm you!"

"Quiet, young lady," Ex yelled.

Pointing Eve's knife at me, the Extractor yelled, "Listen, Hunter Wainright. Since you've proven you can't solve the dumbest of riddles, I'm gonna make you my final offer."

"Offer me anything you want scumbag. I'm not taking it!"

"Allow me to change your mind."

Ex clapped his hands. Chax and three grizzsects rushed forward to seize Eve and me. The powerful beasts separated us, holding our arms behind our backs.

In the tri-moonlight, Ex moved *Arthame* toward us. The sacred knife floated through the air toward Eve.

While she struggled to free her arms and legs, the knife blade moved against her neck.

Eve stop moving when the razor-sharp tip touched her throat. Her defiant eyes glared at the empty space in front of her.

"Join me, Hunter Wainright, or I kill the girl."

While battle cries and death screams echoed into the gorge, beads of sweat formed on my forehead. Everything went silent.

God, what am I going to do? I thought. *I have to make a decision...a choice. Remember what Morph said, the highest choice is the only choice. Don't give in to his demands.*

I shouted, "No! Nothing can make me join you!"

Tears formed in Eve's eyes. She nodded at me with admiration. Her expression confirmed that I had made the highest choice.

"One last chance," Ex yelled. "I'll spare her life if you join the Extractors and come with me, now."

Thought about my situation. If I joined Ex, he'd probably kill us both anyway.

"Wainright, I need an answer. Now!"

I glared in Ex's direction and shook my head, *no.*

"Fool. You were an Extractor on Earth, and you'll be an Extractor on Millennium. My promise is, you'll eventually come over to our side; it's only a matter of time."

Ex clapped his hands three times.

"Get the girl ready, she needs to get away from this frightened little boy."

Chax dragged Eve across the flat rock, held her down, and gagged her mouth with a strip of burlap cloth. Using leather ties, the monster bound her hands and feet to the wooden

crossbar of the hang glider.
She laid on the cold rock,
struggling to free herself. I
saw the terror in her eyes.

The harder I struggled, the
tighter the grizzsects pinched my
arms and legs. "Let her go, or I
will—"

"Silence!" Ex shouted. "We
gotta' special guest."

The grizzsects bowed
and saluted. Bodvar the
Berserker had entered The Point,
interrupting Ex. "The battle has
gone as planned. We're winnin'."

"Did you kill the
dragonram yet?" Ex
asked.

"No. The winged
Utopian doesn't fight fair.
He flies aroun' with that
lightin' rod staff."

"If you can't kill Pendragon soon,
retreat to the forest. I have what I want.
We're done here."

"I ain't retreatin'," Bodvar yelled,
growling. "We're gonna' kill every last one of them."

"Do as I say!" Ex shouted.

Bodvar roared, "Never tell me what to do!" The Berserker
turned and stormed back across the Open Road to the battlefield.

"I'll take care of that bearman later. Insubordination results
in severe punishment," Ex yelled, picking up the hang glider's
support bar.

Eve's body lifted into midair, upside down, hanging by her
hands and feet. Her black hair fell straight down, touching the
granite rock.

She looked at me with terror in her eyes.

"You maniac, untie her!" I shouted, struggling to free myself.

419

"Do not kill the boy!" Ex shouted. "He'll soon change his mind and come crawlin' on his knees to me. I know a weaklin' when I see one."

The Master Extractor ran down the granite outcropping toward the pointed ledge. Eve floated through the air upside down. Her ruby necklace dangled around her neck; the Triamulet gleamed in the light of the three moons.

The glider plunged off the pointed ledge and disappeared down into the gorge, into the starry night.

I held my breath, thinking, *Where is she? What's happened? Has Eve crashed?*

Within moments, the glider's wings appeared in the moonlight. Ex rode the night thermals in a southerly direction.

Chax dragged me in front of the stone bench.

Struggling to free myself from my captors, I heard a sickening sound, instantly feeling a sharp pain on the back of head.

A white flash and the roar of utter silence overcame me.

I felt myself slump forward.

Grimnir stood on the stone bench with his wooden club in his paw.

"Sth-serves you right, you sth-stupid alien!"

The aardvark crawled down off the bench, kicked gravel in my face, bowed to Chax, and scurried back toward his two moleipeedes.

Semi-conscious and disoriented, I laid on my back, groaning from the excruciating pain in my head.

The back of my skull felt warm. I knew I laid in my own blood. All I could think of was how I had to get up and save Eve.

Touched the solid rock with my hands. The surface reminded me of my awakening on Time Island. Turned my head to my right and saw Grimnir fleeing north on the moleipeedes, up the Open Road.

Blurry-eyed, I watched Chax throw *Aroundight* against the granite boulders. Orange and yellow sparks exploded off the steel blade.

The grizzsects pointed skyward and marched away behind Chax, abandoning me.

The screams and the clashing armor and the battle cries seemed a million miles away when I spotted the silhouette of Pendragon soaring overhead, zooming across the red and black starry sky.

He's my friend, he'll save us, I thought, my mind spinning.

Dizzy, I closed my blurry eyes and opened them again, trying to focus on the red and black sky converging directly above me.

Felt myself drift into unconsciousness.

I remember thinking, *It's an X...the red sky is crossing under the black sky...I see a giant X in the sky.*

DAYNIGHT OF THE SCORPION

Aries the 16th
Year of the Dragon

"Weapons are instruments of fear;
they are not an enlightened being's tools.
Use them only when you have no choice.
May peace and quiet be dear to your heart,
and victory no cause for rejoicing.
If you rejoice in victory, then you delight in killing.
If you delight in killing, you shall not fulfill yourself."
—Metamorphosis

Chapter 22
Open Road

Barely conscious, I opened my eyes to see a bright blue sky. I squinted from the glare of Sol and Helios, focusing my vision on the two shadows hovered over me. A numb pain in the back of my head brought a grimace to my face. A long, white beard laid across my chest.

"Wake up, Hunter," Metamorphosis said, cradling my head in his arms while he held a water bag. "You are going to be fine. Here, drink some amrita."

With the sage's help, I sat up, shaking my head. I gained my bearings as I guzzled amrita from the water bag.

Pendragon stood over me, spreading his blue-grey wings to block the bright light. Holding the back of my matted, blood-stained head, I looked around. The moment I saw the Utopian River Gorge, I struggled to my feet.

"Take it easy, young man," Pendragon said, "we need to treat that wound."

"He took her," I yelled. "Ex has taken Eve."

Running toward the edge of the cliff, I stopped to pick up Eve's knife. Morph and Pendragon followed me to the end of the rocky point.

"Took her where?" Morph asked.

Without any fear of heights, I looked down into the gorge. I spotted the remains of the burned vardo on the rocks below.

"It was dark; Ex took her *that* way," I replied, pointing south, down the Utopian River.

"How?"

"She was tied to a hang glider," I replied, running my fingers through my tangled hair. "What are we going to do?"

Morph told Pendragon, "When I dove into the gorge, I saw deck lights down river. Probably the *Walrus* or the *Jolly Roger*.

The ship was heading south. I should have known they were waiting for Ex."

"Have Malagig organize the troops," Pendragon said. "I'm going down river to see if I can locate the vessel."

"Be careful," the sage said, "Captain Kyash's ship has cannons on board. Tyrannus can be dangerous if it's Kraken's vessel."

Pendragon nodded and dove off the end of The Point. Flapping his grey dragon wings, he gained altitude, flying south along the east rim of the gorge. Soon, the Utopian faded into the distant horizon.

"Come," Morph said, handing me *Aroundight*. "We need to get you cleaned up."

"But, what about—"

"My son, relax. Breathe deeply. There is nothing we can do about Eve this moment."

Morph picked up her bow and arrow pouch off the ground, turned and walked toward camp. I slid my sword into its scabbard and caught up with the sage crossing the Open Road.

Walking across the yellow cobblestone, I looked southeast past the junction. The remaining boar soldiers attended to the dead and wounded. Black smoke billowed into the air from a dozen burning fires—funeral pyres.

Tucking *Arthame* into my belt, I walked across the camp site. I noticed pools of dried blood covering the gravel. Nothing was left of Blunderbore's body. I picked up Vindalf's watch; I mean, *Andvari's* gold pocket watch.

The watch, still ticking, showed 15:00 o'clock. I realized it was mid-day, not morning, that I'd been unconscious longer than I thought.

"Look, our guitars," I yelled, pointing to the dust-covered instruments. "Broken in pieces."

"Yes, the guitars did not survive the grizzsect attack," Morph said, handing me a towel. "You may clean up over there."

A stack of food, water and supplies still stood where Vindalf had parked the wagon. The sage pointed to a copper wash tub next to the stack of supplies. I put the pocket watch in my breeches and washed my face in the tub, submerging my head under the clear, cool water. Shaking my hair like a wet dog, I dried my face with the towel. I noticed dark-red stains on the white cotton cloth.

"Shall we sit in the shade and gather our thoughts?" Morph asked, holding food and two water bags of amrita in his four arms.

Grabbed my artist satchel and followed the sage to a wooden bench underneath a stone monolith on the east perimeter of the campsite. Morph laid *Gandeeva* and the arrow pouch against the boulder and sat with me. The wind had picked up, blowing ashes and white smoke into the Palatine Forest. The smell of burning hair and flesh made me gag.

"They have finished the funeral pyres," Morph said. "The air shall clear soon."

I drank amrita, sorting my thoughts.

"Hey, what happened?" I asked, seeing a blood-stained bandage on the bottom of Morph's tail.

"I was struck by a misguided arrow during all the confusion."

"Doesn't that hurt? You don't seem to be suffering."

"Pain is natural, but suffering is a choice," the sage said.

"Is Malagig okay?" I asked, reaching into my black tunic to make sure my Triamulet still hung by its gold chain around my neck.

"The paladin left for Doubting Castle. He shall return soon."

Gazing out across the Utopian River Gorge, I sat and rubbed my gold Triamulet between my thumb and index finger.

Now what? I thought. *Where do we go from here? How are we going to get Eve back? How long will* ***that*** *take?*

I opened the flap to my leather satchel and asked Morph, "What daynight is it?"

"The sixteenth of Aries," Morph said, pointing to the Daynight of the Scorpion on the calendar.

I closed my eyes and clenched my fists. I'd been gone eight daynights, four hundred fifty Earth days, a year and three months. It was going to be Thanksgiving soon, and then Christmas, and then—

"May I answer any questions?"

"I'm trying to make sense of everything."

The sage tapped my shoulder and pointed north. "Here comes a surprise for you, my son."

Galloping down Doubting Castle Road, Sir Malagig had emerged from the Palatine Forest in full armor.

"Is that a horse behind him?" I asked.

"Pegasus," Morph replied as he stood up.

A magnificent white stallion with wings ran behind Malagig.

"The *real* Pegasus?" I asked, standing with the sage.

"The one and only," Morph replied, waving his wand and walking into the clearing to greet the knight.

Sir Malagig galloped toward the sage. "I bequeth thee Pegasus," the knight yelled, pulling up on the reins of his black stallion. "I beseech thee that I may join my brothers-in-arms."

Morph gestured, *thank you*. The knight rode across the junction to the boar soldier camp.

Pegasus flared his nostrils and snorted, pawing the ground with his silver hooves. Larger than any horse I'd ever seen, the stallion kept his white feathery wings folded vertically above his back. The winged horse of human mythology wore a black leather saddle behind his ivory wings.

The sage pointed skyward. "Excellent timing. Pendragon has returned from the gorge."

Shielding my eyes with my hand, I watched the winged Utopian land on the Open Road. Taking twelve long strides, Pendragon quickly stood in front of Morph and me.

"You were correct," Pendragon said. "The ship is indeed, the *Walrus*. The strong current has allowed her crew to sail past Phoenix Hill to the Gates of Dawn. I did not see the girl on board; she might be below deck. I could not get close, the beastmen and hobgoblins had the cannons pointed at me."

"Thank you, my friend."

Pendragon pointed toward the junction with his divine

staff and said, "I must assist Malagig. We shall devise a plan to rescue the Epiphanite."

The winged Utopian nodded his head to me, turned and ran across the junction road toward the encampment.

"My son, you must make a choice," Morph told me. "The recent events prevent us from remaining on your Earthly time schedule. I do not know when I can return you to Fog Harbor should you continue south on the Open Road. We have yet to see Octilogy's first treasure, Anthera, the Eternal Rose."

"What does that all mean?"

The sage pointed at the winged horse. "Pegasus can fly you to Time Island within six hours. As I promised, the Triamulet you wear allows you to go back to sleep and awaken safely on Earth with your family."

I raised my eyebrows. "Wait a minute. Why didn't we just fly on winged horses in the first place? Are you telling me we could have made it from Fog Harbor to *here* in six hours?"

Clenching my fists, I yelled at Morph, "For God's sake, why didn't we just take the flying horses? I wouldn't have had to walk the crater trails, or crawl through the dark Underworld, or be thrown into the Dungeon of Fire and be tortured, or have to tolerate Grimnir. Andvari would still be alive. Eve would be with *me* right now. We could have avoided all those problems if only we had—

"Calm yourself, my son. Relax. I see the frustration on your face. Did we not discuss the importance of the journey, that all things happen in perfect order? Contentment comes from the journey, not the destination."

Closing my eyes, I thought, *This is crazy...what in the hell is going on...how could Eve's kidnapping be part of some perfect order...now he expects me to calm down and make an decision and—Stop!*

I'm not like that any more...that's not like me...I'm in control of my thoughts...Hunter, calm down...he's offering you the chance to go home...stop complaining and—

"Please, sit here and think it over," Morph said. "There comes a time in everyone's life when they must make a life-changing decision. I know you shall choose wisely."

"Wait." I frowned. "I'm not sure what to do. I'm confused. Can you give me some advice? You know, some words of wisdom. Please, Morph, help me."

"Your request is my command." The Sage of the Ages looked me in the eyes. "First of all, your arrival here on Millennium has happened at the perfect time. When this experience comes to a closure, you shall know it absolutely. All my messages have arrived in your life at just the right time."

I gazed into Morph's tranquil eyes.

"Should you decide to return to Earth, I know you shall live the wisdom I have taught you the past eight daynights. I see in your eyes that you hear the silent music in my words, the music of the cosmos. Practice the ten Universal Truths, the Secrets of Time & Space, and your life shall be turned completely inside out and upside down. You shall not recognize your former life, your previous way of thinking. You have discovered The Great Way, the path to happiness. Follow it, my son, and you shall successfully navigate the storms of time and space."

"Wait, I don't remember you telling me the tenth Secret."

"It is only a secret to primitive beings. The tenth Secret of the Universe is, 'Love Teaches All.'"

"That's easy to remember. It's a song."

"Should you decide to return home to your family, embrace love as your mantra. Remain at peace with yourself and do not allow the dark forces, the Extractors on Earth, to affect you in any way. Remember, you have no enemies; I speak of those who suffer from the emotional virus. Forgive them; they know not what they do. They have yet to travel the Open Road, the high road, and learn to live The Great Way."

The sage held up a quieting hand.

"Should you return to Earth, become a great teacher. With calm words and actions, with confident humility, speak grandly so that others feel your love and wisdom, so they follow you down the highest road. Should you return, do not complain or make excuses for yourself or your government. Change the way things are; be a champion of change. Make a difference by seeking the supreme truth. Live life as a leader."

I nodded and said, "I will."

Morph smiled and placed his upper left hand on my shoulder.

"At the beginning of your journey you asked for the truth. Now that you have been enlightened, I believe you know how to use that wisdom to change your thoughts, and therefore, others. The unenlightened you would kill things without remorse or compassion. *Aroundight* has blood stains on it; however, I see the compassion in your eyes for all creatures, large and small.

"When I first met you, you seemed afraid. Afraid of your own thoughts. I no longer sense fear in you. As a fearless being, you shall bathe in the warm waters of eternal bliss.

"When I first met you, you wanted to be rich and famous. I believe you now have a different view of success, and happiness.

"When I first met you, you lived your life without purpose. All intelligent life forms have a dharma, a goal, a purpose in the universe. You have discovered your dharma. Now, live it.

"When I first met you, you lived your life in darkness and fear. Having emerged from the darkness, you now embrace the Light. You see the truth in all things.

"When I first met you, you wore shackles and saw shadows on the wall. Now, you see only reality. The Light.

"When you arrived on Millennium, you were lost; one of the lost people of Earth. Now I feel differently about you. I know you have found yourself, your *Self*, on this journey."

I nodded, *yes*.

"My teachings are very easy to understand and very easy to practice; yet so few in this universe truly understand, and so few are willing to practice. Those who know me are rare indeed."

Morph grinned and placed his right upper fist on his chest, over his heart. "I love you, Hunter Wainright. I wish you all the happiness in the universe."

"I love you too, Metamorphosis."

I placed my right fist on my chest and tapped my heart.

Morph opened his four arms. "I shall always be here with you. All ways and for all time."

Opening my arms, I hugged the sage.

"Have a safe journey home, my son."

He brought his two upper hands together so the thumbs and index fingers touched, forming a triangle.

Looking through the triangle, he said,

"Live Life as a Leader."

The Sage of the Ages pointed to Pegasus.

"The horse of legend awaits you. Godspeed."

Morph turned and walked toward Malagig's camp. Pendragon met the sage on the road. While they talked, I scanned the Millennium landscape. The fires had burned to ashes. The blue sky looked bright and clear. Rising thunderheads hugged the southern horizon. Behind me, a fiery-red sky loomed over the eastern hills. Beyond the gorge, a black sky appeared on the western horizon. The sweet smell of pine trees filled my lungs with fond memories. Home beckoned me.

I pulled the gold chain up around my neck, held my gold Triamulet between my fingers, and went into deep thought. *It could take months to find Eve...in six months another twenty-five years will have passed on Earth...My parents will be seventy years old...maybe dead...I won't recognize my family...things will have changed so much I won't recognize anything. But, I love Eve...I can't stop thinking of her...she needs my help...she loves me. But, I can be home in seven or eight hours...back with my family...back to normal...back in my home and my own room with all my stuff and—Stop!*

What am I thinking? My God...Eve is with that invisible monster...she needs my help.

The mythical stallion stomped the ground and flapped his ivory-white wings.

Think, Hunter...what is the highest choice...the truth...what choice takes you on the high road?

I held the gold Triamulet up to my face. The medallion gleamed in the solshine.

Then I realized, *I already know the highest choice!*

"Wait!" I shouted, walking toward the sage. "Morph, I've made my decision!"

The sage walked calmly back to me. We met next to Pegasus. I held my backpack, artist satchel, and Eve's bow and arrows.

Our eyes met. I nodded at Morph.

The sage returned my nod and said, "The high road awaits us, Hunter."

He gave Pegasus a hand signal, then said to me, "Let us go find your friend, she needs our help."

The magnificent horse of legend neighed, folded his wings and ran to Morph.

"Please mount up, we are going to Escalot, then Hermopolis.

"Why?

"Because Pendragon's messengers have confirmed that the *Walrus* has been spotted rounding Cape Taenarum and heading north through the Sea of Esteem."

"So, which way is that?"

"East, my son. We shall fly toward the red sky."

"On Pegasus?"

"Yes. While I gather our gear, 'saddle up' as you say in your Wild West adventures." He pointed at Pegasus.

I turned and the mighty horse had bowed down to one knee, his white wing touching the ground. I climbed up onto the black saddle, grabbed the leather reins and turned to find Morph. He stood behind me, placing leather bags over the flanks of the horse, behind my saddle.

"Ready?" Morph asked, as he jumped up onto the horse, directly behind me.

I nodded, *yes*, clutching the reins.

Morph whistled and Pegasus took off, his wings outstretched, galloping at full speed toward the gorge. Talk about exhilarating, I had never ridden a horse that ran so fast. Held my breath as the mythological beast lifted his wings and leaped off the edge of the cliff in full flight.

Surprised myself by not closing my eyes. I felt balanced and suddenly had no fear of heights. Soaring through midair felt magical. The winged stallion leveled off and began to flap his massive wings.

"On to Escalot!" Morph shouted.

Soaring high into the blue Millennium sky, Pegasus made a full turn and flew southeast.

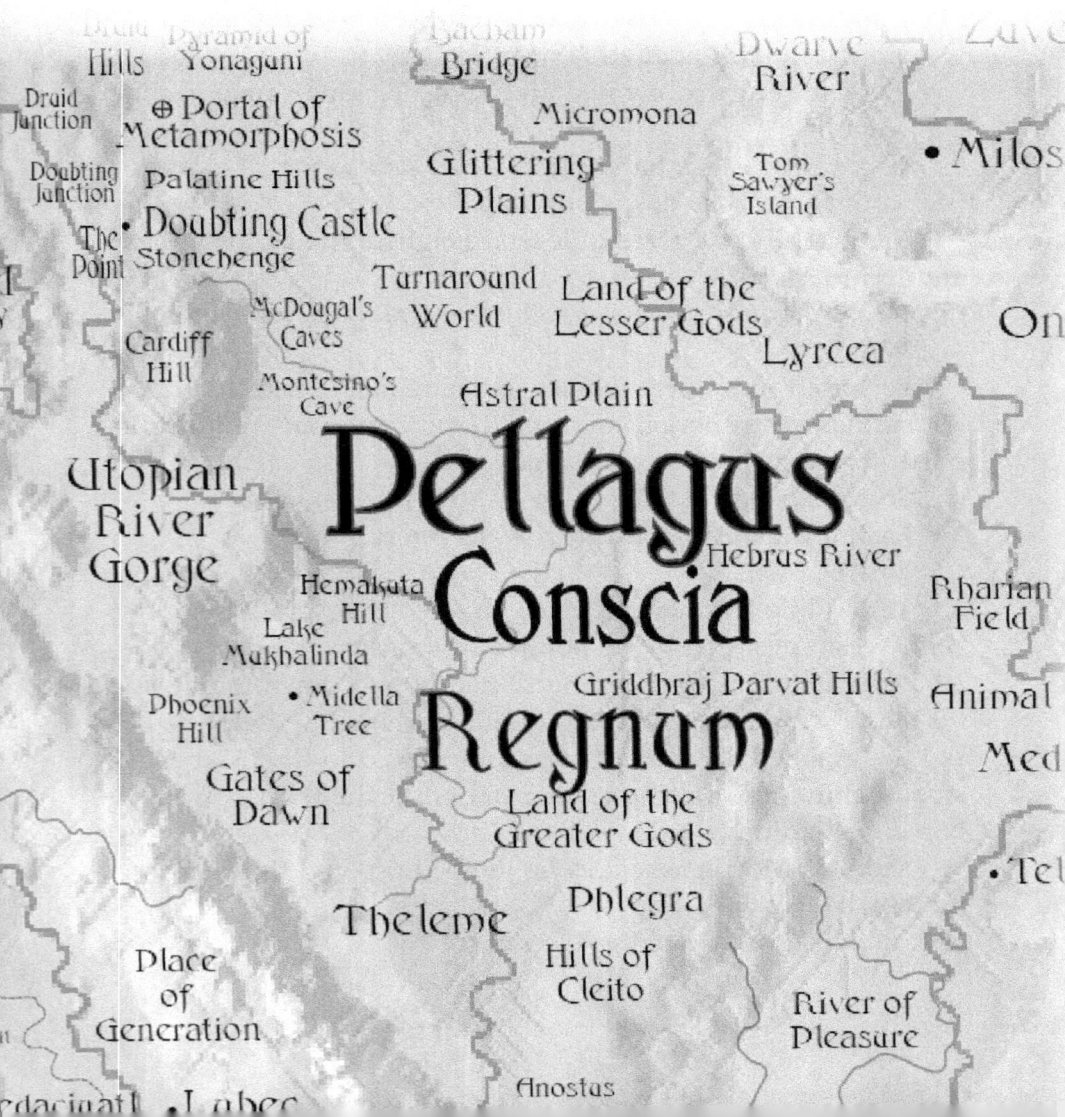

Chapter 23
Escalot

oubting Castle disappeared behind the forest of towering pine trees. Heading southeast under a blue Millennium sky, Pegasus soared over the Palatine Hills and down into a sea of green and gold grasslands teaming with herds of extraordinary animals. Wildlife with multiple tusks and twisted horns and armored plates roamed over the rolling terrain, what Morph called, Glittering Plains. Kangaroos with orange and black stripes jumped through the sea of swaying grass. Mammoths and giant ground sloths rested in the shade of towering acacia trees that dotted the great plains.

The breathtaking scenery and tri-colored sky did not distract me from thinking of Eve.

Don't worry, Eve, I thought, *we're coming to save you. We'll be together soon. Ex is afraid of Morph and—*

"Escalot awaits us," the sage said, pointing his wand.

Flying over the Kingdom of Pellagus, Morph pointed down to McDougal's Cave at Cardiff Hill and farther south, the Cave of Montesino. We turned inland and followed the Hebrus River for two hundred miles, flying over Phlegra, where, according to the sage, the god Zeus overthrew a race of giants.

We gained altitude as the red sky crept over us, giving the landscape an eerie, crimson hue. The grasslands gave way to evergreen forests and rocky hills with pointed pinnacles.

Pegasus glided past Vulture Peak, the tallest point in the Griddhraj Parvat Hills. Soaring down out of the steep slopes, we entered a vast rift valley between the River of Grief and the River of Pleasure.

Morph told me that if one eats the fruit growing along the river banks, that the person begins reverse aging and dies as an infant.

Realizing that the places we had flown over had been documented in human mythology by previous visitors to Millennium, I asked about the fairy tale lands that Father and Professor Johan had described. Morph explained that the majority of the fairy tale kingdoms and castles and story-book characters existed to the far north, in Nemoria, where the Grimm brothers, Jacob and Wilhelm, had explored during their visit. I told Morph I wanted to see all the fairy tale lands that I had read about as a child in Father's library.

He said, "All in good time, my son."

We followed the River of Pleasure for another three hundred miles as the black sky crept overhead, turning the landscape into moon-lit shadows. For the entire flight, I thought about how we would rescue Eve from Ex and the Extractors. For some reason, I felt less fearful of the Invisible Villain.

As the blue sky brought the morning sunrise, Morph reminded me it was Aires the 17th, Daynight of the Boar. He pointed ahead, shouting, "There she is again, the Open Road."

The sage instructed me to pull down on the leather reins and Pegasus dove toward the yellow cobblestone road. We followed the Open Road, the Great Way, while he explained how the famous road, a major trade route, looped around the entire Sea of Esteem peninsula, past Never-Never Land and the Lost Boy's House at the southern end, then up the eastern coast past Black Hill Cove, Argo Bay, Hermopolis, Kallipolis and eventually, Escalot.

As the red sky filled with purple and yellow clouds, the sage announced, "Escalot Castle ahead."

The winged stallion neighed, flapping his white wings faster and faster.

The Open Road wound its way down the steep foothills, through ancient forests of twisted oaks and willows. Beyond the treetops, Escalot perched precariously on the weathered cliffs of the great Sea of Esteem. Looking like a medieval fortress, stone towers emerged from the four corners of the walled city. A central dome with a copper roof rose from the castle's interior.

Morph yelled, "Hang on," as Pegasus swooped down and landed at the gated entrance. A wooden draw bridge crossed a murky moat filled with crocodiles. Beyond the bridge stood the timbered gates of the coastal city.

I asked Morph why we didn't fly into Escalot, over the stone walls.

He pointed up at a tower.

Guards, clad in armor, stood with long bows pointed at us.

"The archers would shoot us out of the sky," the sage replied.

The massive gates creaked open and we entered the castle city by foot, walking Pegasus behind us.

Escalot, bustling with activity, looked like a medieval town that I read about in my *King Arthur, Robin Hood* and my role play books.

Morph told me the seaside metropolis was a major trade center located on the Open Road. Escalot reminded me of Carmel By-The-Sea, because the city had been built on ocean cliffs. We traversed the narrow cobblestone streets lined with two-story buildings that looked like homes and storefronts and stables and taverns.

Everywhere I looked, bizarre creatures roamed the streets or tended the windowed storefronts. Dwarves and elves and boggarts and brownies and sea faeries carried on conversations as they bartered on the street corners.

Spotted oxen with spiral horns and armored wombats pulled creaking carts and wagons filled with wood, coal and sacks of grain. A giant and swamp elve sat in front of a shop playing chess with a half-orc and forest dwarve. The odd-looking foursome drew Gametasia cards from a deck, moved their chess pieces and exchanged gold and silver treasure coins.

I wished I had my camera to photograph all the unearthly two-legged creatures sporting horns, or four arms, or wings, or tails, feathers and fur. No one looked human.

We turned down a labyrinth of narrow cobblestone streets until we reached the east side of Escalot, to a row of rustic buildings standing next to the city's fortress wall.

Morph stopped in front of a two-story-tall inn with a brown thatched roof. The wooden sign above the door read:

Two crisscrossed harpoons formed an X.

Morph tied Pegasus' reins to a hitching post and led me through the inn's front door. The noisy tavern fell silent as my eyes adjusted to the dark, smoky room. The sage escorted me to a wooden booth by the fireplace. Sitting in the shadowed light, I found myself surrounded by a cast of bizarre characters with fur and scales and tusks and claws and antennae. Every eye in the place focused on me, the only human being in the room.

Morph ordered two mugs of mango juice from the cyclops waitress, a one-eyed giant with orange hair, who waited on our booth.

"Stay here," Morph said, "I must find Pendragon."

"Pendragon? What's he doing here?"

"He had to meet with one of our messengers to find out how our new guest on Time Island is doing."

"From what planet?"

"A human female from Earth."

"Why are you so concerned about the new arrival?"

"Just as we were concerned with *your* arrival on Time Island, we always make sure the Extractors do not meet our esteemed guests before we Utopians do."

Before I could ask another question, the sage excused himself and walked up the stairs.

Watching the Utopian climb the stairs, I grabbed the handle of my sword and tried to act normal, unafraid. Within moments, the strange patrons ignored me, going back to their loud conversations and ale drinking and card games and wagering.

Through the smoke and haze, the cyclops waitress brought two pewter mugs to the table. She held out her huge hand.

"Ya owe me two red scruples an' a white frugle, dearie."

"I have no money," I said, shrugging my shoulders.

"Ya weird humans never got treasure coins on ya," she yelled, frowning with her one bushy orange eyebrow.

She rolled her green eye, lumbered away and screamed up the stairs, "Morph, you owe me fer them drinks!"

Sitting by the blazing fire, I held the cold mug with one hand and my sword handle with my other hand. Keeping a watchful eye on the crowd of unearthly characters, I waited impatiently for Morph's return. I looked at the pocket watch and the time was 10:00 o'clock. That meant the sky was still red outside.

At 11:00, the cyclops waitress stopped at my table and told me to go up the stairs, to the first room on the right.

I made my way through the smoke-filled tavern, past the rowdy guests, up the creaking stairs, down a narrow hallway, and into a banquet room with oil lamps lining the walls. Behind a wooden table in the middle of the room, Morph stood in front of a floor-to-ceiling rock fireplace.

"Please, have a seat," the sage said, "we need to talk."

The sage patted my back as I sat down in the wooden chair by the fire.

Have you ever had that feeling where you know something unusual is about to happen? That's how I felt.

Before I could speak, Pendragon entered the room and asked to see Morph alone, that he wanted to share good news about the female visitor.

The sage excused himself and left me sitting at the table.

Anxious, I stood and walked to the second-floor window. I opened the shutters to breathe the fresh Millennium air.

With a crackling fire at my back, I gazed out the window at the surreal landscapes of the Andromeda planet.

DAYNIGHT OF THE BOAR

Aries the 17ᵗʰ
Year of the Dragon

*"They who know others are wise.
They who know themselves
are enlightened."*

*"The wise talk because
they have something to say;
fools talk because they have to say something."*
—Metamorphosis

Chapter 24
Julia

Now you know how I arrived on Millennium, and why I'm standing *here*, in the Crossed Harpoons Inn. Staring out the window at the three moons crawling across the red sky, my thoughts are focused on one thing, Eve. I'm getting anxious to leave, wondering what's taking Metamorphosis and Pendragon so long. They've been gone for almost an hour.

Wait. I hear footsteps. Finally, here is Morph.

"We're back," he says as he enters the room with Pendragon. The sage points to the table and says, "Please sit down."

The crackling fire casts a shadow on their Utopian faces as they sit down with me, one at either end of the table.

"Hunter, we have a surprise for you," Pendragon says, grinning from horn to horn.

My heart skips a beat. "Did you find Eve?"

"No, but we *do* know that the *Walrus* has recently sailed past the Isle of the Eternal Rose," Morph says. "That means we should be able to catch up to her with our fastest ship, the *Argo*."

The sage puts his hand on my shoulder and says, "Our good news involves the human female visitor who arrived three daynights ago on Time Island."

"Someone my age?" I ask.

"Yes," Morph replies, "*exactly* your age."

What does he mean, exactly?

Suddenly, it dawns on me.

"Julia?" I ask.

Morph and Pendragon both nod, *yes*.

"But, she didn't have a Triamulet."

"Well, she's wearing one now," Pendragon says. "Would you like to see it?"

"What do you mean?" I ask, confused by his question.

"Julia is here to see you," Morph says. "She has something important to share with you."

Still in a state of shock hearing my twin sister has arrived on Millennium and has found me at Escalot, I wonder, what could be so important that Julia has traveled all the way across the universe to find me?

"Where is she?" I ask.

"Downstairs," Pendragon says.

Hearing a knock, Pendragon gets up and opens the door. There stands Nyx, one of the Utopians I saw in the *Magnum Opus.*

She hugs the sage and Pendragon. I like her furry-white face, hands and legs. Her body is covered with silver-blue and green fish scales, the translucent color of abalone shell. A blue dorsal fin rises from the forehead and runs between her upright ears and down her back. Her mermaid-like tail fin almost touches the ground. Six red gills, three on each side, protrude from under her jaw line. She holds a spear and carries a unicorn knife in her belt.

Her upright ears are pierced with eight gold earrings, four in each ear. She's wearing a gold chemise with a gold Triangulum buckle on her braided rope belt.

She stares at me and grins. Nyx's blue-green eyes look hypnotically tranquil as her pink nose twitches, making her translucent whiskers move up and down.

"Greetings, I am Nyx," she says, holding out her furry white hand with five, human-like fingers.

Stepping forward, I shake her hand and say, "Hello, I'm Hunter Wainright."

"You look just as I thought you would," Nyx says. "We have been searching for you since the Daynight of the Spider."

"Is something wrong?" I ask. "Is my family okay?"

"As far as I know, everything is as you left it at home. I shall let Julia update you on your family."

"Take me to her; we need to talk."

Nyx points at the door and says, "Please, follow me."

The sage looks at Pendragon and says, "You had better check on our supplies for the morning." The dragonram strides out of the room, leaving the door open.

Morph follows Nyx out the door, with me right behind them. We make our way down the hallway to the stairs. The rabbitfish prances down the tavern stairs with the sage and me at her heels.

Through the smokey haze of the crowded tavern, I spot her, sitting in a booth by the fireplace.

Julia!

Julia Rose, my twin sister!

The moment she sees me, she jumps up and runs toward me, making her way through the crowd of bizarre characters.

I can't believe my eyes.

There is my twin sister, dressed in medieval attire—black breeches, a long-sleeved white chemise with crossed-laced leather ties and a red bodice. Her gold Triamulet hangs just above the top laces. Her knee-high snake-skin boots are topped with brown fur. On her side, she's wearing a sword with a jewel-studded handle.

Unable to contain myself, I run past Morph and Nyx into her outstretched arms.

We hug each other tightly. We both have tears in our eyes as we laugh and kiss each other's cheeks.

My sister has grown taller since the last time I saw her, the night before our seventeenth birthdays.

"What in God's name are you doing here?" I ask, feeling my smile turn to concern.

"I came to find *you*," she replies. "Bring you home."

Before I can respond, Morph interrupts us, saying, "Come my children, let us move to a quiet location."

Turning to the sage, I say, "This is my twin sister, Julia."

"Ah, another Wainright on a mission," he says, extending his hand in friendship.

"Your father must be proud of his two oldest children."

She looks at me while she shakes Morph's hand. We both grin.

"No, Father's not real happy with Hunter right now, or me," Julia says. "Momma's *really* upset."

Julia hugs me again and we follow Morph and Nyx up the creaking stairs, down the narrow hallway, and back into the rustic banquet room with oil lamps lining the walls.

A blazing fire pops and crackles in the rock fireplace.

Julia

442

"This will do nicely," Morph says, gesturing, *sit down.*

The four of us sit at a wooden table in front of the fire, Morph at one end, Nyx at the other, and Julia across from me.

Julia says, "If I didn't know any better, I'd say Mom dressed us both today."

We both laugh. My twin sister and I are wearing similar clothes.

"Just like in third grade," I say.

Julia tells Morph how my mom would dress us in matching outfits when we were in grade school. How we both hated it, but learned to joke about it as we grew older.

Can't take my eyes off my sister. The warm flames of the fire cast a shadow on her face. She looks so mature, grown up.

The cyclops waitress brings us four cups of hot tea. She collects twelve treasure coins from Nyx and rumbles out the door, slamming it shut.

"Now, what brings you to Millennium, young lady?" the Sage of the Ages asks Julia.

Pointing at me, she replies, "I'm here to bring *him* home. Momma is really sick and Hunter needs to return before she gets worse. Our house is in foreclosure, the terrorists have bombed the foundation's headquarters and kidnapped all the doctors."

Her voice cracks as she holds back her tears. "Father's life is in danger. The terrorists are trying to kill him."

"What are you talking about?" I ask.

The sage holds his hand up, preventing me from speaking.

"Calm down, young lady," Morph says. "Let us focus on the events here and now, before we deal with your situation at home."

"Relax, Princess Julia," Nyx says. "Take a deep breath."

Glancing into the Morph's blue eyes, Julia sighs deeply and nods with an *I'll-try-to-calm-down* look.

The sage asks, "How was your galactic trip to Time Island?"

"Fine," Julia replies. "But, can't we talk about more important things than my trip?"

"Of course," the sage replies, gesturing toward me. "Perhaps we should allow Hunter to share his experiences on Millennium before you demand his decision to return home with you."

Julia stares at me and says, "Sorry. I'm in a hurry to get back, before it's too late."

"First of all, it is never too late for anything," Morph tells her. "I say this because all things happen in perfect order. There is nowhere to go. Nowhere because we are now here. They are one in the same word. Therefore, let us enjoy this moment in time together, right now."

"That's what Nyx has been telling me," Julia says.

The sage grins. "This perfect moment together is all there is. There is no time but this time; no moment but this moment."

He moves his white beard off his lap with one hand and holds his tea cup with the other, while his third and fourth hands rest calmly on the oak table.

Everything he is saying is going right over Julia's head. I don't think she's listening to him. She just keeps staring at me.

"I'm sorry things are such a disaster back home," I say. "Sorry, but I can't help the family, even if I return tomorrow. Father has to solve his own problems. So does Mom. Believe me, I think about Mom all the time, but, I've made the highest choice. What I mean is, I must stay here to rescue Eve, my true love."

While the blazing fire warms us, I explain to Julia how I have met Eve of Epiphany aboard the *Skipbladnir*. That the girl from another planet is the most beautiful girl I have ever seen. That I have fallen in love with her. That Metamorphosis has taken me and Eve on a journey to visit the first Great Treasure, Anthera, the Eternal Rose. But we never made it that far. Told my sister how we traveled through the Forest Primeval and fought the hobgoblin pirates, ventured into the Underworld to defeat Vulcan and the dungeon trolls, and then killed a monstrous grizzsect at the Battle of Doubting Junction.

Listening to myself talk, I sound like I am reading a fantastic adventure story straight from a science fiction book or fantasy novel.

My voice sounds calm as I describe how Ex has captured Eve and taken her captive on a pirate ship, the *Walrus*. I announce to Julia that I will soon rescue Eve.

"Morph has taught me the Secrets of Time & Space, the Universal Truths," I say. "I'm so much wiser now. I've discovered what's important in life. I'm beginning to understand who I really am."

"Are you coming back with me, or not?" Julia asks.

I pause, staring at her exhausted expression.

"Sorry, Julia," I reply. "I'm not sure if I'm *ever* coming home."

Looking stunned, then upset, she reaches across the table and grabs my hand.

"Oh, Hunter. Don't say that. It will break Momma's heart. We all miss you so much. Father told me that you can be an artist, anything you want to be. Just come home. He will not interfere with your career."

Tears fill her eyes, as though the weight of the world, both worlds, have come down upon her shoulders. I feel really bad for her, but my mind is made up.

"I have to go, Julia," I say. "I'm wasting time sitting here. The longer I wait, the farther away I am from Eve."

She stands and steps around the table.

Standing up, I hug her, tightly.

"Are you going to stay here, on Millennium?" I ask her.

"No, I've got to get back home" she replies. "There's nothing for me here."

"*Everything* is here," I say. "Come with us. Morph can teach you things you've never dreamed of. You will visit places you can only imagine in your dreams."

She arches her eyebrows. "I can't, Hunter. I've got to go home. Momma and Daddy and the children need me."

Shaking my head back and forth, I say, "Always taking care of everyone but yourself."

Kissing her cheek, I say, "I'm going to get my backpack while you talk to Morph. He'll help you feel better."

Leaving the room before I start to cry, I miss my family. Miss being home. Miss my sister, but I can't be with her right now.

I walk to my room, close the door and gather my backpack for our voyage on the Sea of Esteem. I finish packing and sit at the wooden desk in front of the window. Finding my satchel, I take out a sheet of parchment, my quill and ink bottle.

As I draw, my thoughts are wild and free, full of adventure and positive energy. I tell myself, *Eve is not far away...she will be safe in my arms soon...as for Julia, there is nothing I can do to help her. She's going to have to save Mom on her own...I can't believe my sister is here on Millennium...it sounds like my father's Millennium report has got him in serious trouble...I hope he can keep the family safe from harm... I hope that—*

A knock on the door interrupts my deep thoughts.

Finished with my illustration, I open the door. It's Nyx, asking me to rejoin our group. Julia needs to see me one last time. I grab the backpacks and follow Nyx down the hallway.

Reentering the banquet room, I tell the sage, "Here's your stuff, Morph," setting a leather backpack on the floor.

It's difficult to look at Julia. I don't know what to say, or how to comfort her.

The sage pats my sister's hand and says, "Julia, you have noble work to perform on Earth. People desperately need your positive energy and your unconditional love."

She thanks Metamorphosis, turns, and runs across the room to hug me.

We embrace, maybe for the final time. I look into her sad eyes and say, "I made something for you." I open the flap to my leather satchel and pull out the drawing I had just finished.

Julia stares at the illustration of her wearing her Millennium outfit, holding her sword. I made my sister look like a heroine, a superhero.

"You always asked me to draw fantasy characters for you," I say. "This time, the fantasy is *real*."

Tears run down her cheeks. "I wish you'd come home with me. I'm going to really miss you."

446

Squeezing her tightly, I say, "Please tell everyone they are always in my thoughts. Give them my love. I have this feeling I will see you again, Julia. Be safe."

With tears in my eyes, I kiss her cheek. Unable to speak, I sling my leather backpack and satchel over my shoulder and hurry out the door, down the hallway and out the front door of the inn.

A crowd has gathered around Pegasus, gawking at the mythical beast. It doesn't take long for Morph to exit the Crossed Harpoons Inn, point to the winged stallion and say, "Come, my son. The *Argo* awaits our arrival."

The onlookers move away from the white horse, allowing the sage and me to secure our packs, mount Pegasus, and ride out of town, through the gates, and south onto the Open Road.

Morph whistles and white stallion gallops down the yellow cobblestone road, picking up speed until he spreads his magnificent wings and lifts off the ground.

"Where are we going?" I ask.

"To Hermopolis, only 600 miles southeast," he answers.

With the wind whistling in our ears, we remain silent, following the Open Road south. The scenery, as always, inspires me. To the north, a black sky moves toward us. To the east, the Sea of Esteem stretches beyond the horizon. To the west, the Melody Mountains tower into the blue sky. Ahead of us, a red sky casts a crimson glow on the coastal valleys below.

Time seems to stand still as we pass the ruins of Cavershall Castle and arrive at the outskirts of Kallipolis, a medieval-looking castle perched on a bluff overlooking the Sea of Esteem.

Not as large as Doubting Castle or Escalot, the three-story stone castle at Kallipolis has been constructed from grey granite block. I count two main towers with conical spires, the major features of the castle. The pitched roofs are covered in grey slate shingles. White smoke pours from the main chimney. Battlements and balustrades encircle the tops of the outer walls. Behind the battlements, armored guards walk the walls.

Pegasus lands on the Open Road and Morph picks a spot to rest, under an oak tree, one hundred yards from the entrance to the castle. On the opposite side of the cobblestone road, a row of merchant tents and temporary thatch structures have been set up along the entrance to the castle. The merchants and traders and drifters include the usual gathering of Millennians and bizarre creatures. I see no humans.

The sage tells me that we must wait for Pendragon, who will join us on our flight to Hermopolis.

"Since we have some time, can I tell you my plans?" I ask.

"Certainly, my son."

"I can handle ridicule. Don't laugh, but I plan to become a sage when I get back home."

"My, you have set your goals high. Excellent."

"Do you think I'm being realistic?"

"You have free will, freedom within. You shall decide your own destiny. Your personal freedom allows you the luxury of being a cosmic traveler in the infinite universe. You are a slave to no master."

"Okay, how do I begin?"

"The moment you no longer have to ask that question, your journey as a sage begins."

I grin and drink from my water bag, bathing in his warm words of wisdom.

"Your first step to becoming a sage is to change your thoughts by asking questions. Admit that the only thing you truly know is that you know nothing. Never accept the word or teachings of others."

"Wait. Does that include *your* teachings?"

"Yes, mine included. Continue to seek wisdom so you may decide for yourself. Make up your own mind. Do not allow others to think for you. Ask yourself, 'Is the information Metamorphosis has shared with me the highest truth?'"

"And if I discover your words *are* true?"

"When you know the wisdom to be true, ask yourself the ultimate question, 'Whenever I have to make a decision, what choice puts me on the highest road?'"

"What's the highest road? Please explain that again."

"The path of truth, my son. The high road. The Great Way. The Open Road. During your childhood on Earth, you were mistakenly taken down the low road, the path of deceit, the fast road to ruin. You have traveled the low road most of your life. Do you feel me?"

"Feel what?"

"The truth."

"Allow me to enlighten you," the sage says.

"Each time you have to make a choice, you stand at the crossroads of decision. One direction takes you down the low road; the opposite direction takes you up the high road. The low road is the road to confusion, the path to greed, profit and exploitation, the road to self-indulgence. This is the favorite road of humans. The high road is the path of honesty, the highest truth. The highest road is, of course, The Great Way, our winding and unfolding Open Road. You humans often call it the 'road less traveled'."

"Does Earth have an Open Road, a Great Way?"

 Morph nods, *yes.* "It is universal."

"Then, why can't humans find the right road?"

"Humans live in a low self-esteem fog and cannot see the high road. So, they choose the low road, the easy way. When they stand at the crossroads of decision and face a choice of which road to travel, they avoid the high road paved with truth because they believe the low road is easier, less work, less pain. But eventually, the low road, full of ruts, ends in anxiety and fear."

"I understand the road thing, but I'm still a little lost. What question should I ask to take the high road?"

"You are not as lost as you think. You have already asked the enlightened question, 'How do I become a sage?' The ultimate question you must always ask yourself is, 'What is the highest choice I can make right *now,* at this moment in time?' If answered truthfully, this most basic of questions changes your life instantly."

"Just be honest with myself?"

"The truth shall set you free. Choosing the highest truth is the ultimate free-me experience. You shall never take the low road again. You shall never be lost. Your life path shall follow the cosmic wheel on its eternal journey through the cycle of life. You shall close the circle. Once you travel The Great Way, true contentment is yours forever. The bliss of eternity can be found in your contentment."

"I will have to dedicate myself, really focus."

"The Great Way of which I speak requires the mindset of a scholar. A great scholar hears of The Great Way and begins diligent practice. The middling scholar hears of The Great Way and retains some and loses some. The inferior scholar hears of The Great Way and roars with ridicule. Without that laugh, it would not be The Great Way."

"I know I can become a great scholar."

"You already *are*, my son."

"Thanks, Morph. Then, I *can* be a sage like you someday?"

"Anything is possible."

"If I return home, is it really possible for me to make a difference, change the world?"

"As I have said, all things are possible when you put your mind to it."

"Anything?"

"Just imagine all the possible possibilities. Your desire to change your world is but one possibility, one, of the endless possibilities. Change your thoughts and the world changes with you. Miracles happen every moment in the universe. If you stop and observe, you shall see the miracles. When you return home, be in the awe of the miracles around you."

I nod in approval, knowing that if, or when, I return to Earth, I can make a difference.

Morph points up at the river of stars and announces that we cannot wait any longer for Pendragon.

Just as we are preparing to leave, we spot the dragonram landing on the Open Road.

Pendragon joins us with a worried look on his face.

"Sorry I am late. I bring bad news," he tells us. "Hunter's sister, Julia, has been captured by Captain Kraken, whose ship, the *Jolly Roger*, is docked off the coral reef opposite Goblin Grotto. Malagig and his boar soldiers are on their way."

"Now what are we going to do?" I ask. "God, if anything happens to Julia, I'll never forgive myself."

The sage tells me to calm down and stop worrying, then he

tells Pendragon, "Fly to Hermopolis and make sure the *Argo* is ready for boarding. Hunter and I shall return to Escalot and make sure Julia returns safely to Earth."

Pendragon nods, turns and takes flight, soon disappearing into the southern black sky.

Morph and I mount the winged stallion and lift off, soaring into the starry night.

Back to Escalot.

Daynight of the Jaguar

Aries the 18th

Year of the Dragon

"They who know The Great Way
can walk without fear of rhinoceros or tiger.
They will not be wounded in battle.
For in them, rhinoceroses can find
no place to thrust their horn,
tigers no place to use their claws,
and weapons no place to pierce.
Why is this so?
Because they have no place for death to enter."
—Metamorphosis

Chapter 25
Goblin Grotto

aybreak. It is the Daynight of the Jaguar, the 18th of Aries, Year of the Dragon. We have just arrived at Escalot, landing on a seaside bluff just above Goblin Grotto. A Millennium sunrise has painted the clouds pink and orange. My eyes adjust to the morning light as Nyx, Malagig and two of his boar soldiers greet us. We position ourselves on a cliff overlooking the grotto, hiding behind a rock outcropping, staring down into the sea cave.

Crystal-blue water splashes up onto the rocky ledge of the grotto. Two wooden skiffs, tied to a mooring on the rock outcropping, bob up and down in the gentle waves. A natural rock archway forms an entrance, a passageway, to and from the grotto. Beyond the arched-bridge opening, the lagoon reveals a coral reef that has created a barrier, protecting the grotto from the crashing waves of the Sea of Esteem.

"In our dreams the dragons stir."
—Metamorphosis

Beyond the reef, a hundred yards off shore, a lone ship with black sails has set anchor. Morph tells me it is Captain Kraken's ship, the *Jolly Roger*. We believe the pirates did not spot Pegasus land.

Malagig and his archers draw their longbows and silently sneak down the path to the cove below.

Morph taps me on the shoulder and points to the grotto.

Captain Kraken stands there with two beastmen pirates. Next to them, the beastman commander, Barbus, points his silver hook toward the skiffs and yells, "Aye, Captain, you got five o' me best mates, so I be returnin' to the ship an' preparr to sail."

453

Captain Kraken nods in approval and waves his sword at two beastmen pirates. Eight feet tall, they raise their spiked clubs above their horned heads. The pair of monsters snarl, showing their white fangs and lower tusks.

Scanning the grotto, I see her in the shadows.

I nudge Morph's arm and point below.

"There's Julia," I whisper. "She's being held by three pirates."

The hobgoblins holding my sister look like the pirates who had attacked us in the Forest Primeval.

Kraken rushes to my sister and grabs her arm, pulling her away from the three pirates. He forces her to stand next to the grotto wall facing a circular fire pit built into the stone floor of the sea cave. The flames of the blazing fire sway back and forth in the sea breeze, casting shadows on the grotto walls.

The beastmen pirates lumber over to Julia and grab her arms. Standing on either side of her, the hoofed monsters snarl.

Julia looks defiant, not frightened.

Barbus wades into the water to his wood skiff. He turns and says, "I hate to miss the fun, but I gotta' get back to me ship."

As Barbus rows away, Captain Kraken raises his saber and shouts to his crew, "Stand at attention, mates!"

The lizardman captain sticks out his chest and struts across the cave, pointing at Julia with his curved black nails and yells, "Here's the ugly girl from Earth. Over here, Master Ex."

Ex is down there! I can't see him, but I sense the Invisible Villain is near my sister.

"Welcome to my planet, Julia," Ex says. His low voice echoes off the grotto walls. He must be six feet from Julia.

I can see she's confused by the voice without a face.

"How do you know my name?" she asks.

"I know *all* things," Ex replies.

"I doubt that," she yells.

"Ah, we got ourselves another spirited human, full of defiance. Just like her cowardly brother."

"I've done nothing wrong. Let me go free."

"Freedom is hard to find in my part of the world," Ex says. "I'm willin' to set you free, but I ask one small favor."

"What's that?"

454

"Tell me where that pesky brother of yours is. Might he be with that pathetic sage with the mangy beard?"

She frowns at the voice with no body. "I don't know where Hunter is."

"Well, we gonna' help you get your memory back," he says.

"You'll have a long wait," she says, sneering in the direction of the evil voice.

Captain
Kraken

"Tell me where Hunter Wainright is, or I'll burn your pretty little face."

The beastman on her right side lets go of her arm, bends over and picks up a glowing, red-hot poker from the blazing fire, holds it up for all to see, then, jams it back into the flames.

A flurry of orange sparks flies into the grotto air.

Barbus

The three hobgoblins clap their hairy hands, hissing and showing their sharp yellow teeth.

"That's not fair!" she screams. "I've done nothing to hurt you, or your friends. Let me go, now!"

"I'm fair as they come!" Ex shouts.

The hobgoblins laugh in their high-pitched voices.

"Silence!" Ex shouts.

Once the goblins settle down, he says, "To show my fairness and generosity, I'll give you a chance to gain your freedom. If you can solve a simple riddle, I'll let you go."

"What if I can't guess the riddle?"

"Then, my alien visitor, you'll end up with a face that only a mother could love."

"Okay, go ahead."

"The riddle is, 'Lighter than what I am made of; more of me is hidden than is seen; I am the bane of the mariner; a tooth within the sea. Speak my name.'"

Julia turns red with frustration.

"Well?" Ex asks in a deep, sinister voice.

"I don't know."

Ex chuckles. "Captain Kraken, tell the dumb girl the answer."

"Iceberg!" the lizardman screams, sneering. His black iguana eyes gleam in the morning light. He snarls and spits a glob of green seaweed phlegm onto the grotto rocks.

She scowls and shouts, "That's a stupid riddle!"

The hobgoblins laugh and point their swords at Julia.

"Quiet, you fools!" Ex shouts.

The pirates hiss and groan. Brown, tobacco-stained drool drips down the front of their waistcoats as they hang their heads in reverence for the Master Extractor.

Kicking the beastman's shins with the heels of her boots, Julia yells, "I've done nothing to hurt you. Let me go home."

Ex yells, "Even though you proved your human stupidity, here's my final offer. Forget your stubborn brother and join me, become an Extractor. I'm offerin' you one last chance to pledge your allegiance to me."

My twin sister stares defiantly in Ex's direction and shakes her head, *no.*

"Ya have chosen poorly, young lady!" Ex shouts. "Ya'll soon regret your decision!"

The gold chain and medallion around Julia's neck moves up and over her head, floating in mid air.

"Give that back!" she screams. "You have no right to take my Triamulet!"

The gold chain and medallion float through the air and remain motionless six feet off the ground. I can see that the Invisible Villain now holds the Triamulet.

Ex screams, "Time to rearrange your young, flawless face to somethin' more appropriate, in case you decide to become an Extractor."

The beastman pirate grabs the glowing iron poker from the blazing fire and raises it slowly toward Julia.

"Hold 'er tight," Ex yells. "After we burn 'er pretty little face, we'll take 'er to the ship. Captain Kraken needs a first mate."

With a cruel look in his wild, blood-shot eyes, the sadistic beastman holds the red-hot poker six inches from her face.

That maniac is really going to burn my sister's face!

Do something, Morph!

She closes her green eyes and holds her breath, praying for her life. Now, the poker is an inch from her face.

I stand and pull the sword from my scabbard. Morph and Nyx hold me back. I push their hands away, ready to scream, stop!

The sound of arrows zipping through the air is followed by two loud thuds, the sound of ripping flesh. The beastman pirate drops the iron poker, grabbing the shafts of two arrows in his chest. Moaning, the monster falls to his knees, writhing in pain.

Below us, the two boar soldiers drop their long bows and charge down the rock path behind Malagig. Their shining suits of scale armor rattle as they grab the iron maces and spiked flails hanging from their metal belts.

The second beastman continues to grip Julia's upper arm with his black fingernails. He draws his saber, waving the shiny blade high in the air.

Morph, Nyx and I run down the path behind the soldiers.

I draw my sword and shout, "Julia! We're coming!"

In front of me, Nyx leaps from the rocks to the cave floor, holding her spear, *Gungnir*, above her head.

"Put the girl on the skiff!" Ex shouts.

Three screaming hobgoblin pirates charge Malagig and the boar soldiers as they cross the grotto.

Nyx attacks Kraken. The Extractor swings his saber at the Utopian, who reflects his powerful blows with her royal spear.

The sounds of clashing metal echoes off the cave walls.

Morph swoops down with his scepter in his lower right hand and hits Kraken on the back of his reptilian head. The captain stumbles and backs up, looking for his second attacker while he swings his saber at Nyx.

I sprint straight at the beastman gripping Julia's arm.

Jumping high in the air, I kick the pirate in the face.

The stunned beastman releases his grip on Julia's arm as I land awkwardly on my back.

Grunting, the monster raises his saber above his head and swings the glistening blade down at me.

Helpless on my back, I hold my sword up to defend myself.

White sparks fly as the beastman's saber strikes *Aroundight*, knocking the weapon out of my hand.

He raises his saber and roars loudly, staring down at me with his demon eyes.

In the corner of my eye, I see Julia running and jumping high in the air. She kicks the beastman in the ribs. Screaming, "Geeehaaahp!" she smashes her boot into the pirate's side.

He groans, grabs his ribs and looks over his shoulder at Julia.

She motions with her hands, *come get me*, as she jumps onto a flat boulder. The flaming fire pit lies directly behind her.

461

With no place to escape, my sister positions herself in a martial arts stance.

The growling beastman lumbers straight for her, swinging his gleaming saber above his head.

I climb to my feet and run toward my sister, screaming, "Stay down, Julia!"

Before he reaches her, I jump on the beastman's back and cling to his neck.

Julia karate-kicks the pirate's face with the heel of her boot.

Warm blood drips from his bleeding nose down onto my forearm.

Really pissed off, he reaches back to grab my head, taking a swipe at me with his black claws.

I pull Eve's knife, *Arthame,* from my belt and run the steel blade across the beastman's neck, slitting his ugly throat.

Letting go, I jump down to the grotto floor.

The beastman stares at Julia and me with a look of disbelief.

He drops his saber and grabs his bloody neck with both hands. The moaning beastman stumbles forward, loses his footing and tumbles into the fire pit, head first.

A geyser of roaring red flames, sparks and black ash explode into the grotto air while the burning beastman screams in agony.

"Arrrggghhh!"

The smell of burnt flesh is sickening.

"Kill the inferior humans!" Ex shouts.

Malagig swings his mace and flail at a pirate.

Another hobgoblin, holding Julia's sword above his head, charges us, screaming and showing his sharp yellow teeth.

Julia shouts, "Give me my sword back, you little creep!"

She pushes me out of the way and runs straight at the pirate.

Launching herself through the air, she karate-kicks the pirate in the chest.

Dazed by the blow to his chest, the hobgoblin stumbles backward, trying to catch his breath as Julia leaps and spins full circle in midair, striking the pirate on the side of the head with her boot.

The sword flies out of his hand and hits the grotto wall.

The pirate drops to the rock floor.

His face cut and bleeding, the wounded pirate crawls toward the water, leaving a trail of blood.

Julia runs and picks up her sword while I pick up *Aroundight*. She glances at me.

This moment will be a memory I never forget.

Here I stand with my twin sister on another planet, dressed in medieval clothing, holding swords in our hands, fighting hobgoblins and beastmen and Extractors.

Julia runs to the crawling pirate and stands over him in a victory stance, raising her sword above her head.

The hobgoblin holds his hairy arms up and begs for mercy. "Sparrre me life, missy."

She lowers her sword, pointing the blade in the pirate's face and shouting, "Tell Ex I want my Triamulet back, or he's next!"

The bleeding pirate scrambles to his feet, scurries across the grotto and jumps off a rock ledge into the water.

I run to her, grab her arm and tell her, "Great job, Julia. You put that pirate in a world of hurt."

"I should have killed that pirate," she says.

"No. You did the right thing."

I scan the grotto for Ex and the floating Triamulet.

Across the cave, the boar soldiers drive the pirates back toward the water.

Swinging a spiked iron ball on the end of a chain, Malagig strikes a hobgoblin on the side of his unprotected head with the lethal flail. Blood splatters down the pirate's waistcoat as he crumples to the ground, dead.

When the last standing pirate sees the crushed skull of his ship mate, he turns and leaps off the rock ledge into the lagoon.

On the other side of the grotto, Captain Kraken swings his saber at Nyx, then Morph, then Nyx.

The winged sage hovers above Kraken, just out of reach, using his scepter to harass the frustrated captain.

Kraken stops cursing the two Utopians and shouts, "Help us, Master! The girl's gettin' away!"

Ex screams, "Destroy the sage's wand first!"

"Ya no-good coward!" Kraken shouts. "Take care of the sage yourself!"

The bewildered captain swings his saber one last time at Nyx before he turns and leaps off the ledge, diving into the waves below the grotto.

Morph shouts, "There it is, the Triamulet!" pointing his scepter at the medallion floating near the edge of the grotto.

Morph flies toward the necklace. Toward Ex.

The crystal ball on the end of his scepter glows with pulsating ultra-violet waves. The astral glow from *Joyease* exposes a shape moving toward the water.

Shielding my eyes from the glare, Ex's shape is exposed again, just as it was in the Dungeon of Fire.

This time, Julia gets a look at the two-legged creature with fiery-white eyes, covered with armor-like scales.

Ex still wears his feathered cloak and the dog-skin helmet with white feathers.

"Metamorphosis, I'll get you next time!" Ex screams, pointing his dagger-like fingernails at the Utopian.

The Master Extractor vaults high into the air and flies through the archway, soaring into the blue Millennium sky.

Amazed at how fast Ex can fly, we all watch her medallion disappear above the Sea of Esteem.

I walk over to Julia and hug her.

"Are you okay?" I ask, holding her shoulders and looking into her eyes.

"My Triamulet," she says, breathing heavily. "How am I going to get home?"

"Don't worry, Morph will have an answer," I say, leading her across the grotto to Nyx and the sage.

Suddenly, Captain Kraken explodes from the water, sneering and flicking his purple forked tongue.

Riding Tyrannus, he points his saber at us and shouts, "See you soon, Metamorphosis. You won't be so lucky next time!"

Malagig commands the boar soldiers to raise their long bows.

They release their arrows in unison.

One arrow misses Captain Kraken's head by inches.

The second arrow strikes Tyrannus in his tail fluke. The flying sea monster lets out a loud roar as he soars through the rock archway, over the pirate skiff and toward the ship.

We watch Tyrannus dive into the sea next to the *Jolly Roger*.

Barbus and his crew pull anchor as Captain Kraken climbs up a rope ladder on the starboard side of his pirate ship.

Nyx looks at my twin sister and asks, "Princess Julia, are you all right?"

She nods, *yes*.

"My, young lady," Morph says, "you certainly know how to defend yourself."

"Thank my mom," she tells the sage, knowing she means the martial arts lessons we took together as children.

"Julia, do you still want to go home?" I ask.

"After this experience, more than ever," she replies, staring at the dead beastman lying in a pool of blood.

"Then, you shall," Morph said, patting her shoulder.

With tears of frustration in her eyes, she asks, "How. Nyx told me to never lose my Triamulet, or I could not return home. It's gone. Ex has it."

The two sages look at each other and nod.

"Nyx wanted to make sure you knew the importance of the sacred medallion," Morph says. "However, I have something superior to the one you lost to Ex."

Morph reaches into a pouch on his belt and pulls out a Triamulet necklace with a sparkling crystal in the middle.

"That's like the one Elizabeth Dow wears," she says, staring at the medallion.

I remember the name, Elizabeth Dow. My father and Professor Johan talked about her all the time. As a previous visitor to Millennium, she was the focus of their Coma-X study.

"Ah, Elizabeth," Nyx says, "She stayed quite a long time. We treasured our moments together. We hope to see her again."

"What do you mean, *again*?" Julia asks. "Isn't a Triamulet good for one trip only? That's what you told me. That's what my father's Millennium report had in it. One time only."

"These Crystal Triamulets allows intergalactic travel an unlimited number of times," Morph says, placing the gold chain with the sacred medallion around Julia's neck.

She looks down at the gold talisman on her chest and says, "You mean, I can return to Millennium whenever I want?"

"Anytime you choose, Princess Julia," Nyx says, smiling.

"Only a few humans have taken advantage of the eternal power of the Crystal Triamulet," Morph says.

"Who was the last one to do that?" Julia asks.

"Hunter, you tell her," Morph says.

"William Shakespeare," I say. "He visited here, first as Francis Bacon. Then, he showed up the second time, returning as Shakespeare the playwright."

Erda & Ava

"Willie was perhaps one of my favorite humans," Morph says. "He loved to sit by a fire and have philosophical discussions. Unfortunately, like all humans, he acted impatient, in a hurry to get back home. He said he had a lot of writing to do, so he decided to leave."

"Speaking of leaving," I say, "I'd love to stay and talk to my sister more, but we have to go."

"To find Eve?" Julia asks.

I nod, *yes*.

Morph nods and says, "The Open Road awaits us, my son."

Nyx whistles and points at the sea cliffs above us. Within seconds, a four-legged creature soars downward, directly at us. Silhouetted against the red sky, the magical beast turns its black-feathered wings forward, slowing down for a landing.

A magnificent gryphon!

The gryphon touches down with its four bizarre legs. The two front legs have black feathers with fleshy-orange eagle's legs with brown, curved talons. The back legs and tail look like a golden-haired lion.

"She's gorgeous," I say, awestruck by the eagle's head, feathered chest and wings that adorn a lion's muscular body. The gryphon stands twelve feet tall at the shoulder and she must be at least thirty feet in length, head to tail.

"Her name is Ava," Nyx says, as the gryphon rears up on her hind legs on the grotto floor.

A little person is riding on the gryphon's upper neck.

"Who's that riding on Ava?" I ask.

"Erda, the gryphon master," Nyx replies. "The gnome is the finest trainer of the flying beasts in all of Millennium. She will get us back to Time Island in no time."

The gnome sits on a miniature saddle strapped on the gryphon's upper neck, just behind the white-feathered head.

Holding the reins with one hand, she pulls her goggles over her leather cap. Her braided pigtails fall to her shoulders. The freckled-faced gnome's smile reveals a missing front tooth.

Julia says, "We flew on Ava to get to Escalot."

Erda pulls out a sword, scanning the cliffs for signs of trouble while the gryphon flaps her wings, clawing the ground.

Erda takes a gold pocket watch from her vest and yells, "Aye, we best put spurs to the nags, the black sky's a comin', she is."

"Be right with you, Erda," Nyx yells.

Erda waves to us from her gryphon saddle.

I hug Julia tightly, telling her, "Please give my love to Mom and Dad and Ruby. Tell Alexander, Zachary, Emily, Grace, Astrid and Pearl I miss them. Hug Crystal and Sebastian for me. Please tell them all how much I love them."

Looking out across the Sea of Esteem, I say, "I don't know how long it will take us to find Eve."

"Think positive, Hunter," she says. "All things happen in perfect order."

Morph looks at me and we smile together.

The sage says, "Your wise twin sister has discovered a Universal Truth, one of the Secrets of Time & Space."

I hug Julia and kiss her cheek.

Pointing to the gryphon and ask her, "This time, do you think you can make it home safely?"

Julia bursts into tears.

"I'll be careful," she says, sobbing and hugging me tighter and longer than she ever has.

"Come, Princess Julia," Nyx says. "Our ride awaits us."

Julia turns and hugs Metamorphosis. The sage holds her with four arms, patting her shoulder with one hand, holding the side of her face with the other hand, while his two other arms hold her waist.

He lowers his bearded chin and looks in her eyes, saying, "Julia Wainright, I wish you all the joy that a person can wish."

She wipes the tears from her eyes, turns and hugs me one last time.

"I love you, Hunter."

"I love you too, Julia."

The sage points to Ava. "The gryphon of legend awaits you, young lady. Godspeed."

Nyx takes my sister's hand and leads her across the grotto.

Through the rock archway, I see the black sails of Kraken's ship fade over the horizon, into the fiery-red sky.

Julia mounts the gryphon, along with Nyx.

"Aye, 'tis a good day to fly," Erda says, pulling her goggles and leather cap over her braided red hair.

The mighty gryphon runs and leaps off the grotto's ledge, soaring through the archway.

Holding onto the saddle, Julia looks back at me.

Raising my sword, I wave goodbye.

The blade of *Aroundight* gleams in the two daystars.

Julia waves back.

Taking a deep breath, I bid my twin sister a safe trip home as she rides the gryphon into the western horizon.

I'm happy for Julia that she's returning home. Sad, because I might never see her again.

Malagig and the two boar soldiers escort Morph and me up the rock path to the top of the grotto.

Pegasus waits for us, pawing the ground with his silver hooves.

"Let us go find Eve," the sage says.

"Yeah, we've wasted a whole lot of time," I reply.

The sage looks at me with that *did you hear what you just said* stare.

I grin. "Excuse me. I meant to say, 'All things unfold at the right and perfect time.'"

Julia

469

DAYNIGHT OF THE RAVEN

Aries the 19th

Year of the Dragon

"Showing off does not reveal enlightenment.
Boasting shall not produce accomplishment.
They who are self-righteous are not respected.
They who brag shall not endure."

"Fill your house with jade and gold and it brings insecurity.
Puff yourself with honor and pride
and no one can save you from a fall."
—Metamorphosis

Chapter 26
Cloud of Emergence

Pegasus has been airborne more than fourteen hours. Strong trade winds rising from the Sea of Esteem have prevented us from making better time. The black sky has moved behind us. The emerging blue sky welcomes the twin stars, Helios and Sol. The beginning of another glorious daynight on Millennium. We have finally arrived at Argo Bay.

As we descend, my mind drifts to thoughts of Eve, how she must be suffering; thoughts of Julia, how she must be on Earth by now; thoughts of home, how everyone and everything has changed; and my father, how he always controlled my life, until now.

Having kept track of Earth time on my Millennium calendar, I know it is December, Christmas back home. Julia is home safe with our family. That makes me feel good. Mom is so much happier with Julia around. Father has learned that I'm alive and well. Now he can stop worrying and take care of his family.

The past eleven daynights have allowed me to experience the highest, and the lowest, of emotions. I've traveled across the universe to fall in love, been enlightened by a great sage, fought hobgoblins, trolls, beastmen and Extractors, and reunited with my twin sister. No matter what happens to me, I feel like I lived an entire lifetime.

You can imagine how I feel, can't you?

I know I've got a long way to go, but that's how I feel.

"There is Hermopolis," Morph says, pointing straight ahead to a speck of land rising from the Sea of Esteem.

"Do you think Julia is home by now?" I ask.

"Most certainly," Morph says. "Once she gets to Time Island, her journey home happens at the speed of thought."

The sage taps me on the shoulder and says, "Look behind us, above the Discordia Crater."

I turn my head to see a gigantic, swirling cloud, like a hurricane, rising above the great crater. The colossal cloud has all the colors of the rainbow.

"What is that?" I ask.

"The Cloud of Emergence. It is a cosmic phenomenon that occurs every time one of our previous visitors returns to Millennium and awakens in the Place of Emergence."

"How does that happen?" I ask.

The sage explains that whenever a returning visitor awakens in the Place of Emergence, the brass and iron doors in the side of the crater cliffs are opened by the giants guarding the cave, allowing a magical wind to escape.

The wind swirls in a clockwise motion around Time Island, forming a vaporous mist. The mist gathers momentum to become a thousand-mile-wide swirling cloud, rapidly spinning as it rises to the top of the Discordia Crater. By the time the cosmic vapor emerges from the crater, it contains all the colors of the rainbow, a celestial kaleidoscope.

Morph says, "The swirling Cloud of Emergence rises above the crater, eventually disappearing into Millennium's cosmic rings."

"How do you find out *who* has awakened?" I ask, staring at the atmospheric phenomenon.

"We Utopians are always the first to know. Word travels fast with our messenger system in place."

"So, how many people are asleep in the cave, in the Place of Emergence?"

"Let's see, with all eight planets we have eighty-two individuals asleep in the cave at this time. Oh, excuse me, someone has just awakened, so the number is now eighty-one."

Still staring over my shoulder at the mystical Cloud of Emergence, Morph says, "Look, my son, we are about to land on the *Argo*."

As I turn my head around, Pegasus finishes his decent, straight down. We emerge through a cloud formation and the ship of legend comes into view. Beyond her sail looms the city of Hermopolis, one of the major ports and trade centers on the Sea of Esteem. I learned that when I read the *Magnum Opus*.

Morph reminds me that the ship is built for speed, that she can reach 11 knots on the open sea.

"We'll be able to overtake the *Walrus*," he says.

Within seconds, we land on the top deck of the *Argo*.

Pegasus touches down on the wooden gangway that runs down the center of the ship. The crew members, dressed in soldier armor, helmets with bronze breastplates, lower their heads as the wings of the white stallion pass over them.

Morph and I dismount. We walk toward the stern of the ship. The crew salutes us as we pass by. I can see their faces through the openings in their helmets.

I recognize them as half-orcs, grotesque looking, but just like the *Skipbladnir's* crew, loyal to Morph.

Before I can ask a question, Morph yells, "Captain Jason, it is good to see you again."

"Metamorphosis, my friend," Jason says, "I have prepared the ship with a full crew to sail at your command. The Argonauts are ready to challenge the *Walrus*."

The two shake hands while I stare at the crew, imagining how the Greek legend, the story of Jason and the Golden Fleece, made its way back to Earth.

"This is my guest of honor, Hunter Wainright," Morph says.

"Hello," I say, shaking the commander's hand. A human hand.

"Welcome to the *Argo*," Jason says.

Before I can ask a question of the first human stranger I've come in contact with, Morph says, "Excuse me, I must speak to the captain for a while. Please, keep an eye out for Pendragon."

"Okay, Morph," I say, watching him and Jason enter the aftercastle door.

I turn to watch the crew prepare the ship to sail.

The red and gold military ship is a sixty-oar galley with a mid-ship mast, one sail.

Although similar to the *Skipbladnir*, the ship is narrower and has no forecastle, only the aftercastle above the rear quarterdeck.

With sixty oars are mounted on the top deck, she was designed for stealth speed during battles.

We are anchored one hundred yards off shore. I can see the mouth of the harbor, and behind it, the city of Hermopolis. She looks like an ancient Greek city with her rows of stone-columned buildings built on a grid of narrow cobblestone streets. Built on the side of a hill, I can see the center of the city where a white temple towers

Hunter

474

over the acropolis. That's a word I learned in history class. Or maybe one of my role play games. Anyway, the outskirts of Hermopolis is lined with houses constructed of clay brick and plaster with roofs made of thatch and tile. The streets are teaming with all sorts of people. Some are tall, maybe humans, but most of the inhabitants look smaller, perhaps dwarves or gnomes. I'm too far away to get a good look at anyone.

Several Argonauts point to the sky and wave.

It's Pendragon!

Diving down from the clouds, the Utopian prepares to land.

The ship's crew cheers as the dragonram lands hard on the gangway, his hoofs pound loudly against the oak planks.

"Hello, Hunter," Pendragon says as he approaches the aftercastle.

I nod, noticing a look of concern on his face.

"Where is Morph?" he asks.

"With Commander Jason," I reply.

"I have news that concerns you, and only you."

"What's wrong?"

"Nothing is *wrong*. I would rather have Metamorphosis tell you the news."

"Is it Eve?"

Pendragon shakes his head, *no*, saying, "A human has awakened in the Place of Emergence. Please excuse me, I must find the sage so we can talk."

"No," I say. "I need to know what's going on. I don't need Morph to hold my hand like my father used to do."

Pendragon stares at me and says, "Very well. The exact words you just spoke reveal the name that concerns us all."

Looking deep into his dragon eyes, I ponder his words.

What did I just say to him?

Then it hits me.

No way!

I ask, "My *father* is here?"

Pendragon nods, *yes*.

He places his hand on my shoulder and says, "Wayland Wainright has awakened in the Place of Emergence. He wears a Crystal Triamulet."

Overwhelmed, my mind is filled with negative thoughts.

What's my father doing here? What does he want? This will kill my mom. What about my brothers and sisters? I hope Julia is home with Mom.

"How did he get the Triamulet?" I ask.

"Our messenger told me he borrowed it from his daughter."

"There's no way Julia would let my father have her Crystal Triamulet."

"Wayland and I have not spoken; therefore, I have no idea how he obtained the sacred medallion. That is irrelevant at this time. He is here, on Millennium, and our messenger tells us he is looking for his oldest son, Hunter Wainright."

Pendragon says, "Excuse me while I find Morph."

He turns and disappears through the aftercastle door.

I look over my shoulder at Hermopolis. Beyond the city lies the dark and mysterious Sea of Esteem.

Eve is out there somewhere.

At this moment, I will not allow my thoughts to be negative.

I forgive Father. I am no longer angry with him. But the reality is, *my* reality, that I just traveled 200 million light years across time and space to get *away* from my father!

And here he is, looking for me!

I refuse to let him ruin my plans. I don't want to see him right now. I'm not sure *when* I'm ready to see him.

You understand. Don't you?

Sorry, Father, you're on your own.

I must go find Eve.

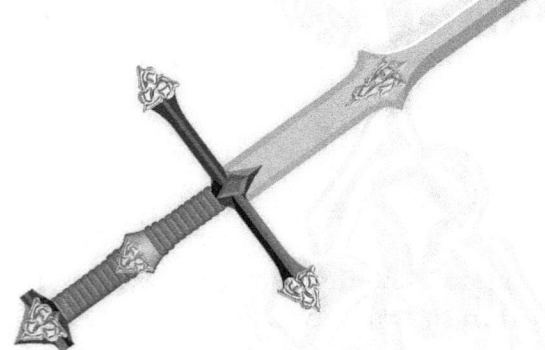

"Of birds I know that they have wings to fly with;
Of fish that have fins to swim with;
Of wild beasts that they have feet to run with.
For feet there are traps; for fins, nets; for wings, arrows.
But who knows how dragons surmount wind and cloud into heaven.
This day I have met Metamorphosis, and he is a dragon."

Universal Truths

Secrets of Time & Space

I
"Like attracts like."

II
"Nothing, no thing, happens by accident."

III
"Thoughts are the most powerful force in the universe."

IV
"All things happen in perfect order."

V
"You get what you think about, whether you want it or not."

VI
"Now is all there is; live in the moment."

VII
"Enjoy all things, need nothing."

VIII
"What you do to others, you do to yourself."

IX
"There is no way to happiness; happiness is the way."

X
"Love teaches all."

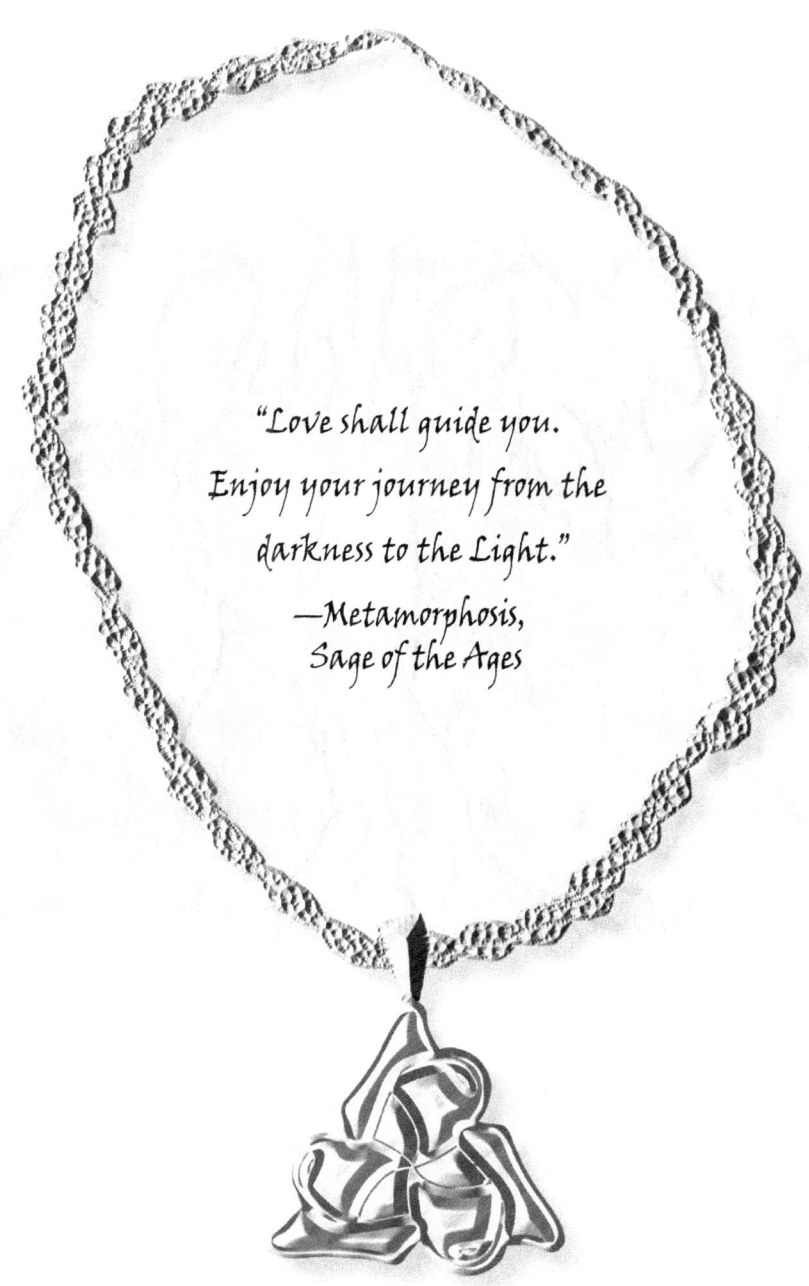

"Love shall guide you.
Enjoy your journey from the
darkness to the Light."

—Metamorphosis,
Sage of the Ages

More Books, Novels, Maps and Videos by

Mel Wayne

- Atlas of Millennium -
- Heroes From Earth -
- Julia Wainright: Girl In Two Worlds -
- The Great Way: 81 Oracles -
- The Great Way Tarot & Cards -
- Morph: Sage of the Ages -
- Esteem: Discover Who You Are -

Hunter Wainright Deluxe Edition

Hunter Wainright: The Way is also available in a full-color, illustrated edition featuring the characters, maps and landscape scenes of Millennium. Soft-cover, 8.5" x 11", 368 pages.

Atlas of Millennium

Atlas of Millennium depicts more than 3,548 mythological names shown on full-color physical, political, and parchment maps, including characters and landscape scenes of Millennium. Illustrated, 8.5" x 11", 224 pages.

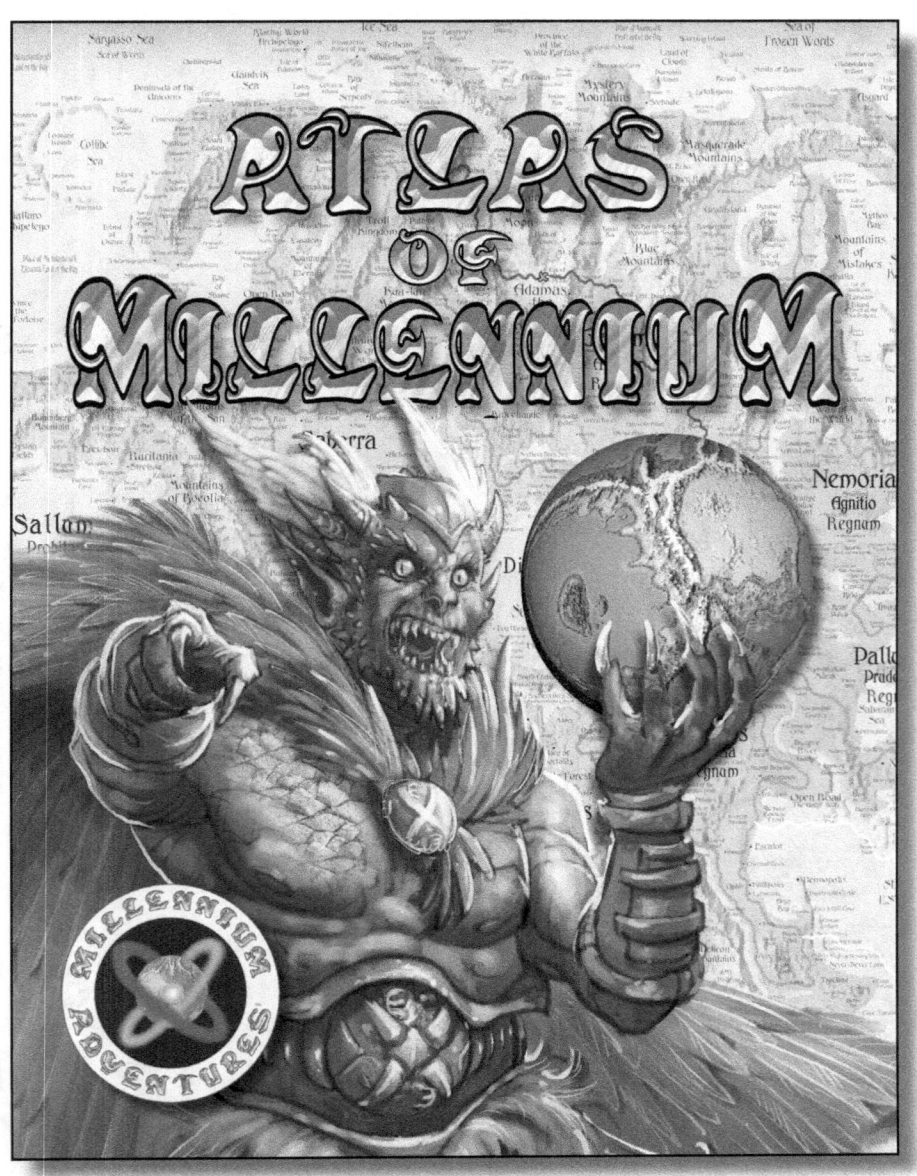

Heroes From Earth

Heroes From Earth ~ Book One: Nemoria is an Role Play Game book featuring the story world of Millennium in a fusion of pen and paper with modern game master aids featuring videos and grid maps. Illustrated, 8.5" x 11", 128 pages.

Julia Wainright:
Girl In Two Worlds

Written as a companion book to *Hunter Wainright: The Way* by Mel's creative partner, Pamela Wayne, this adventure novel tells the story of Julia Wainright, on the same time line as Hunter. Illustrated, Deluxe Edition, 8.5" x 11", 236 pages.

The Great Way:
81 Oracles

The Great Way, told by Metamorphosis, Sage of the Ages, unlocks the ancient mysteries of his 81 oracles. The book comes in two editions, the 6" x 9" black and white edition, and the illustrated, full-color, 8.5" x 11" Deluxe Edition, 308 pages.

Esteem:
Discover Who You Are

Esteem: Discover Who You Are, begins your quest for life~long health and happiness as you find out who you truly are. The illustrated, 8.5" x 11" book features 144 full~color pages. A motivational Ebook is also available.

"I wish you all the joy that you can wish."

—Metamorphosis, Sage of the Ages